For Alison

HERO OF ROME

Douglas Jackson

CORGI BOOKS

TRANSWORLD PUBLISHERS
61–63 Uxbridge Road, London W5 5SA
A Random House Group Company
www.transworldbooks.co.uk

HERO OF ROME
A CORGI BOOK: 9780552161336

First published in Great Britain
in 2010 by Bantam Press
an imprint of Transworld Publishers
Corgi edition published 2011

A CIP catalogue record for this book
is available from the British Library.

Addresses for Random House Group Ltd companies outside the UK
can be found at: www.randomhouse.co.uk
The Random House Group Ltd Reg. No. 954009

The Random House Group Limited supports The Forest Stewardship Council
(FSC®), the leading international forest certification organisation. Our books
carrying the FSC label are printed on FSC® certified paper. FSC is the only
forest certification scheme endorsed by the leading environmental organisations,
including Greenpeace. Our paper procurement policy can be found at
www.randomhouse.co.uk/environment

Typeset in 11.5/14.5pt Sabon by Falcon Oast Graphic Art Ltd.
Printed and bound by CPI Group (UK) Ltd, Croydon, CR0 4YY

2 4 6 8 10 9 7 5 3

Historical Note

Hero of Rome is a work of fiction but the story of the two hundred men sent from Londinium to reinforce the veterans at Colonia in the face of Boudicca's avenging army is recorded by the historian Tacitus in his *Annals*.

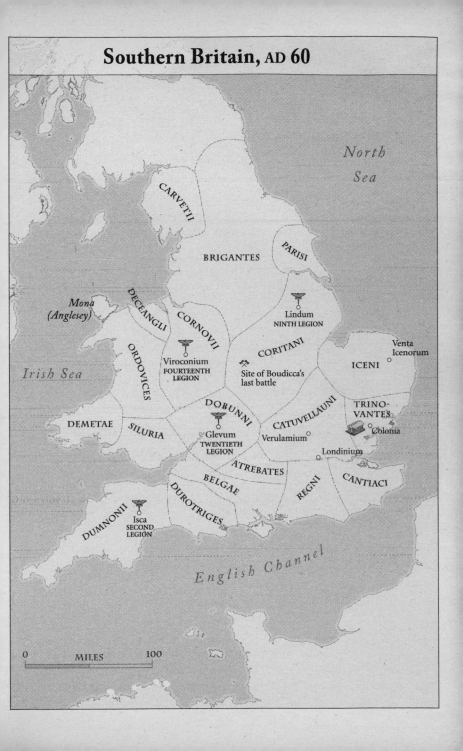

Southern Britain, AD 60

North Sea

CARVETII

BRIGANTES

PARISI

Mona (Anglesey)

DECEANGLI

CORNOVII

Lindum
NINTH LEGION

CORITANI

Venta
Icenorum

ICENI

ORDOVICES

Irish Sea

Viroconium
FOURTEENTH
LEGION

Site of Boudicca's
last battle

TRINO-
VANTES

DOBUNNI

CATUVELLAUNI

DEMETAE

SILURIA

Glevum
TWENTIETH
LEGION

Verulamium

Colonia

Londinium

ATREBATES

BELGAE

REGNI

CANTIACI

DUMNONII

DUROTRIGES

Isca
SECOND
LEGION

English Channel

0   MILES   100

Prologue

The flames reached out to him like a lover's arms as he walked naked between the twin fires. He felt their warm caress upon his skin but knew they could not harm him, for they were the flames of Taranis and he was the god's servant. Another man's flesh would have been scorched and shrivelled by their heat yet he remained untouched.

When he reached the far side of the chamber, Aymer, high priest of the sect, awaited him with the clothing he would wear on his journey, cleansed and blessed in its turn. The druid was very ancient, a shrunken husk of a man, dried out and worn down by all the long years of toil and study and abstinence in the great oak-walled halls of Pencerrig. But the life force was still strong in him and Gwlym felt it now, along with a palpable expansion of his own mind as the milky, faded eyes locked on his. No words were spoken as Aymer passed to him the knowledge that would take him to his goal, but he saw the path ahead clearly. The black mountains, with their deep gorges and narrow paths along foaming, rock-strewn streams. The great river, swirling, deep and dark, which he must cross unseen. Then, more dangerous still, the flat green pastureland with its well-worn tracks and curious inhabitants, before he reached the final sanctuary of the forests and the faraway sea.

'It is done,' the priest said, his voice brittle with age. 'The cleansing is complete.'

Gwlym dressed quickly and followed the druid into the darkness where the ponies waited. They picked their way through the night along hidden trackways until they reached the edge of a low cliff overlooking a narrow beach. From below came the gentle hiss of waves breaking rhythmically against a pebble shore and he saw a shadowy figure working on the fragile wood and animal-skin craft which would carry him across. The light, or lack of it, made the sea a dull, leaden silver, and beyond it was visible the darker, more sinister contour of the mainland. Shorter routes existed between Mona, the sacred isle of the druids, and the country of the Deceangli, but they would undoubtedly be watched.

'They will come for us soon.' Aymer's words were barely audible. 'By then you must have completed your task.'

Gwlym nodded. There was nothing more to say. He understood he would never see Aymer again after this night. Soon, the legions of Rome would march through those same mountain gorges to destroy the last stronghold of the druids and break their power for ever. He felt the dull ache of regret at the knowledge he would not share the fate of the priests who had trained him and nurtured his unceasing quest for knowledge. But he had his own mission and it was more important still. For even as the spears of the legions descended upon Mona, he would fan the embers of the long-neglected fire that was Celtic pride and create a conflagration that would consume every Roman and every Roman-lover on the island of Britain. Shame and resentment and humiliation would be his greatest weapons. After sixteen years of conquest and debasement the tribes were ripe for rebellion; all they needed was a spark and a leader. Gwlym would be the spark, the gods would provide the leader.

'Carry the word. Carry it far, but carry it with care. You must not be taken.' Aymer paused, allowing Gwlym time to reflect on the grim reality of his last words. 'Counsel patience. When the time is right the gods will send a sign: the wrath of Andraste will rain from the sky and the people of Britain will rise from their bondage and sweep the usurpers from our land in a maelstrom of blood and flame.'

'The wrath of Andraste.' The younger man whispered the words to himself as if they were a prayer before he picked his way carefully down to the beach without a backward glance.

13

I

What was the ruin of Sparta and Athens, but this, that mighty as they were in war, they spurned from them as aliens those whom they had conquered?

Claudius, Emperor of Rome, AD 48

Severn Valley, Siluria, September AD 59

Could it only have been ten minutes? Gaius Valerius Verrens gritted his teeth behind his smile and his eyes locked on his opponent's, but the message, if message there were beneath those hooded lids, was the opposite of what he wanted to see: the bastard was mocking him. He breathed hard through his nostrils, drawing in the sharp pine scent of the freshly cut stump on which his right elbow rested. At the same time he felt the agony that had been tearing the big

15

muscle in his upper arm ease a little. He channelled the relief up into his forearm and along his inner wrist to the fingers of his right hand. The increase in power must have been infinitesimal – he barely registered it himself – but he noticed a slight movement as Crespo's eyebrows twitched and he knew the centurion had sensed it too. So. The hand that gripped his – the elbow resting precisely to the left of his own – was horny and calloused and had all the yield of a hypocaust brick. Fingers like talons clasped with a force designed to break bone, but he resisted the temptation to meet the challenge. Instead, he directed all his own strength into moving Crespo's fist to the left; any movement, even a hair's breadth, would do. So far, Crespo hadn't yielded even that. But then again neither had he. The thought made him grin, and the crowd of legionaries ringing the tree stump cheered encouragement at the sign of confidence. Arm wrestling was a favoured pastime in the First cohort of the Twentieth legion. All you needed was a flat surface and the inclination. Sometimes they wrestled for fun. Sometimes to gamble. And sometimes because they hated each other's guts.

The First had been in the temporary camp in the lee of the Silurian hill fort for six days. When the cavalry patrol had failed to return two weeks earlier, the legate's reaction had been immediate. Reprisal in force. Three thousand men – five legionary cohorts and a mixed unit of auxiliary infantry and horse from Gaul and Thrace – had marched behind their standards down the River Severn, then west into the rough hill country beyond. They had found the heads, twenty of them, still in their helmets, like marker points on a trail. A few unfortunate Celtic peasants picked up along the way and put to the question had led them here. It had taken five of those six days to dig the ditch and rampart around the base of the rugged hill which now entirely isolated the fort's inhabitants from either help or escape. When the legionaries weren't digging they spent the time on guard, drilling, exercising or patrolling, but during their occasional rest periods they were able to sit outside their leather eight-man tents and do the things soldiers always do: mend and polish their equipment, gamble their pay away and grumble about their officers, or just sit and stare at the sky and the blue-grey haze of the distant mountains.

Valerius concentrated on his right arm, attempting to will more power into it. The big muscle bulged below the short sleeve of his tunic as if it were trying to burst free from the skin and he could see the twisting snakes of dark veins beneath the tanned surface. It had swelled to the size of a small melon and matched that of Crespo, who was judged the strongest man in the cohort. The forearm was broad, tapering towards the wrist, where the tendons stood out like tree roots. His wrist was bound firmly to Crespo's by a strap of red cloth, so that neither man could shift his grip and win by trickery. But he knew Crespo would try, because Crespo was a cheat, a liar and a thief. But he was also a senior centurion, which made him untouchable. Almost.

He had discovered Crespo beating one of the new recruits, young Quintus from Ravenna, with the gnarled vine stick he carried as the traditional badge of his rank. Every centurion disciplined his men, because discipline was what made a legion a legion. But Crespo confused discipline with brutality, or maybe he just enjoyed brutality for its own sake, because he had beaten Quintus half to death. When Valerius ordered him to stop, Crespo had looked him up and down with those expressionless ice-chip eyes of his. The two men had a history, of sorts, but one that was more animal wariness than physical hostility. The first time they'd met had been like two dogs coming together on a narrow path: a rising of the hackles, a sizing up of strengths and weaknesses, a quick sniff and a moving on; gone, but far from forgotten.

Now he stared into Crespo's features from two feet away. Did he sense uncertainty? By the gods, he hoped so. The fire which had started in the crook of his elbow was moving up into his shoulder and on into the base of his neck and it was like no pain he'd ever experienced. Crespo's washed-out eyes glared back from a long, narrow face that had somehow stayed pale while the sun turned most men's walnut brown. Valerius could make out a pattern of individual pockmarks dotting his opponent's forehead and chin, evidence of some childhood disease unfortunately survived. His nose was long and sharply angled, like the blade of a pioneer's axe, and below it hung a thin, rat-trap mouth that reminded Valerius of a viper's. Oh, he was a handsome fellow was Crespo. But handsome or not, he was a sword hilt taller, and, though Valerius was broader in the chest and shoulder, the centurion had the wiry strength of fifteen years in the legion; the kind of strength you didn't get from running errands in the law courts. Still, growing up on his father's farms had given Valerius his own strength, and the confidence to use it.

The sweat started at the very edge of Crespo's hairline: tiny, almost invisible diamonds of moisture among the untidy dark stubble the unit's barber had left him. Valerius watched, fascinated, as they slowly grew in size, until two or three joined and formed a clear drop which trickled gently down the centurion's sloping forehead until it reached the point where it joined his nose. And stopped. He felt disappointment. The droplet had seemed an omen. If it had carried on and run down the blade of the axe to the tip, he was certain it would have foretold victory. Now he wasn't so sure. Still, it was a sign of something. Was there a loosening of the talons, a sense that the opposing force, though it felt as relentless as ever, had passed its peak? Or was Crespo luring him into a trap? Allowing him to think he'd won and then producing a burst of energy he'd kept in reserve for the moment he had him slightly off balance? No. Wait. Patience.

'Tribune?'

Valerius recognized the voice but tried not to let it affect his concentration.

'Tribune Verrens?' The tone was a little more officious than was proper in a double-pay man addressing a Roman officer, but when the double-pay man was clerk to the Twentieth's commander it seemed sensible to ignore the potential slight.

'Had enough yet, pretty boy?' Crespo's lips barely moved as he hissed the words through clenched teeth. The thick Sicilian accent grated on Valerius's ears as much as the insult.

'What is it, soldier?' Valerius addressed the man behind him but kept his eyes on Crespo and his voice steady. The joined fists remained as motionless as if they were carved in rock.

'You are to attend the legate, sir.' The announcement brought groans of disappointment from the dozen legionaries crowding around the tree stump. Valerius could have groaned with them. He sensed that the contest was there to be won. But you didn't keep the legate waiting.

Which posed a problem: how to extricate himself without giving Crespo something to crow about? He knew that the instant he relaxed the centurion would force his arm over and claim victory. A small thing, a minor defeat which a man could easily bear and would cost nothing but a little hurt pride. But he wasn't prepared to give Crespo even that satisfaction. He thought for a few seconds, allowing Crespo to anticipate his moment of triumph, then, maintaining his grip, rose smoothly to his feet, drawing the puzzled centurion with him. Crespo suppressed a curse and glared at Valerius as the young tribune used his left hand to untie the cloth binding their wrists. 'There'll be another time. I had you where I wanted you.'

Valerius laughed. 'You had your chance, centurion, and I have better things to do.' As he pushed through the grinning crowd of off-duty legionaries at the heels of the legate's messenger he heard Crespo boasting dismissively to his cronies, the senior men he kept loyal by handing out light duties: 'Too soft. They're all the same, these rich boys, just short-timers playing at soldiers.'

It took Valerius twenty minutes to wash the sweat from his body and don his uniform over his tunic and *braccae*, the calf-length trousers the legions had adopted after their first winter in Britain. First the dark red over-tunic, then the belt round his waist with the decorative apron of studded leather straps that were meant to protect his groin, but in reality wouldn't stop a goose feather, never mind a spear. Over the tunic, his orderly helped him strap the *lorica segmentata*, the jointed plate armour that covered his shoulders, chest and back and *would* stop a spear, but was also light enough to allow him to move fast and fight freely. The short-bladed *gladius* hung from the scabbard on his left hip, the weight comfortable against his upper leg, ready to be cross-drawn with

21

that musical hiss that always made the hair stand up on the back of his neck. Finally, the heavy polished helmet with its neck protector and cheek pieces, topped by the stiff scarlet horsehair crest. He knew he was testing the legate's patience, but Marcus Livius Drusus was a general in the mould of the great Gaius Marius and anything out of place would be noted and remembered.

When he was satisfied, he marched the short distance from the bivouac he shared with another of the legion's six military tribunes to the tented pavilion which doubled as the commander's living quarters and the *principia*, the legion's nerve centre. The surroundings were comfortingly familiar. Neat rows of tents, divided into units of centuries and cohorts, the *via praetoria* stretching off to the point where it was bisected by the *via principalis* just before the *principia*, and beyond that the supply area, workshop tents and horse lines. Glevum, the Twentieth's permanent headquarters, lay forty miles to the north-east, but since he'd arrived in Britain all those months ago, fresh-faced and nervous at the port on the River Tamesa, he'd spent more time on the march or on engineering detail than in the fort. Marching camps like this, hardly varying in any way, were more home to him now than his father's villa. From the first, soldiering had come perhaps not easily but certainly naturally to him. In those early days he'd often lain wrapped in his cloak, exhausted after a long day on patrol, and wondered at the fate which had brought him here, where he belonged. He knew instinctively that his ancestors had fought at Romulus's side, marched with Scipio and stood with Caesar at Pharsalus. It was there, *inside*, in every nerve and sinew.

He recognized the two legionaries on guard outside the *principia* as permanent members of the legate's bodyguard. The man on the right raised his eyebrows, warning of the reception he was likely to receive. Valerius grinned his thanks then switched to his expressionless soldier's mask. Inside, the general bent low over a sand table at the rear of the tent, flanked by a pair of his aides. Valerius removed his helmet and stood for a few seconds before clashing his fist against his chest armour with a loud crash.

'Tribune Verrens, at your service, sir.'

Livius turned slowly to face him. The afternoon heat had left the inside of the *principia* airless and clammy, but even so he wore the heavy scarlet cloak that marked his rank over his full dress uniform, and by now his puffy, patrician face and balding scalp matched it almost to perfection.

'I hope I didn't disturb your games, Verrens?' The voice was excessively cultured and the tone almost solicitous. 'Perhaps we should have our tribunes wrestling in the mud with the common soldiery every morning? It would raise their morale considerably to inflict a few lumps and bumps on their officers. We might even lose a few, but then tribunes aren't much good for anything in any case. Yes, good for morale.

But . . . not . . . good . . . for . . . discipline!' The final sentence was barked out with all the venom Livius could inject into it. Valerius picked out a worn spot on the tent wall behind the legate's right shoulder as he prepared to ride out the inevitable storm.

The legionary commander spat out his words like a volley of ballista bolts. 'Discipline, Verrens, is what has allowed Rome to conquer every worthwhile part of this world and to dominate what's left. Discipline. Not courage. Not organization. Not even the untold riches of the Empire. Discipline. The kind of discipline that will keep a legionary holding the line while his comrades fall one by one at his side. The discipline that will keep him in the fight until he has not another drop of blood to give. The kind of discipline which you, Gaius Valerius Verrens, by your childish desire to impress, are in danger of fatally weakening. Do you think you made yourself more popular by challenging Crespo? Do you want to be *liked*? Show me a legion whose officers are *liked* by their soldiers and I will show you a legion ripe for defeat. This is the Twentieth legion. This is my legion. And I will have discipline. The only thing you achieved, tribune, was to diminish a centurion's authority.'

Without warning the tone softened. 'You're not a bad soldier, Valerius; one day you may become a very good one. Your father asked me to take you on my staff to provide the military experience you require to make a career in politics and I fulfilled my obligation

24

because our families have been voting side by side on the Field of Mars for ten generations. But the one thing I have learned in our time together is that you are no politician. Flattery and dissembling are not in your nature, nor is a natural desire to curry favour. You lack true ambition, which is essential, and you are honest, which is most certainly not. If you follow the political path you will fail. I have already tried to tell your father this, but perhaps I was overly subtle for he still sees you in the Senate some day. What age are you? Twenty-two? Twenty-three? A quaestorship in three years, atop some desert dung heap. Twelve months spent attempting to prevent your rapacious governor or proconsul from ruining his province and its people.' Valerius was surprised enough to allow his eyes to drop and meet the legate's. 'Oh, yes, tribune, I have been there. Counting every *sestertius* and gasping at the man's greed, then counting them again just to be sure he hasn't stolen a few more. And after that? A year back in Rome, perhaps with an appointment, perhaps not. That is when your future will be decided, and by then it will be in your hands.'

Valerius could see the two aides still staring at the model on the sand table and trying to look as if they weren't listening. The legate followed his gaze.

'Leave us.' The two men saluted and hurriedly made for the door.

'Come.' Valerius followed his commander across the dirt floor towards the sand table. 'There will be a day, Valerius, when your soldiers are mere coins to be

25

spent. What will you do then, when you know you must order them into the abyss? The truth is that they do not seek your friendship, but your leadership. Here.' He pointed at the sand table, which held a perfect miniature replica of the hill and the British fortress.

'Sir?'

'It is time to end this.'

II

The Silurian chieftain looked down from the wooden ramparts towards the symmetrical lines of the Roman encampment and fought back an unfamiliar panic. He was puzzled, and, yes, frightened. Not frightened for himself, or for the impetuous warriors who had brought this upon him, but for the people who had come to this place seeking sanctuary, but were instead facing annihilation. Within the walls of the fortress stood perhaps a hundred and fifty thatched roundhouses, clustered in the lee of the ramparts or around the little temple in the centre of the compound dedicated to the god Teutates. The inhabitants farmed the fields in the surrounding countryside, hunted and fished and traded the surplus to the less fortunate communities, of which he was also the overlord, in the rugged hills to the west. Normally the fort would support fewer than five hundred people – today all the warrior strength he could gather and an additional thousand refugees scrabbled for space among the huts and fought for water from the single well.

The ambush on the Roman cavalry patrol had been carried out at the orders of the High King of the Silures, who had in turn received 'guidance' from his druid, who had no doubt received similar guidance from the leaders of his sect in faraway Mona. He had been against it, but how could he, a lowly border chieftain, refuse his king? In any case his young men were eager to test their mettle against the enemy who paraded across their hills and their valleys as if they were their masters. But the High King was a long way from the soldiers who now threatened his fortress. One tribe would feel the power of the Romans' revenge and it would be this one.

He had always intended to fight; his honour and his authority depended on it. But initially he had intended to fight and run. This was not the first time he had seen a Roman legion prepare for battle. Ten years before, in a valley not three days' ride away, he had stood with the Catuvellauni war leader Caratacus when the long line of brightly painted shields crossed the river and the last great alliance of the British tribes had smashed itself against them the way a wave breaks against a rocky shoreline. He knew what the Romans were capable of. His puzzlement had begun when the legionaries started digging, and by the time he'd worked out why, his opportunity to run had gone. Now his people were in a fortress within a fortress. Trapped. But the puzzlement only turned to fear when the messengers he sent to ask for terms and offer hostages failed to return. Such offers had always been accepted in the past. The reason this one was not became clear when the leader of the ambush explained the fate of the Roman auxiliary cavalrymen, and clearer still when the heads of his two messengers were sent back by a Roman catapult.

'Father?' At first he didn't acknowledge the melodious high-pitched cry because he needed every ounce of courage and he knew that even to look at her would weaken his resolve. 'Please, Father.' He turned at last. Gilda stood at her mother's side: part child, part woman, liquid doe eyes beneath an untidy fringe of raven hair. For a moment their combined beauty cast aside the bleak shadow that blanketed his mind. But only for a moment. The thought of what might happen to them in the next few hours placed a lump of stone in his throat and he barely knew his own voice.

'I told you to go to the temple,' he said to his wife, who, for reasons only a woman would understand, wore her best grey dress on this of all days. 'You will be safe there.' He could see she didn't believe him, but what could he tell her? Another man would have given her a dagger and instructed her to use it. But he wasn't that man. He had spoken more sharply than he intended and Gilda gave him a look of reproach as they walked away hand in hand. When he turned back to the ramparts and the Roman preparations below, his vision was strangely blurred.

Valerius stared up at the fortress on the flat-topped hill. He had seen native *oppida* like it many times but this was by far the largest and the most skilfully constructed. He studied it carefully, impressed by the engineering. The approaches had been cunningly designed to force attackers to assault the palisaded walls from an angle, so that they would be more exposed to the slings and spears of the defenders. He could see those defenders now, a silent line of heads silhouetted against the sky above the first of the three ramparts that encompassed an area measuring as much as two legionary encampments.

The legate called for his chief engineer, who had been summoned from Glevum when a siege became inevitable. 'It may look formidable,' Livius growled. 'But this place is no Alesia and I do not have Caesar's patience. How long before the heavy weapons are ready?'

The man chewed his lip but Livius knew him well enough to be certain he had the answer to hand. 'One hour for the onagers and ballistas, perhaps two more for the big catapults. We had a little trouble at the last river crossing . . .'

'You have two hours to put everything in place' – he also knew the engineer well enough to be certain

30

he had built in the leeway to be able to meet his general's deadline – 'two onagers, two ballistas and a single catapult between each pair of watchtowers.'

Later, the heavy chopping sound that was instantly recognizable as the discharge of a ballista brought him from his tent. He looked up at the sun and a particularly sensitive watcher might have noted the shadow of a smile cross the stern features. Two hours less perhaps ten minutes. Good.

'A ranging shot, sir, short by a dozen yards,' the engineer announced. 'A waste of a bolt, but we'll do better this time. More tension on the rope there!'

Valerius hurried across to join them and watched as the weapon's commander hauled on the winch, and the two front arms of the ballista bent noticeably back as the ratchet turned noisily. It was a big bow, really, one that shot massive, five-foot arrows with heavy, needle-pointed iron heads. A big mechanical bow encased in a wooden frame and mounted on a cart for easy transportation. They called the arrows 'shield-splitters' and he had seen the destruction they could do to an enemy battle line. They would be equally deadly when they fell among the British warriors and the shambling mob of refugees who had sought the false security of the fortress walls. Those walls were now ringed by twenty ballistas and the same number of onagers, the little stone-throwing catapults. Experience told him the onagers would struggle to hurl their ten-pound projectiles over the walls of the inner rampart, but they would add to the chaos and the panic. There would be no such problems for the big catapults. The long, fifteen-foot arm could throw a boulder five times the size of a man's head from one side of this hill to the other.

'Weapon armed and ready, sir.'

The engineer scuttled round to the rear of the ballista and stared along the launching ramp towards the fortress. 'Another elevation.'

The ballista commander lifted the central beam of the weapon a notch and stood back as the engineer again checked the aim, the calculations twitching one by one across his furrowed brow. Eventually he turned back towards Livius. 'You have the honour, general.'

The legate nodded. 'Ballista . . . fire!'

From the eastern gateway of his fortress the Silurian chieftain heard a soft thud at the base of the hill and detected a flicker of movement against the green and brown of the earth below. In the same second some force disturbed the air close by his left shoulder, plucking at the heavy cloth of his cloak, and a moment later he heard a shriek from within the fortress behind him. He turned, knowing what he would see. At first he wasn't certain whether it was one person or two writhing in the dust. They must have been standing face to face when they were hit. Mother and son? Brother and sister? Lovers? It did not matter now. The ballista bolt had taken the man in the centre of the back, punching through his spine on the downward arc of its trajectory. The impact of the strike had thrown him forward and the point of the five-foot arrow had pierced the woman's lower body, so that now they squirmed and gasped and quivered in some obscene parody of the act of love.

It had begun.

Livius nodded to the engineer to continue and turned to Valerius. He looked the young tribune up and down. Yes, the boy would do – a credit to his father, even if the father was not a credit to him. Of medium height, but powerfully built with it. Crow-dark hair cropped short beneath the polished helmet, a strong jaw and a sculpted chin with its almost invisible central cleft shadowed with the slightest stubble. Serious eyes of a deep, aqueous green confidently returned his stare. But look a little closer and there was something slightly disturbing about those eyes; a hint of what might be cruelty that would attract a certain type of woman, and hidden in their depths the unyielding hardness which made him the right man for this mission.

He had his orders, but no harm in reinforcing them. 'Rome does not generally place her tribunes in peril, but in your case I have decided to make an exception. You attack in two days, at dawn. Our Gaulish auxiliaries will carry out a diversionary assault on the western gateway. It will provide you with your opportunity. Once they have engaged the enemy and drawn their reserves you will assault the eastern gate with three cohorts of heavy infantry – more than fifteen hundred men. I have studied the east gate. Once the catapults have done their work it will not hold you for long. Remember, take the fight to them and do not stop killing until there are no more warriors left to kill. That is the price they pay for murdering Rome's soldiers. The women and children will be taken as slaves. Anyone too old or too sick to march . . . well, you know what must be done. For Rome!'

For the next two nights Valerius watched as the bombardment battered the rebel defences. He had seen what the artillery could do; the casual, arbitrary malevolence that turned one family into bloody scraps fit for nothing but the dogs, and the next second immolated a dozen warriors in an all-encompassing fireball that left them blackened, smoking imitations of the human form. It was the big catapults, of course, with their boulders that would take out a section of wall or gate and everyone behind it, and the fiery missiles that stank of pitch and sulphur and consumed hut and flesh alike. The assault continued spasmodically through the night, the impact of each death-bringer preceded by the distinct sound of its passage: the almighty, whooshing surge of the giant rocks and the peculiar *whup whup whup* sound of the fireballs as they spun through the air. Against the awesome violence of the catapults the more numerous projectiles of the smaller weapons would seem almost puny by comparison, but still they would take their toll among the packed ranks of the refugees and the doomed warriors who stood on the ramparts, defiant, as if flesh and blood alone could halt the Roman assault. He tried to blank out images of the exposed bones of shattered children; tried not to imagine the screams of the dismembered or those impaled or blinded by splinters as the wooden palisades and the once mighty gates were smashed flat.

On the morning of the third day, an hour before dawn, the three cohorts of the assault force formed up amid the flickering torchlight on the camp's parade ground. Valerius stood silently at the centre of the square beside the legion's eagle and the individual unit standards held aloft by the *signiferi*, their rank and role emphasized by the wolf-fur cloaks they wore. Each man here had signed up for twenty-five years in the legions. As a military tribune, Valerius had joined for six months, served sixteen because the life agreed with him, and would be sent home in another eight months at most. He gazed slowly round the square, attempting to judge the mood, but in the darkness every face was lost in the shadow of a helmet brim. *I'm leading an army of the dead*: the thought entered his head before he could suppress it and he shuddered. Was it an ill omen? He made the sign against evil and took a deep breath.

'You all know me.' His firm voice carried across the parade ground. 'And you know I'm only here because your Primus Pilus twisted his leg the other day. He regrets his absence, but not as much as I do.' A few of them laughed at that, but not many. Valerius knew that some of them would be glad the legion's feared senior centurion would not be there to hound them up the hill, but the veterans understood that the loss of experience could cost lives. He noticed Crespo, in his distinctive helmet with the curved transverse crest, scowl. 'You've all done this a hundred times before and there's nothing on that hill you have to fear. When we go, we go fast and we stop for nothing. Anyone who's wounded on the way is left behind, and that includes the officers. Stay tight, because the tighter we are, the safer we are. I'll be up front with the First cohort and where I lead, you follow. They won't be expecting us to come knocking on the front door, so it should be simple.' This time they did laugh, because they knew it was a lie. The sides of the hill were too steep for a direct assault on the walls. Only the two gateways to the east and the west were vulnerable and the enemy would be waiting behind both. 'Once we're inside the gate, it's over,' he ended decisively. 'These people may know how to fight, but they don't know how to win. We know how to win.'

They cheered him, and pride rose up inside him like water from a spring. He felt a bond with these men that was stronger than family; a comradeship of the spirit, tempered in the heat of battle. They had marched together and fought together, and there was a fair chance that when the sun came up they would die together, their blood mingling in the mud of a British ditch. All of them knew that some of the men who marched up that hill would not be coming down again. But instead of weakening them, the knowledge gave them strength. That was what made them what they were. Soldiers of Rome.

He issued detailed instructions to each of the unit commanders in turn, finally approaching Crespo, who was to lead the Second cohort. He found it difficult to hide his dislike for the man, but the hour before an attack was a time to put aside petty rivalries. He could see the pale eyes glittering in the darkness, but he couldn't read what was in them.

'May your god protect you, Crespo.' The centurion followed Mithras and somewhere in the camp was the hidden shrine where he would have made a sacrifice to the bull-slayer. It was a secretive cult but anyone who survived the initiation was worthy of respect – for courage at least. Soldiers did well not to ignore the gods, but Valerius worshipped them the way most men did, doing just enough to keep them happy and calling on them in time of need. 'Stay close on the way in. Once we're past the gates, the First will hold the enemy in position while you punch a hole through their line with the Second. When you're beyond them, turn and we'll crush them between us.' It was a good plan, but its success depended on many different factors. He had fought the Celtic warriors of western Britain before and, for all his confident talk about their weaknesses, he knew them for courageous fighters prepared to die in defence of what was theirs. Today, they would have no choice, because they had nowhere to run.

Crespo grunted suspiciously. 'So we do the fighting and dying while you hide behind your shields and take all the glory?'

Valerius felt the anger rise in him, but bit back the words that accompanied it. No point in getting into an argument with the embittered Sicilian. 'Dying is what we are paid to do, centurion,' he said, and turned away before Crespo could reply.

III

The barrage paused and for a few seconds the soft, false light of the grey predawn was accompanied by an unearthly calm, the serenity broken only by the crackle of burning wood from the hilltop. At the head of his men, Valerius closed his eyes and tried to read the sounds. At first, nothing. But a moment later he heard the muted growl he knew was the start of the auxiliary attack. He kept his eyes shut a little longer, enjoying a final moment of peace, and when he opened them a fire arrow arched through the sky like a shooting star.

Now!

He led the legionaries at the trot, eight abreast in their centuries. The legate had placed a screen of archers to the right and left of the assault point and, as the spearhead of the attack passed them, the bowmen loosed a flight of arrows that harvested the defenders from the first of the three ramparts. Valerius had spent the two days preparing for the attack, examining every inch of the eastern slope, and he had noted something that gnawed like a maggot at his brain. The most obvious route to the gate had a very clear entrance, but no apparent exit. Of course, the way out could be hidden, a tunnel perhaps, but that, even in a fortress of this size, would be the expenditure of enormous effort for very little gain. The longer he looked at it, the less he liked it. The anomaly might have a perfectly innocent explanation but, in Valerius's experience, nothing in war was innocent. Now he made his choice, knowing he was gambling his soldiers' lives on the result. He led his men swiftly past the first opening and on to a sloping platform running parallel with the fortress walls, and when it took a sharp uphill turn he followed it. The route brought the first legionaries within range of spears hurled from the palisade that topped the second rampart. 'Form *testudo*!' At the order, each man in the first century locked his shield above his head with those of the man next to him. Only those in the front and rear ranks and the men on the edges of the formation kept their shields vertical. The result was a solid carapace which made the eighty men inside the *testudo* invulnerable to attack from above. Behind him, Valerius knew each century in the attacking cohorts would be following his example. Now he was operating on pure instinct, following the well-worn path upwards, and praying the Silurians had placed no more false exits or hidden traps; a dozen knee-deep pits could shatter a *testudo* in less time than it took to draw his sword. No. A fortress this size must be a place of commerce as well as refuge, and commerce meant ease of access. Whoever had designed the defences would have been forced to make that compromise. His chest was heaving, his arm ached from holding the heavy shield above his head and the breath rasped in his throat. Sweat blinded his eyes in the little oven of his iron helmet, with the big cheek flaps that restricted his vision but wouldn't save him from a blade to his throat. The clatter of spears and arrows against the outer surface of the *testudo* was almost constant now, like a heavy shower of rain. Death was everywhere around him but he had never felt more alive.

He thought of his father, mouldering in semi-retirement on the country estate in the pretty, wooded valley close to Fidenae and making his plans to revive the family's political fortunes; plans which had Valerius at their very heart. Next year he would have to return to resume his legal career, touting for minor cases outside the Basilica Julia; snapping up the crumbs left by brighter minds. It wasn't that he disliked the law; to sit and listen to one of the great practitioners wield logic and rhetoric the way a champion *retiarius* wielded net and trident was one of life's pleasures. But to stand up before a court didn't light a fire in his belly the way he knew it must do in a Cicero or a Seneca. Only combat did that, and— The gate! They had reached the gate!

'Ram to the front.' The missiles had destroyed the gate structure beyond recognition, but the Britons had used the smashed timbers to form a makeshift barrier. It wouldn't take long to clear, though it would delay the assault, and he'd seen what happened when attacks became delayed. The battering ram was with the second century, but the legions practised re-forming the *testudo* under fire until it was almost habit, and the big rectangular shields quickly formed a tunnel that allowed the ram squad forward. Most legionaries were small men, iron tough but more gristle than muscle. Compared with them, the soldiers who wielded the legion's battering ram were broad-chested giants; they had to be to handle the specially reinforced oak trunk that was their stock-in-trade. Still it took too long and he heard the inevitable crashes and screams that told him the Britons were making good use of the boulders the catapults had hurled at them. Now they were dropping those stones, some of them weighing as much as a small ox, on to the *testudines* following him. The defences were sure against light weapons, but a big boulder would smash a gaping hole in the shields, and then the spears and arrows could seek out the soldiers below. The *testudo* would reunite quickly enough but, behind him, he knew men were dying.

At last! He stepped sharply aside to allow the ram

to do its work, the massive head of carved stone surging forward with the strength of twenty men behind it to smash the pathetic blockage aside. One. Two. Three. Yes, three, that would do it. 'First cohort, with me. For Rome!'

As he turned to lead the way through the breach in the British defences, he glimpsed a line of snarling moustached faces from the gap between his helmet's cheek pieces. A shower of burning fat thrown from his left spattered his legs and he screamed a curse. Now he was inside the fortress and his men filed past him to make the line and he stopped thinking and allowed training to take over.

'Forward.'

The curve-edged shields of the leading cohort's first and second centuries locked in one solid defensive wall, and the weight of the attack was multiplied by the addition of two further lines. At the far right of the first line Valerius tightened his fist on the wooden grip at the rear of the shield boss, bunched his muscles in the arm straps and butted the edge against that of the man to his left. He knew every man to his rear would be holding his shield aloft to protect the front line from spears and arrows fired by the defenders. The Romans had their own spear, the *pilum*, a four-foot shaft of ash tipped with an arm's length of tempered iron. But no one carried one today, because they were long, heavy and awkward and would only have slowed the attack, creating more casualties than they caused. This was a day for swords.

The momentum of the initial breakthrough had pushed the defenders back a dozen paces but now they counterattacked in a single howling mass four or five hundred strong. Valerius flinched as an arrow nicked his helmet an inch above his right eye and he braced himself for the impact of the charge, his eyes searching the barbarian ranks for the man who wanted to kill him. There was always one: the single individual who hungered for *your* blood more than any other; who saw in *your* face everything he hated most in this world. It took a moment, because his eye naturally fell upon the British champions, the big men made even taller by hair lime-starched into spikes and horns who were the pick of their tribe and carried long iron swords or broad-bladed ash spears. They fought bare-chested to prove their courage and decorated their skin with blue tattoos that told the story of their heritage and their bravery in battle.

But the man who wished to kill him was no champion. Short, with lank, dirty-blond hair and a slight frame from which hung a filthy, ragged shirt, he looked almost harmless in that warrior throng because he didn't carry a sword or a spear, only a curved dagger with an edge that gleamed blue from constant union with the whetstone. But his eyes told a different story. They burned with an enmity beyond hatred: a mindless promise of violent, painful death. All this Valerius noted in the time it took his enemy to cover a single pace. He knew that the man's lack of height could be an advantage in this kind of fight, and it made him doubly dangerous. For the battle would be fought above the belly and he would come in low, under the big shield, and that gleaming blade would seek out the Roman's unprotected genitals or try to hamstring him. Valerius experienced a chill in his lower guts. Yes, it would be the balls. The haunted eyes told of a loss beyond bearing. A loss that could only be avenged by inflicting horror upon its perpetrators.

A mighty crash announced that the first Britons had collided with the centre of the Roman shield wall. He felt the impact shiver along the line, bringing with it a roll like thunder as hundreds of swords began hammering at the painted oak shields, as if by obliterating the Twentieth's emblem of a charging boar they were obliterating the men themselves. Above the rim of his shield he watched his enemy come with the extreme left of the British attack. To the man's right were warriors bigger and better armed, but still Valerius's instinct told him this was where the true danger lay. When the burning eyes disappeared below the level of the shield he counted the heartbeats: *one*, he would have covered another pace; *two*, he was crouching, preparing to roll under the shield and stab upward, the blade seeking the big artery in the groin; *three*. With the strength of his shoulder behind it, Valerius smashed his shield forward and down so that the rounded iron boss struck the charging Briton above the bridge of the nose, smashing flesh to instant pulp, the impact forcing his eyeballs from their sockets and splintering skull bone deep into the brain. The blow numbed Valerius's left arm, but as it was struck his right was already moving, a lightning flick of the *gladius* that ripped out his enemy's throat in a spray of scarlet. He felt the flame of exultation explode within him as it always did when he took a life and he tried to still it because he believed the savage, atavistic joy shamed him. He would never reveal or try to explain that feeling beyond the brotherhood of the battlefield. Only those who had experienced it could understand that most elemental of human reactions to the most basic of human experiences: to survive and to kill. The inner fire flared and was gone, replaced in an instant by cold calculation. From his left, a Silurian spear sought out the weak point below his armour. He brushed it aside with the strengthened edge of the *scutum* and, snarling defiance, he was back in line, the shield rim hooking behind his neighbour's.

With the breath rasping in his chest, he took time to listen, attempting to gauge the battle and noticing for the first time the throat-filling stink from the burning huts and granaries, the rubbish pits and animal dung and human excrement that lay in haphazard piles all around. The main force of the British attack had struck the middle of the Roman line, and it was here that the howls of impotent rage and screams of the maimed and dying were centred. For the moment, Valerius was happy that his legionaries could contain the enemy. Crespo could not be far away.

He heard the call he had been waiting for. 'Cornicen!' The trumpeter who had been hovering behind the line appeared at his shoulder. Valerius spoke to the man on his left side, shouting to be certain he was heard above the clamour of battle. 'On me, wheel right ten at the signal.' He gave time for the order to be passed along the wall of shields. 'Sound the command.' The trumpeter pursed his lips and hesitated for a second before the circular horn blasted out its message.

The manoeuvre Valerius had ordered was complicated and potentially dangerous, and he would only have asked it of men he trusted with his life. It meant the entire Roman line would pivot on his position like a door opening. Simple for the legionary two or three along from his commander who only had to move forward half a step, but not for the unfortunate soldier on the far left of the line who would have to put his shoulder to his shield and smash his way ten paces forward, aided by the power of the two men at his back, and all without losing formation. But ten paces could be the difference between defeat and victory.

Because through the gap – if he had timed it correctly – Crespo was now charging with his centuries in wedge formation. Arrow-headed human battering rams that would hammer their way through the enemy ranks, utterly destroying their cohesion, and then turn and attack them from the rear.

An increase in the intensity of the battle told him

he'd been right. He stepped back and allowed the man behind him to take his place in the line. A few yards away, the ruins of a shattered roundhouse gave him a vantage point from which he could view the entire length of the British fort. Studying the smoke-wreathed hilltop, he realized that Crespo had added a refinement to his plan, or perhaps deliberately disobeyed orders. Two of his eighty-man wedges had punched all the way through to the west gate, and from there the auxiliaries of the diversionary attack were now pouring into the fort, killing as they came and not distinguishing between fighters and the women and children the legate had ordered taken captive.

Now, the Britons Valerius had faced were trapped; hundreds of warriors corralled between the two legionary forces and the fortress wall. Some attempted to escape by climbing the rampart, but there would be no refuge from the bowmen posted at the base of the hill. Sharp cries rang out from within the midst of those remaining, and Valerius knew they were calling for mercy. But there would be no mercy. Only the long slumber of the Roman peace.

A Roman legion was a killing machine and now he watched that machine at work. No amount of Silurian courage would change the outcome. In the confined space, the long, curved swords of the Britons had little or no room to swing and when they did they expended their force against the three layers of hardwood that made up a legionary shield. The *gladius* was different. Jabbing between gaps in the shield wall, the short, razor-edged swords ripped into belly and groin then twisted free, creating a gaping wound that left a man praying for death. Then the big shields smashed forward and the swords flicked again. The legionaries of the First cohort worked with a studied concentration that made no distinction between old or young, brave or fearful. The Celts were beasts to be slaughtered. At first, Valerius was fascinated by this utterly disciplined lack of humanity, the relentless rhythm of death which eventually left the prospective victims slack-jawed with horror and sapped of the will even to defend themselves. But the fascination faded as the individual details of the butchery burned themselves on to the surface of his brain. The moment he felt some fragile barrier in his mind threaten to crumble he turned and walked away through the chaos of victory.

Surviving women and children huddled for protection amongst the wreckage of the wattle-and-daub huts by the south wall. Close by, the bodies of the elders who had stood with them only a few moments earlier still twitched in an untidy heap. Valerius studied the prisoners, but none would meet his eye. He was reminded of cattle marked for slaughter, disturbed by the smell of blood from those who had gone before but helpless to escape their fate. Meanwhile, fighting continued all around him: small skirmishes involving groups of warriors who had defended the west gate; individual Britons fleeing for their lives from a dozen legionaries still lost in the frenzy of battle. The air was filled with screams. But one scream was different.

It was a child's scream of pure terror.

He knew he should walk away: what was another child's life in this slaughterhouse? But the scream was repeated and he realized it came from one of the few surviving huts less than twenty paces away. Two legionaries stood in the doorway with their backs towards him beside the crumpled body of a woman in a torn grey dress. He dropped his shield against the fence of a nearby animal enclosure and advanced to place the point of his *gladius* below the closer man's ear. The legionary froze.

'First rule of war, soldier,' Valerius said quietly. 'If you don't keep your mind on the job, you get yourself killed.'

The second legionary turned with a nervous grin. He looked towards the first soldier questioningly, but Valerius shook his head and maintained just enough pressure on the sword to keep him honest.

'Nothing in there you'd want to see, sir.'

'I think I should decide that for myself, soldier. What century are you?'

'Third of the Second, sir. We—'

A muffled cry of distress interrupted his words and Valerius pushed past him and stepped into the hut. At first he could see nothing in the darkness, but as his eyes acclimatized to the gloom he heard a rhythmic shuffling and traced it to a white blur at the rear of the hut. On closer inspection the blur was identified as a pair of male buttocks heaving and thrusting at something below it. He gave the buttocks a sharp kick and the heaving stopped. The man turned his head and stared up at him. The pale eyes were no longer expressionless. They could have been those of the Briton Valerius had killed earlier. The only difference was that in Crespo's the killing rage was more controlled.

'Go and find your own whore.' The centurion's voice was slurred with lust and contained a clear warning. He turned contemptuously away and began deliberately thrusting his hips back and forth in a brutal, almost violent motion. Over his shoulder Valerius could see two terrified, pain-filled eyes. He remembered the screams and wondered why the girl – she could be no more than twelve years old – now stayed silent. Then Crespo moved again and he understood. As he held his victim down with one hand, with the other the centurion had forced a dagger between the girl's lips, the point at the back of her throat. He only had to shift his weight and she would be dead. Valerius almost gagged on the wave of disgust that swept through him. He turned as if to walk away, then spun and with all his strength swung a kick that took Crespo on the side of the skull, pitching him clear off the girl and catapulting the dagger from his hand.

The kick would have knocked a lesser man

senseless. Crespo only shook his head and launched himself across the hut. Valerius was able to half side-step the charge, but Crespo caught him with just enough force to throw him off balance and send his own sword flying. A fist landed a glancing blow below Valerius's left cheek and he felt fingers clawing for his eyes. He retaliated with a punch of his own that took the centurion square on the chin and knocked him backwards, so he stumbled and almost fell. When he stooped to the floor Valerius thought he had stunned or disabled him, but Crespo straightened with the knife glittering in his right hand.

The Sicilian didn't hesitate. He came in fast, hold-ing the dagger low, point upwards, and feinting right and left, but Valerius knew he would go for the soft flesh of the lower belly just below the armour. He had no doubt that Crespo wanted to kill him, but he felt no fear at the sight of the blade. It was what made him a soldier. He knew instinctively he was quicker than his opponent. He allowed the centurion to come in close before twisting his body so that the thrust slid down his left side. The blade scored his hip and he gasped at the lightning streak of pain, but the sacrifice had been worthwhile. As he pivoted he grasped Crespo's knife arm with both hands and used the man's momentum to swing him against the centre post of the hut with a force that shook the whole structure. The centurion's unprotected face took most of the impact and he reeled back spitting blood and teeth, with one eye already swelling closed. Still he retained the strength to stagger towards Valerius. Would the man never give up? The tribune allowed Crespo to take two tottering paces then stepped forward and smashed the reinforced cross-brace of his helmet into the centurion's forehead, dropping him like a poleaxed bull.

Valerius picked up his sword and stood over the prone body. He remembered the feeling of power when he had killed the Briton and fought back the urge to experience it again. It would be neater. Crespo was capable of anything. He would never forgive or forget the disgrace of a defeat. But the moment passed quickly and all Valerius felt was a curious emptiness.

A sob attracted his attention and he turned to see the girl standing naked against the rear wall of the hut with one hand to her mouth and the other covering her sex. Fresh blood stained her inner thighs and Valerius had to look away. 'You!' he snapped to the two men staring wide-eyed from the doorway. 'Cover her up and put her with the rest.' He took a last sickened look at the figure on the floor, noisily snoring through a broken nose. 'When he wakes up tell him to report to the legate.'

IV

'You are a fool, Valerius. You should have killed him and had done with it. Instead you burden me with trouble I don't need and paperwork I don't have time to deal with.' Valerius stood at attention in front of the legate's desk, exactly where Crespo should have been standing. The general pursed his lips and frowned. 'Did you really think I would arrest Crespo? The man may only be a centurion but he has powerful friends. When I took command of this legion I received letters of commendation about him from my three predecessors. Look!' He waved a document he had been reading. 'One of them is now a consul, another a military adviser to the Emperor. I do not need enemies like that.'

'He raped—'

'I know what you say he did, but where is your

evidence? The two soldiers you say watched him claim they saw nothing.'

'The girl—'

'Is dead.'

Valerius remembered the helpless, sobbing figure being led from the hut. Of course. The legate was right. He'd been a fool.

'Even if what you say is true – and I don't doubt that it is – I would remind you that this is a punishment expedition. The men of this tribe murdered twenty of my cavalry and they have paid the price for it. Some would say the price was light and that centurion Crespo was only carrying out the punishment in his own fashion. He may have overstepped his orders but I'm too short of experienced officers to lose him. Tribunes come and tribunes go but our centurions are the backbone of the legion.'

'But the law,' Valerius protested. 'We came here to bring these people under the protection of the Empire. Are they to be denied that protection? Allowing Crespo to do what he did and go free makes us as much barbarians as the Celts.'

A spark of anger flared in the legate's eyes. 'Do not try my patience, tribune. Not only are you a fool, but you are a naive fool. There is no law on the battlefield. Keep your high-minded arguments for the courts. You talk of civilization, but you cannot have civilization without order. We came to this island to bring order and order can only be achieved by the use of force. Rome has decided the tribes are a resource to be harvested. If we must flatter their kings to get the best crop, we will do so. If flattery fails, I am prepared to exterminate as many as it takes to ensure the message is heard and understood. If you do not have the stomach for the work say so, and I will have you on the first ship home.

'It is important that we demonstrate to the Silurians who rule here. The scouting party they ambushed was no ordinary patrol. It included a metallurgist sent directly from Rome. Somewhere out there,' he waved a hand to indicate the hills to the west, 'is the primary source of British gold. It was his job to find it. Instead, he ended up with his head on a pole.' He paused and stared out of the tent to where the legionaries and auxiliaries were busy dismantling the camp around them. 'I had intended to continue this demonstration, but that is no longer possible. I have received orders to retire to Glevum and prepare for a major campaign next year. We will march on Mona.'

The name sent a shiver through Valerius. Every Roman had heard of the blood-soaked Druids' Isle and the terrible rites that took place there.

'The druids are at the heart of every obstacle we face in Britain,' the legate continued. 'But by the time next year's harvest ripens there will be no more druids. Governor Paulinus intends to attack the sect's stronghold with two legions, including the Twentieth. We will wipe the island clean of the vermin priests and every Briton who follows them, and when that phase is completed we will turn south and destroy the power of the Ordovices and Silures once and for all.'

He turned to face Valerius. 'You will take the First cohort to winter at Colonia Claudia Victricensis. A season repairing roads in the snow is just what they need to keep them battle-ready. Work them hard and, when they're not working, train them hard. They are my best fighting troops and you are my best fighting officer. Do not let me down.' Valerius opened his mouth to protest. Colonia, Claudius's 'City of Victory', lay a hundred miles to the east and was the last place he wanted to be posted when the legion was preparing for an important campaign. It had been the site of the British surrender to the Emperor, when it was known as Camulodunum, and was the first Roman city created in Britain, although it was becoming increasingly overshadowed by the new port and administrative centre at Londinium. Livius continued before he could interrupt. 'Centurion Crespo will only be fit for light duties for some weeks.' The legate suppressed a smile, remembering the battered face and outraged protestations of innocence. 'He will accompany the main unit to Glevum where he will be given duties commensurate with his standing and his rank. Under normal circumstances he would take over the First cohort when you return to Rome, but that may not be ideal. I will think on it.'

For a moment Valerius thought he had misheard: he'd been certain the summer campaign meant a reprieve. The legate read the look on his face.

'Oh, yes, Valerius, you cannot escape your destiny. In the spring you will return the First to Glevum and then await a ship to take you back to Rome. I will be sorry to lose you, my boy. I did try to intercede on your behalf but it would take more than a legate and an impending battle to alter what is written on a bureaucrat's scroll.'

Four days later Valerius led his men in full marching order past the wooden walls of Londinium, and smiled as he heard the subdued muttering behind him. The city called to him just as loudly as it did to his soldiers, but where the legionaries heard the siren sound of the inns and the brothels along the quay, Valerius craved only his first proper bath in three months.

'They're restless.' His second in command, Julius, a twenty-year veteran who had replaced Crespo as the unit's senior centurion, rode at his side. Auxiliary cavalry scouts ranged ahead and on the flanks, and behind the two commanders the cohort marched in its centuries.

'They're not alone,' Valerius agreed. The men knew that the slaves captured at the hill fort would bring them a month's pay each and a soldier never liked to keep money in his purse for long. 'But we've been ordered directly to Colonia and that means another two hours on the road and two more with a shovel before we can rest. A pity; I'd have liked to visit Londinium again. It's surprising how the place has grown in only a year.'

Julius followed his gaze. From behind the wooden palisade the smoke from hundreds of cooking fires hazed the sky. But Londinium had already overflowed the boundaries set by the engineers who had sited the port and the fortress which guarded it. Upstream and down, new buildings of wood and stone fringed the bank of the broad River Tamesa. Where once only willows had grown now stood the homes and the workshops of merchants of every sort, drawn to the town by the scent of profit. At each of the three gates a settlement of huts and shops clung to the edges of roads along which the bounty of an empire passed each day. It must have been close to here that Claudius had fought the decisive battle which destroyed the might of the southern tribes. Valerius had heard fifty thousand men died that day, but he knew the figure would be exaggerated. Soldiers always inflated their successes and then the politicians inflated them a little more. No matter, it had been a great victory, one which had won Claudius the triumph that cemented his next dozen years on the throne. Now he was dead, and the Emperor was Nero, a man just a year younger than Valerius. Nero's mother, Agrippina, had died only a few months earlier. He'd heard whispers she had been murdered, but that wasn't something a lowly tribune dwelt upon if he valued his career.

The cohort had marched from the Silurian border on the military road through the Corinium gap, then on to the easier going of the gentle rolling downlands inhabited by the Atrebates, most Romanized of all the British tribes. Military roads were designed to allow the legions swift passage, elevated on a bed of earth and compacted stone, and paralleled by two deep ditches. You knew Rome was here to stay when such roads spread their tentacles across the land. They were the ropes that bound a vanquished nation; ropes that could become a noose if circumstances required it. A legion in a hurry could march twenty miles a day along these roads, but Valerius had set a more leisurely pace. The men deserved some rest after their efforts in taking the Silurian fort.

'You were here with Claudius?'

Julius shook his head. 'Not with Claudius. With Aulus Plautius. Claudius didn't arrive until the main battle was over. It was the Twentieth and the Fourteenth who forced the bridges, but if I'm being honest the Second did most of the fighting.'

'I thought the Ninth were there as well?'

Julius spat. 'You know the Ninth: last on the battle-field and first off it.' Valerius grinned. The rivalry between the Ninth and the Twentieth was legendary; any bar where off-duty soldiers of the two met was certain to become a battleground.

A decurion approached and reported that one of the recent recruits to the fourth century was struggling to keep the pace. His centurion requested a short halt to allow the man to recover. Valerius opened his mouth to agree, but then he remembered the legate's words of a few days earlier. Did he want to be liked or did he want to be a leader?

He shook his head. 'I won't stop the cohort because one man can't keep up. Assign two of his section to help him. If he's still lagging we'll leave him at the next way station. He can rest there and follow on to Colonia in his own time.'

'But—' Julius interrupted.

'I know,' Valerius said sharply. If they left the man behind without written orders he'd have trouble persuading any military post to feed him and might well be accused of desertion. 'This is the First cohort of the Twentieth, not a parade of Vestal Virgins. When he gets to Colonia make sure he gets extra training. Think, Julius. Think what would happen if he was left behind in some valley on the way to Mona.'

Julius nodded. He had seen the result when Roman prisoners fell into the hands of the Britons. He remembered a night on guard on a river bank: screams from the darkness and a terrible, flaming figure. And in the morning blackened lumps of charcoal that had once been men he had called friends.

They reached the halt by late afternoon; the scouts had already marked out the position of the cohort marching camp. Each legionary took his place without thinking in a combined effort they had carried out a thousand times before. Men dug, erected palisades or put up tents. A fortunate few formed hunting parties to seek out hare or deer to supplement the monotonous legionary rations. They

61

had only covered a dozen miles since dawn but Valerius was satisfied. He knew they'd reach Colonia in four more days and he was in no hurry. The only thing that awaited him there was barrack-room walls and boredom.

He was wrong.

V

They approached from the west, on the Londinium road, through a gap in one of the great turf ramparts which had once defended Cunobelin's Camulodunum. Colonia's origins were clear the moment the city itself came into view. It stood on a low, flat-topped rise above a river crossing; a classic defensive position designed to dominate all the country around. What had once been a continuous ditch, backed by a turf wall and topped by a wooden palisade, surrounded the city, but much of it was now obliterated by new buildings and orchards. To the north, beyond the river, the ground rose in a hogs-back ridge that stretched for miles from east to west. Once, the ridge must have been wild land, wood and bog, but it had been tamed by the dozens of farm-steads and the occasional small villa that dotted the hillside. At the eastern end of the ridge Valerius could just make out the distinctive outline of a military signal tower. The layout of the farms was almost entirely Roman because they were occupied by Roman citizens. The men who had won this land – cleared it, ploughed and sown it – had been granted that right by the Emperor Claudius in honour of his victory on the Tamesa. They were twenty-five-year veterans of the four legions who had conquered Britain. Men who had reached the end of their service and been rewarded either with twenty *iugera* of prime land or a share in the legionary fortress they had turned into the first Roman colony in Britain. In return they pledged their service as militia and vowed to protect what they'd been given. That had been eight years earlier and from a distance it looked as though they had used the time well.

Beyond the broken walls lay the familiar grid of streets that had originally been home to a legion. Once, those streets would have been lined with tents, then permanent legionary barracks, but now *insulae*, apartment blocks, some of them three storeys high, jostled the roadways. Valerius's attention was drawn to a small group of soldiers gathered beside the western entrance, an honour guard to welcome the cohort to its temporary home, and he instinctively straightened his helmet and adjusted the plate armour beneath his cloak. Behind him, he heard the centurions and decurions closing up the ranks. He smiled. Of course, they would want to make a show before the men of another unit.

But as he approached the legionaries at the gate, he sensed something odd. A Roman soldier's equipment had changed little over the last thirty years, but the armour and weapons of the men arrayed to welcome him appeared curiously dated. And something else was missing: a legionary had a certain posture, a straight-backed solidity that hinted at strength and stamina. These men looked to have neither. They stood ten to each side of the roadway beneath a modest triumphal arch that was in the latter stages of completion, and as Valerius rode towards them a soldier wearing a centurion's crested helmet stepped smartly into the road in front of him and saluted.

Valerius reined in and dismounted, returning the salute. 'Tribune Gaius Valerius Verrens commanding the First cohort of the Twentieth legion, on assignment to Colonia for the winter,' he announced formally.

The man pulled back his shoulders. 'Marcus Quintus Falco, First File of the Colonia militia, at your service.'

Valerius attempted not to stare. The militiaman facing him was like no soldier he had seen before. For a start, he was an old man, perhaps more than fifty, with a well-trimmed beard peppered with grey and a substantial paunch that bulged over his belt beneath the oft-mended chain-mail vest that covered his chest and shoulders. His helmet was of a pattern that Valerius only recognized because he'd seen it on altar stones dedicated to the men of Julius Caesar's legions – men who had last worn those helmets a hundred years earlier. The cloak he wore had been washed so many times the original vibrant red had faded to a sickly pink, and the leather of his scabbard was worn through at the point. Each member of the welcoming party shared their commander's failings to a degree. Slumped shoulders weighed down by out-of-date, rust-pitted armour. Lined faces staring out from beneath antique helmets. The hands that held the spears were veined and wrinkled.

'Your scouts brought word this morning that you were on the way.' Falco ignored the stare. 'No soldier is more welcome here than a ranker of the Twentieth. We have prepared ground for your men's tents in the old horse lines, but we hope that you personally will accept our hospitality and stay as a guest of the town.'

Valerius opened his mouth to refuse, but Julius appeared at his side before he could speak. 'Centurion Julius Crispinus makes his greetings,' he rapped out, and there was a respect in his voice that surprised Valerius. It took a lot to win Julius's respect. 'How are you, Primus Pilus?'

Falco squinted, focusing on the newcomer's face. 'Julius? An officer? No, it cannot be. I knew a Julius once who was only fit for cleaning out the latrines.' Valerius waited for the eruption that would inevitably follow this insult, but Julius only laughed.

'And I knew a First File once with shoulders like a bull, not a belly like one.'

With a grin, Falco reached forward to take the centurion's hand by the wrist and drew him forward into an embrace that was more father and son than a meeting of military equals. 'By the gods it's good to see you again, Julius. A centurion, and a proper centurion too.' He reached out to touch the medals that hung from the younger man's chest. 'Where did you win these *phalerae*?'

Julius mumbled something and blushed like a boy and Valerius decided he'd better rescue his centurion. 'You will have the opportunity to continue this reunion later,' he suggested. 'I'd like to get the cohort settled in and fed. Julius? Find the granary and organize the replenishment of our stores.'

'Sir!'

'I can take you. If you'd agree, tribune?' Falco offered. 'My men will lead you to the camp ground. No digging for the Twentieth tonight. The defences are prepared and the latrines ready.'

Valerius nodded. 'In that case we'll fall them out once they're fed. They deserve something after a week on the march. Three hours on the town should do it. But make sure everyone knows I want them back by dark or I'll have the skin off their backs.' He paused, remembering previous nights. 'And I want them back alone. Defaulters to stand guard.'

Falco shook his head. 'No need for guards here. My men will cheerfully do duty for you. In any case, this is Colonia; you won't find a quieter place in the whole of the province.'

'That may be, sir,' Valerius said mildly. 'But the First is my cohort and no cohort of mine beds down for the night without a guard. Not in Colonia; not if we were in the Forum in Rome.'

Falco acknowledged the censure with a smile. 'You shame me, tribune. As you can see it is a long time since I served. Ten years ago I hope my reply would have been exactly the same. Come, Julius, we have much to discuss.'

Valerius followed the honour guard through the arch and on to the *decumanus maximus*, Colonia's main street. Once they were within the town he glanced at his surroundings. The *insulae* had walls of white plaster punctured by small, shuttered windows. Many of the ground floors were occupied by shops offering the kinds of goods you would find anywhere in the Empire: fine glassware and jewellery, cloth and linen of every colour and quality, *garum*, the fish sauce without which no meal was complete, fruits, even figs that he knew must have been imported from far in the east, and of course wine by the *amphora*, without which any Roman colony would grind to a halt within a day. Competing vendors called out their prices and leatherworkers and potters showed off their wares. Everything spoke of a prosperous, thriving and settled community. His nostrils were assaulted by the sharp stink of a tanning yard and the strong smell of piss told him a dyer was at work nearby. The legate of a legion once ruled here, but now Colonia would be run by an elected town council. A crowd lined the street and children cheered as the men passed and he knew the legionaries would have their chests puffed out and the centurions would be snarling in their ears if they put a foot out of place. A small triumph in its way, but any triumph was to be savoured. Soldiers generally had a wary relationship with the civilian population. Profits could be made, but soldiers meant extra mouths to feed and more taxes, and civilians didn't like taxes. Colonia was different. This was an army town, with army wives and army children. They knew how to treat a fighting man. Valerius's soldiers might be weary after days on the road, but he could sense their excitement at the chance to spend time in proximity to civilization.

But was it truly civilization? His eyes strayed again to the buildings around him, and he noted that many were simply reused barrack blocks, subdivided into homes. Even those that had been rebuilt showed signs of having been thrown up in a hurry. He'd thought Colonia a true example of a Roman provincial town, but now he studied it he realized it was a caricature of one. It had none of the comfortable solidity or deep roots that could be found even in Gaul or Espana. The feeling grew as they turned left on to what had been the *via principalis*, past the Forum and the *curia*, which was simply part of the original headquarters complex, extended and with an extra storey added. Here the town's toga-clad elders gathered on the steps, but he kept his eyes to the front and marched the cohort past with only a covert glance. A protocol must be followed. First, he would settle in his men. Then he would wait for their invitation, which would arrive in its own good time.

Falco had been as good as his word. The tent lines were laid out with symmetrical precision and it would be the work of a few minutes to erect them. No ditches to be dug today. And here at least the defensive wall was intact, probably because the area had yet to be earmarked for development. The old soldier was right; they were as secure as they would be in the fortress at Glevum. Still, he thought, there will be a guard tonight and every night. Civilization could make a soldier soft and he would not allow that to happen. They needed to be hard for what awaited them in the spring. He would make sure they were.

Beyond the flat, hardened earth of the camp ground was the beginnings of a semicircular structure which must be the town's theatre. And beyond that again, something which astonished him.

The Temple of Claudius.

Of course, he had heard tales of its grandeur, but nothing had prepared him for the reality. It was the glory of Britain. Constructed of creamy white marble and glowing like a beacon even in the flat light of an early autumn afternoon, the temple dwarfed every-thing around it. Wide, fluted columns five or six times the height of a man supported an enormous triangular architrave with a decorative marble frieze showing a bull being led to the sacrifice, and another depicting the Emperor Claudius riding in a chariot. Gold statues of winged Victory rose tall at each corner of the pitched roof. The temple stood in the centre of a walled precinct perhaps a hundred and fifty paces square with the entrance in the middle of the southern wall, which was set back from the line of the main street. Building plots and vegetable gardens dotted the area around the precinct, but the isolation merely served to emphasize the structure's immense scale. Intrigued, Valerius left his officers to set up the cohort headquarters and walked to the front of the precinct to take a closer look. Here the wall was lower and he was able to see the massive building in its entirety. He had been taught to admire the balanced symmetry and perfection of form of fine architecture, and in the Temple of Divine Claudius he found it manifested in a place he would never have expected.

'Wonderful, isn't it?' He turned to discover a tall, balding figure in a pristine white toga standing behind him. The man studied him complacently. 'The Emperor sent an architect from Rome to supervise the building and every ounce of marble was carried here from the quarries at Carrara. It is of similar design to the temples at Nemausus and Lugdunum in Gaul, larger than the first, but slightly smaller than the second. Tiberius Petronius Victor, *quaestor* and adviser to the council,' he introduced himself.

Valerius smiled to show he was impressed, but

something in the man's voice – a certain unnecessary arrogance – irritated him. Pride was something he understood, but it was as if Petronius wanted him to believe he'd personally laid every stone.

'Tribune Gaius Valerius Verrens of the Twentieth. I lead a detachment of the First cohort. We will be based here for the winter.'

Petronius smiled in his turn, showing an array of white teeth that were so unnaturally perfect they might have belonged to another, much younger man. 'I knew of your coming, of course. I myself served with the staff of the Second.' The words were accompanied by a certain inflexion that made Valerius aware their status among the equestrian classes was approximately equal, but also raised an intriguing question in the younger man's mind. Normally, a *quaestor* would serve on the procurator's staff for two years, but Petronius gave the impression of being a permanent member of the city's bureaucracy. 'We have much to do here, as you see. Colonia should be the pride of Rome, yet we have barely started. In the beginning we were encouraged to be ambitious, perhaps overly so. Projects were begun but never properly completed, public buildings commissioned but never built. The veterans,' his tone made it clear he didn't care to be included among them, 'preferred to spend their money and their time on the land. Even then, we might have succeeded, but the temple . . .'

Naturally, when the Emperor had ordered the construction of the temple which would bear his name, every *sestertius*, every *denarius* and every *aurius* must be dedicated to it. Such funds could be diverted, of course, but there was an unspoken admission that it would take a braver man than Petronius to do it.

'Yet, as you say, it is wonderful,' Valerius said politely.

Petronius gave a tight smile. 'You are invited to join us tomorrow at the eighth hour, in the banqueting hall in the precinct.' He indicated a doorway in the eastern wall.

Valerius nodded his acceptance. 'I will be glad to attend.'

'When will your men be ready to start work? As I said, there is much to do here and the rains will begin soon.'

Valerius realized that Petronius expected his legionaries to carry out construction work in Colonia itself, and he almost laughed. 'I'm sorry, *quaestor*,' he said, allowing his voice to take on an edge of irritation. 'My men are soldiers, not house-builders. They carry out military projects. We have a warrant to repair the roads and bridges to the north of here.' With a curt nod and one final look at the temple, he returned to his men.

VI

Three hours later Julius lurched into the cohort's administrative tent to find Valerius sitting in the lamplight at his collapsible desk with a writing block in front of him and a stylus in his hand.

'My apologies, tribune, I understood you were staying in the town. If I'd known . . .'

Valerius looked up. 'No apologies required, Julius. That's exactly what I intended to do, but I wanted to see the men settled in, and I rode out to visit the cavalry *ala* at the auxiliary camp to the south-east. They're Thracians who've been here since just after the invasion and their prefect is a very conscientious young man – Bela, son of one of their tribal chieftains. His troopers showed me some tricks on horseback that would make your hair stand on end. Tomorrow will be time enough to seek out my billet. I'll be happy in a tent tonight.'

'Falco . . .'

'Falco is an unusual officer.'

'A good officer. The best.'

Valerius accepted the unspoken reproach. 'They tell me he has three thousand men under his command?'

Julius shook his head. 'Perhaps nominally, but he gives the figure as less, nearer two thousand. But two thousand veterans who were once the cream of the legions. The Colonia militia. They don't look like proper soldiers, I'll grant you. But that doesn't make them bad soldiers. I served with many of them. As long as they can walk and carry a sword they can still fight.'

'As long as you don't ask them to walk far.'

Julius laughed. 'Yes, I wouldn't like to march them much more than a mile. But I'd venture they're still good, and they'll stand. You'll see.'

'I'll see?'

'He – Falco – requests that you inspect them. He'll have them on parade on Saturday, on the old cavalry exercise ground by the river. Will you agree, sir?' There was a hint of appeal in Julius's voice and Valerius realized that Falco was seeking a chance to prove himself and his men. Saturday was five days away: plenty of time to polish armour and sharpen swords.

'Of course. What was he like . . . as an officer?'

'A complete bastard.' Julius laughed again. 'But the toughest, hardest-fighting bastard in the entire Roman army. You'd have liked him.'

'I think I do like him.'

'Now he's a wine merchant. Rich. He imports Faustianum wines from Falernia and sells them to the British aristocrats and legionary messes across the south. A good man to know.' The words came out a little slurred and it was clear Julius had sampled his old friend's wares while they'd been reminiscing about old times.

'You should sleep, Julius. I want the men ready for a full inspection at dawn as usual. Then we'll put them through their paces. No reason why we shouldn't give old Falco and his militia something to think about over the next few days. It'll do them good to see real soldiers sweat.'

Julius yawned. 'You're right, sir. Perhaps a little too much of the good vintage.' He turned to leave. 'Oh, I almost forgot. You are invited to a dinner at the temple tomorrow. Apparently the council is eager to meet you.'

'I know. Just what I need: four hours of boring provincial gossip and a sore head the next morning. I'd rather storm another hill fort.'

The centurion smiled. 'For once I'm glad I don't have your social advantages. Good night, sir.'

Valerius rose before dawn. He detected an unfamiliar chill in the air that hinted at more than autumn, and he shivered as he washed and dressed. By the time he left the tent the men were already turned out in their sections and centuries on the parade ground. Eight hundred legionaries, five double-strength centuries rather than six normal ones because this was the First cohort, twenty eight-man sections to each century, the elite of the legion; the shock troops who would go where the danger was greatest and the fighting hottest.

He gave them a long look. Marius's Mules they called themselves. Lean and tough: mostly men of only medium height, but strong and hardy. If necessary they could march twenty miles in a day, carrying the sixty-pound loads of their gear, rations and weapons, and be ready to fight a battle within the hour.

But on closer inspection the First was not quite the perfect fighting machine it appeared. He walked along the ranks with Julius at his side, pulling at straps to ensure the armour was tight and pointing out an occasional imperfection on a weapon or a piece of equipment. Not that there was much to point out. As usual, the turnout was exemplary. He knew how difficult it was to keep armour bright in the damp British air and the constant attention required to stop leather from rotting. No, it was the legionaries themselves who were out of condition. The eyes that stared through him as he walked along the lines were red-rimmed and buried deep, like slingshot pellets fired at a mud bank. The rank smell of stale wine assailed his nostrils. He heard the sound of vomiting from one of the rear centuries, but decided not to notice.

'Your name and rank, soldier?' he barked at a bleary-eyed specimen who stood out because he was taller than any man in his unit.

'Decimus Lunaris, *duplicarius*, front rank, second century, sir.' The answer was equally brisk. A *duplicarius* was a double-pay man, a senior legionary with a trade.

'So, Lunaris. My orders were to return to the camp before sunset. Were those orders obeyed?'

'Sir!'

'They were, sir. I counted them in myself,' Julius said helpfully.

Valerius stared at him, but Julius had been as helpful as he was going to be.

'You don't look like a man who returned to camp before dark, Lunaris. You look very much like a man who spent the entire night drinking. How do you account for that?'

Lunaris opened his mouth, then hesitated.

'Speak freely, legionary. You're among friends here,' Valerius said smoothly, allowing a note of sympathy to coat his voice. Lunaris grinned. He was among officers here, and he knew an invitation to walk into a trap when he heard one.

'I look like a man who's *had* an entire night's worth of drink, sir.'

Valerius raised an eyebrow.

'You specified the time, sir, but not the volume. The second century likes a challenge, sir.'

Valerius stifled a laugh. 'Six merit points to the second century for enterprise, centurion.' He watched Julius note the award on his writing tablet. 'So, Lunaris, the second century likes a challenge?' The legionary studied him warily. 'I want the second century to be ready in full battle order in five minutes; *scutum* and a pair of *pila*, do you think, Julius? Then the second century will lead the cohort on three full circuits of the outer walls . . . at double pace.' He looked up at the sky, which was now a deep, cloudless blue. 'That should be enough of a challenge before noon.'

Lunaris had barely completed half a circuit at the head of the unit by the time Valerius caught up with him, but sweat was already pouring down the *duplicarius*'s face.

'That must be almost pure wine. You shouldn't waste it.'

Lunaris looked across, surprised. Most tribunes weren't prepared to suffer with their men. But then he'd heard this one wasn't like most tribunes. Valerius wore his full armour and carried his shield on his left arm and a pair of the heavy *pila* in his right hand. Normally a legionary on the march bore his shield in a leather cover on his back, and, unless there was an imminent threat of danger, a handy mule transported the majority of the unit's spears. The shield was big and heavy and needed constant adjustment to stop it obstructing its bearer, and the two spears had a habit of crossing so that the lead weights which gave them their accuracy and power wanted to go in different directions. Added to the difficulty of jogging across uneven ground with a large pot on your head, cooking in an iron shell, it made for an interesting exercise.

'Not wine . . . vinegar.'

Valerius shot him a puzzled look.

'The bars here,' Lunaris grunted. 'The wine they sell is pure vinegar.' He grinned and gradually stepped up the pace, but if he thought he would leave the tribune behind he soon found he was mistaken. Valerius's long, powerful legs covered the ground in a loping stride that never seemed to falter. His armour had been fitted by an expert and allowed him greater ease of movement and less chafing than the *segmentata* worn by the rank and file. It was lighter too, but just as strong, because the armourer had chosen iron with a greater carbon content. By the second circuit, Lunaris was drawing in the warm air in prolonged, shuddering gasps, and Valerius could hear groans from the ranks behind him. He slowed imperceptibly, allowing the grateful *duplicarius* to drop back with him. As he ran, he studied Colonia's walls and defensive ditch.

'What do you think of the defences, soldier?'

Lunaris spat. 'What defences?'

'My feelings entirely,' Valerius agreed. 'I think we'll double the guard tonight, just in case. Second century to supply the first watch.' He moved away so he wouldn't hear Lunaris cursing under his breath.

VII

She was tall, was that his first impression? No, it was her eyes, he decided; he was drawn to her eyes, which were wide and curious and framed by long lashes. Irises of a deep chestnut brown contained a message which was at once challenging and mocking, and, perturbingly, left him feeling quite naked. Lustrous, shoulder-length hair which matched them was swept back from a broad forehead, leaving tendrils to highlight the perfect oval of her face. The nose perhaps a little too delicate, the mouth a little too wide for classic beauty, but in her they combined to create something more. She wore a full-length crimson dress, the design of which said Roman but something about the way she wore it said not. All this in the time it took for an arrow to leave the bow, or a shot the sling. As he stared into them the eyes changed shape and became serious and he realized the military commander Falco was talking to him.

'. . . And this is Lucullus, our foremost Briton, a lord of the local tribe, the Trinovantes, and a long-time friend to Rome.'

A short, rotund man bowed and smiled ingratiatingly. Valerius would have moved on – the local Britons were of little interest to him except as potential enemies – but Lucullus stood his ground and waved the girl forward.

'My daughter, Maeve,' he said.

Maeve?

Valerius turned to acknowledge her but she was already walking towards the gate of the temple complex. He stared at the slender retreating figure and was rewarded with a venomous backward glance aimed, fortunately, at her father. He felt an almost unstoppable urge to follow her, but Falco took his arm and steered him round the still smiling Lucullus with a sniff of irritation.

'Tiberius Petronius Victor, whom I understand you have already encountered.' Valerius's mind remained focused on the girl but he noted the hint of disapproval in Falco's voice. 'He is Colonia's senior magistrate, the procurator's personal representative here and one of our leading citizens.' The militia commander gave a brittle smile. 'And he has a tight grip on the town's purse strings.'

Petronius produced a laugh equally devoid of humour. Clearly little love was lost between the two men. 'Each of us has our priorities, Quintus. Mine is to ensure we create a Colonia worthy of the Emperor's name it holds. We have real soldiers, like the tribune here, to keep us safe in our beds. Why should we spend a king's ransom so that your little army can strut the streets like peacocks?'

Valerius expected the insult to provoke a violent reaction, but it seemed this was an argument so well rehearsed it had lost its power to inflame.

'Come.' Falco led him away from the *quaestor*. 'I will introduce you to the head of the *ordo*, our council of one hundred leading citizens.' When they were out of Petronius's earshot, he explained. 'He means why should we have shields that don't splinter at the first blow and why must we complain when we wear the same rusty swords we carried all the way from the Rhenus to the invasion all those years ago.'

'Every army has supply problems . . . even little armies,' Valerius said. He recognized the older man's frustration. Shortages were part of life in the legions. A soldier, even a Roman soldier, had to fight for everything he could get.

Falco looked at him sharply, wondering if he was being made fun of.

Valerius smiled. 'Perhaps while we are here we will lose a few shields and a few spears. My men are some-times careless.' There would be no shortages for a unit taking part in the governor's campaign against Mona, that was certain, and in any case he would be back in

Rome before the legion's quartermaster worked out what had happened.

The militia commander slapped his shoulder. 'Now I understand why Julius likes you. Come, we will share some wine. You should have been with us on the Tamesa: Catuvellauni warriors seven feet tall who took a dozen cuts and still wouldn't fall. I have nightmares about them even now . . .'

Still talking, he led the way into a long, narrow room with a patterned mosaic floor and walls painted with lifelike scenes of an emperor, who must be Claudius, carrying out his imperial duties as fawning courtiers looked on. Two of the paintings immediately caught Valerius's eye. In the first, the Emperor was depicted sitting high on the back of a gold-clad ceremonial elephant as a dozen splendid barbarian figures bowed before him. He realized this must be the surrender of Britain, which had taken place close to this very spot. The second took up an entire end wall and showed Claudius standing proudly on a hill above a broad river surveying the crossing of his legions and the hazy battle beyond.

'The Tamesa,' Falco whispered. 'Claudius wasn't even there. Didn't arrive until the next day. He was a fraud, old Claudius, but we didn't love him any the less for it.'

Valerius looked around to see if anyone was listening. Criticizing emperors, even long-dead emperors, was not something to be done lightly. But Falco only winked.

'If he was going to strike me down he'd have done it long ago, lad. I sweated and bled for him and now he's taking care of me in my old age. But he's still an old fraud.'

The room had been set for twenty-four people, with couches round the walls and a gilt table in the centre. Valerius found himself between Falco and Petronius, and opposite the Briton, Lucullus, who called for wine to be brought.

One by one he was introduced to the men who ran Colonia; bland mercantile faces his brain refused to accept had once been seasoned soldiers of Rome's finest legions. A few names stuck in his mind: Corvinus the goldsmith, wide-shouldered, dark-visaged and improbably handsome, who had turned his trade as the Twentieth's armourer into a more profitable business; Didius, tall and thin and with shifty eyes that fitted all too well with his profession as one of Colonia's foremost money-lenders; and Bellator, who seemed out of place because his exotic name and relative youth identified him as a freedman, and who now prospered by taking a cut of the rent from the *insulae* he administered for his former master. All had one thing in common. They were rich. They had to be, because membership of the *ordo* didn't come cheap, as Falco explained in his dry monotone.

'It has its compensations: prestige, which counts for little unless you are a certain type; access and patronage, which counts for more, particularly when that patronage comes from the Senate. We have our say upon who gets what contract, which buildings must be demolished and which must stay; we adjudicate in land and water disputes, all of which can be lucrative and creates a bank of favours which will one day be returned. But the cost . . .'

'Yet not so onerous as election to the *augustales*,' Petronius interrupted from Valerius's left.

'Easy for you to say, since a *quaestor* is above such lowly appointments,' Falco huffed. 'No payments to the treasury or public munificence from you, eh, Petronius?'

'*Augustales?*' Valerius enquired. The title was new to him. A slave brought wine in a silver cup and he accepted it, vowing only to sip, watered or not. The ripe, fruity scent reached his nostrils. No vinegar here. This was as good as anything that would be served at his father's table.

'The priests of the temple, those who officiate in the annual ceremonies central to the cult of Divine Claudius,' Petronius continued airily, taking a deep draught from his cup. 'It is a great honour . . . if you are a certain type.' Valerius noted the repeat of Falco's pointed phrase of a few moments earlier. 'However, it also carries great responsibilities.'

Valerius knew that in Rome to be elected to the priesthood of one of the great temples – Jupiter Capitolinus or Mars Ultor – brought with it substantial power and that such an appointment was only open to the knightly classes. 'Yet even at a price, it must be greatly sought after by the members of your council,' he said.

Petronius laughed, but Valerius felt Falco shift uneasily behind him. 'No Roman citizen would be foolish enough to accept it. We leave that honour to the Brittunculi.' Falco drew breath and the conversation in the room went quiet. Valerius saw the smile freeze on Lucullus's face, but Petronius carried on as if nothing had changed. 'For them, it is as close as they will ever come to *being* a Roman. Ah, at last. The food.'

Valerius watched as the dishes were set on the table. In Rome, a banquet like this would be an opportunity to show a flair for the exotic; peacocks still in their livery, swans artfully displayed to seem almost alive. But this was wholesome, rustic fare. Sizzling cuts of beef, venison and suckling pig. Duck, pigeon and partridge, and birds smaller still which looked like particularly plump sparrows. A great fish, probably from the river below, and oysters and crabs from the coast, which he knew to be just a few miles downstream. He set to with a will. Army rations could always be supplemented, but somehow they were still army rations. It had been many months since he'd sat down to such a feast. His companions, too, ate greedily; all except Lucullus, who nibbled at the food, still wearing his fixed smile.

Petronius raised his cup theatrically. 'Your health, sir. Would that we supped like this every day. No toast required with this wine.' The comment provoked a burst of laughter. Toasted bread was often crumbled into inferior wines to disguise the bitter taste.

He saw Valerius's look of surprise. 'Oh, yes.' He lowered his voice so the young tribune had to lean towards him to hear his next words. 'Lucullus, our British friend, is responsible for everything you see around you. Food and drink, the couch you lie on and even the upkeep of the building. He is a fine fellow. A friend of Rome and an *augustalis*. He cannot be a member of the *ordo* because although he has chosen a Roman name he is not a Roman citizen, nor ever will be. But as one of the priests of the temple he enjoys great honour among certain of his people and even influence in the Roman community.'

'He must be a very fortunate man.' Despite himself, Valerius was impressed. He considered the Celts rough tribesmen. A martial race of hut dwellers. Yet here was a Briton who had adopted Roman ways and already contributed to the new society that a Roman Britain would become.

'Fortunate?' Petronius gave a quiet belch. 'He has a villa on his farm on the hill yonder,' he waved a hand in the vague direction of the river, 'and he owns property in town. So, yes, I suppose he could be called rich.' He smiled and turned towards the neighbour on his left, leaving Valerius to study the figure across the table.

The appellation 'portly' could have been coined for Lucullus, but he carried his bulk in a way that told you he took pride in it; that it was, in some way, a measure of his success and position in life. He was short and rounded, with a fringe of mousy hair which circled the back of his head like an untidy laurel wreath. Valerius noted that he shaved his face in the Roman fashion, yet it shouted out that it would never be complete without the moustache his people habitually wore. Lucullus met his eyes and raised his cup in salute. His smile took on a sad, almost resigned aspect. Valerius had seen the look before in clients he had represented in minor court cases – the clients who inevitably lost. In that instant something like pity replaced the natural disdain he felt for the Trinovante. He raised his own cup in reply and wondered what Lucullus was thinking. He didn't have to wait long to find out.

'You must come and visit my estate,' the little man offered loftily in a clipped, unnatural Latin which had a curious singsong lilt. 'The hunting is good. No? You are not a hunter, then? Perhaps a man of culture. I have many fine pieces – from Rome itself, and even from Aegyptus. The man who painted these walls painted my own. I have a copy of the surrender in my *atrium.*'

Valerius knew he should decline the offer, but a beautiful face flashed into his head. *She* would be there, and this time she wouldn't be able to run away. 'If my duties permit it I would be happy to visit you.' He became aware of a change in the atmosphere, as if a shutter had been opened to allow in the sun. The fixed smile disappeared and a different Lucullus emerged; a Lucullus whose eyes twinkled with surprise and genuine pleasure. 'My estate manager will arrange it, then.'

For the rest of the meal, Valerius found himself the hub of attention for the members of the *ordo*. Was it true that his soldiers were to waste their time building roads when they had so much to complete in Colonia? How did he think the town compared with Londinium? What was the latest news from Rome? There was a rumour that Burrus might be out of favour. Had he heard the druids were returning? It was true: Corvinus had it from a trader, who had it from a merchant, who had it from a customer, who had it from . . .

He fended off the questions with polite, harmless non-answers until Falco concluded the proceedings. The banquet broke up with men leaving in pairs, one or two clinging to each other as a result of the effects of the wine. Valerius was surprised to see Lucullus walk out deep in conversation with Petronius.

Falco insisted on accompanying him back to the camp. 'Then I will guide you to the townhouse where you will stay while you are with us. It is owned by Lucullus, and very comfortable, but the *ordo* will provide the slaves. Better to be spied on by a Roman, eh?' He laughed.

'I thought your charter denied the Celts the right to own property in the town?'

Falco gave him a sideways look. 'The charter was drawn up in different times. Much has changed. It is true that technically no Briton should own property here, but if a man has money there are ways such technicalities can be circumvented. Third party agreements, for instance.'

'And who would the third party be in this case?' Valerius knew he was pushing the boundaries of their short acquaintance, but even the small amount of wine he had drunk had loosened his tongue.

The look again, longer this time. 'Let us just say that Lucullus would do well to be wary of his business partners.' The militia commander laughed. 'Of course, I am one of them. Lucullus provides transport for me. He has the largest wagon business in the province.'

'Julius told me you were a wine merchant.'

Falco's lips pursed as if he wasn't sure what he was. 'I suppose I am. I have a monopoly to supply every legionary mess and public office from here to Isca and from Noviomagus to Lindum. A shipload of *amphorae* in from Ostia every two weeks. How else would a simple soldier be able to afford to break bread with the likes of Petronius?'

Valerius had a feeling the older man was anything but a simple soldier, but he risked another question. 'When Petronius talked of the Brittunculi I had the impression he was referring to Lucullus.'

Falco nodded. 'It is a term that has become popular among a certain type of Roman; a term that is meant to belittle the Celts. For myself, I believe we must live and work with them, and that to insult them only stores up trouble for the future.' He paused, and Valerius knew enough to hold his tongue. 'Things were done, when Colonia was founded, that do none of us credit. Land fever, greed and envy all played their part. Our colonists are good men. They fought for Rome for twenty-five years and knew nothing but hardship. Who could deny that they deserved this land their Emperor had given them? But when a legionary sweating to dig up tree roots in parched ground looked across his boundary and saw a Celt picking rows of fine vegetables while his cattle drank sweet water from a dew pond, what was he to do? He was the victor, they were the vanquished. He took what he believed should be his. And if a Celt died,' he shrugged his shoulders, 'it was no real matter.

'Now people like Petronius look at Colonia and see the glory of Rome; invincible and sustained by the power of four full legions. And he has a point. We have had eight years of peace since Scapula stirred up his hornet's nest by attempting to disarm the tribes. Our farms and estates prosper and grow, and with them the town prospers and grows. The local Britons, those such as Lucullus who are prepared to work and trade with us, have done equally well, but . . .' He hesitated, and his face took on a troubled aspect. 'But I fear we take advantage of their good faith.'

It was the temple.

'Six years ago, when work began on the temple, Colonia was not the place you see now. Claudius was generous with his grant of land in the *territorium* around the city and each of us had our pension, but a farm needs investment and a town needs businesses and such things would drain the resources of even a rich man. Yet, when the Emperor was declared divine and we knew this was to be the centre of his cult in Britain, we were proud. He was *our* Emperor. But we reckoned without the priests. Those they sent from Rome created a Roman institution, with Roman rules and a Roman bureaucracy, to be run on Roman lines and to make a Roman profit. But Britain is not Rome. Colonia is not Rome. There is no old money here. No great fortunes garnered from hundreds of years of slaves' sweat on grand family estates. To accept the role of *augustalis* would mean ruination. Did you know that Claudius himself paid eighty thousand gold *aurei* when he entered the priesthood during Gaius Caligula's time?' He shook his head, as if the sum was beyond his wildest imaginings. 'Only one class could be persuaded . . . no, *flattered*, into accepting nomination: the British kings and aristocrats who had supported the invasion and therefore had the most to gain from being *magis Romanorum quam Romanorum* – more Roman than the Romans. King Cogidubnus, who rules the Atrebates and the Regni, was the first. One taste was enough for him, but he had set the precedent. Others followed, and now Lucullus, a prince of the Trinovantes who once held these lands.'

'But surely Lucullus could not . . .'

'No, of course Lucullus could not afford such

sums. But there are those in Rome prepared to lend them, even the Emperor himself, and members of his court; Seneca for one. It was he who loaned Lucullus the money to buy into the priesthood and provide the community with the theatre you see yonder. It should have been enough, but Lucullus believes he is a man of business. Where another might have seen the jaws of a trap he saw opportunity. He borrowed more to buy his wagons, which was a good investment. And more still to purchase six *insulae* in Colonia, which may or may not be. He pays commission to a Roman partner who nominally owns the buildings, who collects and passes on the rents. Like Bellator, though neither would thank me for making the comparison. On the surface, Lucullus is one of the richest men in Colonia. In reality he is rich only in debt. We are here.'

The townhouse stood in a street close to the Forum and not far from the legionaries' camp, which Valerius knew Falco, 'simple soldier' that he was, would have insisted upon. Part of him wished he had refused the offer to sleep beneath a solid roof in a soft bed, but refusal would be seen as bad manners. He would live with the guilt. It wouldn't make the men any more comfortable in any case.

Double doors opened on to the *atrium*, which in turn led to an open courtyard surrounded by a covered walkway, from which further doors gave access to other dwellings that no doubt shared the courtyard. He sensed a stillness to the place that spoke of lack of inhabitation, which suited Valerius perfectly but did not bode well for Lucullus's rents. The house itself turned out to be a modest enough place, pleasingly bright with unpainted walls and comfortable, functional furniture, and decorated in the Roman fashion with a few busts of notables who were unlikely to be related to the Briton but had probably been bought as part of a job lot. Pride of place – as he suspected it always would in Colonia – went to a flattering, painted marble likeness of Claudius.

'Your sleeping quarters are through here, and the latrine is beyond the courtyard.' Falco apologized for the lack of a bathhouse, but Valerius said he was happy enough to use the public facility. His effects had already been delivered, so as soon as the militia commander left he settled down and retrieved the copy of Thucydides' *History of the Peloponnesian War* he always carried. The Greek writer had served in the military, that was certain, but he was no soldier. Not quite Homer, on whose tales of Troy Valerius had been weaned, but an improvement on Herodotus, who was much too wordy for his taste. Later, he fell asleep haunted by a female face which never quite came into focus, and a sweet, tuneful voice he had never heard before.

VIII

It was the eyes, rather than the words, the chieftain thought. They made a man feel important, even a man who only held sway over a few farmsteads worked by his clan, a minor western sub-tribe of the Catuvellauni federation, and had little influence beyond his farthest field. The priest's eyes were the colour of the old amber the chieftain's wife coveted in the market down at Ratae, and hooded like a hawk's. Not that the chief visited the place often. He preferred the smell of cowshit to the perfume of the Roman-lovers who lived there in their palaces. For the first time in a decade his fingers itched for a sword. He had once been a warrior. The amber eyes made him feel like a warrior again.

Gwlym studied the group around the fire. Most of them were too old or too young to be truly useful in a fight. But not too old or too young to hate or too old or too young to die. The old remembered the days before the Romans came, when any man with a shield and a spear was his own master. The young knew nothing beyond the boundaries of the little settlement but their minds were open to his subtle arguments and persuasion. He talked of life before the Romans: before the roads and the watchtowers and the cavalry patrols, and before the taxes which guaranteed that no matter how good the harvest their bellies would still be empty before winter's end. He talked of the countless thousands marched off in chains to be worked to death in Roman mines, of the lands that had been stolen from them, and, to a growl of approval, of mighty Caratacus betrayed and brought low before being degraded for an emperor's pleasure. By the end, their eyes blazed as bright as the flames of the council fire, and the young men – those few who could be forged into warriors fit to face a legion – clamoured for the weapons they needed to take their revenge.

They wanted to act now, but the time was not yet right. This was the art they had taught him on Mona. How to tend the fire and keep the flame burning until the moment it was needed. He looked at the faces round the fire again, seeking the man who would continue the work when he moved on. Not the chief; too many years at the plough and too ready to sacrifice himself and his people. No, he needed someone more subtle, more obedient. The quiet, dark-haired peasant three rows back. Young, but not too young. Watchful, intelligent eyes; determined, but not over-eager. Yes. He would talk to him later, alone.

'Wait,' he ordered. 'Have patience. Organize. There will be a sign.'

And always they asked: what will be the sign?

And always he told them: the wrath of Andraste.

His mission had almost ended before it had begun, in the savage mountains of the Deceangli, for he could not risk contact with the people there lest word of his coming reach the Romans. Close to starvation, he had turned south and crossed into the country of the Cornovii just north of the Roman fortress at Viroconium, beyond the bend of the great river. There, he had forced himself to wait until he was beyond range of the daily cavalry patrols before begging food and shelter at a rough farmstead. Under the thatched roof, with the cattle lowing gently in the background, he had listened while the farmer, a man more used to conversing with his beasts, recounted news and rumour from a dozen miles around. Only when the tone and the manner had told him what he needed to know did he begin to talk.

The first farmer had passed him to another, and another, and from there he had reached the local lord, who told him of other lords of similar persuasion, with similar complaints and similar ambitions. He would arrive at a farm or a village after nightfall, gather those he could trust, and talk until it was time to sleep. The following day he would spend at the plough or the whetstone or gathering in the harvest. He used his skills as a healer to foster trust and to bind them to him, even though it placed his life in danger. Tales of a medicine man would spread and multiply where those of an itinerant farm labourer working for bread and beer would soon be forgotten. He was always at risk, but he was never betrayed.

By now he realized others followed the same path. Quite often he would arrive at a household to discover he had been preceded by another of his sect. No one said so aloud, but he could see it in the puzzled eyes, and in the answers they gave to his questions. All over southern Britain men like him were spreading a message: fanning the embers of an almost forgotten fire.

IX

Valerius spent his first few days in Colonia drawing up work schedules with Julius and directing squads of legionaries out into the network of roads around Colonia to identify the areas which required immediate attention and those which were less of a priority. Julius presented a local quarry-master with a warrant for the supply of the materials they would need and Valerius set himself the task of providing the wagons required to carry them. Which took him back to Lucullus.

The Trinovante welcomed him effusively to his office in the centre of town, apologizing for the humbleness of his surroundings. 'Of course, I carry out most of my business at the temple or the baths, like a true Roman,' he said.

When Valerius explained the reason for his visit,

Lucullus was delighted to be of service. He asked for information on the quantities of material to be hauled and the distances they had to be carried and swiftly calculated the number of wagons needed and the teams of oxen to pull them. 'You will need spare teams, of course. No point in having a wagon lying idle just because an ox needs to be rested.' He named a price, a time and a place for delivery and Valerius presented his warrant. He noted that the figure Lucullus wrote down bore no relation to the one he had just given.

'Now,' the Briton said. 'Do not think I have forgotten my invitation. I am holding a gathering a week today. Just a few people whose company I enjoy. I think you would find it interesting and perhaps illuminating. Would the fourth hour after noon be acceptable?'

Valerius agreed that it would, then asked the question that had been on his mind since he entered the room. 'And is your family well?'

Lucullus's face darkened. 'Families are like taxes, a trial to be tolerated. A son, perhaps, I could have guided. His father's success would have provided him with a path to follow. But I have no son. A daughter?' He shook his head sadly. 'Of course, you have no children yourself?'

Valerius smiled at the unlikely thought. 'I am not married.'

'Then you are doubly welcome.'

When he returned to the cohort headquarters,

Julius reminded him that the following day was Saturday, when he had agreed to watch the Colonia militia being exercised by Falco. Valerius grimaced. It had seemed a reasonable request at the time, but now there were so many other things requiring his attention. Still, it was a duty he couldn't avoid, not least out of respect for Falco.

They gathered on the flat ground between the broken remnants of the city walls and the river to practise close-order drill and arms. Two thousand men, once the elite core of the legions of Rome, with battle honours that stretched from Scythia to the Silurian mountains.

'Jupiter save us, will you look at them,' grunted Lunaris, who had accompanied Valerius as part of his twelve-man escort. 'Not one of them is under fifty. I'm surprised they could find their weapons, never mind use them.'

It was true there were few who appeared to own a full set of armour. Most had lost some piece of equipment since they last took the field almost a decade earlier: a breastplate, a helmet, a set of greaves. In those years they had grown used to the life of the farmer, the trader and the small-town politician, and nothing could disguise it. They were a mixture of the pot-bellied and the scrawny, the snowy-haired and the bald. Some of them hung heavy with the fat of success, others were bent by years of labour. They had one thing in common. They were old men.

But as Valerius watched from the top of the slope he realized his first impression had been flawed. There were other things that united them. What armour they did have and the weapons they carried were well cared for, no matter their antiquity. And although they were old, they were still legionaries: the barked commands were as familiar to Valerius and his men as the call to break fast, and it was apparent in every manoeuvre the veterans carried out. They moved from line to square to wedge, and from defence to attack, with the practised ease of a lifetime's experience. Every man knew his place, every shield and every sword was positioned exactly where it should be, and Valerius felt the pride rise in him as it always did when he witnessed professional soldiers at work.

He saw Falco, who he guessed wore the same ancient uniform as his men out of choice not necessity, watching him, and the wine merchant gave an order to the officer at his side. The legionaries came together smoothly into their centuries and in a single swift movement each of the eighty-man formations transformed into the unbreakable armoured carapace that was familiar to every Roman soldier.

'They'd give you a run for your money forming *testudo*, Lunaris.'

The big man grinned. 'I doubt they'd want to run for anything these days, sir.'

Valerius grinned back, but a warning in the legionary's eyes told him Falco was approaching. He turned and saluted the militia's Primus Pilus. 'I congratulate you on a fine display of arms, sir. Your militia does you great credit.'

Falco smiled his thanks. 'Only two afternoons a week, but we work hard – those of us who attend regularly, at least – and there are some things you never forget. It becomes more difficult with every passing year, and we grow fewer, but most regard it as a sacred trust. Claudius gave us a home and a living and we will serve him to the grave.' The words would have been falsely sentimental coming from another man, but from Falco they were a simple statement of fact. 'Come, take a closer look at them.' He lowered his voice, so that Lunaris and the escort wouldn't hear. 'I confess they have made an extra effort for you. We do not normally shine quite so brightly.'

They marched down to where the militia now waited in their silent lines facing the fortress. The exercise ground stretched away behind them, broad and flat, to the river bank where Colonia's main bridge carried the north road across to the long slope on the far side.

A single shout brought the militia to attention and Valerius followed Falco along the ranks. The lined faces beneath the helmets were pink-cheeked and sweat-slick and shoulders heaved from the earlier exertions, but the veterans straightened their backs and sucked in their bellies behind their shields and Valerius's stare was met by a hard-eyed confidence he hadn't expected to see. They might be farmers and shopkeepers now, but they would never forget what they had been.

It took an hour to complete the inspection, Valerius murmuring compliments where they were due and Falco following behind tutting at some minor fault only he could see. When they were done, to Valerius's surprise, the militia commander called out twelve of his men by name to line up in front of the formation.

'Would you like to try them out?' Falco invited. 'A dozen of yours against a dozen of mine?'

Valerius opened his mouth to refuse, for these were old men and his escort was the pick of the Twentieth legion, but there was a challenge in Falco's eyes and in his voice and Valerius – though it had occasionally cost him dearly – had never turned down a challenge. Only now did he notice that the men Falco had chosen were among the biggest and fittest on parade, and that they included Corvinus, the goldsmith, who was attempting to stifle a grin. Perhaps it wasn't the mismatch he'd thought.

'What do you think, Lunaris? A gentle workout?'

'Wouldn't like to hurt these old gentlemen, sir,' the *duplicarius* said.

'Chicken more likely.' It was an old soldier's trick to talk without moving the lips but Valerius thought the stage whisper probably came from Corvinus.

Lunaris's eyes narrowed and he grinned and ran his eye along the line of older men. 'Maybe just a gentle workout, then. But I'm not carrying them up the hill when we're done.' He drew his sword and tested it ostentatiously with his thumb.

'Oh, no swords,' Falco said hurriedly. 'We don't

want your fellows being hurt. A simple exercise of shield against shield.' He heard Lunaris's snort of derision. 'Well, perhaps practice swords, then.' A practice sword was a replica *gladius* made of hardwood. It had no edge or point, but it weighed twice the real thing and was perfectly capable of cracking bone or denting skull.

Lunaris and the men of the escort accepted shields from the closest century and practice swords were issued to each of the twelve men in the two lines, who stood directly opposite each other. The younger legionaries bristled with confidence and joked to one another, while the veterans waited calmly, conserving their energy. Cries of encouragement rang out from the rear ranks of the massed militia formation. Valerius cast a warning glance at Lunaris; he had a feeling this contest might not be as straightforward as it appeared.

'An *amphora* of my best wine on the outcome, tribune?' Falco suggested innocently. Now Valerius was certain he'd been lured into a trap. But Lunaris and the escort were veterans in their own right; surely they had nothing to fear from these pensioners. Falco saw him hesitate. 'At cost price, of course.'

Valerius nodded. 'Of course.' Something told him he was unlikely to get a chance to taste Falco's finest tonight.

Falco positioned himself at the end of the gap between the two lines. 'When you are ready . . . attack.'

It should have been so simple. Lunaris kept his

shield hard against his neighbour's and could feel the pressure as the man to his left did the same to his own. He kept his head low and his left shoulder tight to the rear of the shield boss, the sword ready in his right hand to dart between the shields when the chance came. He knew it wouldn't come at once, because this wasn't a fight against barbarians who could be depended on to expose themselves to the sting of the *gladius*, but he was sure it would come eventually. The twelve legionaries were younger, stronger and fitter than the men facing them. It would be a shoving match, but a shoving match they would win. And when they won he intended to take his revenge against the old bastard who had called him a chicken. 'Keep the line tight,' he shouted as the two walls of shields were about to meet. '*Now.*'

The younger men rammed their shields forward, square on to the enemy, using brute strength to hammer the veterans backwards with the almighty crash of two galleys colliding. Except the veterans didn't go backwards. The wall of shields rippled as they absorbed the power of the attack, but the line held, and no matter how hard Lunaris pushed he couldn't budge the man in front of him. After a minute of intense effort he allowed himself to relax just a fraction.

'Don't get too comfortable there, sonny. We don't want to be here all day.' It was the same voice that had insulted him earlier, infuriatingly calm and unflustered from behind the shield in front of him. He grunted and put all his strength into pushing again.

'Don't worry, Granddad. You'll soon get all the rest you want. A long, long rest.'

Similar confrontations were taking place along the entire shield line, and Lunaris could feel the puzzlement in the younger men. He heard Messor, so slim that his tent-mates had nicknamed him 'Pipefish', but with a wiry strength that belied his slight frame, cursing under his breath, and Paulus, the First's *signifer*, handing out useless advice. Still, it would be all over soon. They were trained to keep this up all day and these old men would soon tire.

But something strange was happening. The angle of the shield facing him kept subtly changing and it became difficult to maintain the force against it. First to the left, then to the right, top and bottom, but to no set pattern and never for long enough for him to take advantage of it. He tried to analyse what was happening but instinct and training told him to hold his ground and maintain the pressure where he could.

'Heave, lads, we'll soon have them.' His shout was echoed by grunts as the legionaries used all their frustration to increase the pressure on the men in front of them. Lunaris felt a slight change, and he knew he'd won. Only he hadn't. The shield in front of him disappeared and he found himself sprawled on his back at the far side of the veterans' shield wall with a wooden sword at his throat and a grinning, swarthy face in his. 'Soon have who, sonny?' Corvinus asked conversationally.

The veterans' ploy had been repeated by every second man along the line, and the contest collapsed in disarray with men struggling and wrestling with each other.

'Enough!' Falco shouted. He turned, grinning, to Valerius. 'An honourable tie, I think.'

Valerius nodded and watched as Corvinus helped Lunaris to his feet.

'You wouldn't have got away with that in a proper fight,' the *duplicarius* said evenly. He knew he'd been tricked, but better to be tricked on the training ground than on some heathen battlefield.

'That's right. We wouldn't,' Corvinus agreed. 'But it wasn't a proper fight. You fashion your tactics to beat whatever's facing you.'

'You're good,' Lunaris admitted. 'For your age.' He held out his hand.

Corvinus studied him suspiciously before gripping Lunaris by the forearm. 'If we weren't good we wouldn't be here. Every man you see survived twenty-five years in the legion. Twenty-five years means as many battles and twice as many pointless skirmishes that are even more likely to kill you. Twenty-five years of blood and sweat and seeing your tent-mate dying by inches with his liver in his lap, and twenty-five years of dozy patrician officers like him who don't know what they're doing.'

Lunaris followed his gaze towards Valerius. 'Oh, no. Not like him. Not like him at all.'

X

Two days before the dinner at Lucullus's villa, Valerius visited the daily market beside Colonia's Forum. It was here the local farmers brought their surplus and the craftsmen who plied their trade in the workshops on the hill to the west of the town came to sell their wares. Out of curiosity he had walked up the hill and found a bustling place of sparks and smoke, curious metallic smells and the clang of blacksmiths' hammers. Among them he found Corvinus, which surprised him, for this was a place of artisans and the goldsmith now counted among Colonia's elite. But the Twentieth's former armourer explained: 'I have my shop in Colonia, but our charter doesn't allow manufacture within the walls.' He pointed to a nearby smith's glowing forge. 'Too much risk of fire. The things I sell have to be made somewhere, so I set up my workshop here. I have slaves, of course, but I keep my hand in, and I do the special commissions myself.'

The memory of the encounter started a thought in Valerius's mind, but he decided to leave it for another day. Now he walked among the stalls of vegetables, hanging joints of meat, bulging sacks of barley and spelt, arrays of duck and hen eggs, perhaps fresh and perhaps not, and fish silver-bright from the river and the sea, taking in the sights and pungent scents of home-grown herbs and exotic imported spices and ignoring the pleas and flattery of the vendors. For a while he carefully studied a basket of scrawny chickens, clucking and fussing among their straw, but none was quite right. The sound of bleating drew him. Perhaps? When he reached the farmer's pen, he cursed himself for a fool. Of course, there would be no lambs at this season of the year. He imagined leading a ewe on a rope through the streets. No, it wouldn't do. He returned to the chickens.

'I'll have the biggest one, with the white patch on its wing.'

He carried the squawking bird by the legs, its wings flapping impotently, along the main street until he reached the temple gates. Today a queue stretched from the temple steps and he had to wait his turn behind a wrinkled, elderly woman with a white scroll and a small leather bag clutched tightly to her chest. It was several minutes before she stood before the priest at a stone altar set in front of the marble stairway. The transaction should have been private, but the woman had a loud voice that reminded Valerius of the chicken's squawking and he couldn't help but overhear.

'I wish the god to place this curse on whoever stole my sheets when they were drying. It was my neighbour, Poppaea, I'm sure, but I will know for certain when her feet and her hands turn black, the thieving bitch. In pursuance of my petition I leave this offering.' The priest took the leather bag, opened it and studied the contents before accepting the scroll with a curt nod. The woman bowed and walked away, muttering to herself.

Valerius took his place at the altar while the priest noted something on a waxed writing block. Despite the authority with which he'd dealt with the woman and the earlier supplicants, the priest was little more than a boy, with narrow, pinched features and a nose that marked him out as Roman. At first Valerius was puzzled, but as he waited – a little longer than he needed to – he realized that the people who actually operated and managed the cult of Claudius were unlikely to be major benefactors like Lucullus. Every organization needed its fetchers and carriers, and he recognized one before him.

He coughed, and the priest looked up as if only just noticing his presence. Valerius wore a simple tunic over his *braccae* and he knew he'd been mistaken for an off-duty legionary or perhaps one of the farmers in town for the market.

'I wish to make a sacrifice to the god,' he said, holding out the chicken.

'That?' the boy asked, frowning.

'Yes, that,' Valerius agreed, aware of growing restlessness behind him.

The boy studied the chicken, and Valerius wondered if he had ever conducted a sacrifice. Probably the task was normally carried out by the more experienced priests.

'Perhaps you might like some help?' he ventured.

The boy looked at him seriously, then back to the chicken. 'Oh, no.' He paused. 'Will you require an augury?'

Valerius thought for a second. Did he really believe this child had the gift? He was almost certainly wasting his money. Still, why had he come here, if not to find out whether the girl was part of his future?

'How much?' he asked, and was quoted a price that made his purse squeal in protest. At these rates the Temple of Claudius must be the most profitable enterprise in Britain. He handed over a silver *denarius*, which the boy placed in a basket beneath the altar, then the chicken, which the young priest expertly held down with one hand while reaching into the basket with the other and producing a lethal-looking house knife. With a flick of his wrist he slit the bird's throat. The chicken jerked and its wings fluttered in an involuntary spasm. The boy studied its dying movements until it went still, then, with another expert flick of the blade, made a long cut in its belly and allowed the inner parts to spill on to the marble surface.

Valerius stared at the remains of the chicken but all he saw was a heap of feathers and a mess of entrails and watery blood. The priest used the point of the knife to move a curling clump of guts to one side and let out a prolonged sigh as he uncovered the liver. He sighed again as he found the gall bladder, which he studied intently. Valerius leaned closer as the signs were explained. 'The path you follow is not the one you wish to tread,' the boy said cautiously. 'Yet there are many ways to reach the destination you seek. Not all are straightforward, but each, in its own fashion, will take you where you want to go.' He paused, studying the entrails more closely still while Valerius attempted to decipher the message he was being given. Was the boy talking about his pursuit of the girl, or the path that would take him back to Rome against his will? Or both? Or neither? He raised his head to find the priest studying him, a curious look in his dark eyes. 'You may face a great challenge, or you may turn away from it. Your fate is tied to that decision. It is not clear, but I believe you have much to gain but more to lose if you continue along the road you have chosen.' He reached into the basket and his hand came out with the silver *denarius*. 'Here. I have told you nothing you did not know.'

Valerius shook his head. 'No. Keep it . . . for yourself if not for the temple.'

As he walked away deep in thought, he looked

back to see the priest staring at him, ignoring the line of petitioners waiting to avail themselves of his services.

The villa of Lucullus was set high on the slope opposite Colonia and about a mile to the west of the city. It lay at the centre of his 'estate', which as far as Valerius could see consisted simply of another tract of British farmland, dotted randomly with patches of forest and the flea-infested, thatched roundhouses the tribesmen lived in. A Roman villa would have been identified by an ostentatious gateway and landscaped gardens, but he had only been able to find his way here because of the precise directions Falco had provided, passing through and by another dozen farms on the way. At first sight the villa was a disappointment: a simple, single-storey structure, with white walls, shuttered windows and a red-tiled roof – it could have been home to any subsistence farmer on the shores of the Mediterranean. Still, he approached along the narrow, hedged trackway with his heart thumping against his ribs. His mind conjured up conflicting visions of his coming meeting with Maeve and he found he could barely remember her face, which placed an icy orb of fear in his belly, yet her eyes were as familiar to him as his own mother's. How would she be dressed? He remembered the slim form walking away from the temple. Perhaps not so slim; a narrow waist, but her hips and . . . His mouth went suddenly dry, and he licked his lips and forced the seductive memory from his head. Why did he feel more nervous now than when he had been about to lead the attack on the British hill fort? Was nervous even the correct word? No, it was more than that. He was afraid. Not afraid of dying, or failing, but of disappointing, or of being disappointed. Yet the fear was just as real. It didn't matter that he had cast eyes on the British girl only once. All that mattered was that he should see her again.

He was not inexperienced with women, but that experience had tended to be with a certain type, or, more correctly, types. There had been servant girls, of course, perhaps prompted by his father – surely not his mother? – who had led him along the delicate path towards maturity. And when he had donned the *toga virilis* of adulthood his father had taken him into Rome on the obligatory visit to a brothel of the better class, where he had been introduced to delights that made his rough fumblings behind the kitchens somehow inconsequential. Then there had been the army and the soldiers' women, many of them, readily available but only fleeting erotic experiences untouched by passion or tenderness. For the first time he realized he had never known love.

Lucullus stood smiling in the courtyard in front of the villa, along with a groom who took Valerius's horse and led it towards the stables. 'Welcome to my humble house,' the little Celt said formally, but Valerius could see he was almost dancing with excitement, the way his father had sometimes been when some particularly auspicious guest was about to arrive.

'You were very kind to invite me to dine with your family,' he replied, with equal formality. 'You have a fine estate, Master Lucullus.'

Lucullus waved dismissively, but his smile said he appreciated the compliment. 'This? This is nothing. The best land is beyond the hill, land my ancestors have cultivated for generations – the gods thank them – and beyond it are my hunting grounds. You are sure you do not hunt? I must tempt you. A fine stag? Or a boar? Surely a boar would be a worthy adversary for a soldier?'

Valerius shook his head, and Lucullus laughed and led him towards the house, chattering about the animals he had hunted and killed. They entered through an arched doorway which led into a hall, where a slave surprised Valerius by ushering him to a bench so that he could remove his sandals and have them replaced by a pair of soft slippers. It was something he would have expected only in the most fashionable houses in Rome and seemed out of place in this rough provincial outpost. He looked up to find Lucullus watching him, seeking his approval, and he smiled his thanks. Suitably shod, he followed his host into a sumptuously furnished room lit by perfumed oil lamps. The room measured around thirty paces by ten and the plastered walls were painted a dramatic deep ochre made more striking by the broad gold horizontal stripe which divided them, and the colourful scenes that took up most of each end of the room. The floor was basic *opus signum* covered in rugs, apart from the centrepiece, a patterned mosaic of blue, red and white, with the familiar figure of Bacchus at its centre, surrounded by grapevines. Again, Valerius was impressed; clearly Lucullus took his culture seriously enough to lavish considerable expense upon it. Two men and a woman stood talking in front of a marble bust and he felt a sting of disappointment when he realized the woman was not Maeve.

Lucullus introduced them. 'My cousin Cearan, and his wife Aenid. They are of our northern neighbours, the Iceni.' Valerius bowed politely. Cearan and Aenid were one of the most striking couples he had ever seen, with looks so similar they might have been brother and sister. Cearan's features had the perfectly balanced symmetry Valerius remembered from statues of Greek gods, only with a sharper edge. His golden hair fell to his shoulders and his eyes were a startling, delicate blue. Aenid was blessed with her husband's high cheekbones and full mouth, but she wore her hair long, cascading to the middle of her back. Their clothing somehow managed to bridge the cultural divide between Roman and Briton without offending either; Cearan was in a plain cream tunic and *braccae*, with a thin gold torc at his throat, while Aenid wore a long dress of pale blue that covered her neck and arms. It took a second glance to realize that they were older than they appeared, probably only a few years younger than their host.

Valerius was still staring at them when Lucullus introduced the second man. 'Marcus Numidius Secundus,' he said. 'Numidius constructed the Temple of Claudius.' His eyes twinkled as if to say, *See, I recognized your interest and this is my gift to you.* It seemed that everything with Lucullus came at some sort of price.

Numidius nodded, and Valerius noted that, although he was standing beside Cearan and Aenid, he couldn't be said to be *with* them. He held a silver cup in both hands with his arms tight to his sides as if to avoid any inadvertent contact with the two Britons. Dark, watchful eyes peered myopically from a thin, almost malnourished face, but they lit up, indeed almost caught fire, when the engineer realized he had found a fellow Roman citizen. He marched across the room and took Valerius's right arm like a drowning man grasping at a piece of passing flotsam. 'Come, Lucullus tells me we have a common passion. You must sit by me.'

He steered Valerius towards a low table at the far end of the room surrounded by comfortable padded benches. Lucullus's face took on the same fixed smile it had assumed when Petronius mentioned the Brittunculi. 'Yes, it is time to dine. Cearan, Aenid?' He ushered the Iceni couple towards the benches, which Valerius noted with a flutter in his stomach numbered six. Lucullus placed Valerius and Numidius on one side of the table, opposite Cearan and Aenid on the other. He took his place to

119

Numidius's right, leaving the couch next to Valerius vacant.

When they were settled, he called out something in his own language and Valerius thought he caught the word Maeve amongst the burst of unintelligible syllables. He looked up, hoping to see the British girl, but Numidius tugged at the sleeve of his tunic.

'Lucullus tells me you are interested in the temple?'

'I am interested in all architecture,' Valerius admitted. 'I think the Temple of Claudius is a fine example. The workmanship, if not the scale, stands comparison with anything in Rome.'

'Anything in the Empire,' the engineer said complacently. 'I worked to the instructions of the architect Peregrinus, who was sent from Rome by Claudius himself to oversee the construction. We had previously completed the temple in Nemausus together, but this was an altogether different task.'

Valerius nodded politely, torn between genuine interest and hope that Maeve was about to walk into the room and take the seat next to him.

'It was the foundations, you see,' Numidius explained in a voice as dry as an empty *amphora*. 'The site chosen was entirely inadequate, but they insisted because a shrine to one of the heathen Celtic gods once stood there. Peregrinus did not think it could be done, but I discovered the answer. Foundations so strong they could bear the Capitoline Hill itself. It took two hundred slaves to dig the pits and we had to face them with timber or they would have collapsed on the men working in them. When they were completed we poured mortar by the ton into them, then more in a thick layer over the area between them, so that when the material hardened we had created four huge earth-filled vaults of astonishing strength. Even then, Peregrinus had his doubts until the priests sacrificed a fine bull to Jupiter and predicted the temple would stand for a thousand years.'

Finally.

Today, she wore white, and from the chestnut-brown hair swept into a fashionable pile on her head to the handmade shoes that cradled her delicate, manicured feet she looked every inch a Roman. Her dress was long, the diaphanous material clinging to her body, its folds full of shadows and promises, but it left her shoulders bare and her pale skin shone in the yellow light of the lamps. Valerius noted that she had used powder to turn the healthy glow that flushed her cheeks to a subtle pink, and today her lips were the colour of ripe strawberries. He wondered how old she was and a voice inside his head answered. Eighteen.

XI

Maeve walked into the room at the head of a line of servants and only when they had placed the dishes they carried to her satisfaction did she take her place opposite her father and to Valerius's left side. He must have eaten, but he would swear he neither saw nor tasted anything placed before him. The murmur of conversation continued, but if a single word was addressed directly to him he did not hear it. She lay so close that his head swam with the scent of the perfumed oils she wore, but frustratingly her face was hidden from him. If he moved his eyes to the left when she reached for some morsel on the table he caught a glimpse of the downy golden hairs that covered her lower arm. It took a long time before he realized she was no more aware of him than any of the busts that lined the walls and that, although he felt her presence like heat from a winter fire, to her he might as well have been made of the same cold stone.

She concentrated all her attention on Cearan, talking quietly in the language they shared but which left Valerius an outcast. He felt a tide rising within him and, unfamiliar though it was, knew it for jealousy. It was unreasonable, madness even – he had not spoken a word to this girl, this woman – yet he found he couldn't tame it. With that realization came anger; anger at himself for accepting Lucullus's invitation and anger at the Briton for making it. And with the anger the room came back into sharp focus and he heard Numidius still droning on about the temple.

'. . . the dimensions are perfect, of course, according to the principles of Vitruvius: the length exactly one and one quarter times the width . . .'

Valerius looked up to find Lucullus staring at him. 'Maeve, our guests,' the Trinovante said sharply.

'Lord Cearan and I were discussing horses.' The voice, in a Latin endowed with a gentle, almost musical quality, came from behind. Valerius knew it was directed at him, but for some reason he was reluctant to turn and face the source. 'Our British stock is sound of wind but short in the body and the legs. They would benefit from the introduction of some of your Roman bloodlines.'

Now he had no choice but to turn and look into her eyes, which had the qualities of a Tuscan mountain stream: deep, dark and full of intriguing mystery. 'I am sure that would be possible,' he said, knowing it was anything but and wondering why his voice sounded like an old man's.

'Then I will call on you tomorrow, and we may be disappointed together.' Cearan laughed. 'For ten months I have been trying to persuade your commander of cavalry at the fort south of Colonia to give me the use of a single breeding stallion. For a week. Even for a day. But all he does is try to sell me his broken-down pack mules and assure me I am getting a bargain.'

Valerius felt that honour demanded he defend Bela, his auxiliary counterpart. 'No doubt he has his reasons. A cavalry prefect will always be careful of his mounts, and he is a Thracian and therefore will be more so. Perhaps, with time, you can win his trust? You have common interests, after all.'

He heard a sharp clicking sound to his left that told him Maeve didn't agree, but Cearan slapped the table. 'Well said! And you are right. If it were only he and I, we would get drunk together and boast about the stallions we have known and mares we have broken, and in the morning he would say to me, "Cearan, take this fine beast and return it when its duty is done," and I would give him the first foal of its many unions and he would be satisfied. But it is not he and I. He has his orders, he says, and it would be more than his life is worth to disobey them. Trust.' The cheerful voice turned serious and the pale eyes bored into Valerius's. 'It is this matter of trust that comes between us. I have traded with the farmers in the *territorium* for five years and each of us has benefited from it. They trust me to deliver the ponies I have promised and I trust them to pay me when the crops are sold and they are in funds. Lucullus deals with these men every day. He is a priest of the temple and he has won their respect.' Valerius had a vision of Petronius's drink-swollen face and his derisive reference to the 'little Brits' and wondered if that was entirely true. 'But still there are Romans who look upon us and see us as their enemy.'

'It is true,' Maeve interrupted with passion. Now he was able to turn towards her again, and the breath caught in his throat like a fishhook because she was angled towards him, her face only inches from his own. She wore the fierce expression of a mother defending her brood and the pride burned through the powder on her cheeks. 'It is sixteen years since you came here. We have accepted Roman law and wear Roman clothes. We eat from Roman plates and drink Roman wine. Your gods are not our gods, but we have accepted them, even . . .' she paused and Valerius sensed some warning glance from either her father or Cearan, 'even though some of them are alien to us. What more do you need before you give us your trust?'

Valerius remembered the Celtic tribes in their dark mountains west of Glevum, and the tattooed warriors who had thrown themselves on the swords of his legionaries. He studied Lucullus, plump and content on his padded couch, his eyes hidden in the shadow, and Cearan, not quite comfortable in the almost Roman tunic that clearly hid a physique as impressive as any Valerius had seen on the Silurian battlefield. Rome had trusted barbarians in the past. Arminius, of the Cherusci, had been an officer in the legions, and had used what he had learned to destroy three of those legions in the Teutoburg Forest. Caesar himself had made common cause with the tribes of Gaul, only for them to try to stab him in the back. The trust of Rome was not easily earned. The Iceni's horses would never have the bloodlines of Roman cavalry mounts because no Roman commander would risk the chance of meeting British cavalry on horses that could match his own for strength and stamina on the battlefield, even ten years away.

'You have this Roman's trust, lady,' he replied. But if he hoped flattery would pacify her he was mistaken.

'You trust us, yet you come to Colonia at the head of almost a thousand soldiers. Do a thousand spears signify trust in Rome?'

'The number is eight hundred, and I bring road-builders, not soldiers,' he said evenly. 'Soon we will begin work on the roads and bridges between Colonia and the north. A well-mended road is good for trade. Your father,' he bowed his head towards Lucullus, 'will save on axles and wheels and his wagons will be able to travel further and faster. That in turn will mean more profits to spend on this wondrous villa.'

He knew he'd made a mistake when he saw her eyes narrow. Fortunately Cearan stepped in to save him from the retaliation.

'But surely the primary purpose of your roads is military? A legion travelling on a metalled road can cover twice the distance of one marching over open country. Was it not Aulus Plautius, the first governor of this province, who said that his roads were the chains that would bind the barbarians for ever?'

'You have me at a disadvantage, sir. I never knew Aulus Plautius, though I understand he was a fine commander.'

'Cearan met him, though, didn't you, Cearan?' Lucullus's voice was slightly slurred and Valerius noticed Maeve's eyes widen fractionally, but Cearan himself only nodded thoughtfully.

'Once was enough. Caratacus believed he would destroy him on the Tamesa, but it was Caratacus who was destroyed and the rest of us with him.' He smiled sadly. 'I rode to battle with eight thousand men, and returned to Venta with fewer than six thousand, and counted myself fortunate.'

Lucullus lurched to his feet, and Maeve rose from her couch and brushed past Valerius to lead him from the room, whispering in his ear. Numidius lay back with his eyes closed, snoring gently. Valerius took the chance to study Lucullus's painting of the surrender. It was a remarkable piece of art. The painter had cleverly used the ranks of the surrounding legions to focus attention on the group at the centre. Claudius wore a cloak of purple and sat high on the back of an elephant resplendent in golden armour. Before him knelt eleven figures, ten male and one female, and the artist had somehow contrived, with only the slightest embellishment, to convey their royal lineage. Their expressions ranged from mild concern to outright fear.

Cearan came to his side. 'Prasutagus, my king.' He pointed to a figure in the centre of the kneeling line. 'His wife Boudicca stood at his side that day so that she would share his burden, but the artist has overlooked her.'

'And she would thank him for it!' The voice belonged to Aenid, who now sat upright on her couch, picking at an arrangement of honeyed nuts on the table in front of her. 'Boudicca needs no reminding of her people's dishonour.'

'Forgive my wife. She is a remarkable woman but sometimes she forgets her place,' Cearan said with a smile.

'Do not believe him, tribune,' Aenid interjected. 'She knows her place very well. But unlike one of your Roman wives she is entitled to her opinion and has the right to voice it.'

'And this,' Cearan pointed to the picture again, 'is King Cogidubnus, whose rule now extends over the Atrebates, the Regni and the Cantiaci. I once thought to kill him.' The last sentence was said matter-of-factly, and at first Valerius thought he'd misheard. Cearan smiled sadly. 'He betrayed us, betrayed

Caratacus. If the Atrebates had stood and fought with the rest, who knows, perhaps . . .' He gave a little shrug. 'But that is in the past. We must deal with life as it is, not how we would wish it to be.'

Valerius's eye was drawn to the figure in the flowing blue gown. The artist had made her beautiful in a way no real woman was beautiful. 'And who is this?'

Cearan hesitated and Valerius had a feeling his eyes flicked towards his wife. 'That is Queen Cartimandua of the Brigantes,' the Briton said. Valerius heard Aenid snort derisively behind them. 'She came late to the ceremony but was among the first to recognize the benefits of Roman rule.'

'She is a traitor.' Maeve's voice came from the doorway and seemed unnaturally loud in the small room.

'My wife is not the only lady who does not know her place,' he said mildly. 'You should attend your father, child.' Valerius saw Maeve's nostrils flare at the word child, but Cearan's authority was strong enough to overcome her anger. With a last lightning flash of her eyes she turned and swept from the room again, with Aenid at her heels. Valerius felt cheated.

'Now I truly ask your forgiveness, and your forbearance.' Cearan frowned and glanced towards Numidius, but the engineer was still oblivious of anything around him. 'It would go ill with Lucullus if it were known in Colonia that his daughter had used that word in connection with Cartimandua. None is held in higher honour by the Romans than she, though, since I count you my friend, and a very special Roman, I will say that her reputation among her countrymen is less savoury. Maeve is young, and the young, at least among our people, like to have their voices heard, even if what they say is occasionally foolish or hurtful.'

He turned back to the painting. 'Our world changed that day, but some of us still do not recognize the reality. I have often wondered why my cousin should wish to have a depiction of his people's greatest shame on his wall. He says that it is a fine painting by a fine artist, and there is some merit in that. But I think the truth is that he needs to remind himself each day that the life he once knew no longer exists, and that he must don his Roman clothes and step into his Roman shoes and take his place in Colonia as a Roman, because there is no other path open to him.'

With a nod, Cearan went to join his wife. Valerius reluctantly walked out into the night and waited as his horse was brought from the stables. He stood beside the animal for a moment, enjoying the cool night air. The light of a full moon bathed the country-side in silver and in the distance he heard the mournful screech of a hunting owl.

'We believe the owl is a messenger from the goddess.' She was part hidden in the shadow of the doorway where she must have waited until the servant was gone. 'To encounter one can be a good omen – or a bad.' Her voice had a honeyed quality; the angry outburst of a few minutes earlier might never have happened.

'It sounds very much like a message from our gods,' he replied, thinking of the augury by the temple steps. 'The signs can be good or bad but they are never clear. Sometimes you have to decide for yourself.'

He felt her smile. He wished she would come into the light.

'I have been told to apologize for my behaviour.' Now the voice was a parody of a small girl's and the words held a slight tremor. It had a strangely unsettling effect on him. 'You are my father's guest and he feels I have insulted you in some way. I did not intend to. My uncle tells me I must learn to control my tongue.'

'Your uncle is a good man.'

A slight hesitation. 'Yes, but sometimes he is too honest.'

Now it was Valerius's turn to smile. 'Can a man be too honest?'

'Oh, yes. Because all honesty comes at a price.' The girl's voice was gone and it was said with a woman's certainty. 'One day Cearan may find it too high.'

'May I see you again?' He wasn't even sure that he had spoken the words; certainly he hadn't formed them in his head. But they must have been said because she let out an audible gasp of surprise. When he looked at the doorway it was empty, but he sensed she was still there, in the shadow. He waited and almost a minute passed.

'It would cause ... complications.' The whisper came out of the darkness. 'But . . .'

'But?'

Another long pause made him think she had gone. 'But if you truly wish it, you will find a way.'

The ride back to Colonia seemed much shorter. At one point a ghostly shape crossed his path a few hundred yards ahead. He decided it wasn't an owl.

XII

The last rays of the dying sun caught the roof of the ramshackle Temple of Juno Moneta, which shared the summit of the Capitoline half a mile away across the Forum with the much grander house of Jupiter Capitolinus. For once, Lucius Annaeus Seneca agreed with his Emperor's view of the ruinous state of much of central Rome. Still, this was hardly the time to raise the subject.

'And Britain?' he asked.

'Britain?' The pale eyes were a shadowy curtain for whatever was happening behind them. The cherubic face tilted slightly to indicate puzzlement. A hint of a smile touched lips the shape of a cupid's bow, but there was the faintest air of petulance which carried a warning. Seneca smiled back.

'Our island province is the final subject of the day,

Caesar, surely you haven't forgotten?' The smile stayed in place but Seneca noted the eyes appeared to harden. He had played this game many times, but the boy – strange that he still thought of him as a boy even though he was almost twenty-two years old – was an emperor now, and playing games with emperors, however familiar, could be like playing touch with a viper. Agrippina, the boy's mother, had forgotten that simple rule and he had made her pay the price after one of the most ludicrous, botched assassination attempts ever devised. When his collapsing boat failed to do the job, the Emperor's hirelings had resorted to the simple and much more effective expedient of stabbing her to death.

'Remind us.' Lucius Domitius Ahenobarbus, known as Nero, nodded for Seneca to continue. No offence had been taken.

'Conquered by your respected stepfather, a feat for which Rome awarded him a triumph in recognition of his military prowess.' The curtain lifted for a second as Nero attempted to reconcile the vision of weak-minded, doddering old Claudius with the victorious general, hailed *imperator* twenty-two times, whom the arch on the Via Flaminia commemorated. 'Your rule is imposed by four legions: the Twentieth and the Second in the west, soon to be joined by the Fourteenth, and the Ninth to the north, to which they have yet to bring Rome's bounty.'

'And the east?'

Seneca paused. This was more dangerous ground.

'Pacified. The conquered tribes accept your rule without question. The Colonia which Emperor Claudius founded on the fortress of the Trinovantes thrives and its people prosper. It is an example to all Britain. The temple dedicated to the cult of your divine stepfather is a masterpiece worthy of Rome itself, but . . .' he hesitated in deference to the delicate decision he was placing before the boy, 'there is, of course, the question of whether it might be rededicated.'

'I will think on it. Continue.'

'Your new port of Londinium continues to grow . . .' Seneca allowed his voice to drop to a low murmur as he listed the virtues of the province. This was another part of the game. He had found that a combination of pace and pitch could mesmerize the boy and he could let his mind drift on to other subjects while his tongue rolled off the facts and figures he had learned by rote in a few short hours earlier that day. It was, he thought, a singular talent, but one he would never boast of, unlike those other talents for which he, and the world, must be for ever thankful: his genius for oratory; his subtlety of argument; the way he could turn a simple subject upside down and inside out and find a satisfactory conclusion that would have eluded any other man. Today his thoughts turned to Claudius. There too had lain a sort of genius. A genius for survival. Yet at the end he accepted death as meekly as a sacrificial lamb in the Temple of Fortuna. Not only accepted it, but embraced it. Claudius had known Agrippina's purpose, Seneca was certain of it. So why, when it would have been so simple to plead fatigue or insist another took the first bite, had he supped the fatal portion with such enthusiasm? Was this a case of a life so well lived that the man who lived it had recognized his time? Surely not. Proximity to Claudius and the nest of serpents he called his advisers had been almost as dangerous as proximity to Caligula of reviled memory. Between them the pair had cost him nine years of his life; nine long years of heat and wind and dust spent in exile on Corsica. A small twinge – part guilt, part annoyance – reminded him of his own complicity and he struggled to suppress it. It was a sensation he had felt often over the years. How could a man so . . . astute? Yes, astute: one must be accurate with words . . . how could such a man succumb to a momentary folly, or perhaps not so momentary, which would endanger not only his career, but his very existence? But self-analysis, like self-pity, could be corrosive and he forced himself to concentrate. Too late.

'So we still do not know the source of the island's gold?' The sharp voice interrupted his thoughts. He realized his tone must have faltered, allowing the spell to be broken.

'That is correct, Caesar,' he acknowledged smoothly. 'But we have barely scratched the surface of the Silurian heartlands. Even now your engineers are seeking out the fountainhead.' The truth was that the Empire's expectations should have been met years earlier and would have been, but for the obstinacy of the rebel Caratacus, who had held out in the Silurian mountains for almost a decade before his capture.

Exploitation. One could cloak the reasons for a military campaign in any guise one wished – there were still suspicions about the true motive behind Claudius's invasion of Britain – but the primary purpose would always be exploitation. Exploitation of natural resources. Exploitation of land. Exploitation of peoples. And the late and much maligned Claudius had proved a master of exploitation. Better still, the exploited were unaware until the hook had been set or the trap closed. First subsidies – or loans: the one as good as the other, indeed, the one capable of being mistaken for the other, and who would know the truth by the time the loan was called in? Gifts that bound the warrior kings of Britain to Rome. Gifts that brought with them obligations. And with obligations came taxes, which meant more subsidies, more loans: more debt.

'Yet the cost of maintaining our legions is barely covered by the tax revenues.' It was as though the Emperor had read his mind. He should have learned by now never to underestimate the intelligence behind the child's mask. 'The profits of our enterprises slim or non-existent. The initial outlay enormous, but unrecouped. I see little profit in Britain. Perhaps it is time to withdraw?'

Seneca nodded in acknowledgement and allowed himself an indulgent smile, though the blood froze in his veins. Nero was not the only actor in the room. 'But does history not teach us that patience is the investor's greatest virtue? That haste can be an expensive business partner?'

The young man frowned and leaned forward in the gilded throne, one hand – the right – raised to stroke the smooth, almost baby-textured flesh of his chin. The thinker's pose. A ruler deliberating on matters most momentous. Eventually, he spoke. 'Perhaps, but patience does not fill bellies. Did you not also teach me that filled bellies and a full arena are what keep the mob from the streets?'

'Of course, Caesar.' In fact it had been Claudius who had imparted that rather brutish wisdom. Seneca allowed the daintiest touch of annoyance to seep into his tone. 'I merely counsel against a precipitate decision. Grand strategy should not be decided like two beggars haggling in the streets. You have other advisers. Perhaps the Praetorian prefect is more qualified to provide guidance in military matters.'

The eyes narrowed. 'Your most intimate friend, Afranius Burrus?'

'Your governor of the province, then. Gaius Suetonius Paulinus. Surely no decision should be taken without having first been discussed with the man most able to enlighten. Summon Paulinus home and question him as you have questioned me. Perhaps his answers will be more palatable than my own humble opinions.'

Nero laughed; it was a child's laugh, high-pitched and easy. 'Have I offended you, dearest Seneca? Does the pupil's lack of understanding grieve the teacher? Then you have my apology. Sometimes the cares of the Empire drive your teachings from my head. Let us lay down the subject of Britain for a moment. Come, explain to me again why an emperor's greatest need is for compassion and mercy. Would not wisdom in all things suffice?'

Seneca shook his head. 'First, a Caesar can cause no offence, only concern – and Britain should rightly be a matter for our concern. But, to mercy. Your step-father, Divine Claudius, showed mercy when he reprieved the British war leader Caratacus from the strangling rope. Yet he also showed wisdom, and statesmanship. For in allowing a mighty warrior to live – one who had knelt before him in defeat – he gained a living monument to his greatness, and thereby enhanced both his own and Rome's security. Since with security comes stability, did not all, from the lowest slave to the highest senator, gain from it?'

'But . . .'

An hour later Seneca left the room and turned past the twin figures of a pair of anonymous Praetorian guards into the corridor. Once he was certain he was alone, he put one hand against the painted wall for support and choked down the bile that filled his throat. Sweat matted his hair and the stink of fear from his own body filled his nostrils. Nero knew. Of course he knew. It was time to act. He must call in his

British investments immediately. If the legions withdrew it would be lost. All of it. What could he do to ensure his fortune was safe? An idea formed and he saw a face, a thin, beak-nosed, miserable face. Could he trust him? Could he afford not to? Yes. It would have to do.

Self-interested panic receded and he considered the wider, appalling consequences if Nero proceeded with his threat. Billions of *sestertii* wasted on sixteen years of folly. A dozen potential allies turned in an instant into certain enemies. He listed the tribal king-doms of the province in his head and attempted to calculate the cost of withdrawal. The legions would strip them of each and every vestige of wealth, every bushel of grain and every cow, taking tens of thousands of slaves and hostages to ensure their future compliance. Compliance! The island would starve and the legacy of that starvation would be enmity for a thousand years. And they were so close. The gold mines of Siluria and the Brigantian lead reserves would change everything. No, it must not happen. He could not allow it. But first he had to retrieve his fortune.

He closed his eyes and tried to compose himself. Marble busts of Claudius, Caligula, Tiberius, Augustus and Divine Julius, the pantheon of Rome's great, stared at him from their alcoves as he walked quickly past them. Emperors all, a trio, at least, of tyrants, and each, he thought, had left Rome worse than he received it. Could Nero be different? Had he,

Lucius Annaeus Seneca, been in a position to *make* him different? It was cool here in the heart of the palace complex and he felt the sweat chill in his hairline. His mind went back to the earlier conversation. Yes, he knew.

XIII

Gwlym could see only a few faces in the glow of the fire, but he knew that beyond them a hundred others sat on the damp leaf mould listening to his words. They were the elders of the northern Catuvellauni, at least those he thought he could trust, and he had gathered them in this forest clearing so that they should understand that they were not alone. This was the most dangerous time, the time when he had to persuade the doubters and the timid. Now they could see that they were many, that they were strong, that they were part of a great movement.

But attending a meeting in a forest glade by night did not mean a man would pick up his spear and march against his oppressors. They had courage, of course, and they hated, but sometimes it required more than that and he needed to know that when he moved on they would return to their homes and set up the secret furnaces and workshops that would help them rearm their tribes.

'This was once a sacred grove,' he said, his voice soft but strong enough to be heard clearly by every man among them. 'The Romans hacked down the oak trees which grew here for a hundred years and slaughtered the guardians so their blood soaked the ground we sit upon. But that blood was not wasted,' he pointed to a ring of small saplings, barely a year old, 'for the grove has been replanted and one day the rites will be renewed here. One day the gods will return to their rightful home.'

He paused to allow them to consider his words. He knew that certain of the rites he spoke of were not universally loved. Sometimes it was necessary to dispatch a messenger to the gods to ensure an appeal was heard and understood. Normally the message carrier was a prisoner or a slave, but in times of true emergency the gods would only accept a more treasured candidate: a chief's first born, or the well-favoured daughter of a lord.

'But the gods will only return when they are certain that you have not forsaken them. What did you do when the Romans came with their axes and their swords?' He let his hawk's eyes rove over the men in the inner circle and then the darkness beyond them, so that each became the focus of his words and felt the shame they evoked. 'Did you fight or send your sons to fight? Did you stand and say: this is the sacred ground of Taranis and Teutates, of Esus and Epona? No, you did not, for you are still alive. Yet, though you failed them, the gods have not forsaken you. The message I bring is this. Prepare: for the time of release is upon us. Arm: for strength is the only message the Romans understand. Wait: for only when the gods send their sign will the time be right.'

And they asked: what will be the sign?

And he answered: the wrath of Andraste.

XIV

Five days before the festival of Armilustrium, when his soldiers would hold the annual ceremony to purify their arms, Valerius received a surprise summons from the camp prefect of the Londinium garrison. Technically, he remained under the command of the Twentieth legion and the *praefectus castrorum* had no authority over himself or his troops. In reality he knew that with the governor immersed in preparations for the spring campaign the man was de facto commander of the south-east. He had a momentary panic that he was being posted home immediately, but quickly realized that order would have come in a simple dispatch.

He made preparations to leave at once, then changed his mind. He had more than one reason for making the trip. He made the short walk to Lucullus's offices.

'I am sorry you were inconvenienced.'

Lucullus looked up at the young tribune from the scroll he studied. For an unguarded moment his face was blank, before it automatically took on the fixed smile he wore as if it were part of a uniform.

'On the contrary,' he said cheerfully. 'I apologize for being such a poor host. You were fortunate you did not have the oysters. They had been kept a day longer than was good for them – or for me. My factor's back now bears the scars to ensure it will not happen again. It was kind of you to come here to enquire after my health.' The last sentence held the slightest hint of a question.

'You have been very kind to me,' Valerius said obliquely. 'But that was not the only reason for my visit. I must leave for Londinium tomorrow and I have a favour to ask. Part of my supplies – engineering equipment – has failed to arrive. I could send a letter, but it would only give birth to an extended family of paperwork. Would it be possible to hire another of your wagons? I know it is short notice, but I would happily pay a premium.'

'Pah! Do not talk to me of premiums,' the little Trinovante blustered. 'For my friend Valerius there are only discounts. I will give you it at half rate, although, of course, you must provide an acknowledgement for the full amount. Your Roman auditors . . .' He shook his head solemnly as if a visit from the auditor was like the arrival of the first plague spot.

146

Valerius reluctantly agreed to what he knew was tax fraud and arranged for Lunaris to collect the wagon, before turning the conversation to the true subject of his visit. 'You very generously invited me to hunt over your land. At the time I was busy, but I would be honoured to take up your offer whenever it is convenient.'

Lucullus's smile visibly transformed itself from lie to truth and he came round the table and clapped Valerius on the back. 'Wonderful! Send word when you have fetched your shovels. I promised you good sport and you shall have it. There is a boar in the far wood who has been digging up my fields. My factor says he is as big as a pony. If he's that big he can feed fifty people. We will have him on a spit in time for Samhain and feast till the sun comes up. I remember . . .'

He was still boasting of the beasts he had taken when Valerius left ten minutes later, but the young Roman could only think of one thing. He would see Maeve again. As he made his way back to the camp he felt someone fall into step beside him and he turned to find Petronius at his side.

'Falco tells me you are doing business with our tame Briton. I hope he isn't cheating you?' The words were accompanied by a smile that suggested they were said in jest, but Valerius felt like a plump trout being tempted by a dangling worm. Somewhere in the sentence was a barbed hook.

'Surely the *quaestor* would not allow such a thing?'

he replied guardedly. 'In any case Falco tells *me* that you also do business with Lucullus.' Falco had done no more than offer a hint, but Petronius was not the only one who could dangle a bait.

'We have an arrangement,' the lawyer admitted airily. 'The Celt has his uses and we must at least be seen to try to make common cause with the natives. And if I benefit, does Colonia not also benefit to an even greater degree?' The boast puzzled Valerius and it showed on his face. Petronius laughed. 'You have not heard? Poor Lucullus. He talks much more than is good for him. How else would I know what the Celts from here to the River Abus are thinking and planning, who is happy with his lot and who is not?'

Valerius increased his pace. Clearly Colonia formed part of the great military and civilian spy network that blanketed southern Britain. One of the reasons Paulinus felt secure enough to launch an attack on the druids on Mona was that his spy-masters had assured him no danger existed to his rear. In any case, how would the Empire decide whom to tax and by how much if they did not know to the last egg and the smallest bushel of corn what the British chieftains were worth? He doubted very much that Petronius was the intelligence mastermind he appeared to want him to think, but the *quaestor* was a hard man to shake off.

'You have met his daughter?'

Valerius almost stopped, but that would have

betrayed his interest. Maeve was his business and no one else's. 'His daughter?'

Petronius was amused. 'The skinny, dark-haired one. She was with her father outside the temple.'

Skinny? Valerius shrugged and tried to give the impression that, to a soldier, one woman was very much like another. From the corner of his eye he caught Petronius giving him a sly glance.

'But you must remember her? I believe someone – perhaps it was old Numidius, the engineer? Yes, I'm sure it was him – mentioned that you dined with the Briton and his friends only two days ago. Surely she must have been on hand? I'm surprised he hasn't already tried to marry her off to you.'

This time Valerius did stop. He gave the *quaestor* a look that would have silenced any of his centurions, but Petronius only laughed.

'Do not look so shocked, young man. You are unmarried and of means, and therefore eligible. You are a Roman citizen, which makes you doubly so. If you were the Emperor himself you could hardly make a finer catch for a Briton with ambitions beyond his status. Far better certainly than many he has tried to tempt her with. It is little wonder she had no interest in the attentions of some toothless farmer who still has the manners of the marching camp. But a young man of your lineage . . .'

'I am here to do a job, sir,' Valerius said stiffly. 'Not to find a wife.'

'Of course not,' Petronius said sympathetically. 'I

merely thought to warn you, tribune. Your Briton is a cunning fox, and Lucullus more cunning than most. Do not be misled by that inane grin he wears: there is a mind behind it that could almost be Roman were it not that slyness must never be mistaken for intelligence nor playing the fool for wit. Still, you know of the trap now, and I doubt you will fall into it. I bid you a good day.' He bowed and walked off in the direction of the Temple of Claudius.

The road between Colonia and Londinium was the most important in the province and Valerius made good time, assisted by the dispatches he carried and the military warrant which allowed him to change horses three times at state-run way stations. When he arrived at the city's east gate, the guards directed him to an officers' *mansio* where he could rest and wash off the accumulated dust and sweat of the journey.

Londinium, even more than Colonia, was a place of bare wooden beams, wet plaster, half-tiled roofs and piles of bricks. Streets echoed to the rattle of hammers as carpenters swarmed over the skeletal beginnings of public buildings, houses and apartment blocks. One stood out among the rest, a massive squat structure with a pillared entrance and two separate wings. It was still far from complete, but the guards surrounding the building indicated that the governor, Gaius Suetonius Paulinus, had already taken up residence in his new palace. Like Colonia, the city had begun life as a fort protecting a river crossing; then, when the restrictions of Colonia's river access became clear, protecting the port that was the driving force behind Londinium's bustle of economic and commercial activity. The fort still remained, up by the wall on the high ground to the north-west, but the city's heart was here in the ordered grid of streets by the river, and in particular on the main street between the Forum and the timber bridge linking the city to the communities which had already sprung up on the southern bank.

Valerius crossed the stream known as the Wall Brook and walked north towards the fort, where he knew the camp prefect had his headquarters. After presenting his orders at the gate, he expected a formal interview and was surprised to be ushered into a small room off the *principia* and offered wine. Two minutes later the prefect bustled in, throwing out a stream of orders over his shoulder. When the curtain closed behind him, he sat down with a sigh and poured himself a liberal cup and raised it in salute.

'Health,' he growled. 'Though at your age you've still got it. After sixteen years in this swampland I have aches that will never leave me and I'm as stiff and creaky as a siege tower.'

Valerius warily acknowledged the exaggeration. Decimus Castus had been a soldier before he was born, had risen through the ranks and held every senior centurion's post in the Ninth legion before being promoted again to his present position, where he outranked even senior tribunes with lines of senatorial relatives dating back to before Caesar. He answered only to his legate and to his governor. Normally he would still be with the Ninth at Lindum, but it was a measure of Londinium's growing importance that the fort was under the authority of a battle-hardened veteran instead of the young auxiliary prefect who would normally command a post like this.

'Wondering why I dragged you away from your bumps and bridges, eh?' Castus beckoned Valerius forward to where a map lay pinned to a wooden frame. 'You're based in Colonia, here,' he indicated, 'with a full cohort and a complement of mounted scouts. I take it you've made contact with the prefect in charge of the auxiliary cavalry wing billeted to the south? Yes. Good. You'll need to work closely with him.

'Now, see here, here and here?' He pointed to three positions marked across the centre of the map. 'Just east of Pennocrucium, to the south of Ratae and about twenty miles from Durobrivae. We've had word of unusual activity in all these areas. Nothing solid. Nothing you can pin down, but, shall we say, a change of attitude among the natives. Notice the dates?' Valerius looked more closely and saw each site was marked with a date about a week apart, with the latest three weeks before. 'Now, governor Paulinus is not minded to take these reports seriously, and he's probably right, but I'm old enough to remember what happened when we disarmed the tribes back in Scapula's time. One minute they were quiet as dormice, the next they came screaming over the battlements like wolves. Never underestimate your Briton, young man. He can be subdued, but he'll never be tamed. There's a pattern to these changes that makes my old wounds itch.' He waved a hand over the eastern sector of the map, as yet unmarked. 'If that pattern continues, we'll have word from around Lindum, where I've already asked the Ninth to quietly keep an eye on things, then further south-east, which brings us to the point. I want you to work with your cavalry commander to carry out aggressive patrols to the north and north-west of Colonia, with particular emphasis on the country where the boundaries of the Trinovantes, the Catuvellauni and the Iceni meet.'

'The *quaestor*'s opinion is that this area is quiet,' Valerius ventured.

Castus grunted. 'So I understand. The next thing you'll be telling me is that the Celts enjoy being taxed and they think the price we pay them for corn is fair.'

Valerius smiled and resumed his study of the map. It seemed a small thing to be getting so exercised about. Still, Castus knew his business better than most. 'Spies can be wrong,' he agreed. 'I'll issue the order as soon as I return to Colonia. The cavalry commander, Bela, is a good man and his troops are keen.'

'You should pay particular attention to the Iceni,' Castus continued. 'They're our allies and old

Prasutagus is on friendly terms with the governor, but that doesn't make them any more trustworthy and it means we know less about them than we do the other tribes. It's more difficult to spy on your friends than your enemies. Anything you can discover would be of help, but you'll have to be subtle.'

When the interview was over Valerius walked the short distance to the quartermaster's depot by the north gate. There, his business looked likely to take longer thanks to a clerk who insisted that a mistake wasn't a mistake unless it was confirmed in writing and endorsed by three seals, and he wouldn't budge on that even if it happened to be the governor at the other side of his desk. Fortunately, the clerk's overseer was a decurion who had served with the Twentieth and recognized Valerius.

'If the tribune says the shovels didn't turn up, they didn't turn up, and if the Twentieth needs shovels, the Twentieth gets shovels. Anything else you require, sir?' he asked with a wink. Valerius left with an assurance that when his wagon arrived it would be loaded with a dozen shields and swords and fifty *pila* to replace those 'lost' during the summer, which would go some way to paying his debt to Falco.

Lunaris wasn't likely to reach Londinium with the wagon until the next day, which gave him a night to kill. He didn't want to be alone, but equally he didn't want to be with the type of woman available to a soldier in a city like this. In fact, the only woman he wanted to be with was Maeve. Eventually, he settled for a night in the *mansio* drinking wine with a few fellow officers either passing through on their way to join a legion, or travelling back to Rome. It amused him to listen to the veterans' hair-raising stories of the prowess of the Celtic warriors from the western tribes he had faced earlier in the year. He watched one of the younger newcomers grow paler and paler and finally took pity on the man.

'I don't believe they were actually seven feet tall,' he whispered. 'And they bleed just as easily as the next man. You have nothing to fear if you keep your shield up and your sword sharp.'

'But do they truly burn their prisoners alive and eat their still-beating hearts?'

He smiled. 'Only in the north, and I believe your unit is in the west.'

'They burn their prisoners in the west, too.' The growl came from a rough-hewn centurion sitting by the fire in the corner of the room. 'At least the druids do. But not for much longer. I was on the staff of the Fourteenth and we're going to settle them for good. They think they're safe on their little island but the only way they'll leave it alive will be if they swim for it. We'll be waiting to welcome them on the beach, then we'll see who burns. Come the summer there won't be a druid left in Britain, and good riddance to them.'

Valerius looked around to see who might be listening. Talk like this was universal among soldiers but hearing the man trumpet details of an impending military campaign made the hairs on the back of his neck rise. The servants in the *mansio* were all British slaves and he doubted they could be trusted. He had heard many stories about the druids' merciless cruelty but beneath those stories lay an unlikely respect. These men, these priests, were the mortar which had bound the British tribes until Claudius had shattered their unity with a combination of military might and subterfuge. They might have been herded back on to their sacred island, but they were still organized. It wasn't only Rome that had spies. He shot the centurion a warning look, but the man refused to be silenced.

'Everyone knows, and why should they not?' he said defiantly. 'If the Britons fight, so much the better. The more of them who try to stop us, the more of the vermin we will kill.'

Valerius had a sudden image of a pair of fire-filled eyes and a flashing knife; a man who wanted to kill him more than he loved life itself.

'What if there are too many of them for you to kill?'

XV

The following day he woke before dawn and joined legionaries of the Londinium garrison in the fortress exercise yard. An hour sweating with the practice sword had become as much part of his life as eating and drinking and he'd reached a stage where he enjoyed the small agonies which accompanied pushing his body to the very limit. He knew Lunaris was unlikely to arrive until late afternoon and while he laboured against his opponent's shield he decided to spend the morning at the public baths, down by the waterfront close to the inn where he had arranged to meet the *duplicarius*. There he spent a few pleasant hours listening to desultory and no doubt scurrilous gossip in the baths and wondering at the good fortune that had allowed him the pleasure of the *caldarium* and the *tepidarium* twice in as many weeks after so long an abstinence. Later, a slave oiled his body before scraping the skin clean with a sharp-edged *strigil*, and by the time he emerged he felt more relaxed than he'd been for months.

Still surrounded by a pleasurable euphoria, he reached the tavern, happy to see that it hadn't been subsumed in one of the many building projects going on around it. It occupied the ground floor of a three-storey *insula* and was identified by an *amphora* hanging at an angle from two chains above the doorway. A painted poster beside the open door advertised the finest imported wines, but Valerius knew that anyone who thought they'd find them in a place like this was destined to be disappointed. Inside, oil lamps flickered from the walls but seemed to produce more smoke than light. It was busy even at this hour of the day, as he'd guessed it would be. This was a sailor's town and sailors between voyages only had two interests. Judging by the laughter and the high-pitched female squeals, both were available here. He took one last deep breath of relatively clean air and plunged inside.

Lunaris had made the choice, and Valerius could see why, but it wasn't a place he would have selected for himself. The room he entered had a low ceiling and measured about thirty paces by fifteen, with five or six seated alcoves where a man might conduct his business in relative privacy. In another establishment the sight of an officer's uniform would have caused a hush in the conversation, but here his fellow customers ignored his presence. A glimpse of scarlet in the gloom told him he was not the only army man among all these seamen. He pushed towards the bar through the crowd vying for the attentions of a few heavily painted and only partially dressed women.

'What'll you have?'

Lunaris had said the inn was owned by a retired legionary veteran who had sold up in Colonia and moved to Londinium. 'I'm with the Twentieth,' he said, as he'd been instructed.

'I don't give a bugger if you're with the camel-humpers,' the barman laughed. 'What'll you have?'

Oh well, it looked as if the place was under new ownership. 'Whatever's good.'

'Now you're talking. We had a shipment in from Sardinia last week. Cost you a couple of *sestertii* more for a jug, but you won't regret it.' He turned to go, but Valerius grabbed his sleeve.

'If I do, I won't be the only one.'

The man laughed, unconcerned at the threat. 'Suit yourself. You'll get a seat over there.' He pointed to a darkened corner. 'I'll get the slave to bring it over.'

Valerius pushed his way to the corner and sat down with his back to a doorway which, from the smell, led to either the kitchen or the latrine – or possibly both. A young man with a cast in one eye brought him a jug filled to overflowing with dark liquid and placed a chipped cup beside it. The slave reached to pour the wine, but Valerius waved him away. He studied his surroundings, already regretting the impulse that had brought him through the door. The noise and the smoke after his hours at the baths made his head spin slightly. He'd just resolved to leave after a single drink when a slight commotion erupted behind him as two drinkers collided in the doorway with a muttered curse.

The sound of one of the voices rang a warning bell in his head and he half stood, reaching for the knife on his belt. Too late! An arm wrapped itself round his throat and he felt a calloused hand on the back of his head in a classic wrestling hold that he knew could snap his neck as if it were a dry twig. He tore at the arm with both hands, trying to break the iron grip that was already choking him, but the pressure on the back of his skull increased and his vision began to go. I'm dead, he thought. In the same instant, the grip slackened and as he gasped for breath a roar of laughter assaulted his ears. A tall figure in a red tunic stumbled into the seat opposite him and stared across the table with peering, reddened eyes.

'Got a drink for an old pal, pretty boy? I'm just about out of cash. SLAVE! Slave! Another cup, and bring another jug while you're at it.'

Crespo.

'Thought I had you there, eh? Just one twist and – crack – you were a goner.' The Sicilian chuckled. 'Killed a man like that once. Looked as if he had his head on backwards. SLAVE! About time.' The boy arrived with a second cup and another overflowing jug and retreated with a scared glance at Crespo as the Roman poured the wine carefully into the two cups.

'*Ave!*' He raised his cup in salute. 'The Twentieth and victory.'

Reluctantly, Valerius picked up his own vessel and repeated the toast. 'The Twentieth.'

'And damnation to the Brits, and all their disease-ridden sluts.'

Valerius stared, but the grin on Crespo's face never wavered.

'Maybe I should have killed you. Caused nothing but trouble for old Crespo, you did, pretty boy. Had the legate on my back for a month. Might have been kicked out. But Crespo's too clever for them.' He tapped his nose. Valerius noted that it hadn't set well; the axe blade now had a distinct notch in it. 'Too clever. Got myself a transfer.' For a second, the eyes glazed over and the centurion rocked back and forward from the waist, his head wobbling gently on his long neck. Crespo had clearly been in the bar for some time, possibly all night judging by the crumpled state of his clothing and the dark shadow on his chin. Valerius recalled the scene in the Silurian hut. It was as well he'd come across Crespo cheerfully drunk and in daylight.

The same thought had evidently occurred to his unwanted companion.

'Maybe I *should* kill you,' he growled, pulling a dagger from inside his tunic and stabbing it into the already scarred table top. The noise attracted the attention of everyone in the bar and Valerius saw the barman reach below his counter where he undoubtedly kept a large cudgel specifically for situations like this. He caught the man's eye and gave a slight shake of his head. An unspoken question. You sure? Valerius answered by pinning Crespo with the friendliest grin he was capable of.

'Why would you want to kill me? We had a little misunderstanding, that's all. Things like that happen all the time in the heat of battle.' He remembered the Silurian girl's terrified eyes staring at him over Crespo's shoulder. In one movement he could take the dagger by the hilt and put the blade through Crespo's right eye. The centurion would be dead before he could blink. Everybody in the bar had seen Crespo pull the knife. There might be a few awkward questions but he'd worry about that later.

Crespo frowned. He had both hands on the table top and Valerius decided that if the right hand moved towards the knife he would kill him.

'Misunderstanding? Sure. Heat of battle.' The hand moved. But only as far as his cup. He took a deep draught and wiped the back of his hand across his lips.

'Tell me about the transfer,' Valerius suggested, hoping it was somewhere far away and very dangerous. Germania, or even Armenia would do. A couple of seasons playing tag with the Alamanni was just what Crespo needed.

'Secret,' Crespo said, tapping his nose again.

'Old tent-mates don't have secrets, Crespo. You know that. We've fought in the same shield line and shared a latrine bench. How could we have secrets?'

'Procurator's office. On his staff. He's a miserable little shit, Catus Decianus, but he's got the right idea. Squeeze them until they bleed.' He paused and Valerius watched his brain fight the wine in his system. 'You won't tell anybody I said that?'

Valerius tried not to show his disappointment. The procurator's office meant Londinium. Much too close. 'What, that he's a miserable little shit?'

'Not that, the other thing. Squeeze them. It's a secret.'

'Squeeze who?'

'Squeeze the Celts,' Crespo said, as if the answer was obvious. 'They've been feeding off Rome for years. Subsidies and tax breaks. While me and you were sweating and bleeding, they've been rolling in it. Now they want it back.'

'Who wants it back?'

'Big people.' The centurion winked. 'Powerful people. Subsidies and tax breaks. Only now they're all loans.'

Big people? Powerful people? Just like Crespo to talk up his new job. He knew as much about subsidies and tax breaks as Valerius did, which was precious little. It sounded as if he'd got out of the Twentieth just in time and he seemed inordinately proud of his appointment. But what was he? Just another blood-sucking debt collector. So a few

Britons had got behind with their tax payments? Maybe someone would have their farm taken away from them. Well, Crespo was just the man for that. But what really mattered at the moment was that he was drunk enough to be harmless and Valerius decided it would be better to keep him that way, at least until Lunaris arrived. He poured wine from the jug into the two cups, ensuring Crespo's was full to the brim.

'Tell me about Glevum . . .'

It was dusk when he left the bar, with Crespo staggering in his wake, banging from one side of the doorway to the other and muttering about vengeance. He still had his knife and Valerius considered taking him down towards the river and finding out whether he could swim with a bellyful of wine, but all he really wanted to do was get away from the man. Proximity to Crespo had left him feeling dirty. Every soldier had his dark places, but Crespo's went to the very centre of Hades itself. The rape of the Silurian girl evidently hadn't been the first. Not by a long way. And there were hints of even more terrible crimes.

'Who's the drunk?' He looked up to see Lunaris lounging in the doorway of an apartment block opposite the bar.

'An old friend. Don't you recognize Centurion Crespo? And aren't you supposed to salute an officer?'

'Sir!' Lunaris rapped his arm against his chest armour with elaborate ceremony.

'I thought we were going to meet inside?' Crespo had slumped against the wall of the tavern and Valerius removed the knife from his hand and threw it into an alleyway.

'Didn't fancy the company . . . sir.'

'Mine or his?'

'Not sure, sir. What are we going to do with him?' The legionary's tone made it more of a suggestion than a question. Maybe the river wasn't such a bad idea. Valerius looked around. No. Too many witnesses, and if Crespo was truly on the procurator's staff there'd be an investigation. He had a better idea. 'Let's give him a nice soft bed for the night,' he suggested, pointing to a large midden that steamed noxiously beside a stable a few yards down the street.

They picked Crespo up between them and carried him to the dungheap.

'Ready?' Lunaris asked.

'On three. One, two, three.'

Crespo's body landed face down among the horse and mule shit, and, if Valerius was any judge, the contents of the owner's latrine pit.

'That'll do nicely. He's among friends,' Lunaris laughed.

'Wait.' Valerius picked up a stick leaning against the stable door and prodded the manure around Crespo's face until he had space to breathe. 'No point in killing him.'

Lunaris snorted. 'I wouldn't be so sure about that.'

XVI

Valerius, dearest son and a father's pride, I greet you and salute you. Livius sends word that you are in good health and do your duty. Do not trouble yourself on behalf of your father; his joints may creak these days but he thrives like the olive trees on the southern slope beyond the river, a little more gnarled with each passing year, but still productive in his way. Granta and Cronus send their greetings, too.

The letter had followed him from Glevum and must have been written two months earlier. Valerius smiled as he read the opening again. A typical father's missive to his son; replete with familial pleasantries but containing a rebuke in every line. The fact that Livius had sent word of his condition was meant to remind him that he had not. The creaking joints were a hint that his father was feeling abandoned. Granta and Cronus were the two freedmen who managed the estate. He struggled to find the hidden message in their inclusion, but he had no doubt it was there somewhere. He read on.

I still await the reply from the Emperor in connection with my request for an appointment. It has been several months, I know, but I retain some hope of advancement and a resurgence in the fortunes of our family. The Emperor is a fine young man, with many responsibilities, but I have taken steps to ensure my application is brought before him.

Valerius felt his heart sink as he read the last sentence. Even in faraway Britain it was clear that dabbling in politics in Rome under Emperor Nero could be as dangerous as a night patrol in a Silurian swamp. His father had prospered thanks to his friendship with the Emperor Tiberius, but that had been long ago. He had only survived Caligula by retreating to the estate and resolutely ignoring the blandishments of every competing faction. There had been a brief revival under Claudius which ended with some indiscretion his father would never discuss, which had left him with an enduring hatred for the old Emperor's freedman, Narcissus. Now was not the time to be making a political comeback. The problem was that Lucius believed he had friends at court.

I had a most pleasant encounter with your old tutor, Seneca, just the other day, and he brought me up to date with events in Rome and in the Senate. Valerius groaned. As a boy he had studied under the great man and the philosopher now owned an estate in the next valley to his father. Seneca, in his early sixties, could be a wonderful dinner companion, entertaining and erudite, fashioning arguments that could turn a man's head inside out and have him debating against himself. He was also reckless and dangerous to know. One clever remark too many had lost him Caligula's patronage and might easily have cost him his life. Yet just when his star was in the ascendancy again a flagrant affair with the now-dead Emperor's sister, Julia Livilla, had seen him sent into exile by her uncle, Caligula's successor, Claudius. Claudius's wife Agrippina had rescued him from obscurity in Corsica to tutor her son, and now that same son ruled the Empire and Seneca sat at his side.

Seneca advises that you consider leaving Britain at once – these things can be arranged, he says – and resume your legal career. It appears that your island province has not met the Emperor's expectations. He sees only huge expenditure without tangible result and only his respect for his late stepfather's achievements there maintains his interest. My friend fears that interest may not be

168

indefinite. He hinted that if I had any investments in Britain it might be wise to withdraw them and direct them elsewhere. But my only investment is you, my son [Valerius imagined he could see a stain on the letter where a stray tear had dropped], *and the thought of that investment ending its days on the point of some savage's spear undoubtedly shortens a tenure already sadly decreased by life's manifest burdens . . .*

More of the same emotional blackmail followed before the letter descended into a catalogue of complaint directed against the weather, the slaves, the worthy Granta and Cronus who were the only reason the estate remained in profit, the price of olive oil, which was down, and the price of cattle feed, which was up.

Valerius put the letter aside before he had finished reading it, knowing it would undoubtedly end with another plea for his return to Rome. But his mind dwelt on the contents. The old man's ambitions were worrying enough, but what about the hints of high politics? Could Nero truly be considering abandoning Britain? It seemed impossible that such an enormous investment in gold and blood should be cast aside so lightly. No, it was *not* possible. He was here, in Colonia, the tangible proof that Britain *was* Rome. A city with an emperor's name and a god emperor's temple at its heart. And Seneca's suggestion that Lucius should withdraw his non-existent investments: how did that square with what he had heard about the huge stake the philosopher had in the province? No, his father must have misunderstood.

Later, Valerius dispatched Lunaris to deliver the swords and shields to the militia armoury. 'Then you can take the shovels out to the second century on the Venta road. You should be back by nightfall. Get a good night's sleep. We're going hunting in the morning.'

Lunaris gave him an old soldier's look. 'Hunting?'

'You said you were bored mending roads.'

'That depends what we'll be hunting.'

'Boar, I think.'

The legionary brightened. 'And we get to eat what we kill? Where?'

'On the estate of Lucullus, the Briton who is *augustalis* of the Temple of Claudius.'

Lunaris frowned. 'Are you sure it's only boar you're after?'

Now it was Valerius's turn to look concerned. 'Why? What have you heard?'

The big man shrugged. 'Just tent talk. You were out there the other day, and the *quaestor*, Petronius, was sniffing around, asking questions.'

'You should have speared the bastard. What kind of questions?'

'The kind of thing you toffs are interested in. Who your father is. If you have any friends in high places. Ask Julius. I only got it from his clerk.'

'Who'll lose the skin off his back if I have anything to do with it.'

Lunaris hid his smile. He knew Valerius wasn't the type of officer to have a soldier whipped. The young tribune was an easy man to like and they'd become as close as people of their very different classes could become on the slow journey back from Londinium. Valerius had tied his horse to the ox cart and they'd walked together for most of the way. For all his ancient bloodlines and high education the tribune was a country boy at heart. He had pointed out animals and sign of animals that Lunaris, who had been brought up in the festering backstreets in the valleys between the seven hills of Rome, would never have seen without his help. A sleek otter gliding along the depths of a river pool with silver bubbles streaming from its flanks, and shy fallow deer peering from the shadows of a roadside copse. An old dog fox that crossed the road just ahead of them with one of his cubs in its mouth. Lunaris, in his turn, had told of surviving by his wits among the child gangs of the Vicus Bellonae in the Subura, stealing apples by sleight of hand or drawing a baker's attention while a fleet-footed accomplice lifted a loaf that would be shared later. By the time they arrived outside Colonia's gates they had become friends, which allowed Lunaris a certain leeway when they were alone. But he was a legionary and Valerius was a legionary officer and there were limits that both understood.

'I'd best be going if I'm to be back by dark, sir,' he suggested.

Valerius waved him away and set off in the direction of the west gate. The goldsmith's shop formed part of a villa fronting the main street, not far from Lucullus's townhouse. It didn't look much from the roadway, but looks could be deceptive. A villa like this might take up an entire city block, with a labyrinth of dozens of interconnecting rooms and courtyards behind the unimposing façade. More likely it was less grand – Corvinus didn't strike him as a man who needed to parade his wealth – but certainly enough to show that the former armourer had invested his pension and his talents wisely. The thought brought Lucullus to mind, and from Lucullus, Petronius. No doubt he had his reasons for asking questions about a lowly visiting tribune, but the *quaestor*'s interest had planted a seed of concern.

Corvinus awaited him inside the shop as they had arranged. 'Your business in Londinium was concluded successfully, I hope,' he said politely.

Valerius mentioned the brand-new swords and shields he had prised from the quartermaster in the city, and the goldsmith's face lit up. 'You wouldn't have got away with that in my day, but, by Mars's beard, I thank you for it. That's a dozen rusty spikes that call themselves *gladii* I'll never have to put an edge on again, and a dozen shields only fit for the practice ground I can replace.'

Valerius smiled. 'Is the work complete?' he asked, changing the subject.

'It is,' Corvinus said. 'I have it here.' He reached up

into the top row of a many-drawered cabinet behind him and pulled out a leather bag, which he placed on the counter between them. 'I hope it is to your satisfaction.' He picked at the drawstrings of the bag and poured the contents into his hand. 'I could have fashioned something finer – added a chain perhaps – but the time . . .' he said apologetically.

'No. It is exactly what I wanted.'

It was perfect. Hanging from a thin cord of soft leather was the tiny figure, worked in gold, of a charging boar, a replica of the insignia which decorated the shields of the Twentieth. The craftsmanship was astonishingly delicate and Valerius could barely believe it had been created by the massive, workman's hands which held it. The pendant shone with a lustre that belied its size and was an object of incredible beauty. It had cost him a month's pay and was worth every *sestertius*, because it would not look out of place at a queen's throat. By tomorrow night, he hoped, it would be hanging at Maeve's.

'I congratulate you,' Valerius said. 'The workmanship is the finest I have ever seen. But how . . .'

Corvinus might have been insulted, but he only laughed. 'Sometimes a man spends a lifetime battering swords on an anvil, but knows deep inside that he has the skill to create finer things.'

Valerius paid the agreed sum and Corvinus placed the necklace carefully back in its leather pouch. 'Your lady is very fortunate. Tell her to bring it back here and I will fashion a chain for it. Free of charge. I have not forgotten your handsome new swords. But, of course, she will be in Rome?'

Valerius picked up the pouch, and smiled his good-bye. 'No,' he said. 'She is not in Rome.'

When he was gone, Corvinus reflected on the tribune's final words, and chewed his lip. Should he have said something? No, it was none of his business.

Lunaris didn't suit the horse. And the horse didn't suit Lunaris. It was Valerius's spare mount; a Gaulish mare with handsome thoroughbred lines and a playful nature made more playful by the fact that she hadn't been ridden for more than a week.

'Don't keep tugging on the reins. She has a delicate mouth,' Valerius admonished him, wishing he'd put the *duplicarius* on a pack mule instead.

'I've got a delicate backside. If I don't keep tugging on the reins she'll be in Brigante country, and you'll be hunting on your own.'

'I thought you said you could ride?'

'I said I had ridden,' Lunaris announced with dignity. 'I didn't say I'd ridden a horse this big.'

Valerius tried to imagine the legionary on anything smaller. 'When was that?'

'When I was six or seven. But there are some things you never forget.'

Valerius studied him again, hunched low over the mare's ears as if he could control her by sheer force of will. 'Yes, there are some things you never forget,' he agreed.

'We won't be hunting on horseback?' said Lunaris worriedly.

'I hope not.'

They arrived at Lucullus's villa in the fine grey drizzle Valerius had come to realize was Britain's standard morning welcome. Lunaris grunted with relief to see the hunting party waiting on foot, but Valerius suppressed a curse when he saw how they were dressed. A Roman officer's dignity wouldn't allow him to appear before his barbarian host in anything but full uniform, including his scarlet cloak. The dozen men awaiting them – he noted that they were all Britons – were dressed uniformly in clothing of brown and green: heavy cloth shirts and trews that would fend off the largest bramble, perfect for blending in with the landscape and thick with lanolin to keep out the rain.

'At least we'll be able to find each other,' Lunaris muttered from his side.

'Welcome, my friends.' Lucullus emerged smiling from the house and Valerius was pleased to see he was accompanied by Cearan, the Iceni nobleman. He looked beyond the two men, searching for Maeve, but she was nowhere in sight. The Trinovante continued: 'You have eaten, I hope? Good. We will not eat again until the eighth hour, but I have arranged to have food brought to us on the hunt. We are civilized people, you see.'

Valerius saw Cearan studying him with a sympathetic smile. He came close to the horse's side and patted it on the flank. 'A fine beast. From Gaul? Good for racing – and fighting – but not for hunting.' He lowered his voice. 'Like your uniform. If you and your comrade follow me indoors I believe I will be able to find you something more suitable.'

The two Romans glanced at each other and the handsome Celt recognized the look that passed between them.

'Do not be concerned. Your fine weapons and armour will be safe under Lucullus's roof. We are not all thieves, despite what your people seem to think.'

Valerius felt the heat of embarrassment on his face. 'I'm sorry. We did not mean to give that impression. But we are soldiers and these things are precious to us.'

'As they are to us,' the Iceni said graciously. 'I will place your sword beside mine and your helmet with my arm and neck rings.'

He led them to a room where they could change their clothes and showed them where to put their armour and weapons. Lunaris finished dressing first, grunting as he squeezed into a pair of checked woollen trews which struggled to fit around his substantial backside.

'I'm putting you on half rations for a month,' Valerius joked. 'Get out there and find out what's happening. I'll join you in a moment.'

The shirt and trews were of heavier cloth than the

equivalent Roman tunic and *braccae*, but he could move much more freely than in chest armour and a helmet. He left his *gladius* with his armour, but retained his belt and the short dagger attached to it. The belt also carried a small pouch and he carefully placed the leather bag with the boar amulet inside and ensured it was secure. He felt outlandish in the unfamiliar Celtic clothing and wished he had a mirror to see what he looked like, a thought he immediately banished. Fool. You look exactly like everyone else, only with shorter hair and no festering moustache.

He hurried into the corridor and collided with someone rushing the other way. His first sensation was of softness, then of strength: of warmth, followed by fear. Maeve gasped when her body felt the touch of his and her eyes widened with surprise when she saw the handsome young man in the familiar Celtic clothing. It took a moment for her to recognize Valerius. The look was quickly replaced by another that was gone before he could decide what it was. Valerius willed his legs to move, but for some reason they wouldn't obey. His chest tightened and his flesh seemed to tingle in a way he had only experienced once before, when he was caught outdoors in a lightning storm. She wore her hair loose today, and her long dress was of dark blue wool, belted at the waist in a way that emphasized the weight of her breasts and the breadth of her hips.

He took a step back and bowed. 'Maeve.'

She gave a little frown and lowered her head. 'Tribune.'

He wanted to reach out and raise her chin so that she was looking into his eyes, and tell her that his name was Valerius, but all he said was: 'Will you be joining us on the hunt today?'

The creamy skin of her forehead wrinkled slightly and he knew she was smiling. 'Not all British women are the mighty Amazons of your mysteries, sir. We cook and we weave, but we do not hunt – or fight.'

'I apologize.' They seemed to be forever apologizing to each other. 'You must think me uncultured.'

She raised her head and stared at him. 'No, I do not think that.'

He reached for the pouch at his belt, but she sensed his purpose and placed her hand on his. The heat of her touch felt like a brand. 'You must hurry. They are waiting.'

'Will I . . .'

'If the gods will it. Remember the owl.'

A shout from the doorway summoned him. He looked at her and nodded. Then he was gone.

She stared after him, trying to divine the conflicting feelings that raged within her; knowing they were the most dangerous of human emotions, but not which would win the fight.

XVII

Lucullus led the way along the muddy, thorn-lined trackways dissecting the fields of his estate. Most of the enclosures were devoted to raising sheep or pigs, although a few were grazed by scrawny, dun-coloured cattle. Small farmsteads dotted the countryside, each with a roundhouse and its pen for livestock, and around these the currently barren spaces that would be planted with crops in the spring.

Valerius and Lunaris walked together, and Valerius wished Cearan could join them. A Roman hunt would be governed by traditions dating back hundreds of years, and he had little doubt a British hunt was the same. But the Iceni walked ahead with their host and it seemed unlikely they'd be enlightened by their closer companions. The Britons paid the two Romans little heed, apart from an occasional quizzical glance, chattering excitedly in their own language. Behind the hunters came the servants and slaves, each carrying a long spear.

'What happened while I was inside the villa?' he asked Lunaris.

'Mainly they wondered what was keeping you,' the *duplicarius* said. 'What was keeping you?'

'There must have been something.' Valerius allowed his impatience to show.

Lunaris gave a shrug. 'The little lord, the fat one, paired everyone off. You're with him, and I'm with the tall friendly one. After that he gave a speech in that noise of theirs, and they cheered him.' He glanced around him. 'They're a rum lot. One minute they're as docile as sheep, the next they're roaring like wolves. I wished I'd had my sword.'

Valerius smiled, remembering Castus's similar comment. 'We're safe enough with Lucullus. In any case, I used to hunt wolves on my father's estate.'

'Not these wolves you didn't! Watch your back when you're out in the long grass. We'll look silly if we end up with some druid prodding at our livers to find out if it's going to rain tomorrow.'

By now they were approaching a broad stretch of woodland guarded at intervals by small groups of men, each of whom held a pair of snarling hounds. Valerius heard Lucullus call out his name, and a guide ushered them forward.

He studied the animals, remembering tales of British fighting dogs trained to rip out a man's throat.

Lucullus noticed his interest. 'My boar-hounds,' the little man said proudly. 'I bred them myself. They have been out since dawn tracking down our quarry. I instructed my forest wardens that only the largest beasts were of interest – in your honour, of course.'

Valerius bowed his thanks, but there were other honours he'd rather have received.

'It seems they have penned a boar in this wood. A few dogs have been lost, and no doubt he will be rather torn, but he will still provide us with good sport. I think I have hunted this boar before, but he has always bested me. He tore up the green shoots in the spring, and more recently he has destroyed the corn on the ear. He has been an expensive guest.'

'So we wait until the dogs have cornered him properly and then surround him?'

'Oh no,' Lucullus said seriously. 'This is not one of your arenas. That would be much too simple and there would be little honour in it. The boar must have his opportunity, as we will. You are different from us, you see; we esteem the birds and the beasts we hunt, for each of them possesses a soul, just as each man possesses a soul, and the gods watch over them as they do us.' He smiled sadly. 'Let us hope that the gods – both our gods – are with us today.'

The men split into pairs, and Lucullus accepted a team of hounds from one of the handlers. Valerius found Cearan at his side. 'You will take the first boar, as the guest of honour,' he said quietly. He stepped aside as a servant handed Valerius a spear, seven feet in length, solid and heavy, with a broad, leaf-shaped blade and a wooden cross-piece a third of the way down its shaft. 'The cross-piece is to ensure the boar cannot reach you with his tusks,' he explained. 'Lucullus will keep the dogs leashed until the last moment. The boar will be deep in a thicket licking his wounds and the warden will place you where he is most likely to emerge. When the dogs find him, he will run. They will stay with him, but when he sees you it will be you he comes for. He knows his enemy, you see. When he comes, his head will be low. That means you must be low too, for the spear has to take him in the chest to kill him. Anywhere on the head and it will glance off his skull, which is like iron. On the flanks, it will only anger him more. Remember, only in the chest.'

'We are ready,' Lucullus announced. Valerius hefted the spear and balanced it between his hands, instinctively finding the most effective grip so that when the moment came he could place the point where it was needed without hesitation or thought. He felt no fear, only the suppressed excitement of the hunt. His heart beat faster in his chest, thudding against the ribcage, and he willed himself to control it because he knew passion was his enemy. He must clear his mind and concentrate every one of his senses on his quarry. Slowly, he followed Lucullus towards the escarpment of brown and gold, the two dogs straining at the leash, alternately snarling and baying as the scent of their prey carried to them on the light breeze.

When they reached the shelter of the trees Valerius saw the forest was much less dense than it appeared from outside, and, as they penetrated deeper, he realized that what he had thought untamed woodland had been carefully managed for generations. Gaps in the trees showed where the different types of wood had been harvested. Oak, for house timbers and making shields; ash, pollarded to provide the long spears the Britons wielded so effectively; hornbeam, yew and horse chestnut. All had their uses. Each clearing quickly filled with scrubby bush and thorn that provided perfect cover for partridge and woodcock, deer and wild ox. And for the giant boar which raided Lucullus's fields.

By now the dogs were permanently on the scent and they threw themselves against their leashes, almost strangling themselves in their eagerness to reach their prey. Lucullus must have been stronger than he appeared or he could never have held them. They were massive beasts, black and tan on the flanks, standing as high as a man's belly, with deep, powerful chests, big heads and jaws filled with fearsome teeth. The Briton's eyes met Valerius's and he grinned, the excitement of the moment as fierce within him as it was in the Roman.

The forest warden ranged ahead of them and they froze as he halted before a large clump of thorn that spread in a broad half-moon across their front. Valerius would swear the man sniffed the air and pointed like one of his dogs before he waved them up and spoke rapidly to Valerius in his own language.

'He says you should go there,' Lucullus translated, and pointed to a spot on the right, about fifteen paces from the bushes. 'He advises you to keep the spear low. You will have only one chance before he is on you. May Taranis aid you and Mercury speed your hand.'

Valerius nodded as Lucullus and the warden moved away with the dogs, leaving him alone. He felt a fluttering in his chest. Not fear, he thought, just a few nerves, and nerves gave a man an edge if he knew how to control them. This was the moment of crisis in any hunt. The moment when everything became clear and the only things that existed were the hunter and the hunted and nothing between. He crouched low and held the spear in front of him, his left hand well forward on the ash shaft and the right close to his body to ensure a steady, direct thrust. As he waited, he stared at the bushes in front of him, a wall of unbroken, dangerous green. Where would it come? Surely Lucullus should have unleashed the dogs by now. He cursed his own impatience. Wait. Be ready. The misty rain had stopped, but his hands were damp, and he prayed his grip wouldn't fail at the vital moment. *Where were the dogs?* He glanced to his left and in the same instant a cacophony of barks, snarls and unearthly squeals shattered the silence. The green wall in front of him exploded as something enormous burst from the undergrowth. His heart seemed to stop. It was huge – he had seen smaller oxen – a black nemesis with burning red eyes and menacing, curved six-inch tusks, already bloodied by its battle with the dogs that now snapped at its flanks. As he watched, it swung its head almost casually and one of the hounds was tossed away, howling, with a fearsome gash in its side and its entrails hanging clear. He recognized the instant the boar became aware of his presence; the subtle change of direction. It came unbelievably fast, its short legs a blur as it crossed the ground between them. Low. He dropped to one knee and forced the butt of the spear into the ground behind him, keeping the point directly on the animal's breastbone. But was he low enough? The massive snout was almost on its chest, and he was close enough to see the long crest of erect, quill-like black hair along the ridge of its spine and the old scars on its massive shoulders from past encounters with dogs. He had no time to change the angle of the spear, he could only hold and pray. The boar's size was its undoing. It was so enormous that when the iron spearhead slipped just under the chin the animal's own momentum forced it deep into the chest cavity, punching through bone and muscle and delivering a mortal wound to the great heart. Valerius had braced himself for the shock, but still the power of the impact astonished him. The force of it surged along the spear and almost catapulted him free of the shaft. He was shaken like a leaf in a thunderstorm, tossed this way and that until he thought his neck would snap. Instinct told him the strike was true, but the boar refused to die. The red eyes still burned as it forced its way inch by inch up the ash shaft, driving the blade ever deeper into its body, until it was stopped by the cross-piece. Even then it fought on, lashing right and left, so that Valerius feared he would lose his grip. Finally, bright heart blood gushed from the gaping mouth and the boar gave an awful shudder and was still.

Valerius slumped, panting, over the spear. He sent a silent prayer to Jupiter and Minerva and willed himself to stop shaking. The exhilaration of the kill would come later, but for now there was only the familiar, dry-mouthed aftermath of survival. The remaining hound saved him. It broke off from sniffing at the enormous carcass to give a sudden, warning snarl.

A second boar, almost as big as the first, erupted from the bushes to his left where it must have lain silent while its brother drew the dogs away. Now it was here to avenge him. No time to retrieve the spear, which was buried two feet in the first animal's chest. Valerius rolled to his right, placing the mass of the dead pig between himself and the attack. He was only just in time. As he huddled in the lee of the boar, attempting to make himself part of the earth, a giant head appeared over the animal's flank: a ferocious apparition of gaping pink mouth, snapping mantrap jaws and slashing yellowed tusks that came within a hair's breadth of disembowelling him. He scrabbled for his knife, knowing it would barely scratch the boar's thick hide, but it was trapped beneath his body. How long would it take the beast to work out that it could reach him more easily from the side? Could he run? No. He had seen the speed with which it had crossed the clearing. He frantically searched the area around him for some weapon, but there was none. He twisted his arm so he could reach his belt, but the movement attracted the boar and now the tusks swung at his face, the great mouth wide and putrid-breathed in front of his eyes and the teeth chopping and gnashing. Another inch and he would be dead. He ignored a stab of pain in his shoulder and concentrated on the belt. At last his grasping fingers found the fastening and gradually he was able to work it round his body until the knife hilt lay in the palm of his hand. One chance and one chance only. He lay with his left side beneath the dead boar's still-warm belly and his head tight against the coarse hairs of its ribs. His right arm was twisted behind him but at least he had the knife. He screamed a mindless battle cry and with all the power he could call upon swung the knife at the beast's gleaming eye, praying to any god who would listen that his aim should be good. The boar squealed with pain and fury but he knew he had failed. The point missed its target by a full inch, ploughing a red furrow across the pig's broad forehead. The thrashing above him took on an even more savage, mindless quality, and he knew that there was no escape. No glorious end on the battle-field for Gaius Valerius Verrens, scion of a tribe with its roots in the very founding of Rome. He would die unremembered in this damp British forest with his nostrils filled with the musky stink of boar. He thought of the golden amulet in his pouch, and that in turn made him think of Maeve. Her face filled his mind and he heard the sound of a familiar voice.

'So one boar was not enough for you?'

He looked up, bemused, to discover Cearan staring at him over the second boar's shoulder, which had now sprouted the shaft of a throwing spear. The great body shook spasmodically and tendrils of dark blood drooled from the beast's open mouth on to the flank of its sibling.

'Please.' The Briton extended his hand. Valerius allowed Cearan to help him shakily to his feet.

'I thank you. You saved my life.' His voice sounded hoarse in his own ears as he stared at the two boars. Between them they would weigh as much as a fully laden ox cart. If the second hadn't been obstructed by his brother's body it would surely have ripped him to pieces. He turned back to Cearan. 'If ever . . .'

The Iceni waved a hand dismissively. 'We are friends. You would have done as much for me. In any case, it was at my suggestion that Lucullus invited you to hunt with him. He became disoriented in the forest once the dogs were loosed, therefore you were my responsibility. It would have been discourteous, not to say inconvenient, if you had died.' Valerius registered the word 'inconvenient' as Cearan stooped to crouch over the first boar, studying the spot where the blade of the spear had penetrated its breast. 'A fine blow, well aimed. He is your first?'

Valerius nodded.

The Briton smiled and when he stood he reached out his fingers, which were red with the boar's blood, and with quick, practised strokes smeared it over the Roman's forehead and cheeks. 'It is our custom,' he explained. 'It marks a man as a man, and only a man could have faced such a giant without flinching.'

A commotion behind them announced the arrival of the rest of the hunting party, led by Lucullus and Lunaris, who stopped in his tracks when he saw the size of the kill.

'By Mars's mighty arse, I've never seen anything like it. Just one of them would feed the cohort with ham for breakfast every day for a month. You could hitch them to a chariot and they'd haul you all the way to Rome. You . . .'

'Could help us butcher them?' Cearan suggested.

'Surely you would not put him to work before he has had the opportunity to best his officer?' Lucullus admonished his cousin. 'There is word of another spoor in a copse to the north.' He suggested that the rest of the hunt move on while Valerius rested and the slaves butchered the two boars. 'You have had your sport, cousin. I will leave you to take care of our guest.'

Lunaris looked suspicious, but Valerius nodded to him and the big legionary allowed Lucullus to lead him off with the others. As the slaves worked on the two carcasses with gutting knives and hatchets, Cearan reached into the pack he had dropped and retrieved a bulging goatskin. 'Here,' he offered. 'You must be thirsty.'

Valerius put the skin to his lips, expecting the contents to be water, but the tepid liquid was some sort of sweet, fruity beer that went straight to his head, instantly reviving him. He took another gulp.

Cearan laughed. 'Not too much or the slaves will have to carry you home along with the boar. It is honeyed ale, but with an infusion of herbs singular to my own tribe.'

The effect was remarkable. 'This must be what your warriors drink before battle.'

'Perhaps the Catuvellauni,' Cearan said seriously, 'or the tribes of the west, but the Iceni do not need ale or mead to give them courage.' He walked to the edge of the clearing, out of earshot of the servants, and Valerius instinctively knew he should follow. 'When I fought the Romans beside Caratacus on the Tamesa I realized a truth that he did not; or perhaps I do him an injustice, and he did realize it but refused to accept it. That makes him a braver man than I, but not, I think, a wiser one.'

Valerius stared at him. Where was this leading?

Cearan went on thoughtfully. 'Caratacus would have had us fight until the blood of the last Briton stained the earth. The truth I learned is that we must find a way to live with Rome or everything that makes us who and what we are will cease to exist.

Our children and our children's children will be brought up either as Romans or as slaves. Our kings will serve Rome, or we will have no kings. You will even take our gods and make them your own.'

'Then you already have your wish,' Valerius pointed out. 'The name of Prasutagus, king of the Iceni, is spoken of with honour in the palace of the governor. He retains his authority in the name of the Emperor and you retain your British ways. You prosper as no other tribe has prospered save the Atrebates, and you worship whom you will and no Roman interferes.'

A momentary glint of triumph flashed in the pale eyes. 'But Prasutagus is an old man. What happens if Prasutagus is no longer king?'

Valerius considered the question. It had two answers, or perhaps three. First, Prasutagus would have appointed his own heir and if that heir were acceptable to Rome he would have the support of the Emperor. If the governor felt the chosen heir was too weak, or, worse, too strong, he might appoint his own king from the Iceni aristocracy. But that would only be done with the aristocracy's agreement. The third answer was so unlikely and unacceptable to Cearan that he would not voice it. Eventually he said the words he knew the Briton wanted to hear: 'Then the Iceni will need a new king.'

Cearan nodded emphatically. 'A king who would maintain our present relationship with Rome. But there are some among my tribesfolk who believe the path Prasutagus treads is the wrong path and would welcome a new Caratacus to follow. Who may even wish to *be* the new Caratacus. They are encouraged in this foolishness by men who come to their farmsteads at nightfall and leave again before dawn. Men who preach a message of hatred against your people.'

Valerius stared at him, remembering the meeting with Castus in Londinium. Was this what had stirred up the midland tribes? 'Who are these men?'

'Druids.'

Valerius froze. 'The governor, Gaius Suetonius Paulinus, understands that the druids are penned on their sacred isle, or in the mountains of the west. The Iceni are a client tribe of Rome and if they welcome a druid at their fires then they place that status at peril. If King Prasutagus is aware of these visits he should hold the druid and send word to Colonia.'

'Prasutagus is a good king and a good man, but his sword arm has weakened with age along with his mind. His strength now lies not on the throne, but beside the throne, where sits his wife Boudicca.' Valerius remembered the name from the dinner at Lucullus's villa. The painting of the surrender. 'Queen Boudicca is not unsympathetic to the old religion. Even if Prasutagus were to seek out the druids it is unlikely he would find them.'

The Roman shook his head. This was the stuff of Paulinus's nightmares. Celtic priests stirring the embers of rebellion in a subject tribe. A weak king with his queen at his side whispering treason in his ear. If, as Castus seemed to hint, the Cornovii and the Catuvellauni were rearming, all it would take was one spark to set the entire country ablaze.

'There is a way,' Cearan said and his eyes turned hard. 'When Prasutagus dies ensure the *right* king succeeds him.'

Now Valerius saw it. He almost laughed. Did this handsome barbarian truly believe a lowly tribune could help him secure the crown of the Iceni?

But Cearan had read his thoughts. 'Swords and gold. The two things that together equal power. With gold I can buy swords and the arms to wield them. I will bring you your druid and you will persuade the governor that Cearan would rule the Iceni not only as a client of Rome, but as a true ally of Rome.' He brought his face close to Valerius. 'You must believe me. I want no more Iceni sons gasping out their lives on some river bank for an impossible dream.'

Valerius took a step back as if distance would diminish the scale of his dilemma. Was the Briton merely another power-hungry barbarian lord? He would not be the first to try to bring down his chieftain with a subtle denunciation. But something told him Cearan was more than that. From the first he had sensed a deep honesty in the Iceni that set him apart. He carried his honour like a banner and Valerius had no doubt that he would die to defend it. But what could he do?

'You ask the impossible. I have no access to the governor and even if I did he would dismiss this as a conspiracy against Prasutagus who has served Rome well. You talk of plots, but where is your evidence? A few cowherds' tales of strangers in the night? Paulinus would have me whipped from his office.'

He expected Cearan to protest, but the Iceni only nodded impassively. 'You are right, of course. I have been too concerned for my people's welfare and do not fully understand your Roman ways. There is time. I believe Prasutagus will see out the winter, but, even if he does not, there will be no decision on his successor until after Beltane. This evidence you seek, what would it be?'

'Bring me the druid. Then I will find you your gold and your swords.'

XVIII

Afterwards, he wasn't sure whether Cearan had engineered it.

The Briton seemed content with the conclusion of their discussion and settled down to supervise the butchering of the two boars, but after a few moments he looked up at the sky, which was still a pale, watery grey. 'My stomach tells me the eighth hour is close, even if the sun does not,' he said. 'They will bring the feast to the forest edge. We are almost finished here; why don't you walk ahead and make sure the wolves don't get to it first?'

'Where food is concerned Lunaris is more dangerous than any wolf.'

'Go then and keep him at bay,' Cearan urged cheerfully. 'Or I must eat one of these pigs raw.'

Valerius left the clearing and set off through the

wood towards the rendezvous point. He wasn't entirely sure of his direction and his head still spun with the effects of the ale and clamoured with images of slashing tusks and a gaping tooth-filled maw snapping within inches of his face. He tried to concentrate on what Cearan had said; the subtle nuances in his voice, the messages in his eyes that had accompanied them. These were not Romans he was dealing with, for all Lucullus's Roman airs. Less than twenty years ago they had been sworn enemies of everything he believed in. How could he trust them after only a few months' acquaintance?

Maeve stepped from the shadow of an ancient oak straight into his path and when she saw him her hand went to her mouth and her dark eyes opened wide in alarm. The young Roman who had set her heart fluttering at the villa had been replaced by a dishevelled, mud-stained vagabond in a torn shirt who stared at her with startled eyes. She noticed something else.

'You're bleeding!'

For the first time Valerius heard something more than polite concern in her voice. She dropped her cloth-wrapped bundle and rushed towards him. He let her come. He would explain that it was the boar's blood later.

She stopped two paces away, wanting to take the next step but not quite knowing how to, and they stared at each other for a few interminable seconds. The long brown cloak she wore over the blue dress hid the curves of her body but couldn't disguise the way her breasts rose and fell sharply with each breath. She had bound her soft chestnut hair in a long plaited tail that draped over her left shoulder. Valerius saw the confusion in her eyes and knew it must be mirrored in his own, but he feared any decision he made would break the spell. An image of the Temple of Claudius filled his head and he recalled the priest's message. The thought made him giddy and he swayed slightly, a movement that made her instinctively step forward to support him. Then they were in each other's arms.

For a moment each was surprised by the other's strength. He held her close so the softness of her body melted against the hardness of his and her head rested lightly on his shoulder. At first, that was enough, but then warmth was transformed into heat and he felt her stiffen. She raised her head and looked up at him in surprise, so he could see the mysterious golden shadows deep in her eyes. Her lips were so close it would have taken only the slightest movement to meet them. Maeve felt the moment, too, but this unfamiliar heat deep within had disturbed her. It conjured up feelings she hadn't realized could exist and half-flashes of something which couldn't be memory, but which was remembered all the same. Her throat went dry and her heart pounded like the beat of a Samhain drum. Another second and she would be consumed. She stepped back.

'You're bleeding,' she repeated, but now her voice was a husky croak.

'It's boar's blood,' Valerius said cheerfully.

'Not your face,' she frowned. 'Your shoulder.'

Valerius glanced down and noticed for the first time the ragged tear in his tunic and a patch where the wool was considerably darker. 'It's a scratch,' he claimed, gingerly touching the area.

'How do you know if you haven't looked at it?' Her voice had recovered its authority now and overflowed with the resigned exasperation women use for men they think are idiots. 'Take your shirt off.'

Valerius hesitated. This wasn't going the way he had imagined it would.

'I am a Celt, Valerius. I've seen men with their shirts off before.'

'You haven't seen *me* with my shirt off,' he protested. 'It would not be seemly.'

She gave an earthy laugh that drove all thoughts of staid Roman maidens from his head. 'What you seemed to have in mind for me a few minutes ago would not have been seemly either.'

Valerius felt a rush of heat in his face. He was a twenty-two-year-old Roman officer and he was blushing.

'Or are Romans different from Celtic men? If so I think I should find out . . . especially if we are to see each other again.'

She kept her face solemn, but her eyes sparkled with gentle humour. He caught her mood and grinned, pulling the woollen tunic over his head and placing it on the ground beside him.

The breath caught in her throat. Yes, she had seen men before, in their many shapes and sizes, but this was different. The young Roman's torso was tanned a deep shade of honey and constant practice with sword and shield had given him heavily muscled shoulders and upper arms. How could hands so powerful have felt so gentle when they held her earlier? His deep, sculpted chest narrowed towards the waist where a thin line of dark hair ran down a flat stomach to disappear somewhere she tried not to think about. She noticed a fresh scar across his ribs and had to stop herself reaching out to touch it. Closer inspection showed other smaller scars: indents and barely noticeable pale lines that spoke of narrow escapes from danger. Disturbingly, the heat she had experienced earlier returned, accompanied by a liquid feeling low in her body.

'Are you going to help me or sell me in Colonia's market?' Valerius asked lightly, conscious of but not unhappy with her inspection. He knew the figure he cut, and took pride in it, but not to the point of arrogance. All the muscle in the world wouldn't stop a well-flighted arrow or the edge of a blade.

She tossed her head, swinging the plaited tail from left to right and reminding him of a colt he had once seen frolicking in a field. 'You were right,' she said dismissively. 'It is just a scratch, but you were a fool to allow yourself to get so close to a boar.'

'Two boars,' he announced, just to see her reaction. He wasn't disappointed.

'Two?'

'Big ones. Enormous.'

'How big?' she demanded, and the wound was forgotten as he described the hunt and how the second boar had come so close to avenging his sibling. She made little 'mmm's of concern at just the right places and her face came closer and closer to his as he talked. Eventually she was so close that it became impossible to do anything but kiss her. When their lips met there was no resistance, just a soft and entirely natural moulding as he tasted her sweetness and the clean tang of freshly torn mint that made him wonder if she had prepared for just this moment. At first her lips stayed closed, but as the seconds passed and the thunder in his head grew louder she opened her mouth to draw him deeper and he felt as if he were being swept away in a swollen river torrent. It seemed right that his hands should move to her waist below the cloak and from there upwards . . .

'Stop!' She took a step away. 'We can't. It is not . . . right.'

'How can it not be right?' He heard the frustration in his voice, and knew that in another six words he would destroy everything he had won so far. But the thunder was still pounding inside his head and his tongue seemed to belong to someone else. 'We—'

She gently placed the first finger of her right hand on his lips, and with her left hand took his.

'Come,' she said, and drew him beneath the boughs of the oak tree, where the sod rose thick over the roots and the grass remained dry despite the rain. She pushed him down and recovered the cloth pack. Among other items it contained a stoppered flask, the contents of which she used sparingly to clean the wound on his shoulder, dabbing gently with a corner of the cloth to clear away the dried blood.

'A waste of good wine,' he protested, reaching for the flask.

She held it away from him. 'A man, a woman and wine are not a good combination,' she said, clearly speaking from a well of experience. 'Later.'

'Later?'

'When we have found my father, or Cearan. When it is more . . . seemly.'

He grinned and lay against the oak, feeling the rough bark against the skin of his back. Her hands worked delicately around the wound and he found himself more at ease than at any time since he had landed on Britain's shores. It was as if they had always been together. Or they belonged together.

'Your father is a fine man.' He said it purely for the pleasure of hearing her voice, but her reply surprised him.

'My father has forgotten who he truly is. He embraces every new Roman fashion and dismisses the old ways. We sacrifice to Roman gods and sleep under a Roman roof on Roman beds. The wine he drinks is shipped from Gaul, but it is Roman wine. The look in his eyes when he talks of his ambitions frightens me. He will never be satisfied.'

'You talk as if you hate Rome, but you are here . . . with a Roman.'

She stared at him and he became lost in the depths of her eyes. 'I am here with Valerius, a young man whose company I enjoy and whose origins I try to forget. It seems to me that Romans think strength is everything.' She reached out absently to stroke the muscle of his right arm. It was a gesture of pure, unthinking affection which instantly took the sting from her words. 'When I was young, I had a friend, the son of one of my father's tenants. We grew up together, played in these woods and swam in the river; I shared my first kiss with Dywel.' Valerius instantly resented Dywel and the time he had spent with Maeve that he could never share. 'He herded his father's cattle, took them out to pasture in the spring and kept them fed during the winter. Then the Romans came. My father had stayed at home when the young men rode off to join Caratacus in the west, so his estate was largely spared. But eight years ago they divided up the land all around us. They said the pasture was no longer my father's to graze his beasts upon and that he could not water them at the dew pond. My father had other pasture and other water, but Dywel's farm was on the far edge of the estate and his father was poor. He defied the Romans.'

'What happened to him?' Valerius asked, already knowing the answer. He remembered Falco's words: *Things were done, when Colonia was founded, that do none of us credit.*

'They cut Dywel's throat with a knife.'

'I am sorry. Your father should have taken his case before the magistrate.'

Maeve gave a bitter laugh. 'That is a very Roman thing to say. Dywel was a Celt. Roman justice is for the Romans.'

He could have protested that she was wrong. That Roman justice was the best in the world: the product of a thousand years of lawyerly debate, discussion and study. But he didn't. Because he realized she was right.

A shout rang out from the woods to their left and Maeve's head whipped round like a frightened deer. 'Here,' she said urgently, thrusting his shirt into his hands. As he stood up to shrug it over his shoulders she poured most of the wine away and took a loaf from the bag she had been carrying and tore it in half, throwing one of the halves into the bushes. She did the same with a large piece of meat. 'Bite it,' she ordered, pushing the portion she'd retained into his mouth. He did as he was told, trying to speak as he chewed.

'Gghwy?'

'Because I stumbled upon you when you were lost. You were hungry and weak from loss of blood and we stayed until you were fed and felt strong enough to move. Quickly!'

She gathered up the cloth bag and thrust the remains of the food inside. When that was done, she studied him critically, brushed some leaves and grass from his back and turned to go.

203

'Maeve?'

She turned back with a look of annoyance that faded when she saw the leather pouch he had retrieved from his belt. He held it out to her, and she hesitated for a moment before taking it, but when she did she smiled and lifted her head to kiss him lightly on the lips. He stood there grinning long after she disappeared into the trees.

XIX

While autumn lasted, Bela the dark-haired young Thracian auxiliary commander kept his men on constant patrol in the forested areas to the north of Colonia, but although he reported occasional signs of disturbed ground and evidence of gatherings in woodland clearings, he found no solid evidence of the subversion Valerius suspected and Castus feared. He passed on the information without comment and drove his troopers all the harder.

When it arrived that year, winter came quickly and it came hard. Frost turned the ground unyielding as stone and the cattle in the fields smoked as if they were on fire before the herd boys drove them into the huts where they and those who farmed them would provide mutual warmth during the following months. The city's aqueduct quickly froze and Valerius ordered a squad of legionaries to be on constant duty at the river below Colonia, breaking the ice as it formed to ensure a supply of water for the citizens. Nature was relentless and the centurions were forced constantly to rotate their shivering, exhausted men. The frost brought the First's road-building duties to an end and Valerius and Julius came up with endless fatigues and exercises to ensure their soldiers stayed fit and alert. Joint exercises with the militia became a regular feature and Valerius's respect for Falco and his veterans grew with each passing week. They even took part in route marches together, though this was one area where the men of the First cohort under-standably excelled both in speed and stamina.

'I pray to Mars and Mithras that the governor doesn't ask us to join him in the spring,' Falco said ruefully as his men stumbled past, faces as red as a legate's banner and breath steaming in the thin winter sunlight.

Valerius smiled and wrapped his cloak closer around him. 'He already has my report. Garrison duties only for the men of Colonia.' But mention of Suetonius Paulinus's spring campaign made him uneasy. Was there anyone in Britain unaware of what was about to happen?

Not Lucullus, certainly.

That winter Valerius developed a liking and a curious respect for the little Trinovante. When the frost was followed by snow unlike anything the young Roman had ever experienced even the exercises ended and the legionaries huddled in their tents or around glowing braziers, attempting to avoid the frost-blight that first turned toes and fingers black and then caused them to fall off. They prayed for the coming of spring or a posting to some paradise where the sun shone for more than four hours in a day, preferably both.

With little of military value to keep him occupied, he worked to repay the hospitality he had received during the previous months from Colonia's leading citizens. It was surprising what a legionary cook could achieve given the time and ingredients, and a string of dignitaries and their matrons complimented him on his table and the service provided by legionary servants, prominent among whom was Lunaris, who would do anything to find some warmth.

Falco and his fat little spouse came often, as did Corvinus, accompanied by his very beautiful and very pregnant wife. Valerius even found time to entertain Petronius, though he was never able to like the *quaestor*, who seemed obsessed by lineage and appeared to have a worryingly comprehensive knowledge of the various well-connected branches of the Valerian family.

Colonia's most influential Briton was occasionally among the guests, and what could be more natural than that he in turn should invite the tribune to his home on the slope across the river. At first, Valerius had regarded Lucullus as a figure of fun because of his terrier-like pursuit of Roman ways. But as he came to know him better, he discovered the ingratiating smile hid a shrewd intelligence and an unfailing generosity. But Maeve was right to be concerned about her father's business dealings. Had the times been different, he would have been rich, successful and respected; but the times were not, and they and his ambition had, despite his outward success, combined to leave him floundering in a sea of debt. A Roman would have kept it his secret shame, hidden in the papers in his *tablinum*, but Lucullus, for all his airs, was not a Roman. He was a garrulous, un-principled Celt, who laughed at his predicament and invited you to laugh with him. Valerius enjoyed his company very much.

Lucullus normally visited Colonia unaccompanied, but when Valerius rode out to the Trinovante's villa Maeve would invariably be waiting to greet her father's guest in the portico. The first time this happened her welcome was excessively formal and, in that nervous way of a man in love, he worried their relationship had already lost some of its lustre.

He was still fretting at the table when Lucullus startled him by wondering how the governor's advance troops would be faring in the mountains of the Deceangli with the snow up to their necks and their toes turning black. But everything else was driven from his mind when he became aware of Maeve's presence over her father's shoulder. The look she gave him sent a shudder of desire through his body and her right hand reached up to touch the golden boar amulet at her neck.

'Are you well?' Lucullus asked, his plump face filled with concern. 'You have gone quite pale.' He picked up a plate and sniffed it. 'That factor! Gereth! It's these damned oysters again.'

It should have been impossible, but they managed to make it only difficult. Snatched conversations in corridors and doorways. Clandestine touches as they brushed past each other on entering or leaving a room. Each encounter only served to inflame the thing growing between them, though it created a frustration that grew in equal measure. She persuaded him to brave the snow and her father's estate wardens and contrived to meet him by chance on a forest ride. At last they could talk unhindered and he found her quick of mind and quicker of temper. She was like no Roman woman he had ever met. She had views on everything – even military tactics, which would have bored any other girl he knew – and she was unafraid to speak her mind, but always it came back to one subject: her people.

She was also practical.

They repeated the encounter a week later. A new fall of snow had thickened the glistening blanket enveloping the land to north and south, transforming it into a world of wondrous sculpted humps and hollows. Large flakes still fell from a sky the colour of an old bruise, turning the air around them into a whirling cascade of white petals. Valerius worried that they might become lost, but Maeve only giggled.

'It will help cover our tracks,' she insisted. 'Come with me.'

Valerius reined back his big military horse to keep pace with the little skewbald pony she rode side-saddle. He found it difficult to keep his eyes off her and as they ventured further into the wood he found his natural caution replaced by a deeper, more visceral anticipation, and an outcome his mind shied away from.

'Here,' she said eventually, laughing when she saw the look on his face. He was staring at a wall of sheer grey rock. 'Help me down.'

He dismounted and took her by the waist, lifting her from the pony and delighting in the warmth of her body, then tied the two animals to the nearest tree. By the time he'd finished she stood at the base of the wall where a large evergreen bush hung heavy with snow.

Something in the way she stood gave him the first hint of what had become inevitable. Then he looked into her face and saw the message there and it felt as if a fire had been lit inside him. The fathomless brown eyes were deadly serious but they contained an un-mistakable challenge, and her cheeks burned with colour that matched her lips, which were sensual, swollen and inviting. When he walked towards her, her eyes never left his, and when he reached her she pulled the bush aside with a flourish that was only spoiled by the snow that fell from the branches on to her head.

'Welcome to my lair,' she said laughing.

It was a cave.

A narrow fissure cut into the rock formed the entrance, which widened almost immediately into an area as large as a legionary's eight-man tent. It must once have been inhabited, because niches and shelves had been cut into the rock walls where she had placed oil lamps that now turned their surroundings into a diamond-studded grotto. Tiny fragments set into the stone glittered in the lamplight like unquenchable sparks of blue, green, red and a dozen other colours he had no name for. The atmosphere, almost religious, gave him a sense of wonder magnified a hundred times by the presence beside him. Smoke from the oil lamps disappeared into the darkness above and he had the impression of a great endless void. But his eye was drawn to the back of the cave, where two large fur rugs lay on the earth floor.

'I wanted us to be warm,' she whispered. 'Do you like it?'

Yes.

Her dark eyes stared back unflinchingly into his and she wiped a tear from her cheek, and raised her lips towards his. The kiss seemed to last an eternity; with every passing second it grew in passion and intensity so that when they finally parted they were both breathless. Now Maeve's eyes filled with something that might have been fear, but quickly faded to shocked surprise at the new emotions burning like wildfire deep within her body.

'Come,' she said, and led him by the hand towards the furs.

Thus far, the day had been Maeve's to command. Now, by unspoken consent, it was Valerius, the more experienced, who took control. A shudder went through her as his fingers plucked at the tie of her cloak and when he had completed the task she lay back entirely still, uncertain of what she should do or not do. Wanting what was to come, but, at the same time, half fearful of it.

Valerius sensed her hesitation. Very gently, he reached down and pulled up the hem of her dress, exposing the length of her ivory-pale legs. She immediately understood what was wanted of her and raised her bottom to allow him to take the rumpled wool underneath her body, then sat upright and raised her arms, so he could remove it altogether.

When she was naked he looked down on her with something close to wonder. Her breasts were full and rounded, with tiny, hard nipples of the most delicate pink. Between them hung the golden boar amulet and it somehow added to the eroticism of the moment. She had a narrow waist which flowed into hips that were seductively wide, but tapered again into long slim legs. He reached out to touch her and then recoiled as if he had been burned. Her smooth skin resonated with life and heat. Impatient, Maeve took his hand and placed it on her breast, then drew it down her body with agonizing slowness that made her draw in her breath sharply.

'Please, Valerius.' She tore at his tunic and when it was gone grasped him to her, desperate for him now. But Valerius would not be hurried. He fought her grip, knowing how much better it would be for her if she would allow him to be patient.

Much later, when he gave her that which she had coveted, but feared, her cry of joy split the air.

There were other times, but when he thought of the cave it was always the first he remembered.

Afterwards they held each other drowsily in the silky warmth of the furs, well satisfied with what had gone before but full of anticipation for what was still to come.

'My father would kill you if he knew,' she whispered sleepily. Valerius opened one eye and looked into hers. She wrinkled her nose in a way that made him smile. 'Well, my father would *try* to kill you if he knew. And you would have to let him. I could never love a man who killed my father.'

She talked of her world, and the way it had changed. Camulodunum had been the capital of the Trinovantes and the family of Lucullus ranked high in the royal line, but that was before Cunobelin, father of Caratacus and king of the Catuvellauni, had usurped Trinovante power and installed himself as their king. Lucullus's father had been spared and exiled to the estate on the hill while Cunobelin took over his palace.

'When the Romans came my father thought to win

back his family's inheritance,' she said sadly. 'But nothing has changed.'

He asked her how women like Boudicca and Cartimandua could hold sway even over great warriors and she shook her head at his naivety. '*Because* they are women,' she said. 'And because, even if Cartimandua is a traitor, they are wise and brave and have the aid of Andraste.'

'Andraste? I do not know that name.'

'The goddess,' she explained, as if to an infant. 'The Dark One who holds power over all men and women and breathes fire in her anger and turns the air to sulphur.'

He told her about Rome and he loved how her eyes opened in amazement at his descriptions of the palaces and the basilicas, the great temples and forests of pillars topped with statues of gold, and the way the whole city looked as if it was on fire when the sun shone in a certain way. 'I would like to visit Rome one day,' she said quietly, and he answered, 'You will.'

She asked him what it was that made the Roman legions so powerful and he explained about the siege weapons he'd seen used against the Celtic hill forts: catapults and ballistas, siege towers and even something as simple as ladders which the tribes had never thought to use for war. She listened intently, frowning when some fact eluded her, and he loved her all the more for the obvious effort she was making to understand him.

Occasionally, Maeve would be away visiting some needy tenant or pregnant estate worker's wife when Lucullus invited Valerius to visit the villa on the hill, ostensibly to discuss business matters or the politics of the province. But these days would inevitably degenerate into marathon drinking bouts which the old man viewed as a challenge to the depth of his wine cellar and the breadth of Falco's stock.

During one wine-soaked afternoon Lucullus allowed the clown's mask to slip.

The *principia*, extended, refurbished and unrecognizable now as the old legionary headquarters, had just been dedicated to the god Claudius with a lavish ceremony which the little Trinovante had funded. But it was its function, as they sat well rested and on their second flask of one of his best Calenian vintages, that drew the sharpest barbs of Lucullus's bleary-eyed bitterness. For the *principia* stood at the centre of a vast bureaucratic network of officialdom that regulated every facet of British life; which weighed, measured and valued everything that was grown, made or reared under its all-seeing eye.

'You Romans . . .' You Romans! This from a man who worked every day and used every deception to try to become one. 'You Romans think you can rule everything in the world, tree and field, bird and beast, man and woman. Everywhere there must be order. Everything must have its place and its price. Everything must be on a list. It is not our way. Not the way of my people.' He shook his head to emphasize his point. 'Before you came we did not have things like this,' he waved an arm distractedly round the room, 'but we did not need them. We lived in huts with mud floors, drank beer from clay pots and ate rough porridge from wooden platters, but still we had more than we have now. We had our honour.'

He paused as if expecting an answer.

'You are surprised that I, a Celt, talk of honour? Yes, Valerius, I know that even you, whom I think of as my friend, consider me a mere Celt. What was I saying? Honour? Yes, honour. You would be amazed at how much talk there is of honour in places not so far from here. We have lost much, but some people' – he said the words with that particular inflection that meant they were a significant 'some people' – 'some people believe it is not too late to restore it.'

By now, Valerius was wishing the Trinovante would stop lecturing him and call one of his slaves to bring more of the excellent wine from his cellar. But Lucullus in full flow would not be halted by anything less than a bolt of lightning.

'Your roads and your fortresses are like a boot across our neck and your temple is sucking us dry. Did you know that the cost even of being a member of the Temple of Claudius is ten times more for a Celt than for a Roman citizen? Ten times! If I told you how much I borrowed to secure the priesthood your head would fall from your shoulders. It is we Celts who must pay back the loans taken out to build it.

We who pay for the sacrifices and the upkeep and for that great golden whore of Victory they have placed upon its pediment.

'While we sit here in this,' the arm was flung out carelessly once more, 'there are men, Valerius, great men, proud warriors, who live in the ruins of their burned-out huts and watch their children starve, because they once had the temerity to stand up for what was theirs. And there are other men, who were once farmers and wanted only to keep what they had, who now have nothing, because you,' an accusing finger pointed disconcertingly straight into Valerius's face, 'stole everything they had: their land, their cattle, their women. Everything.'

Valerius shook his head. 'No. Not me.' Did he say it or only think it? It did not matter. Lucullus ignored him in any case.

'It could have been different. Did you really think you could grind into the dust with a single blow a people who have survived for a thousand years? Did you believe that men whose courage and prowess with sword and spear was their whole life would simply disappear after one defeat? You could have used their skills. You could have taken them into your service; they would have fought even for you. Better, even, that you had killed them all or sold them into slavery, but no, you did not do any of that. Instead, you did the worst thing possible. You ignored them. You left them to sit in their huts, to see the bones in their little ones' faces become more obvious every day, and the breasts of their wives grow empty and dry . . . and to hate.

'They are out there now,' he said, and the message in his voice was matched by that in his eyes. He had seen them, these Roman-haters, and they frightened him.

XX

Saturnalia passed and the snow vanished before the Celts celebrated the rebirth of life in secret ceremonies at their festival of Imbolc. Valerius hadn't forgotten the concerns of Castus, the Londinium camp prefect. By now he was a regular, if reluctant, attendant at meetings of Colonia's *ordo* and, recalling Lucullus's words and Cearan's warning of the previous autumn, he wondered aloud if it was worth checking on who attended the celebrations.

'It does not matter who attends, they will all be drunk,' *quaestor* Petronius said dismissively. 'And when they are drunk they play their childish fire games. You are young, tribune, and must leave such concerns to those who understand them best.'

The exchange was quickly forgotten. Valerius had other things on his mind.

Soon, probably in a matter of weeks, his orders would come through to return the First cohort to Glevum. When he had completed his duties at the legionary headquarters it was certain the legate would send him directly to Londinium . . . and a ship to Rome. The thought sent an unfamiliar shiver of panic through him. Maeve's face continued to haunt him and the need to be with her tantalized his nights. He realized that, whatever happened, he couldn't leave her behind.

A few weeks after Imbolc, he set out north on the Venta road to inspect the work his legionaries had carried out and check for any damage that might have been done by the winter frosts or by the floods that followed the great thaw. He took a patrol of twenty, led by Lunaris, and they rode from Colonia's north gate at dawn on a day when the wind tore in from the coast with the sting of a cracked whip and puffy white clouds scudded like invasion fleets beneath a canopy of leaden grey. Lunaris, marginally more comfortable now on a horse docile enough even for him to control, hunched down in his saddle and wrapped his cloak tightly about him, roundly cursing the British weather.

'I froze all winter and now the damp's eating into my bones, rotting my straps and rusting my armour: why did we ever come here? The people hate us, even the veterans in Colonia resent us being here, eating their rations, drinking their wine, chasing their women and requisitioning everything we want, knowing that the procurator will take six months to pay.'

Valerius smiled at an old soldier's grumbles. If they'd been in Cappadocia or Syria, Lunaris would have been complaining that it was too hot, the wine was sour and the women wouldn't leave him alone.

'We're here because we're soldiers and we go where they want us to go. This is where the Emperor wants us to be. Enjoy it while it lasts. You'll be warm enough come summer, when the Black Celts are chasing you round their mountains. How far to the next bridge?'

Lunaris checked his map. 'About six miles. That's not what I hear.'

'What isn't?'

'That the Emperor wants us in Britain. The word is that we're pulling out soon.'

Valerius turned to stare at him. 'Where does that come from?'

'You know how it goes. The procurator's clerk tells the quartermaster that maybe we don't need to stock-pile so much equipment. The quartermaster tells the armourer to use up the iron he's got. The armourer tells the smith we won't be needing so many *pilum* points and then it's all round the province. Suddenly we're moving out. Probably rubbish.'

Valerius nodded, but he remembered the letter which was still in his chest in the townhouse.

'Why did you bring me?' the *duplicarius* asked, shifting uncomfortably in his saddle.

'Because you have a nose for trouble and an eye for everything else. The last big repair is just short of

221

Venta and I thought we would call on our old friend Lord Cearan.'

'You think there'll be trouble?' Lunaris's hand instinctively sought his sword hilt.

Valerius shook his head. 'I doubt it. But I have a feeling there are things going on we should know about. In any case, Petronius as good as told me to mind my own business, which is a good reason not to.'

It was four days before they reached Venta Icenorum. Valerius took time to ensure every repair had been properly carried out and to arrange for any winter damage to be reported. He also inspected the auxiliary unit manning the signal station which flanked the road between Colonia and the Iceni border. The wooden tower, with its pitch-soaked beacon, stood twenty feet above the flat, waterlogged countryside, within a circular rampart topped by a palisade and surrounded by a six-foot ditch. Its garrison consisted of eight surly, unshaven Tungrians who were as alert as he might have expected after three months watching the same piece of road in the dead of winter. Their commander, a decurion with a hangdog expression, made it clear he thought they'd been abandoned and begged him to send food and proper winter clothing.

'Though it's too late for poor old Chrutius there.' He pointed to a man with bandaged feet and a pair of makeshift crutches. 'Stood guard all night in a blizzard an' lost six toes to the blight.'

Valerius asked if the man had noticed anything unusual in recent weeks.

The decurion smiled bitterly. 'Only you.'

Valerius reined in when he saw the smoke from Venta's cooking fires dusting the northern horizon and Lunaris drew up beside him. 'Why are we so interested in these people?' the *duplicarius* asked. 'Fifty miles from rest and rations, and one lot of tame Celts looks just like another to me.'

Valerius shrugged. 'We're here anyway. It's only right that we should pay our respects to Cearan. In any case, I suspect he knows we're coming.' He pointed to a small group of horsemen by a clump of trees about a mile away. 'I wouldn't call the Iceni tame, but they are fortunate. They fought with Caratacus against Claudius and might have ended up like the Trinovantes and the Catuvellauni, with their young men slaves and their lands confiscated. But that's where the luck came in. Their king, Antedios, died in the fighting and by the time of the surrender he'd been replaced by Prasutagus, who very quickly condemned Antedios as a rebel and asked for Rome's mercy.'

'Clever.'

'We didn't have enough troops to garrison this far north and fight in the west, so Claudius, who was also clever, agreed to make them clients of Rome. Ten years ago they rebelled again, or at least some of them did, when Scapula tried to disarm the tribes permanently. But old Prasutagus blamed it on a minority among the western Iceni and the legions had enough on their hands with the Dobunni and the Durotriges, so they were left alone again.'

'The lucky tribe, then?'

Valerius smiled. 'Or their god favours them.'

As Valerius kicked his horse into motion, Lunaris frowned and touched the silver phallic amulet at his neck. 'Which god would that be?'

'Andraste.'

The road to Venta Icenorum ran along the west side of a winding stream edged by drooping willows and tall poplars. The town itself lay forty paces beyond the far bank, a strange mix of the old and the new. The usual Celtic community consisted of scattered roundhouses surrounded by fields and linked by walkways and drove roads. At first sight, Venta could have been a provincial Roman town. It lay, part hidden, behind a wooden palisade and its streets appeared to be laid out on the familiar grid pattern, with a gap in the roofscape which suggested a central forum. Only on closer inspection did Valerius realize that the houses, with their pitched roofs, were constructed of wattle and daub and that where there should have been tiles there was thatch. Lunaris looked uncertainly at the river, which was in spate and foamed, a sickly reddish brown, just below the trees, but Valerius pointed to a wooden bridge a little way upstream. Where Cearan waited.

'It is an honour to welcome you to my home.' The Iceni sat comfortably on the back of a horse considerably larger than the British ponies with which Valerius was familiar. He managed the not inconsiderable feat of bowing gracefully from the waist and hanging on to a curly-haired child of about three who wriggled in the crook of his right arm. 'My grandson, Tor,' he explained, lowering the boy to the ground, where he scuttled off to chase a foraging chicken among the bushes by the gateway. 'It is also unexpected.' The smile didn't falter, but there was a definite question in Cearan's pale blue eyes.

'We have been inspecting the road to the south,' Valerius explained. 'You invited me to see your horses, but if it is not convenient . . . ?'

Cearan's smile grew wider at the mention of his horses, and he slapped his mount on the shoulder. He sat on the animal as if he were part of it, his long legs hugging its ribs and his hands light on the reins. Valerius had never met a king, but if any man looked and acted like a king it was Cearan. His golden hair was tied at the neck with a band that matched the deep red of his soft-spun shirt, and his long blond moustaches hung below his chin.

'Of course. Ride with me. Perhaps your troopers would like to water their horses,' he suggested diplomatically. When they were out of earshot his face grew serious and he explained: 'You must forgive me, Valerius my friend, but you could not have come at a worse time. King Prasutagus survived the winter, but it has taken its toll on his health. He is close to death, only the timing is in doubt, and the stink of his dying draws the carrion birds. They are all here: Beluko, who has lands in the west; Mab, whose territory you have just crossed; and Volisios, who holds the border with the Corieltauvi. Each thinks he has a better case than the others to succeed Prasutagus and all have good reason to hate the Romans.'

'And Cearan? Gold and swords?'

'I fear it is too late unless you carry them with you, and I doubt twenty riders would be enough. In any case, I never brought you your druid and my honour would not allow it.' The Briton smiled sadly. They passed under the north wall of Venta and Valerius looked up to see fifteen or twenty faces watching from the ramparts. 'See,' Cearan said loudly. 'Here is my herd. Now, if your Thracian would only part with that stallion of his for two days?'

They were fine horses, the finest Valerius had seen on the island, and each a replica of the mare Cearan rode. The herd grazed in a mass at the centre of a broad meadow, which sloped down to where the river swept in a wide curve eastwards towards the sea.

'If not Cearan, then who will lead the Iceni?'

'Boudicca,' the Briton said emphatically.

'Boudicca? But you said . . .'

'I was wrong,' Cearan admitted. 'I have spoken to her. She understands her position and she sees the new reality as I do. Do not doubt me: she despises everything Rome stands for but she realizes that to serve her people best she must retain what they have. Better for Emperor Nero to take half the kingdom's revenues than to have a Roman legion camped beneath our walls and Colonia's *quaestor* dabbling in our politics.'

Valerius turned towards the watchers on the wall. Somehow he knew the queen would be there. As tall as any of the men around her, she stood in the centre, clad in a gown of emerald green, her flame-red hair dancing in the breeze. He couldn't see her face, which was silhouetted against the low sun, but he had an impression of great strength, and though her eyes weren't visible he knew they would be as fierce as any eagle's.

Cearan's voice was taut. 'When the time comes you must tell the governor to favour her petition. Her daughters will be Prasutagus's joint heirs but they are young and she will rule in their stead. She will make a better queen than Prasutagus is a king. The governor will not regret it.'

Valerius nodded. He would try. 'And you?'

Cearan opened his mouth to reply but at that moment a shout came from behind them and Valerius looked round to see two young girls watching shyly from the corner of the town wall. Cearan called them across and introduced them.

'Rosmerta.' He indicated the taller of the two, a pretty red-haired child with a freckled face and an easy smile. 'And this is Banna.' The second girl must have been a year younger, probably around twelve, but Valerius could already see the signs that would mark her as a true beauty. She had a mane of blond hair and delicate features matched with startling green eyes. Both girls were dressed in light linen shifts and walked barefoot. Banna spoke to Cearan in her own language with a look that made Valerius wonder if she was about to stamp her feet.

'I apologize.' The Iceni bowed to his assailant. 'She reminds me that she is Princess Banna and she wishes to be given a closer look at your horse, which she says makes mine look like a pack mule.'

Valerius smiled. 'In that case I would be obliged if they would walk her to cool her down after her long ride and perhaps they would provide her with some oats,' he said courteously.

Banna took the reins even before Cearan had completed his translation and the girls led the big cavalry horse away, chattering together animatedly.

'Her daughters?' Valerius asked. Cearan nodded. 'They are very young.'

'That is why they need your protection.' He glanced towards the walls and Valerius realized at least one of the men he had named was there. 'Your coming has placed me in great danger, but I still have the king's favour – and the queen's support. You need not fear for Cearan of the Iceni, my friend.'

Valerius reached out his hand and Cearan gripped his wrist in the Roman fashion.

'My oath on it.'

The two men made a show of studying the individual horses of Cearan's herd before Valerius retrieved his mount from the reluctant sisters, offering them his thanks. As they rode back, they found Lunaris and the other troopers watering their horses in a sheltered backwater of the swollen river under the hostile stares of a small group of unarmed Iceni warriors. A little way upstream Cearan's grandson, now a muddy-faced urchin only recognizable by his shock of golden hair, teased a family of ducks with a stick by the edge of the river.

'Any trouble?' Valerius asked, eyeing the warriors by the gate.

Lunaris grinned. 'Nobody ever died from a dirty look, but I've had warmer welcomes.'

'We ride for Colonia when the horses are rested.'

The big man nodded, but his face registered his disappointment. Valerius knew his troops had anticipated a hot meal, even a feast, and beer and a warm bed after four nights sleeping under their cloaks.

Cearan disappeared inside the gate and returned with a bulging sack which he handed to the *duplicarius*. 'Perhaps this will make your journey seem a little shorter.'

Lunaris looked inside and smiled his thanks.

Cearan turned to Valerius. 'Farewe—'

He was interrupted by a loud squeal of frustration from upriver and the two men turned to see Cearan's grandson tottering on the bank of the river as he leaned precariously to reach the duck's nest. A moment later a sharp cry rang out. The little boy disappeared in a fountain of dirty river water and the only evidence he had existed was a thatch of blond curls just visible in the torrent as it was carried towards them with incredible speed.

'Tor!' Cearan's anguished cry spurred Valerius into action and he urged his horse towards the river. The instant he reached the bank he leapt from the saddle into the water, thanking the gods it was only knee deep at this point. Keeping hold of the reins for support and anchorage he hauled his protesting mount into the rushing flow, immediately feeling the current plucking at his legs and threatening to pull his feet from under him. The river was narrower here, but also swifter, and he knew if he went under in his armour he was unlikely to surface again. He glanced upstream. The boy was nowhere in sight. All he could see was a gushing, foam-flecked brown torrent. Then he spotted it, less than fifteen paces away and coming at him as fast as a galloping horse. A dull hint of gold just beneath the surface. With a thrill of panic he realized it would pass beyond his grasping hand, and he hauled desperately at the reins to give himself extra reach. He sent a silent prayer to Mars and even as he gave up hope he plunged forward with an enormous splash, reaching with his right arm, and came up with a handful of blond curls, followed by a squirming bundle that resembled a half-drowned hare.

Cearan flung himself from his horse and ran to the

river just as Valerius emerged dripping wet with the little boy clutched to his chest, his eyes screwed tight shut and choking up river water in fountains. The Briton tenderly took his grandson from the Roman's arms and nodded his thanks. 'Now I am truly in your debt.'

XXI

Gwlym knew he was being followed. He had seen out the winter in a Catuvellauni roundhouse close to the place the Romans called Durobrivae, alternately starving and freezing, and looked upon with increasing resentment by his hosts. Boredom had corroded his brain and he fought it by whispering to himself the epic history of his people from the time of giants and the great flood. Generation after generation of fighting and suffering and always moving westwards. The endless name-lists of kings and mighty champions, tales of natural disaster and betrayal by peoples who were inferior but more numerous. It was this prodigious memory which had been recognized by the druids when he was chosen at the age of nine to study among them and be trained in the rites. He remembered the long days of repetition and testing as he prepared for the trials of Taranis, Esus and Teutates. Now he called on the same power that had carried him through that horror. Sometimes he felt so tired he suspected his body was dying from lack of will: only his mission and the inner fire kindled on Mona kept him alive.

For the past week he'd noticed the forest gradually thinning as he travelled further east and he knew he must maintain his vigilance or he'd end up in the hands of one of the Roman cavalry patrols which seemed more numerous here. Strange Romans, dark-eyed and heavy-browed, seemingly part man and part horse for they never left the saddle. That thought had brought him another vision, a man with a horse's face, long and narrow with prominent nostrils and protruding teeth. A memorable face, and yet it was only now he remembered he had seen it twice, at different gatherings separated by several weeks and many miles. The thought sent a shiver through him. He knew he wouldn't last a week without the silence of those who took him into their homes.

He entered an area of scrubby trees, low and thin-trunked but with broad canopies. The trees told him he was close to a river or a stream and with the sun close to its high point he decided to stop to eat his meagre rations, rest, and above all think. He realized belatedly that he'd been careless over the past few days, travelling in a direct line towards his next destination. It was a sign of his tiredness but also of something more. He'd always known he was likely to die before he had completed his task. Now it seemed his mind had accepted it as inevitable and was reaching out to it. He must become hard again, rediscover the iron which had been tempered in the flames of Mona's fiery chamber. Careful not to disturb the vegetation, he moved fifty paces away from the path and deeper into the trees and bushes.

He waited for an hour, sitting in the shadow of a hawthorn bush with nothing in his ears but the buzz of flying insects and the crunch of his teeth on the gritty corn cakes he'd been given at the last farm. Perhaps he was wrong? But no, he knew with certainty he was being trailed. Who were they? Roman spies? It was possible. Every Celt knew the eyes and ears of Rome extended far and wide over this land. It was why he had been so careful at first and why he now cursed himself for his stupidity. More likely they were Britons in the pay of a local petty chieftain anxious to gain approval with the Romans. Handing over a druid would offset a year of taxes and more. One thing was in his favour. They hadn't yet reported his presence or the area would be swarming with patrols.

The sharp crack of a broken twig froze his blood. The sound came from *behind* him. With infinite care he turned his head and recognized Horseface, the man from the meetings, less than a spear's length distant, thankfully scanning the trees to his left, away from Gwlym's hide. Unthinkingly, Gwlym slipped the long, curved knife from his belt, rose and with three quick strides wrapped his hand across his hunter's mouth and plunged the blade deep into his back. He had never killed before and it proved more difficult than he would have believed. Horseface was tall and strong and the sting of the knife point gave his strength a greater urgency. He struggled and shook in Gwlym's grasp, emitting animal grunting sounds beneath the clasped hand. At last Gwlym found the gap between the ribs and forced the knife blade through it, the movement accompanied by a warm flood of liquid over his hand. Horseface shuddered, but still he twisted and squealed like a piglet being hunted for a feast. Somehow the dying man found the strength to turn, wrenching the hilt from Gwlym's grasp and breaking the grip over his mouth. He let out a roar of agony as he clawed at the blade buried deep in his back.

At first Gwlym froze, but a shout of alarm from away to the right broke the spell. He bolted into the trees in the opposite direction from the cry. Too late. He could hear the sound of pursuit and when he risked a glance across his shoulder he saw that his hunter was less than thirty feet behind and carried a long sword. Gwlym knew his exertions of the past months had left him too weak to outrun the man, but what alternative did he have? He crashed blindly through the trees, ignoring the snagging branches and the leaves that whipped his face. His left foot hit thin air. He was falling. A shock like death itself knocked the breath from his lungs as he struck the freezing water of the river and went under. Desperate for air, he fought his way to the surface only to find the spy towering over him with the sword raised to strike. A grin spread across the man's face as Gwlym attempted to burrow into the bank. He was still grinning when his belly erupted in a fountain of blood and guts and he was catapulted over the druid's head into the river with a spear shaft transfixing his body.

Sheltered by the high bank, Gwlym allowed the current to carry him downstream into the shadow of an overhanging tree. He gripped a low branch for just long enough to witness the Roman auxiliary cavalryman retrieve his spear from the corpse and gleefully remove its head, then his numbed fingers slipped and he found he didn't have the will or the strength to fight the river.

XXII

For the first time she could remember Maeve was frightened. Since her mother died when she was six years old, her father had been the cornerstone of her life, dealing with every girlish tantrum and adolescent obsession with the same good humour with which he laughed off the peaks and troughs of his ever-changing fortunes. Even the arrival of her first red moon had been greeted only with a sharp 'tut' and a call for Catia, her personal slave, to explain the intricacies and burdens of a woman's existence. It was for her sake, she knew, that he had stayed on his farm and kept his father's sword in its place on the wall when the young men followed Caratacus to their deaths. As she grew older she had seen the pain the decision had cost him and the damage to his honour that was so clear in the contemptuous glances of

Camulodunum's women. But he had been prepared to bear it. For her.

When Claudius declared Camulodunum a Roman colony and renamed it Colonia, Lucullus had fought desperately to keep what was his. He hadn't always succeeded – he had mourned Dywel as keenly as she had – and some of the alliances he made had cost him more than he would ever admit. But he had protected her. When he took the Roman name Lucullus she had been ashamed, but she never allowed it to show. He was her father and she loved him.

Yet now she barely recognized this shell of a man with empty, staring eyes; a fat man grown suddenly thin.

'I am ruined.' The words were said in a whisper. 'They will take everything, and when they have it all I will still owe them more than I can ever repay. I am ruined.'

It had started when Petronius, the *quaestor*, had arrived at the villa just before noon. At first Lucullus had been genuinely pleased to see his business partner, believing this was at last the delivery of the outstanding rent money for the *insulae* in Colonia. But it took only a few moments for Petronius to reveal the true reason for his visit.

'I have had word from Londinium,' the lawyer said solemnly, handing over a wrapped scroll with a broken seal. A few minutes later the *quaestor* left and her father retired to the room he called the *tablinum*, from which he ordered his business. She found him there four hours later, amidst the innocent bills and records that concealed the labyrinth of his finances and, she finally learned, the bottomless pit of his debt that now threatened to swallow the Celtic trader alive.

They sat together in the little room until the sun drifted below the horizon and they were left in darkness. By then Maeve had long given up her attempts at reassurance, and the only words that passed between them from one hour to the next was the little man's shocked whisper: 'I am ruined.' Every attempt to move him was a wasted effort. He had become a human shipwreck with the jagged rocks of failure buried deep in his belly and every wave dragging him closer to destruction.

Her inability to help him left her feeling a sort of growing paralysis. She had to do something. Anything. Lucullus had insisted she learn to read Latin as well as speak it, so she could assist him with his business affairs, and eventually she left the *tablinum* to study the letter. It was dated a week earlier and as she read it, line by line, she was overwhelmed by first fear, then fury and finally dread. The contents were almost beyond belief. The letter contained a warning from the new procurator in Londinium, Catus Decianus, to his friend Petronius of fundamental changes in the way the province was to be governed and financed.

She had heard the name Seneca hailed by Lucullus as the great benefactor who had set him on the way to prosperity. Now this same Seneca had decided to call in every loan he had made in the province with immediate effect. Catus Decianus was commanded to maximize the return on all his investments, convert them to currency and send them to Rome. And that wasn't all. State subsidies, loans and investments were also being withdrawn. It took time for her to understand the true enormity of what she was reading.

Now *everything* would belong to the imperial treasury and the native rulers of southern Britain would be reduced to penury, and their people with them, robbed even of the chance to pay off the loans with the fruits of the earth they tended and farmed.

If that was not enough, her outrage grew as she realized exactly why Petronius had shown the letter to her father. The *quaestor* had never hidden his greed from his Trinovante business partner; indeed that was what had made him an ideal foil for Lucullus. Now he saw the opportunity to lay hands on the *insulae* in Colonia and – she gasped at his audacity – the whole estate, this house, the farms and the hunting grounds, at a bargain price from his 'friend' Decianus. Worse, when she read the letter again she realized it contained another, more sinister message. It was an invitation to Lucullus to commit suicide. Was that not the Roman way, to avoid disgrace by taking one's own life? And how much more convenient for Petronius's transaction if the former owner was dead.

She felt like riding into Colonia and confronting

that thieving, conniving . . . No. She could imagine the cold stare if a woman, and a British woman at that, dared to challenge the *quaestor*. He might even have her whipped. Only one person could help her. She called for one of the slaves.

'Go swiftly to Colonia and seek out Tribune Verrens. Ask him to call on the trader Lucullus as soon as it is convenient. Hurry now!'

She fell asleep thinking of the young Roman and when she opened her eyes she was lying on a couch in the room with the paintings of Claudius. The light streamed in through the gaps in the shutters, creating intricate dappled patterns on the walls and floor. The familiar setting reassured her and for the first time she felt hope. Valerius would protect them. Her father would normally have left for Colonia by this time but when she checked his bed he was still in it, the coverlet clenched to his chin and his eyes tight shut. She guessed he wasn't asleep but decided to leave him in any case. There would be time later to face the harsh new realities of their life.

She washed and dressed, taking care with her appearance. The blue dress today because it was the one Valerius liked. Would he still love her now that she was poor? With a sudden clarity she realized it didn't matter. She saw that their relationship, which had first smouldered, then blazed into a white heat of an intensity she had never known, was a fleeting thing and, like the snows of winter, must pass in its own time. He never talked of it, but she knew he

241

would shortly be returning to his legion, knew even, thanks to her father, that he was due soon to be recalled to Rome. In the first glow of their love she had dreamed of travelling there with him and becoming the mistress of a Roman household, but as the months passed she understood that it could never be. Her experience of the world was limited to Colonia and the estate looking out over the river, but she had seen the way Petronius and the others of the city's equestrian class looked at her father; the sneering glances and contemptuous smiles. Lucullus accepted their disdain because he had no other option; hid his resentment and his anger behind the mask of his smile. How much worse would it be in Rome? Valerius's family might tolerate her as his wife, but they would never truly accept her. And Rome, for all the wonders he described, was an alien place. This was her land. These were her people.

Two hours later she heard the sound of horses on the track from Colonia and she rushed out to greet Valerius. Her spirits lifted at the sight of the unmistakable figure of a mounted Roman soldier outlined against the low sun.

'This is the house of Lucullus, *augustalis* of the Temple of Claudius?' The voice was detached but the speaker managed to invest the simple question with a measure of threat that sent a shudder through Maeve. Not Valerius, but who? And why? Only now did she notice the other riders who accompanied the soldier, along with four open-topped ox carts trundling along behind.

'Answer me. I don't have time to sit here all day.'

She stared up at the rider. She might be frightened, but she would not be cowed. She was a Trinovante maiden and mistress of this house. 'It is the home of Lucullus,' she confirmed, trying to keep the anxiety from her voice. 'And I am his daughter.'

The legionary grunted and slid from his horse, allowing her to see his face for the first time. The eyes that stared at her were close-set and cold. Very deliberately he allowed his gaze to run over her body, lingering on her breasts and hips. It left her feeling somehow violated, as if his eyes were his hands, which were large and rough with long, dirt-caked fingernails. He had coarse, angular features and at some point his prominent nose had been broken and poorly set. Pock marks dotted his sallow skin. This man has been angry from the day he was born, she thought.

'Good.' He pushed roughly past her. 'Fetch your father out here. Vettius? Get to work. Remember, everything of value.'

Maeve watched in astonishment as the men trooped by her into the house, each carrying a large basket. They were a combination of soldiers and slaves and she had never seen a more brutish-looking group of individuals.

'Wait! What are you doing?' she protested. 'By whose authority do you act?'

The soldier turned slowly and removed his helmet. He looked at her with a slightly pained expression as if uncertain who she was. In the same instant her world pitched upside down and she found herself on her back in the dirt, staring at the sky. Every nerve in her body jangled and her vision was shot with lightning bolts. It took a moment to realize she'd been punched. Her face was a mass of pain beneath the right eye and she could already feel her cheek swelling. Tears blurred her vision as she struggled to sit up.

The pock-marked soldier stood over her and she wondered distractedly if he was about to kick her. 'If I have to repeat myself,' he warned, 'I'll have you trussed up and scourged. At last.'

Lucullus walked stiff-legged from the villa with the bewildered air of a man woken in the middle of a nightmare. He wore the fine toga presented to him when he had been voted to the priesthood and didn't seem to notice that the men were laughing at him. They moved briskly back and forth between the villa and the carts loaded with the household treasures he had collected to make himself more Roman. Now the Romans were stripping him of everything.

Maeve struggled to her feet and ran to her father's side as the leader drew a scroll from a pouch on his sword belt and read from it in a disinterested drawl.

'By the authority of the procurator this estate is now imperial property, held as security for the repayment of one million, two hundred and twenty-three thousand *sestertii* loaned to the merchant Lucullus by the senator Lucius Annaeus Seneca. You have seventy-two hours to repay the debt or such portion of it as you are able, or face certain penalties deemed appropriate by the state. Signed Catus Decianus, procurator.'

Maeve gasped at the magnitude of the debt and Lucullus was jolted from his torpor. 'But I cannot,' he whispered. 'No man could raise such a sum in three days.'

The Roman came close enough for Maeve to smell his foul breath. He smiled and she was reminded of a festering sore.

'Three days, old man. I see no gold in those baskets, so you must have it hidden somewhere else. I've never come across a Celt yet who didn't like the glitter of gold. So dig up your treasure and sell everything you've got and bring the proceeds to the procurator's office in Londinium. Maybe you could even sell yourself.' He laughed. 'We done yet, Vettius?' he shouted.

'Unless you want the furniture.'

'Every stick.'

'And the slaves?'

'Round them up. If we leave them they'll only clear off. They can all carry something. Come here.' Fire streaked across Maeve's scalp as the soldier wrapped his hand in her hair and hauled her roughly towards one of the wagons. She kicked out at him and screamed in fury but she was powerless against his

245

strength. Her father shouted a protest which was instantly cut off and she felt a momentary panic that he'd been harmed. 'Stay where you are, you old fool,' the legionary warned. 'Vettius would like nothing better than to gut you, but you can't pay up if you're dead. You won't be tempted to run if you know she's keeping us company. Three days and you'll get her back, and she might even be in the same condition.' A hand slipped surreptitiously inside her dress and cupped Maeve's breast, making her gasp in outrage. 'Or maybe not,' he said.

They tethered her hands to the rear of the wagon and as the soldiers and slaves completed their task it lurched off slowly in the direction of the Londinium road. She felt an agonizing tug on her wrists and stumbled helplessly behind, with only time for a single glance back to where her father knelt in the mud with tears running down his cheeks.

Her mind still whirled from the blow she had received, but she willed it to think rationally. There could be no question of escape; she was too tightly bound for that and where would she run to in any case? She was a hostage for her father's return with the payment. But he could never pay back the full amount and what if it was true and there was no money? What would her fate be at the hands of these evil men? She remembered the touch of the officer's fingers on her body and her skin crawled. She closed her eyes and a groan escaped her lips. Valerius, why did you not come to me?

*   *   *

Red-eyed and almost sleeping in the saddle, Valerius led his men into the legionary tent lines at Colonia two hours after dawn. They had ridden through the night with the aid of a full moon which showed the road ahead like a shining silver pathway between its pair of ditches. As he rode, he had composed in his mind the report he would send to the governor. Cearan had convinced him that only by supporting Boudicca could Rome ensure lasting peace with the Iceni, but Suetonius Paulinus might not be so easily persuaded. Paulinus had the reputation of a man of bull-headed single-mindedness. He was unlikely to appreciate being distracted from his campaign against Mona by what he would regard as the political gossip of a disaffected Iceni lord.

Nevertheless, the letter had to be written, and when Valerius dismounted he hobbled to the cohort's headquarters tent and called for a stylus and wax tablet before sitting down at the collapsible campaign table. It wasn't until he finished that he realized how exhausted he was. If he could only close his eyes for a few seconds it would help. His last memory was of the golden boar amulet nestling against the opaque marble of Maeve's flawless skin.

An hour later, the clerk found him slumped across the table and called for his centurion. Julius looked down at the sleeping figure with affection.

'Should we wake him?' the clerk asked.

Julius shook his head. 'Leave him. He deserves

some rest. Lunaris reckoned they covered forty miles in the saddle last night.'

'There was the message.'

Yes, there was the message. Julius reached towards Valerius's shoulder, then hesitated. No. The message said he should call on Lucullus at his convenience. It would be more convenient when he woke.

'Let him sleep,' he said. 'It can't do any harm.'

XXIII

By the time Valerius rode up to Lucullus's villa it was past midday. He'd been surprised by the message from the Trinovante but the opportunity to see Maeve banished all thoughts of tiredness. And he had another urgent reason to talk to her. He had made his decision on the long ride back from Venta: he loved her too much to leave her behind. They would be married and he would take her to Rome. He had thought long and hard about the effect the marriage must have on his career and the impact on his relationship with his father. The old man might even disinherit him. But someone who had faced death in a shield wall was old enough to make his own decisions. If he couldn't survive on his legal work, he could take up a commission in an auxiliary unit. All that mattered was that they would be together.

The white-walled building was clearly visible from some distance and it was just a feeling at first, but a soldier's feeling he'd learned not to ignore. The fields stood empty when they should have been full of workers either ploughing or planting. There should be smoke from the villa kitchen, but there was none. Now he noticed the open door that would normally be shut. He rode forward with his hand on his sword, allowing the horse to make its own pace. In front of the house he slid from the saddle and stood for a moment, absorbing an almost breathless stillness that made him reluctant to breathe himself.

'Maeve?' His voice echoed from the walls. The darkened doorway suddenly seemed very dangerous. Carefully, he drew his *gladius* and walked towards it. A sharp snap made him flinch and he looked down to see shards of a broken pot beneath his feet. He recognized it as Lucullus's favourite bowl from Gaul, the red clay one with the gladiators fighting below the rim. He remembered discussing the design with Lucullus; the Briton's eagerness to be a Roman had been tempered by an inability to comprehend a society which delighted in making two men fight to the death. The inner door lay ajar by only a few inches and Valerius carefully used the point of the sword to push it open and give him a view into the next room. Empty. No, it was more than empty. The place had been stripped. All Lucullus's fine busts and statues were gone. The bare end walls puzzled him until he realized what was missing.

They'd even cut the paintings of Claudius from the plaster, leaving jagged-edged cavities as the only reminder of their existence.

'Maeve?' He heard the nervousness in his voice. Please. Not that. 'Lucullus?' He moved through the villa, methodically searching each room and in each finding the same story. Until he reached Lucullus's bathhouse.

Lucullus had always been a tidy man. Even the second set of accounts he kept hidden from the tax collectors was maintained in the fussy, meticulous Latin handwriting he took such pride in, each column of figures straighter than any temple pillar. Clearly he had wished to give whoever found him as little extra work as possible because he had opened his veins while he sat comfortably in the warm water of his bath. Now he lay back, impossibly white in an obscene sea of dark, vinous red, quite dead. Strangely, his face was fixed in a dreamy expression which seemed to hint he had not found his passing too unpleasant after all the harshness that preceded it.

Valerius shook his head wearily. He was far from unfamiliar with death, but he struggled to equate this lifeless milk-white corpse with the jolly little man whose restless mind had leapt from one hopeless money-making scheme to the next with the un-repressed vigour of a meadow full of grasshoppers. What had made him do it? And where was Maeve? The sharp crack as a foot stepped on another of the pot shards in the courtyard alerted him to a new danger. He moved swiftly back through the house and reached the inner door just as a hooded figure entered the room. At first his mind cried out *Maeve!* but he realized the frame was too small. He placed the point of his sword at the intruder's back and was rewarded with a squeal of fear from Catia, Maeve's maid.

'What happened here?' he demanded. 'Where is your mistress?'

'She is gone,' the grey-haired woman cried. 'They took her. They took everything. I hid in the apple store or they would have taken me as well. I—'

'Who took her? When?' he interrupted. When was more important than who but he needed all the information he could glean.

'The soldiers. They were led by the tall one and had carts. Four. They took everything. They took Docca.' She broke down, sobbing uncontrollably. Docca must be her husband, but Valerius didn't have time for sympathy. He grabbed her by the shoulders and shook her roughly.

'When, and which direction did they take?'

'Three hours ago. The Londinium road.'

Valerius released her and she slumped to the floor. Three hours and perhaps an hour to catch up with them if he rode hard. There was still a chance. Whoever had taken Maeve could only move as fast as the carts carrying their booty. That meant two miles in an hour at most, so eight miles. He tried to visualize the road, looking for somewhere he could intercept the convoy. But he would need help.

He lifted the woman to her feet. 'Listen to me, Catia. You must go to the soldiers' camp at Colonia. Ask for Julius, the centurion. This is what you must tell him.'

He chose a place where the Londinium road crossed a narrow river about ten miles west of Colonia and concealed himself in a copse of nearby beech trees to wait. He'd avoided the road, but ridden hard across open country until he was certain he'd overtaken his quarry. Now all he could do was wait. And hope.

The truth was that he had very little idea what would happen next. It seemed clear that the raid on Lucullus's villa had something to do with the Trinovante's business dealings, but what had prompted the drastic step and Lucullus's even more drastic reaction was a mystery. All he knew for certain was that he must get Maeve back. Catia had said the man leading the raiders was a legionary, which meant that Valerius almost certainly outranked him. In that case, he would use his authority to have Maeve and the other prisoners freed. It might take some argument but it should be possible. On the other hand, the expedition could be a piece of private enterprise by one of Lucullus's business rivals, or a partner he had cheated, who had hired the soldiers as enforcers to get their money back. When he turned it over in his mind this seemed less likely. They might show they had some legal right over Lucullus's slaves, but not his daughter, and kidnap was a capital offence to be tried before the governor or his deputy.

If it came to it, he would fight for her. But he couldn't fight alone.

As the minutes passed, the heavy silence mocked him. Nothing but the rustle of the trees, and they whispered that his quarry must have taken another road. After half an hour the horse twitched restlessly beneath him and he sensed its urge to move on, but moments later the creak of an unsprung ox cart brought him the warning he'd strained for. The urge to launch himself towards the sound was overwhelming, but he willed himself to stay motionless. Only when he could hear voices did he urge the mare forward and sweep her round to face them.

The leader reined in sharply at the sight of the unexpected apparition blocking the road. He had just reached the crossing, with four riders at his back, and behind them Lucullus's slaves walked disconsolately among the ox carts. A further six legionaries who had been marching in the rear recognized the threat and double-timed past the convoy to join the vanguard, leaving two to make sure the slaves didn't run.

Valerius scanned the carts for Maeve and was rewarded by a flash of chestnut-brown behind the second wagon. She had her head bowed and was partially obscured by the horseman in front of him. He wanted to shout out to let her know he'd come for her, but realized that drawing attention to her might place her in more danger. He bit his lip and waited, allowing the tribune's uniform and his bearing to announce his authority. Thus far he'd ignored the leader of the soldiers.

'You!' The voice reverberated with disbelief and Valerius's heart sank as he recognized it.

Crespo.

But all he could do was play the part he had created for himself – and buy time. This confrontation was all about power and rank and a legionary's natural inclination to obey a command. He injected his words with a touch of parade-ground authority. 'Centurion Crespo, you have exceeded your orders. Release the prisoners and I'll escort them back to Colonia. Any dispute over the ownership of the slaves will be settled in the courts.'

Crespo stared back at him, gimlet eyes glittering. He remembered the stinking awfulness of waking up on a Londinium dung heap, and the humiliation he had endured in the hut at the Silurian hill fort. This man had been responsible for both. Unfortunately, he was also a tribune of Rome, which meant Crespo had to curb his natural inclination towards violent retribution. Yet something wasn't right here.

'You seem to be all on your own, pretty boy. I wonder whose orders you have . . . if you have any at all,' he said thoughtfully.

Valerius ignored the insult. 'I don't need orders, Crespo. This uniform carries the governor's authority and flouting that authority will see you hung from a cross.'

Crespo nudged his mount forward and reached towards the belt at his waist. Valerius's right hand shadowed the move, hovering over his sword hilt. The Sicilian laughed and carefully retrieved the scroll bearing his mandate.

'My instructions, tribune. Centurion Crespo is ordered to secure any or all of the property of Lucullus, *augustalis* of Colonia, on the instructions of the procurator, Catus Decianus. I think you'll find that includes his slaves. If you don't have something official countermanding my order, I'll ask you to step aside and I'll be on my way.' The thin lips twitched in a humourless smile and his voice fell to a whisper. 'And we'll have our reckoning another time. Because, believe me, pretty boy, there will be a reckoning.'

'His property doesn't include his daughter.' Valerius said it loudly enough for the men at Crespo's back to hear. If he could plant a seed of doubt there was a chance. Crespo's style of leadership was unlikely to have made him popular and if the soldiers who followed him could be swayed . . . But Crespo was a predator, with a predator's instinct for any weakness. Something in the way Valerius spoke awoke the wolf in him. He heard it howl and the smile transformed into a grin of anticipation.

'His daughter. So that's it. You didn't come all this way to round up a few dirty old slaves, did you, pretty boy? You came for the priest's daughter. Full of surprises, you are. Here was me thinking you only liked boys. Vettius, bring the Celt bitch up here.'

One of the riders turned and rode to the second cart, where he untied the rope holding Maeve and used it to pull her, stumbling, to the flank of Crespo's horse. Valerius felt raw anger flare within him when he saw the bruise on her cheek and the half-shut eye. He reached for the rope but Crespo flicked it away from him.

'Not so fast, pretty boy.' He leaned forward and swept Maeve effortlessly on to the saddle in front of him. 'What's she worth to you?'

Valerius froze. He understood that Crespo was trying to goad him into a fight. The other soldiers edged closer and their hard eyes never left him. If he reacted now against odds of a dozen or so to one he might take a few of them with him, but probably not Crespo. And if he died, Crespo couldn't afford any witnesses to the murder of a Roman tribune, so Maeve would die too.

'What's she worth?' the centurion repeated. As his captive struggled in his arms he ran his hands over her shoulders, breasts and legs. 'Not bad. I think I might have her for myself tonight. And after I've had her Vettius and his Mules can have her too. Then she'll only be fit for the dogs, so maybe we'll give her back to you.'

Valerius went cold and his mind moved beyond anger to that place where only Crespo's blood would pay for the indignities Maeve was suffering. Her eyes pleaded with him to act. His heart told him to launch himself across the gap and ram his sword point beneath Crespo's chin and up into his brain. His head said wait.

Thunder filled his ears and he wondered if it was the thunder the British champions heard when they threw themselves against the Roman shields. Perhaps the thunder of Taranis that sent them to a warrior's death without fear of what waited beyond. But it was only the thunder of twenty galloping horses.

Valerius didn't look round. He heard the ragged snorts of mounts that had been ridden hard and knew that behind him was now lined up a troop of Bela's Thracian cavalry wing. Crespo's expression didn't change but the men around him backed away from the long cavalry spears.

'Five hundred *denarii*.'

Crespo frowned.

'I'll give you five hundred *denarii*,' Valerius repeated. 'Take it, or we take her and you get nothing.'

He saw Crespo's eyes counting the spears behind him. Maeve sat very still with her head bowed and he couldn't read what was in her eyes. Eventually the centurion gave a sharp laugh. He knew he'd been outmanoeuvred but saw no sense in crying over it. There'd be another time. He allowed her to slip to the ground. 'You heard him, five hundred *denarii* for the British slut,' he shouted. 'If he doesn't pay, his honour is mine and I will bury it in my latrine where it belongs. March, you lazy bastards. We've wasted enough time here.'

Once the little convoy had moved out of sight Valerius dismounted and helped Maeve to her feet. She stood motionless as he cut the rope from her wrists, revealing a glistening band of bloody flesh. Her eyes had the unseeing stare so familiar in legionaries who had fought one battle too many.

On the way back to Colonia she sat on the saddle in front of him and at one point her body began to shake uncontrollably. She was still shaking when they reached the townhouse her father had once owned. He knew he should tell her about Lucullus's death but feared the news would break her already fragile link with reality. Falco's wife was waiting for them and she cleaned and bandaged Maeve's wounds before putting her in Valerius's bed.

While she slept, he sent word to Cearan – and waited.

XXIV

When Maeve finally woke two days later Valerius sensed a deep change in her that he didn't have the wit to understand or the understanding to approach. She emerged from the bedroom pale and exhausted, still wearing the torn blue dress, with dark shadows around both eyes. Her strength visibly returned with each spoonful of the thin soup the militia commander's wife had recommended, but she would not meet his gaze and spent hours staring into the distance as if she were searching for something.

Valerius fretted at his inability to reach her and in the evening he could bear no more. He took her in his arms and held her, deciding that now was the time to tell her of her father's death. But as he breathed in the sweet, jasmine scent of her hair, she stiffened and began to struggle in his grasp, squirming and cratching, forcing him to release her. When she was free she backed away with a look of disgust that twisted her beauty into a parody of itself.

'Maeve,' he pleaded.

She shook her head wordlessly and a high-pitched keening came from her throat. With a single movement she took the front of her dress in two hands and ripped it to the waist. 'This is what you want,' she hissed, finally finding a voice that was as cracked and broken as one of the pots the despoilers had dropped in her father's *atrium*. 'You want these.' She took the twin bounty of her breasts in her hands and offered them to him. 'You *paid* for them. You *paid* for me.'

'No,' he said.

'Yes,' she spat. 'You made a slave of me. You bought me from that animal . . . and . . . now . . . you . . . own . . . me.' With the last five words she tore the dress still further and she was naked, her lovely body still bearing the marks of her ordeal, the scratches and the bruises and the invisible stains of Crespo's assault. 'So take me. Isn't that what Romans do with their slaves? Take them whenever it suits them. Rut with them wherever it takes their fancy.'

She was sobbing now, but sobs of life-consuming fury.

'Your father . . .' he tried to say.

'Is dead or he would have come for me. *He* would have saved me or died in the attempt, not watched as some foul-breathed pig violated and ruined me.' She shook her head and he knew she was remembering

261

each moment of her shame. 'When I saw you in the roadway I *knew* I was safe. I knew that you would fight for me and that if you died I would die by your side. I would have been glad. Instead, you watched while my honour was stripped from me. *Coward*,' she snarled, and she threw herself at him, nails tearing at his eyes. 'Coward. Coward. Coward.'

Valerius fought her off, grabbing the flailing arms and avoiding the teeth snapping at his face. Her head whipped back and forward as if she were possessed but she was still weak and the savagery of her fury burned out in a few minutes. She went limp in his arms. He picked up her slight body and carried her back to his bed, where he sat in the darkness, listening to the sound of her fractured breathing.

At one point during the night she said quietly: 'You may sell me again if you wish, for I do not want to be a burden to you. But you must call me by another name. I am no longer Maeve of the Trinovantes. I am a slave.'

'I am sorry,' he said, because he could think of nothing else to say.

'You would not understand,' she replied. 'You are a Roman.'

Next day, in the misty stillness of the dawn Valerius stood with Falco as the little merchant's body was carried from the villa to the burial ground beyond Colonia where a square pit, ten paces by ten, had been dug. Maeve was still too weak to attend and did not hear the bard sing his praises or see the things he had loved placed around him by the people he had loved. A few treasures, at least, had survived Crespo's ravages. Cearan was first, carrying an *amphora* of the Calenian wine Lucullus had often shared with Valerius; then Cearan's wife, Aenid, with an intricate gold torc discovered behind a loose brick in Lucullus's storeroom; a slim, dark-haired waif of a girl Valerius didn't recognize carefully placed a gaming board and pieces beside his body; his finest clothes and favourite stool; and finally his father's sword, which he had kept hidden for seventeen years.

Once, a priest would have said the sacred words and made the sacrifices, but the druids had all been driven from the east long ago. Instead, an elder from the settlement by Cunobelin's farm performed the rites, and as he did so Valerius allowed his eyes to wander over the mourners.

Apart from Falco, who was here to represent Colonia's council, the Roman merchants and traders who had profited from Lucullus had discovered more pressing business today. But the Celt's Trinovante cousins had gathered to honour his passing to the Otherworld. They stood in a compact mass, with Cearan at their head, tall, sombre figures, broad-chested and proud. Their dark eyes sent Valerius an unmistakable message as he stood, slightly apart, with Falco. It said they may have been long conquered but they still knew how to hate. He remembered Lucullus's words on the night they were drunk together: *there are men, great men, proud warriors, who live in the ruins of their burned-out huts and watch their children starve, because they once had the temerity to stand up for what was theirs.* Now he was seeing those men with his own eyes. The heirs of Caratacus. Unlike the compliant Celts who frequented Colonia, they wore long belted tunics over tight trews and had thick plaid cloaks draped across their shoulders. He could see how their hands itched for their weapons and their war shields. All they needed to make them an army were their spears and a leader.

'Will there be trouble?' he asked the militia commander.

Falco shook his head. 'I don't believe so. Cearan is no fool and he has influence among the Trinovantes as well as the Iceni. They are angry, as they have a right to be, but they are not organized.'

Valerius wondered if that was true, but Falco knew his business.

'When do you leave for Glevum?' the wine merchant asked.

'My orders came through this morning. The First cohort will march in a week and I'll be with them.'

'And Rome?'

'I'll kick my heels for another month in Londinium. It doesn't seem to matter so much now.'

'Have dinner with us on Wednesday, then. Just the old soldiers, Corvinus and the like. No Petronius, on my honour. How is she?'

He thought for a moment. How to describe the indescribable? 'Changed.'

Falco shook his head. 'That man is a monster.'

'He promised me a reckoning and I've vowed to fulfil that promise.'

Falco placed a hand on his arm. 'Do not waste yourself pursuing Crespo. Go back to Rome and make a new life. Forget him.'

Valerius watched the final planks being placed over Lucullus's grave. Crespo was not the kind of man you could forget. If you did you were likely to end up in a river with a knife in your throat. But perhaps Falco was right. Everything had changed. All the certainties in his life had vanished with Maeve's love. Her reaction had shocked him, somehow turned him inside out. Since then, he had swung between extremes of pain and anger, shame and regret. How could she believe he was a coward? He was a Roman tribune and he had saved her life. If he had been a Briton they would both be dead now, and Crespo would still be in Londinium with her father's treasures. In the end he was faced with the certainty that he had lost her. So, yes, he would return to Rome and leave the procurator and Crespo to continue destroying other lives. He shook his head. It was time to go home.

Before he left the burial ground, he sought out Cearan. He knew the Iceni would not want to meet him but also that he was too well-mannered to refuse. He discovered the tall noble talking seriously with a group of Trinovante elders and Valerius again thought how kingly he looked. Cearan needed no golden circlet to prove his lineage; it was written in the aristocratic planes of his face and in the quiet way he wielded his power. If the gods had been kinder here was the true leader of the Iceni.

Cearan caught his eye and frowned, but a few moments later he came to Valerius's side.

'You were Lucullus's friend, but I wish you had not come.' The Iceni's voice was taut. 'It is difficult enough to soothe the passions your people have aroused without the sight of a scarlet cloak to inflame them further.' He shook his head. 'Sometimes I wonder if your Emperor truly wants peace. Even as I try to douse the fires, your procurator throws fuel on the flames with his demands for the repayment of subsidies that were accepted in good faith, but he now claims were merely loans. Lucullus was the first, and, yes, perhaps the most foolish, but he will not be the last. These people,' he nodded towards the Trinovantes, 'did not need another grievance against the Romans. They look towards the slope yonder and see the land they once farmed being worked by British slaves under Roman masters. Now their leaders, men who beggared themselves to ensure their tribe did not starve and accepted the Roman way because it was the only means to retain their dignity, are to be ruined. Their patience is at an end, tell your governor that.'

Valerius studied his companion. 'And what of your patience, Cearan? Will you abandon your people because of a single setback?'

The Iceni stiffened. 'Not a single setback. There have been others. While I counsel peace, men meet in the forest at night and come back with talk of a return to the old ways and the wrath of the goddess. The priests are among us again. Can you persuade the governor to endorse Queen Boudicca as regent and accept her daughters as King Prasutagus's joint heirs?'

Valerius thought of the report he had written which was still with the clerk. He would deliver it himself and risk Paulinus's anger. 'I can try.'

'You must.'

'What will become of her?'

For a second Cearan was puzzled by the sudden change of subject. Eventually he said: 'I will take her north to share our home. She will have a life. It will not be the life she knew, but it will be a life.'

XXV

Gwlym's first indication that he wasn't dead was the scent of crushed marigold, accompanied by a bitter liquid that burned in his throat and filled his body with a warm, reviving glow. Warmth. That was the true puzzle. He had thought he would never feel warmth again. The last thing he remembered was the chilly embrace of the river overwhelming his body and his mind, and the sensation of surrendering to an all-consuming, but not unpleasant, numbness.

'Can he travel?' The voice seemed to come from a long distance away and the mumbled answer was unintelligible. Mentally, Gwlym tested the fibres of his limbs and came up with his own answer.

'Yes.'

It seemed unlikely, but he must have spoken aloud because a presence loomed over him and he opened his eyes to discover a distinguished silver-haired man of early middle age studying him intently, his expression wary and respectful. 'I am Volisios, lord of the Iceni, keeper of the northern Marches, and I have awaited your coming.'

Gwlym allowed his head to fall back and closed his eyes. He was safe.

In truth, the answer turned out to be premature. It was another day before his legs recovered the strength to allow him to walk, and another still before he felt confident enough to venture beyond the door of the roundhouse whose owner had discovered him beached and freezing whilst collecting stones from the river. Volisios rode ahead to prepare the way, but before he left he provided Gwlym with a pony and an escort of six men. The roundhouse was within the stretch of disputed border land between the Iceni and the Catuvellauni, and though an encounter with a Roman patrol was unlikely it could not be ruled out. Only when they crossed a narrow, muddy stream and he saw the guards relax did Gwlym do the same. But the instinct for self-preservation honed during all the months in hiding had returned, and his eyes constantly roamed the country around him. He found it a depressing, alien place. Low, threatening skies bore down on a flat landscape that seemed more liquid than good solid earth. The ponies squelched their way along soggy paths and through reed beds from one piece of dry ground to the next with a reassuring confidence, but

Gwlym sensed the guards were nervous of him. During the few halts he was left alone with a little food and his own thoughts.

The lands of the Iceni had always been his ultimate destination, if he lived long enough, but his relief at reaching his goal was tempered by new concerns. Firstly, Volisios's apparent foreknowledge of his approach hinted, at best, of over-enthusiasm amongst those he had left tending the smouldering fires of freedom. In one of the villages behind him some Catuvellauni lord had asked the question *Who will lead the rising in the east?* and come up with the name Volisios. From there, it wasn't difficult to imagine a messenger being sent to advise the Iceni to prepare a proper welcome for the wandering druid. A breach of security and a concern, but not the disaster it might have been.

No, what truly worried him was the assumption of ownership immediately apparent in Volisios's every word and gesture. It seemed he was to be the Iceni's druid and no one else's and these guards were as much to ensure that as for his own security. He had encountered this situation before, of course; many a lord had looked upon him and seen his own advantage. Even after the years of the Great Silence a druid still had the power to awe. Some coveted him as an ornament to enhance their own standing, others as a weapon to strike fear. He had dealt with them all – but here and now the presumption had the potential to destroy everything he had worked for. As he rocked in the saddle he pondered the dilemma of how to trap the hare without losing the rabbit already in the net.

Dusk fell, and with it came a damp, lung-clogging sea fog. At the same time, the land narrowed to a promontory little wider than the path they travelled. Gwlym peered ahead towards a ghostly wasteland of dangerous, shale-dark waters, evil-smelling bogs and stunted, moss-grown trees. Just as the ground was about to vanish beneath his pony's hooves, a silent figure rose from nowhere to take the reins. Heart thundering, he turned to his escort, but the men were already riding back the way they'd come, apart from one, who gestured for him to dismount and, once he'd done so, led the pony off into the murk.

A druid knows no fear, he had been taught; where a druid walks, the gods walk at his shoulder. Well, if this wasn't fear it was something perilously close. The man who was now his only human contact in this dank wilderness was one of the ugliest he had ever set eyes on. Short, but very broad, he wore some kind of primitive garment made of half-cured animal skins. His flat, round face had a large upturned nose, with the nostrils facing forward in a way that reminded him of a pig's, and slanted eyes with irises of an unnatural translucent blue. When he spoke, his words were mere grunts, but Gwlym realized the man wanted him to follow.

The bulky figure moved off quickly and silently, making no provision for any weakness or hesitation.

When he reached the darker area that must be the beginning of the true wetlands, Gwlym expected him to halt, but he plunged on without stopping and, surprisingly, without making any kind of splash. Beneath his feet, hidden by the swamp grass but above the water level, Gwlym found himself traversing a narrow walkway made up of short sections of branch as thick as his upper arm. The branches were linked by lengths of plaited reeds which must have been stronger than they looked, because the path wore the marks of frequent use and had obviously been here for some time.

As far as he could tell, it led east towards the sea, but it turned sharply here and there to avoid deeper pools and the odd stand of skeletal trees, and occasionally a fork would veer off to right or left. They walked in silence, the short man through choice, Gwlym concentrating all his being on the next few paces of precariously narrow pathway to avoid falling into the ooze below. He was sweating heavily now, despite the chill of the night. The air was unnaturally still and the stink of the mud foul. A man careless enough to lose his footing here would drown in minutes. His body would never be found and his soul would wander this dank and desperate place for the rest of time.

They had been travelling for an hour, as near as Gwlym could guess, when the guide halted. He listened carefully, then cupped his hands to his mouth and gave what sounded like the call of a marsh harrier. After the count of five he repeated the call, a harsh screech, followed by a less shrill 'yick, yick, yick', which this time brought an immediate echo from the darkness.

As they continued, Gwlym noticed a mysterious muted glow in the mist ahead and the unmistakable sharp clang of metal upon metal. The glow appeared to hang in the air and he assumed it must be on some elevated platform. But, as he approached, he saw they were nearing a low island in the the centre of a sea of fog and that the light was emerging from behind a plaited reed screen erected around the perimeter. Volisios waited where the walkway met the island, a torch in his left hand and a broad smile on his face.

'Welcome,' he said. 'And my apologies for your inconvenience. As you see, we have prepared for your arrival.'

'Most ingenious,' Gwlym acknowledged.

Volisios dismissed the guide and led Gwlym through a gap in the screens to where a dozen forges blazed, each with a smith hammering enthusiastically at a glowing piece of weaponry, either a long, crude sword or a socketed iron spear point. In another area a group of men gathered the completed blades and dipped them into cisterns, where they hissed and spluttered until they cooled; still more fixed the spearheads to shafts or bound leather strips round sword hilts to create crude handgrips.

'We are safe here, but the Romans patrol the coast and we must be careful not to provoke their interest.

In this,' Volisios fluttered a hand at the fog, 'you can see nothing beyond a hundred paces. But if we want to work in daylight we have to light the forges before dawn. When the fires reach their heat there's no smoke, but until then it would betray our position from ten miles away. See here.' He ushered Gwlym towards one of the huts. Hundreds of swords lay stacked against the walls in bundles of twenty or thirty. 'I can arm five thousand men with swords and another ten thousand with spears. With you by my side and the validation of the gods I will lead the Iceni against Colonia, tear down the Temple of Claudius stone by stone and slaughter every Roman there.'

The florid red of Volisios's face grew deeper with each word he spoke and in the orange light of the forges his skin looked almost black. Gwlym could see beads of sweat on his forehead. He understood that Volisios had been manoeuvring for months to replace Prasutagus and had seen a way to strengthen his cause by allying himself with the forces of rebellion. But was that enough?

'You have done well, Volisios. Better than I could ever have hoped,' he said artlessly. 'And when you have burned Colonia, what then? Londinium?'

The Iceni hesitated. It was clear he had not planned beyond the destruction of the Roman colony. 'Yes,' he said slowly. 'Londinium.'

'And you will take the city with fifteen thousand men? Londinium is no Colonia. The walls are high and unbroken. The main Roman strength is in the west, but the city's garrison is still large. And what of the legion at Lindum? Will your men face a full legion?'

'The tribes of the south will rally to my banner.'

Gwlym blinked. Could the man truly believe that the proud war chieftains of Britain would follow some lord of a trackless swamp? Still, for the moment Volisios was all he had. He allowed himself a show of enthusiasm. 'You can lead them? The Trinovantes and the Catuvellauni, the Parisi and the Cornovii? I must be sure.' He stretched out his hands and laid the palms against the sides of the Iceni's head, at the same time closing his eyes and allowing a deep, bass murmur to resonate from his chest. 'Yes, I see it. You have the ambition, Lord Volisios, but do you have the fire? Only one with the fire can unleash the wrath of Andraste.'

He removed his hands and stared into the noble-man's eyes, which were wide with fright. But Volisios had not held the northern Marches of the Iceni for twenty years without a wellspring of courage and resolve.

'Yes, I have the fire,' he declared, recovering some of his earlier bluster. 'I have the fire to ignite the wrath of Andraste.'

Gwlym nodded sternly as if he had no doubt Volisios spoke the truth. 'When the time comes,' he said, 'you and only you will know. Until then, Gwlym druid of Mona will be at your side to advise you.'

Volisios's eyes shone. Gwlym knew the Iceni was

seeing not just Colonia and Londinium, but all of south Britain under his thrall. The new Caratacus.

He had sown the seeds of doubt as he intended and he would nurture those seeds as the opportunity arose. But how to bring the hare to the trap?

XXVI

April AD 60

The march west seemed much shorter than seven months before, when the First cohort had made its way towards Colonia under the dank grey clouds of autumn. The very obvious manifestation of spring put a little more bounce in every man's step. Not even the sixty-pound loads they carried could dent their spirits. Wherever they looked leaves fresh from the bud turned the hedgerows emerald green and buttercups, dandelions and primroses studded the meadows with gold. Each farmer's field had its flock of newborn lambs jostling playfully for position on the nearest hummock of grass and watched over by a shepherd boy ready to fend off any enterprising fox or buzzard, or passing hungry-eyed legionary.

As they marched through the hills towards

Glevum, Valerius heard a familiar bass voice take up the simple cadence of the first verse of the 'March of Marius'.

There was a Mule, he was no fool,
He had a girl in every fort
Another one in every port
In Allifae she was not shy . . .'

By the time they reached the Twentieth's base above the Severn, the Mule had shown much imagination and inventiveness and he'd left a trail of worn-out working girls from one side of the Empire to the other. Lunaris's voice never let up and he was still going strong. Valerius sang along with the rest.

He barely recognized the fortress as the place he'd left the previous year. Supply trains carried a constant stream of equipment and provisions from the river to a separate temporary encampment protecting the mountain of stores gathered for the campaign ahead. Engineers had constructed a series of double-ditched annexes to house the various auxiliary units who would accompany the Twentieth and the Fourteenth to attack Mona: veteran infantry from Frisia, Batavia and Tungria, a five-hundred-strong wing of Sarmatian light cavalry scouts and another of Raetian bowmen.

Travel-stained and leg-weary, the men of the First cohort gathered on the parade ground to say farewell to their tribune. Valerius had never seen a unit more battle-ready or eager. Brick-red, dust-coated faces grinned at him from below their polished helmets, and dark patches of sweat stained their tunics, but every man was honed whip thin and tough as seasoned saddle leather. War held no illusions for them but they had had enough of mending roads and mock fights. He felt a wasp sting of guilt at the knowledge he wouldn't be going to Mona and worse when they cheered him to a man as he dismissed them.

'Good luck, Julius. Look after them,' he said to the centurion. 'I'll announce our arrival at the *principia*, and after that, who knows?'

'There's a pretty whore called Thalia in the brothel up by the gate on the Prata Flaminia. Say hello to her for me and give her a big kiss, or something else.' Julius laughed and took him by the arm, looking up into the young-old face with the wary fighter's eyes. 'I can't imagine you in a law court, Valerius, but you'll scare the life out of the opposition.'

Afterwards Valerius reported to the legate on the status and condition of his men. He was pleased by the general's reaction.

'I know, I watched them march in. They are a credit to you and their officers. They'll have plenty of time to rest. The Fourteenth sets off in a week from their base at Viroconium. It will take a month to force a way through the mountains. We go in after that. That's when the First cohort will be needed. When we reach Mona.'

Valerius nodded his thanks and turned to the request that had been dominating his thoughts for the final five miles of the march. 'I would like to ask for a meeting with the governor, sir.'

Livius pursed his lips and tutted. 'You won't change his mind, Valerius. He won't keep you in Britain.'

'I don't expect him to, sir. It's another matter.' He knew he could ask the legate to pass on the information supplied by Cearan, but there was no guarantee it would reach the governor. He owed it to the Iceni to argue the case himself.

'Very well, I'll arrange it, but I warn you he's in a dangerous mood. He heard this morning that Corbulo heaps success upon success in Armenia. The governor's future rests on this campaign and the Emperor is impatient for victory. It will mean a triumph and a consulship if he wins, but . . . I hope it's good news you are bringing him.'

Staff officers and messengers bustled to and from the governor's headquarters with the regularity of bees supplying a hive. A harassed aide ushered Valerius inside, where he found Paulinus at a plain wooden desk writing unhurriedly in confident strokes across a piece of parchment. It was undoubtedly an important report; normal orders would be issued on the wax writing block at his right hand and transcribed by clerks. Valerius felt the first flutter of nerves. This man had the power of life and death over every soldier and civilian in the province, and he was a man to be feared.

In the silence he considered what he knew of the governor. Paulinus had spent his first campaigning season in Britain in the south-west, annihilating the last remnants of resistance from the Dumnonii and their Durotrige allies in the rugged peninsula where they had fled the swords of the Second legion. The governor counted it a great success, reaping the double benefit of guaranteeing Rome the tin it needed and spreading word of the new total war he had brought to these shores. Every king, prince or warrior who resisted was butchered. Only widows and orphans survived to wail their funeral songs and spread the tale of his coming.

Paulinus had plotted and conspired to win his position as governor, but he hated this island and he despised its people. He combined a hard, unbending and utterly ruthless character with a forensic intelligence. He was also a brilliant soldier who had been the first Roman general to fight his way across the Atlas mountains.

A sharp scrape announced he had completed his correspondence. Valerius drew himself up to his full height. The shaven head lifted and he found himself being studied by two flat, basilisk eyes squinting from beneath a heavy brow. Paulinus maintained his gaze for a full minute, as if he was trying to define what species of life form had dared interrupt him. Valerius felt the first prickle of sweat in his scalp.

'I am told you have important news for me?' The voice was as rough-edged as the face it emerged from, the accent from somewhere to the south of Rome.

Valerius repeated what Cearan had told him about the likelihood of political upheaval among the Iceni when King Prasutagus died, the clandestine meetings in the woods and his certainty that druids were spreading poison among his people.

When he had finished the governor snorted impatiently. 'So, in short, I am expected to endorse the claim of this woman, this Boudicca, over other worthy candidates on the word of some barbarian opportunist.'

Valerius took a deep breath. 'Sir, it is my opinion that Lord Cearan is a man to be trusted. If he has concerns, then I think we should also have concerns.'

The pebble eyes glowered in surprise.

'You would give me advice? Young man, I have so much advice that I am forced to sit at this table twelve hours a day considering it. The Emperor advises me how to squeeze more profit out of this benighted province. My officers advise me their forces are not strong enough yet to take the Druids' Isle. My priests advise me that it is a fine day – as if I cannot see that for myself. And my doctor advises me that if I don't calm down my piles will burst.'

Paulinus slapped his palm on the table hard enough to make stylus and scroll airborne.

'Everything you say assumes that these Iceni seek a war. They would not be so foolish. I would wipe this country so clean of any rebellious vermin that neither their children nor their children's children would pose a threat to any Roman again.'

Valerius suppressed a soldier's instinct to keep his mouth shut and used his lawyer's experience to place a doubt where it would do most good. 'Perhaps we underestimate them, sir,' he said, thinking of the hate-filled eyes of the mourners at Lucullus's funeral.

Paulinus stared at him. Lowly tribunes did not answer back to their commander in chief, but then perhaps this tribune was not so lowly. He cast his mind back in an attempt to fathom what political leverage Valerius might have that made him so brave. It did not occur to him that someone might be brave for its own sake. The family Valerii had once wielded influence on the Palatine; perhaps they would wield it again, and one day that influence might be useful to him. Very well, he would humour the boy.

'I underestimate nothing. The eastern tribes are a toothless, leaderless rabble. Their kings have taken our gold and eat off our plates. The warriors sit in the shade and watch their women plant seeds all day, and they drink beer all night. Their swords are rusted to an edge that would not cut grass, oxen pull their chariots and they use their shields to water their cattle. Am I to fear them? Does Colonia fear them?' He thought for a moment. 'King Prasutagus still lives. I will consider his queen's case if and when he dies, but it must wait until my return.'

'And the druids?'

'If what this Cearan claims is true there would already have been attacks. It is always the way. We old men counsel patience, but the young hotheads cannot keep their swords sheathed. No. Even if a few druids are spreading poison, their work is at an early stage. They are no danger yet.'

'But they could be in future?' Valerius suggested.

Paulinus suppressed his annoyance. 'It is possible, but I will not jeopardize this mission on a possibility. If the tribes were to combine to threaten Colonia, I would know of it. No force of any size could gather without my knowledge in this province. The Ninth are only a few days' march away; they would be there before the rebels reached the gates.'

'And if they were not?'

'Then Colonia must be held by its people.'

'And if they cannot hold it?'

'Then they do not deserve to keep it.'

Paulinus picked up his stylus. Valerius was dismissed. He had failed.

He expected to be ordered to Londinium immediately, but the Twentieth's preparations were behind schedule and an extra pair of hands was not to be lightly discarded. That day and each day thereafter the legate found some new logistical crisis for him to solve, a supply line to unclog or a dispute to smooth over. The armourer went sick and his deputy turned out to be incompetent, and a new armourer must be found. Valerius thought of Corvinus back in

Colonia, but the distance was too far and the time too short. Eventually he bribed the prefect commanding the Frisian auxiliaries to give him the use of a blond giant with a manic grin and Latin that sounded like a bath-house draining. And so it went on.

On the ides of Aprilis he watched with Lunaris as governor Paulinus and his personal bodyguard marched out with the auxiliaries to join the Fourteenth legion, the massed cornicens blowing a strident fanfare and the eagle standard glittering in the fresh morning sunlight. His heart swelled as they passed, rank after rank, with their shields on their backs and their spears and equipment and a week's rations already grating on their shoulders. The letters to their loved ones had been sent, their bellies were full and they were eager: he could see it in the way they stepped out and in the determination on their faces.

Behind them by the thousand came the mules of the supply train; no ox carts on this campaign because no roads existed where they were going, only precipitous mountain passes and boulder-filled valley bottoms that would snap an axle as if it were a tooth-pick. The mules were followed by more auxiliaries than Valerius had seen gathered together in one place. The Frisians and Tungrians had been joined by Vangiones and Nervians from the swamps of Germania, Gauls from every part of that vast land, and lithe, tanned hillmen from Pannonia and Moetia and Dalmatia.

'Better them than me,' Lunaris growled. 'They'll have to clear the hills and force the passes. A Black Celt on every ridge and a boulder on your helmet from every clifftop. At least when we go that job'll have been done.'

'You think they'll fight?' Valerius asked. 'The legate of the Fourteenth has been telling whoever wants to know that the druids will pull them back to the island.'

'They'll fight all right,' the big man said gloomily. 'If the barbarians came to burn down the Temple of Jupiter would you sit and wait at the bottom of the Capitoline? No, you'd block the streets and have an archer at every window and a spearman at every corner and by the time they got to the temple there wouldn't be enough of them left to take it. That's why he's taking so many of the country boys. They'll do the dying and then the Fourteenth and the Twentieth will finish the job and take all the glory.'

'If there's any glory they'll have earned it,' Valerius said, considering the perils of a massed assault on a defended island. Any bridgehead would be paid for heavily in Roman lives. 'Would you rather be staying behind with me?'

Lunaris shook his head. 'No,' he said seriously. 'I've been doing this for a dozen years. Mostly digging and marching and waiting – lots of waiting. Fighting is the best part of it, even with all the torn guts and the tent-mates who don't make it back, because it's what we're paid for and trained for.

And because we always win. Because we're the best.'

The next day they heard that Prasutagus of the Iceni was dead.

Valerius considered riding out after Paulinus and pressing him for a decision on the Iceni succession, but reviewing his interview with the governor convinced him that it would do more harm than good. He thought of Cearan's earnest, handsome face and felt the hollow emptiness of having failed a friend. Yet there was always a chance Queen Boudicca would prevail without the governor's sanction. Paulinus had dismissed her as a mere woman, but Valerius had sensed a formidable presence when he had seen her at Venta. In any case, he had done everything he could.

Another week passed and, although the legate kept him busy enough, he began to have a strange detached feeling of not belonging. Each man in the legion had a definite aim and a place in the battle line, but not him. What they did, they did for a purpose: to ensure they reached Mona with the equipment they needed in a condition that would allow them to use it to the best effect. All he did was fill gaps. He was considering asking the legate for leave to go when he received the legionary commander's summons.

Livius received him in the *principia* with the harassed look of a man with too many problems and not enough time. 'Nonsense,' he snapped, throwing a scroll on to the campaign desk in front of him. 'We are not ready but I am commanded to march within forty-eight hours, so march we must.' He frowned. 'You have done good work here, Valerius, for which I thank you, and if I had my way you would be going with us, but . . .' he glanced at the scroll in front of him and gave a bitter smile, 'orders are orders. However, you can do me a last favour. Your replacement is due in Londinium from Rome in one week on the ship that will take you back there. Mars aid me but we need him. He'll be wet behind the ears and I can't have him wandering around these mountains on his own or some Silurian will eat him and have his skull for an oil lamp. Choose a dozen experienced men from the First cohort as an escort and take them with you. Once they have picked up your replacement they are to follow us as they can. Judging by the governor's dispatches we won't have gone too far. We appear to have underestimated the obstinacy of the Celts defending the passes.'

'Of course, sir. It will be my pleasure.' Which was true. He couldn't think of better company than Lunaris and his comrades from the second century. They might not relish the march, but if they weren't marching east they'd be marching west into the arms of the druids. At least they'd be safer with him.

XXVII

Crespo stared at the thatched roofs of the walled town across the river. He'd made no attempt to conceal the approach and he knew they knew he was here because he could feel their fear.

He heard a sniff behind him and felt a twinge of annoyance.

'Are you certain we will be safe among these savages?' Catus Decianus asked in his nasal drawl.

'Safe as if you were back in Rome, your honour.' They would have been safe with half the force he had at his back. But it made the job all the easier. The men he could always depend on, Vettius and his gang of thieves and bullies, plus a few slave dealers who smelled a quick profit, formed the nucleus of the unit, but this was a big operation and he'd used Decianus's authority to strip the Londinium garrison and form a force of a thousand men. They weren't frontline troops, mostly legionaries nearing retirement and the remnants of shattered auxiliary units, only fit for fetching and carrying, but they looked formidable enough. Which was the point.

'Very well. You have your orders.'

Crespo called his centurions forward. 'First five centuries with me inside the town. The rest fan out and surround the place as we agreed. Anyone who tries to run you hold, or kill, I don't really care. Once we've made our point you march to your assigned sector along with your unit's slaves and carts and strip every farm and every home. If you don't find any gold give the owner a tickle with a spear till he tells you where it is. Because it will be there. But don't kill too many.' It wasn't compassion, purely business. This was the Emperor Nero's land now and the Emperor would need people to work it. The pragmatic King Prasutagus had left half his kingdom to Nero and had named his daughters heirs to the rest, relying on his wife Boudicca to rule until they came of age. But Nero didn't want half. He wanted it all. And Crespo was going to get it for him.

Which was why Queen Boudicca was about to be taught a lesson.

Cearan stood in the main square of Venta beside his queen and waited for the Romans to enter through the double gateway. Boudicca wore a long dress of plaid belted at the waist with a chain of gold links.

She held her noble head high and her long russet hair had been carefully combed to a fine sheen, falling over her shoulders in a fiery cascade. A gold band circled her forehead and a torc of the same precious metal shone at her neck. She looked magnificent, he thought, but in his heart he wished it otherwise. This was not a day for a display of queenly splendour. He was not sure yet what it *was* a day for but it was a day he had done his best to ensure would end peacefully.

Word had reached him of the Roman advance several hours earlier and he had puzzled over it. A force of such strength could only be the escort for the governor or one of his senior officials. Was this Suetonius Paulinus on his way to endorse the queen's proposal and confirm her daughters as Prasutagus's heirs? It seemed unlikely. The Iceni were Rome's clients not its subjects, a separate entity outwith the province of Britain. The endorsement of Rome was needed for the succession, yes, but a simple courier would have sufficed. Such a show of power sent out a message which was disturbing, if not frightening. Worse, this was the best reading of the situation he could arrive at. When he had informed Boudicca of the Romans' approach, the colour had flared in her cheeks.

'They seek to cow us.' Her voice shook. 'But I will not be cowed. As long as I am queen of the Iceni, I will rule as queen. No Roman will dictate to Boudicca what she can or cannot do, but . . .' she turned to him, and for the first time he saw the flicker of uncertainty in her eyes, 'I cannot place my people at risk.'

'There are a thousand Romans,' he replied. 'Give me two days and I could have five thousand warriors at your call.' The lords of the Iceni had travelled from their estates to Venta to discuss the succession and it would have been a simple matter for them to return and rouse their fighting men, but . . . 'But we do not have two days. In any case, it would still not be enough. What arms do we have to face their swords and their spears? Nothing but knives, scythes and a few hunting bows. We cannot afford a confrontation.'

'There are swords,' a voice volunteered to a growl of approval.

Volisios. So his suspicions about the lord of the northern Marches had been correct.

'Not enough and not here, Lord Volisios.' He stared at the queen, a question in his eyes. She looked away and his heart sank, then she turned to meet his gaze and nodded. He sighed with relief. 'You must take the young men to the secret places and conceal them there. If you have swords,' he nodded to Volisios, 'then now is the time to sharpen them. Then you must wait.'

A buzz of disapproval greeted his words and he raised a hand for quiet.

'We cannot fight the Romans here, and we cannot fight them now. They are too many and they are too well armed. They will come, and they will swagger and they will make their demands – and then they will leave. When they leave we will resume this discussion. There is a time for swords and a time for words. I do not believe it is a time for swords yet.'

So why, when the Roman officer with the arrogant, pock-marked face rode in at the head of his men, did he wish more than anything on earth that he had a sword in his hand?

A scuffle from behind distracted him and he saw a flash of gold in the corner of his eye as Tor, his grandson, darted from the crowd and pleaded to be lifted. Cearan picked the little boy up and tenderly kissed his head, remembering the last Romans to visit Venta and wishing that Valerius was among these men. The thought of Valerius made him think of Maeve, who was safe in one of the huts, and he prayed she wouldn't emerge to retrieve the child. But it was a pretty girl with her mother's red hair and the leggy confidence of a young colt who took Tor from his arms. Boudicca's daughter Rosmerta. He smiled his thanks and turned to face the Romans again – and froze. The officer was staring past him at the girl's retreating back and the naked, undisguised lust on his face sent ice water cascading down Cearan's spine. Beside him he felt Boudicca stiffen.

Crespo studied his surroundings. Who did these people think they were? The town might have been Roman if it hadn't been made of straw and mud.

Rectangular buildings with narrow fronts facing the streets. Shops and workshops. A marketplace that aped a forum. And a large building at the far end of the square that was probably Prasutagus's palace. He had noted the handsome, aristocratic Briton standing with the tall red-haired woman in the centre of the square, but his attention had been diverted by the girl. Perhaps today wasn't going to be such a chore after all.

Decianus, who had naturally waited until he was certain he faced no danger, rode in with his escort. At last, they could get on with it. Crespo turned to his officers. 'First century, separate the men from the women and children and herd them outside. Make sure they understand what will happen if they don't behave. Third and fourth centuries, search the houses for valuables, but leave the big house at the end to the procurator and his staff.' That was where the records would be, if these people kept records, and the most valuable possessions. 'The rest of you, stand fast. If there's any sign of trouble, you know what to do.'

A few women cried out as the legionaries advanced into the crowd, selected the adult males and pushed them towards the gate. He noted the absence of men of fighting age. Someone had sent them away and he thought he knew who. He studied the Iceni noble at the queen's side. So much the better.

Decianus slid gingerly from the saddle and Crespo dismounted with him. Together they marched towards the little group and halted three or four paces in front of them. The procurator pulled a thin tablet of bronze from the sleeve of his toga and immediately began reading. Crespo saw the woman frown. Decianus truly was a fool. At least he should have found out if she understood Latin.

The tall man began whispering urgently in the woman's ear, translating as the procurator continued.

'. . . will of Prasutagus, heretofore known as king of the Iceni, clients of Rome, is repudiated and its terms annulled . . . designated sole heir and all others hereby disinherited . . . all monies, lands, properties, minerals, crops, livestock . . . revert to the Emperor Nero Claudius Drusus Germanicus . . . all profits from said goods revert to the Emperor Nero Claudius Drusus Germanicus . . . all future profits from the sale of said crops, livestock, minerals and . . . revert to the said Emperor Nero Claudius Drusus Germanicus . . .'

Cearan was appalled. He could barely believe what he was hearing, the words seeming to tumble in his head, but somehow he managed to maintain the sense of what the long-nosed bureaucrat was announcing. Boudicca's breasts rose and fell with increasing force and he felt her anger grow as she began to fully understand what the little piece of bronze plate signified. Nero was stealing her nation.

'No,' she screamed, spitting a wall of Celtic invective that made Decianus back away before the intensity of her fury. Cearan attempted to translate as she demanded a meeting with the governor, justice from a Roman court and the rights of a queen.

Crespo laughed at the procurator's fear and allowed Boudicca to rave for a further minute for his own amusement before he struck. The full-blooded punch took the Iceni queen on the side of the skull, sending the gold circlet she wore spinning into the air. Boudicca collapsed to the ground, stunned, and when she attempted to rise Crespo placed his foot in the small of her back and forced her into the dust.

'Vettius,' he called to his second in command, 'bring my whip. This bitch needs teaching some manners.'

'Please!' Cearan rushed forward, instinctively defending his queen.

Crespo drew his *gladius* and turned in one movement, bringing the razor edge of the sword down in a savage diagonal blow across Cearan's face. The Iceni shrieked and reeled back with his hands to his eyes, the blood already spurting scarlet between his fingers. Aenid, who had been among the crowd of women, screamed and rushed to her husband's aid, but one of Crespo's legionaries kicked the legs from under her and stabbed down with his sword.

'Not so pretty now,' Crespo laughed. 'Vettius, where's my fucking whip?'

Decianus shuffled uncomfortably at the violence being displayed before him. The procurator had served his six months with the legions but he'd never been at home among men whose first instinct was to strike a blow. He disliked Crespo, indeed found him disgusting, but he had a distasteful mission to accomplish and a man like the centurion was a useful means to that end. He looked down at the Iceni queen wriggling in the dust beneath the soldier's sandal and fought back the urge to intervene. No. She had defied Rome and if she was not taught to fear it there was a danger she would defy it again.

He turned away and walked past the bloodied, kneeling figure of the golden-haired Celt scarcely noticing the dead woman at his side, his mind focused on the more urgent problem of discovering the extent of King Prasutagus's wealth.

Crespo's blunt-faced deputy handed him a whip, but the centurion knocked it away. 'Not that one. Get me my *flagellum*.' The *flagellum* was the heavier whip, made of ox leather. Boudicca would not only feel the pain of her punishment but bear the scars of it till she died. He felt the queen struggling harder now and realized she was recovering from his punch. She was a big woman, and strong, which might be awkward. He looked around the square and his eye settled on a post used for tying up livestock on market days.

'Truss her up to that,' he ordered, hauling Boudicca to her feet. Two men dragged her to the post, her red hair and clothing now matted with dust and her cheeks dirty and tear-streaked. She struggled and twisted between them, but her green eyes, blazing with the fire of her hatred, never left Crespo. She unleashed a string of curses, each predicting a worse death, but Crespo only laughed.

'Now we'll see what a queen is made of.' Boudicca had been tied with her hands above her head and her face against the splintered wood of the post, and he took hold of the neck of her dress and with all his strength ripped it apart until her back was bared. Still not content, he half turned her and tore the garment from her front, leaving her naked to the waist and visible to all.

He hesitated for a moment to admire his handiwork. The sight of her breasts, heavy, milk white and dark-nippled, ignited something within him; liquid fire flooded his loins and he felt a roaring in his ears. He raised the whip and slashed it down on the pale flesh of her back. Boudicca screamed for the first time.

Rosmerta and Banna had watched their mother's ordeal with increasing horror. Now they rushed to her side from the crowd of howling women and children, imploring Crespo to show mercy. Crespo watched them race towards him, his mind already framing the possibilities. So. Not one juicy little peach, but two. He threw the whip to Vettius, who was standing by, grinning. 'Make sure she feels it, and when you've had enough come and take your turn.' He took each girl by the arm and dragged them to the nearest hut, kicked in the door and threw them inside. They stared at him, terrified, cowering against the wall, their eyes showing wide and white in the darkness of the interior. The knowledge of their fear

only intensified his desire. He stared at them, pro-
longing the moment and anticipating the pleasures to
be discovered beneath the plain shifts.

'Now,' he said, his eyes moving lazily between
them. 'Who is going to be first?'

Even through her pain, Boudicca heard her
daughters' screams.

XXVIII

Valerius emerged from the low building that served as the port commander's office and shook his head. 'Every ship that's docked this week has been at least three days late. Apparently there have been poor winds in the bay. The galley bringing our man isn't expected until the end of the week at the earliest.'

Lunaris nodded. His knowledge of ships was limited to the transport that had brought him to Britain but he understood enough of the vagaries of the wind to accept the delay without complaint. 'So what do we do now?' He pointed with his thumb to the men lounging among the bales along the wharf by the Tamesa. 'If we don't keep them busy they'll get up to mischief.'

'I'll report to the camp prefect and have you put on

the ration strength. Three days isn't long, but I'll try to make sure you're on light duties.'

'Watch your back. Crespo might still be around,' the *duplicarius* warned.

'If Crespo's around he's the one who needs to be watching his back.'

Two hours later they met on the wharf and Valerius gathered the legionaries around him. 'You've been excused duties for the rest of the day.' The news raised a small cheer. 'But I've been made responsible for your behaviour and you're to be on parade for inspection before dawn tomorrow.' The cheers faded as they realized there would be no night of debauchery in Londinium's inns and brothels.

When the men had dispersed, Lunaris approached Valerius with a scowl. 'I sent the Mules out to ask around about Crespo. Know your enemy, right?' Valerius nodded. 'The word is that he left eight or nine days ago to do the procurator's dirty work and took half of the garrison with him.'

Valerius whistled. 'That's a lot of dirty work.'

'That's right, but he must have finished the job, because most of them are back now, which is why we aren't up there patrolling the walls.'

'Did anybody say what it was?'

Lunaris hesitated. 'Only that it was up somewhere in Iceni country.'

Valerius froze. He thought of Maeve and Cearan in the little township at Venta.

If Crespo harmed her . . .

The hut stank of fish.

Maeve had bandaged Cearan's shattered face as best she could, but was barely able to look at the torn flesh and splintered bone created by Crespo's sword. Now she sat with her back to the thatch wall, cradling his head as his body shook uncontrollably. She had little medical knowledge, but enough to know that if he did not receive help soon he would die.

Little Banna lay slumped against the opposite wall. Her eyes were closed but Maeve doubted she was sleeping. Beside her, a dark-haired woman spoke quietly as Rosmerta sobbed against her breast. Maeve shuddered as she thought of the horrors they had endured. The Romans had eventually tired of the two girls, but so many . . . She knew they would never be the same again.

She had been certain she would be killed, and every man, woman and child in Venta along with her. The Roman commander was the tall pock-marked officer who had kidnapped her – the man Valerius called Crespo – and she had known better than to expect mercy. She brushed away a tear. What she had suffered was nothing compared with the suffering of the Iceni. When Crespo eventually left the square with the bulk of his men she had rushed from her refuge to Cearan's side. Aenid's lifeless blue eyes had stared uncomprehendingly, but Cearan still breathed and somehow she managed to raise him to his feet. The

Roman guards had averted their eyes as she supported him away and Maeve sensed that some of the soldiers with the procurator were ashamed of what they'd been ordered to take part in. It gave her hope she would survive, but did not quench the fire of her anger. Later she returned to the square with a small party of women and cut Boudicca down and recovered the girls. They had left Venta and journeyed eastwards, the dark-haired woman leading them along secret paths to this isolated community among the endless reed beds and swamps of the coast.

Now the queen sat alone, a coverlet across her scarred back and breasts, staring south through the open doorway, her eyes filled with unnerving savagery.

As the hours passed, the heat became oppressive and the unceasing buzz of insects filled the salt air. Dark clusters of flies settled on Cearan's bloodstained bandages and Maeve was kept busy brushing them away. At one point she must have fallen asleep. When she awoke the queen hadn't moved from her position. From time to time she heard her whisper to herself, a garbled litany of fury. Maeve could distinguish only a single word. 'Andraste.'

In the late afternoon voices outside alerted them. Maeve reached for Cearan's dagger, which was the only protection they had, but it was the Iceni lord, Volisios, who entered, accompanied by a stooped figure in dark clothing, a young man with pale, almost translucent skin that clung to the bones of his face, and eyes that knew you in an instant. He carried no weapon but wore a belt studded with loops holding short cattle-horn containers, each about three inches long and stopped with birch bark. He took in the occupants of the hut at a glance and immediately crossed to where Maeve sat with Cearan.

'I am said to have some healing skills,' he said. 'Perhaps you would allow me to look at his wounds.' He deftly unwrapped the bandage and studied the Iceni without emotion. 'He will lose the eye, I think, but one eye will suffice.' He heard Maeve's gasp and without turning said: 'A man's looks are but an outward decoration. It is what is inside that makes him who he is. Our first task is to fend off the spirits that would enter him and set the wound afire.' He reached into one of the containers at his belt. 'Boil water and place this in it, and when it has cooled sufficiently, make him drink it, every drop.' He left the hut and returned an hour later with a cloth bag. 'This is a poultice which you must place over the wound. The drink will ease his suffering, the poultice will begin the healing process. See, you place it like this.' He manoeuvred the bag, which was damp and gave off an unusual earthy smell, directly over Cearan's ravaged face, taking care to leave the mouth clear. When he was satisfied he lit a small fire in the centre of the floor. Then he unstoppered another of the horns at his belt, took out a handful of what appeared to be dust and scattered it in the flames, where it hissed, sparked and crackled. Instantly, the room filled with a suffocating, evil-smelling smoke that battered Maeve's senses and left her head reeling. The thin man bowed his head over the fire and began to chant a rhythmic, sonorous incantation, and Maeve felt the hut spin around her. At one point she was certain she was taken by the hand and drawn into the sky, to look down upon the land of Britain and all who dwelt there. Strange that she thought not of her father or Cearan, but of the Roman, Valerius.

When she woke for a second time, she felt as refreshed as if she had spent a long night in her own soft bed, rather than a few minutes on a hard earth floor. The healer sat by Cearan, but, like her, he could not ignore the heated conversation between Volisios and Boudicca.

'I have swords, shields and spears and the warriors to wield them,' the nobleman insisted.

'And I am Boudicca, queen of the Iceni.' Self-will kept her voice controlled but Maeve could almost feel the physical force of Boudicca's suppressed rage.

'Boudicca, queen of the Iceni, was dispossessed by the Romans,' Volisios persisted.

Boudicca laughed mirthlessly. 'And you, Volisios, if you were brave enough to return to your estate, would no doubt find a Roman in your bed. I am Boudicca, queen of the Iceni, and if I were not you would not be here, with your talk of warriors and spears.'

'I came here to assure myself of your safety.'

'You came here to assume my authority. To raise yourself above the rest.'

Volisios flinched at the undeniable truth, but he held her gaze. 'And do I have it?'

'No!'

'Then who does?'

'I am Boudicca, queen of the Iceni,' she repeated, and her words rang through the little hut like a voice from another world. 'No man among the Iceni has suffered greater wrong than I. *I* will take the fight to the Romans with sword and spear. *I* will destroy them with fire and with iron. *I* will have my vengeance! Go now and call the war bands. Every man, be he warrior, youth or elder, must play his part. I will wipe the Romans and any who stand with them from this land or I will die in the attempt.'

Volisios stared at her, overwhelmed by her presence and her anger. He snatched a startled glance at Gwlym. Now he understood. The wrath of Andraste. The druid rose to his feet and Boudicca glared at him.

'You are no longer Boudicca of the Iceni,' the priest declared, ignoring the fierce eyes that hooked him like an eagle's talons. 'The spirit of Andraste lives within you. The spirit of the hare and the horse . . . and now of the wolf.'

'And who is it who is so impudent as to gainsay a queen?'

The stoop vanished and the young man's paleness took on an almost mystical light, so his skin shone in the gloom.

'I am Gwlym, druid of Mona, and I am here to guide you.'

He was finely muscled, with long brown hair drawn together by a red ribbon at his neck.

Gwlym watched from his place beside the queen as the guardian of the sacred pool led the young man forward. He had been carefully chosen for his untarnished character; no stain sullied his past or his present. He was a prince of his tribe, and he had come willingly to this place and to his death. The druids of Britain knew they had one last opportunity to drive the Romans from their land and they had sacrificed themselves and their sanctuary on Mona to achieve it. But there had to be other sacrifices. Nothing could be left to chance. Gwlym had sent word by swift horsemen to north and west and south. Now. Now was the time. And from each place, as the forces of free Britain assembled, a messenger would be sent, a messenger of such status as to impress even the most blood-weary deities.

So they had gathered here beside the forest pool, in a place sacred to the Iceni and their forebears since antiquity.

Gwlym led the chants, his powerful voice ringing out through the glade, and they were taken up by each of the elders of the tribe in turn. Once, these men had been acolytes and the keepers of the groves, but they had lost their way when the druids were driven into the west. But they still remembered. A thin cord attached the victim to the guardian, a warrior dressed in a red tunic and plaid trews. The others formed a loose circle on the firm ground by the water's edge.

As he sang, Gwlym watched the moon as it made its unflinching arc across the night sky. When the glowing orb reached the exact centre of the circle in the tree canopy he raised his arms high. At the signal, the sacrifice threw off his cloak to stand naked in the firelight, swaying in time to the rhythm of the chanting.

Gwlym hid his relief. The drug had been administered in the exact quantities. He slipped his hand into the folds of his robe. This was his time. This was what all the years of tests and trials on the sacred isle had been for. He allowed the others to continue the chant and walked forward, talking reassuringly to the young man, as he would to a nervous colt, and as he talked he circled round behind him.

When he was in position, Gwlym swung up the short-handled metal axe and brought it down on the boy's head with such force that everyone round the pool clearly heard the sharp 'thunk' as the blade bit into the bone. The blow would have felled an ox, but, incredibly, the victim still stood, swaying wildly, until a second blow of the axe knocked him to his knees.

Now the young druid stood back to allow the warrior with the red tunic to take his place above the prince. With both hands the man took hold of the noose with which he had led his captive, twisted it round the helpless boy's neck, and pulled it until it bit deep into the flesh of his throat. But still he would not die. Without relaxing his grip, the warrior dropped on one knee on to his victim's back with such violence they clearly heard a rib break. Then he used the extra leverage to twist the ends of the noose until the boy's head suddenly flopped forward as his neck snapped.

The warrior rose, his job done, but two deaths were not enough. Three gods needed to be appeased. Volisios, his face a mask of determination, lifted the dead prince's lolling head by his gore-thick hair and in a final act of mutilation drew the edge of a dagger slowly across his throat.

While the guardian carefully weighted the body and placed it in the sacred pool, Gwlym, breathing heavily, strode to where Boudicca stood in a hooded cloak. The three deaths had been administered exactly as ordained by Aymer and in accordance with all the edicts of the sect. The gods would accept the sacrifice.

'It is done,' he said. 'Unfurl the wolf banner. Unleash the wrath of Andraste.'

XXIX

Crespo rolled the dice. 'Seven,' he announced. 'All right, Vettius, the one with the big tits is yours. But take her into the other room. I'm sick of seeing that great arse of yours bulling up and down.'

Vettius grinned and walked across to where a group of young Iceni women huddled fearfully against the back wall of the main hall of Prasutagus's palace. A plump girl of about fourteen squealed as he grabbed her by the hair and hauled her roughly through a doorway. Her sobbing pleas not to be hurt could be heard clearly through the thin wall before a sharp slap silenced them, but such sounds had become so familiar that Crespo barely registered them.

They had been here for almost two weeks now, supervising the collection of Iceni wealth and cataloguing the extent of Iceni lands by day, and drinking and playing dice for the use of the captured women each night. He reflected on a job well done. The procurator, now back in Londinium, had promised to commend him in his report to the Emperor. Crespo prided himself on being a man who took each day as it presented itself, but such recognition opened doors. He certainly didn't intend to return to the legion. No need to as long as the pretty-boy tribune kept his promise to pay up. He didn't have any doubt Valerius would pay. Why did the honest always have to be so pious? Fool. Then there was the bonus he'd managed to hide away – the golden torc the queen had worn at her neck. The sale of that would make his retirement much more pleasurable. Pity about the girl, though. He would have liked to tup her just to see the look on that bastard Valerius's face.

Yes, it was all very satisfactory. He lay back and closed his eyes, still remembering the way the whip had raised bright red welts against the paleness of Boudicca's skin, and the taut, youthful flesh of her daughters. He felt himself stir. Perhaps he wasn't too drunk after all.

'Smoke!'

He came instantly alert at the shout. Vettius emerged from the room at the rear and pointed at the roof. Crespo looked up to see the slim streamers of smoke replaced by a flare of light as a portion of thatch caught fire and the flames quickly spread to a nearby beam. Vettius and a few others reacted quickly, grabbing swords and armour and making for the doorway, but most of the men just stared at him in confusion.

'Get out,' he barked. 'Gather your gear and leave the women.' He knew how quickly a thatched house could turn into an inferno. He'd burned enough of them in the past. They might only have seconds.

'Fuck.' Vettius was the first man to the door and he screamed and staggered backwards, clutching in disbelief at the ragged gash in his belly. He extended one hand towards his leader in a despairing plea for help before collapsing on his face in the dirty straw.

Crespo stared at the dying man for a split second, his mind racing. Given time they could cut through the walls, but they didn't have time. The flames had already spread across the entire roof and the hall had begun to fill with choking white smoke. For the first time he felt panic. The gods only knew what awaited them outside, but better to go down fighting than to burn. He made his decision. 'Out,' he repeated. 'If we stay here we're all dead.'

A collective wail from the British women was followed by a rush towards the door. A legionary took a cut at one of them as she ran by and she fell, howling, to the floor.

'Leave them,' Crespo ordered. 'Swords and shields. We go as one man and when we're clear of the door we form *testudo*. It's our only chance.' He picked up a shield and hefted his *gladius* in his right hand. He wasn't sure where it had all gone wrong, but it had and now there was only one choice. 'On my order. Now.'

The little group burst from the doorway as the roof of the palace collapsed behind them, but when he saw what awaited him Crespo stumbled to a dazed halt. Behind a circle of spear points an unbroken ring of silent, vengeful faces glistened in the dancing light of the flames.

'Shit,' he said, as his nerve failed him and he fell to his knees. He tried to manoeuvre the *gladius* so he could drive the point below his ribs but his hands were suddenly clumsy. A spear shaft knocked the sword from his grasp and another smashed him into unconsciousness.

'The ship should arrive tomorrow,' Valerius told Lunaris. 'So make sure everyone's accounted for with their equipment all present and correct. We don't want you making a poor impression on your new tribune.'

Lunaris laughed. 'Like as not he won't know one end of a sword from the other. How long before it sails again?'

'A couple of days, maybe three.'

Lunaris nodded. 'I'm sorry you won't be coming with us to Mona.'

Valerius stared out across the river to the settlement on the south bank. 'One thing I've learned, Lunaris, is that you can't fight the fates. When I came to Britain *I* barely knew one end of a sword from the other. But I think I became a good soldier, maybe even a good officer. Part of being a good soldier is obeying orders. They've ordered me back, so back I'll go. Still, I'd like to have fought alongside you.'

He turned to the big man and offered his hand. Before Lunaris had time to take it, they heard a shout from the quayside and a legionary ran up to them.

'Sir, you've to report to the procurator,' he said, belatedly remembering to salute.

Valerius frowned. 'What does he want with me?'

'The Iceni have risen.'

Maeve witnessed Queen Boudicca's terrible revenge.

One by one, warriors nailed the men of Crespo's command to the doorposts along Venta's main street with their arms and legs broken, in a mockery of Roman crucifixion. Crespo himself was last to be fixed. They stripped him naked and carried him to the main gate as he struggled and protested, pleading for a mercy he would never have given. They stretched his arms brutally to left and right and when the carpenter hammered the first of the big iron nails through the palm of his right hand into the wooden boards of the gate he shrieked in agony and called out to Mithras for aid. By the time they had fixed his feet in similar fashion he was delirious with pain but still aware enough to understand what was happening.

Boudicca stood before him as he hung from the gate with every sinew of his body reminding him of his torment. When they brought the cudgels to break his bones, she held up her hand to stop them. She had a more appropriate refinement in mind for the man who had led the rape of Banna and Rosmerta.

'He was very proud when he removed my daughters' innocence. Remove his pride,' she ordered.

Crespo was still conscious when the executioner approached with the gelding knife. His screams split the night.

It was still not enough.

'This place is a stain upon my honour and the honour of the Iceni. Burn it and let the flames which consume Venta be the start of a fire which cleanses all of Britain.'

As the town blazed and his men with it, they pulled Crespo's broken body down and staked it out on the roadway outside the gate. He still lived when the iron-rimmed wheels of Boudicca's chariot crunched across his bones, but by the time the last warrior of her avenging army had passed over him the only evidence of his existence was a smear of blood and bone in the dirt.

Catus Decianus did not inspire confidence. His long nose twitched as he studied the scroll pinned to the desk in front of him and a sheen of sweat glistened on a forehead creased by worry lines. Disdain for the world about him was carved into every line of his pasty, underfed face. He looked up as Valerius entered, but immediately resumed his reading of the document.

After a few moments, he sighed. 'Inconvenient,' he said.

'I beg your pardon, sir?'

'I said this is terribly inconvenient. You are Verrens, am I correct? Tribune Gaius Valerius Verrens?'

'Yes, sir. Late of the Twentieth legion and bound for Rome.'

The procurator emitted an audible sniff and his pained expression grew more pained still. 'Yes, on the ship which should also have carried my report of the successful annexation of the Iceni into the province of Britain. But that report cannot be sent now.' He paused. 'Not until this regrettable misunderstanding can be resolved.'

Valerius wasn't sure if he'd heard correctly. 'Misunderstanding?'

Decianus peered at him with beady, sharp-set eyes. 'Of course. I have here a request from Colonia to provide reinforcements for the local militia. It is the *quaestor*'s belief that a section of the Iceni have risen in armed insurrection against the Empire. This belief, I am certain, is based on rumour and speculation. You served a recent posting in Colonia, I understand?'

'Six months over the winter,' Valerius agreed. 'I found the *quaestor* to be most capable and not a man to be diverted by . . . rumour and speculation.' It wasn't entirely true. He'd found Petronius to be arrogant, divisive and venal but he was also at the centre of a spy network which spread far up the east coast. If those spies reported trouble Valerius couldn't allow Decianus to dismiss it, which seemed to be his inclination. 'I also received information of agitators working among the Iceni, which I passed on to the *quaestor*,' he added to reinforce his point.

The procurator's lips compressed in a tight smile. 'Yet I myself spent time in the Iceni capital not more than two weeks ago and found it peaceful and the people quiescent. In any case, our standing treaty with the Iceni only allows them such weapons as are required to defend their borders. Only one in ten even owns a sword,' he ended triumphantly.

Valerius knew that was true, but treaties could be broken. He could tell where the interview was going now. He was to be part of an expedition against the Iceni. It was not a fight he would have chosen, but it was a fight he was going to have . . . if the rebellion existed.

'Nevertheless,' Decianus continued, 'I propose to send a force which I consider proportionate to the threat under the most senior commander available. These are your orders.' He handed Valerius the scroll he had been reading. Valerius hesitated. His only independent command had been the First cohort on the winter road detail. Still, he could hardly refuse. He studied the orders, which commanded him to march to Colonia with all speed and deal with the situation as he saw fit, which, if he knew the army, was as good an invitation to put his neck in a noose as he'd ever seen. It meant any decision was his and his alone. Any mistake would be his responsibility.

He pointed out the elementary error. 'This doesn't say how many cohorts I'll have under me.'

'Cohorts? I do not believe we need think in terms of cohorts,' Decianus sniffed. 'You will have one hundred and fifty men from the Londinium garrison and such other troops as are on leave or in transit. Enough to provide a stiffening for the militia and stay the panic in the *quaestor*'s heart until such time as the governor considers it necessary to move a vexillation of the Ninth legion to Colonia.' He smiled disdainfully. 'You see, Verrens, I take no chances. The governor is informed, a solution suggested and a reinforcement sent. What more should I do?'

'Sir, with respect, two hundred men is—'

'Appropriate to the threat, and as many as you will receive. Am I to understand that you are refusing this command?'

Valerius shook his head. He could protest that a force of two hundred men was as much use for defending a place like Colonia as two hundred sheep, but the procurator's mind was made up. If the Iceni came he would have to depend on Falco and his veterans.

'No, sir, I will accept the command. But I'd like to request that the men of the Twentieth who formed my escort accompany me.' Decianus frowned and

Valerius continued quickly: 'They know the area around Colonia well and have worked with the militia there.'

The procurator nodded reluctantly. 'Very well. This interview is at an end.'

'So we're not going to Mona?'

Valerius shook his head. 'No, we're going back to Colonia.'

Lunaris sucked his teeth and looked longingly westwards over the rampart of the Londinium wall. 'Mona could make a big difference. Those druids are trouble-making bastards.'

'That's true enough, but if the Iceni really have risen we'll be needed in Colonia.'

'Two hundred of us?' Lunaris scoffed. 'If nothing's happened all we'll have done is waste *caliga* leather. And if they've really decided to try to kick us out . . .'

'Falco will be glad to see us.'

The *duplicarius* shrugged. 'I suppose orders are orders. The Mules will miss us in Mona, though.'

'We're marching at dawn. Have the men ready.'

'With these buggers?' Lunaris nodded gloomily at a pair of garrison rats leaning against the parapet of the nearest watchtower. 'By the time we get there I'll be carrying them.'

XXX

Three days later, after a forced march of sixty miles, Valerius recognized the familiar low outline of Camulodunum's turf walls on the far horizon. They were as impressive as any fortifications he'd seen on the island, yet he knew they'd been given up without a fight when Claudius's invasion force arrived. He believed he understood why. To properly defend walls of that scale would demand a garrison far beyond the capabilities of the Trinovantes, who had held Camulodunum then, even if they had possessed the will to fight for them. On the way from Londinium he'd given much thought to the problems of defence and he had come to one devastating conclusion. The town of Colonia could not be held against any reasonable-sized force by the veterans whose duty it was to protect it.

That conclusion was reinforced when he rode up the hill towards the familiar arch of the town's west gate with the two hundred weary men of his tiny command in tight formation behind him. He noted again the enormous gaps in the walls and the warren of streets behind where an enemy could turn a flank or launch an attack from the rear. He saw only one possibility to defend part of the town and it could only be considered as a last resort.

He thought he could rely on Falco. Petronius and his council were likely to be a different matter.

The *quaestor* stood in the shadow of the arch along with half the town and the cheering began while the legionaries were still a hundred paces away. Valerius bit his lip in frustration. A civic welcome was the last thing he needed. Horns blared and someone had brought out a drum that beat in time to the soldiers' marching feet. When he reached Petronius and Falco, standing side by side a dozen yards in front of the crowd, Valerius could barely hear their greeting. Relief was written clearly on their faces.

'You have come at last.' Petronius's narrow face wore a wide smile, but it was strained and he had aged since Valerius had last seen him. 'The council has voted to select a fine bull to be sacrificed in your honour and to thank Divine Claudius for our salvation.'

Valerius exchanged glances with Falco, who had been straining for a glimpse of something in the far distance. He shook his head imperceptibly, and the older man's eyes widened.

'I fear you may be premature, sir,' he told the *quaestor* quietly. 'We are all the procurator has seen fit to send you.'

Petronius looked as if he might faint, and Falco took Valerius by the arm and whispered furiously. 'This is all? But we asked for four cohorts at least, and cavalry. Fifteen hundred men. What good is two hundred against the entire might of the Iceni?'

The cheers gradually subsided to a confused murmur as the crowd realized no legion followed Valerius's pathetic little band. A male voice demanded to know what was happening and Petronius glanced over his shoulder. Valerius saw that the *quaestor* was frightened. In Petronius that didn't surprise him, but it was a shock to see his expression mirrored by Falco, who had fought his way across the Tamesa and led the charge which had brought about Caratacus's final defeat. 'I need to know everything,' he said.

They met five minutes later in an anteroom of the basilica looking out over the Forum. From the open window Valerius could see groups of veterans practising their swordplay, while others watched, shouting advice and laughing at their efforts, and children waved short sticks to mimic their fathers and grandfathers.

Petronius stood talking animatedly to a short, sturdily built Celt whose bristling grey moustache gave him the look of a surly dog otter. 'This is Celle,' Petronius introduced the newcomer. 'He makes what living he can hunting and fishing in the wetlands by the coast. He is one of my informants and was able to approach close to the Iceni camp, where their queen invokes the spirit of the wolf, the hare and the horse to preach painful death to all Romans. Not close enough, he admits, to gain full knowledge of this Boudicca's thoughts and strategies – he aroused the suspicions of an Iceni scout and was forced to kill him – but close enough to gain worthwhile intelligence upon her strength.'

Valerius studied the man, who looked out of place in a travel-stained cloak and ragged trews against the stark cleanliness of the white walls. 'Can he be trusted?'

Petronius scowled as if his own loyalty had been questioned. 'Celle has no reason to love the Iceni,' he said. 'Five years ago his children were taken as slaves and his wife killed when they raided his camp in some dispute over fishing rights. He has never failed me.' He made a sign to Celle, who spat out an unbroken stream of sentences in a dialect Valerius couldn't understand.

Falco translated, and his words fell into the silence like stones into a tomb. 'He says you should know that the army of Boudicca is reckoned to be fifty thousand strong – fifty thousand warriors.'

Valerius felt the blood drain from his face. It wasn't possible. The entire Iceni tribe numbered fewer than forty thousand; even fielding every man and boy and arming them with scythes and hoes there could not be more than twenty-five thousand.

Falco saw the disbelief on his face. 'This is the message we sent to the procurator. The Catuvellauni and the Trinovantes have rallied to Boudicca's cause. Kings and princes, chiefs, nobles and warriors, even the workmen from the fields. And more arriving every day, including from the Brigantes in the north. Friendship, apparently, is less binding than the scent of loot. Now do you understand why we are afraid? We asked Catus Decianus to send us enough soldiers to hold off the Iceni until the governor could return to meet the threat. Instead, he sent you.' The grizzled veteran smiled bitterly. 'I am happy to see you again, Valerius, but I would have preferred a more substantial gift.'

'The governor is not coming. Decianus will not disturb him.'

Falco grimaced, and Petronius's face went even whiter, if that were possible.

'But why?' Petronius asked. 'My message was plain.'

'He does not believe you.'

While Petronius called a full meeting of the *ordo* and senior militia officers, Valerius walked a circuit of what remained of the walls with Lunaris. He'd learned that, only days before, the council had belatedly agreed the city defences were more important than the feelings of the property developers who had torn down the walls to make way for their villas and gardens. The *duplicarius* shook his head:

'Too late. It would take a thousand men months to make this place defensible again. We'd have to tear down houses, rebuild the walls and demolish every hut for two hundred paces to give ourselves a clear field of fire. Even then I don't think we'd have enough men to defend a perimeter of this size.'

Valerius grunted agreement. 'Falco reckons he can scrape together two thousand of his veterans and a few hundred able-bodied civilians who will be more trouble than they're worth. Bela has had his cavalry patrolling the north road, but I've told him to pull back and form a screen ten miles north of here. They should give us a reasonable amount of warning of any attack and when they withdraw it will give us five hundred more, but I think they'll be more useful on horseback than manning a wall.'

'What about the signal station on the Venta road?'

'They stay where they are and fight their way out at the first sign of trouble,' Valerius said decisively.

'We both know what that means.'

Valerius nodded. He had just sentenced eight men to death. The Iceni would overwhelm them in minutes, but the warning they gave could be decisive. He tried to put the image of the disgruntled Tungrian commander out of his mind but he was haunted by the legate's words of a few months before: *There will be a day, Valerius, when your soldiers are mere coins to be spent.* Well, the day had come sooner than he'd believed possible. 'How are the men?'

'Our people – Gracilis, Luca, Paulus, Messor and

the rest – are good, and the lads from Londinium are prime soldiers, but . . . you've heard the stories?'

'That rubbish about the sea turning red?'

'And the statue on top of the temple falling over.'

'Pushed over is more likely,' Valerius said dismissively. 'Most of the local Trinovantes may have disappeared to hide or join the rebellion, but there are enough left to cause trouble. It wouldn't have taken more than two men with a couple of ropes.'

Lunaris grinned. 'You're right, but you know what soldiers are like. Superstitious.' His hand rose to touch the amulet at his neck.

'Tell them what I said, and the next time someone whispers in their ear have them arrested for spreading rumour and dissent.'

'It's time,' Lunaris reminded him.

'Yes, it's time.'

They were too many even for the *curia*, so Colonia's hundred leading citizens and a hundred more packed into the main meeting room of the temple precinct. Corvinus was there, his dark eyes concerned and seeking out Valerius; Didius, the moneylender, sleek and calculating, but nervous for once; and a dozen others he knew. The men who had driven the city's development since Claudius agreed its foundation and the men who had profited from it since. Perhaps a third of them were in their militia uniforms, the rest in the purple-striped togas that marked their office.

Valerius knew his message wouldn't be palatable for any of them.

'I am going to give up the city.'

The announcement was greeted with uproar. Men clamoured to be allowed to speak, demanding precedence from Petronius who sat slumped in his seat looking bewildered and defeated. Even the veterans, conditioned to a lifetime of authority, appeared close to mutiny and Falco stood among them as grim-faced as any.

Valerius raised his voice above the dissent. 'There is no choice,' he said. 'We cannot defend this city against fifty thousand warriors, or even half that. If the walls were unbroken I would not attempt it with the force we have. You must prepare the old, the sick, and the women and children to leave at dawn tomorrow for Londinium. Provide them with enough food and water for four days. Requisition every cart and carriage in the city, but keep the baggage to a minimum. Lives are more valuable than treasure.'

'Are we cowards that we flee before a rabble of Celts whose arses we kicked twenty years ago?' The voice came from the far end of the room and Valerius had to crane his neck to see who had spoken: a gnarled, grey-bearded farmer who had been a legionary officer and was now centurion of the Second cohort of the militia.

'Not cowards, Marcus Saecularis, and I for one will not flee. If we run they will be on our necks like a pack of jackals. If we try to defend the city they will cut our little army into a hundred pieces and hunt us through the streets like rats.'

'What, then?' It was Falco.

Valerius nodded acknowledgement. He needed this man's help more than any other. Without Falco's co-operation Colonia was doomed.

'There is a chance we can convince them to bypass Colonia. If we make a show of force in the right place and appear to have enough strength they will be wary. The rebellion is in its infancy and its leaders need a quick victory to cement the loyalty of their followers. They won't relish attacking what they believe is a full legion.'

'And if that doesn't work?'

Valerius allowed his eyes to wander over the crowd of faces, so each man would believe he was speaking to him and him alone.

'We will do what a legion does best,' he said and he saw Falco's eyes flash with comprehension. 'We will fight them on our ground and our terms. When we receive word of the barbarians' approach we will march out to meet them. I intend to use the river in place of the walls we do not have. Our greatest strength is our unity and our discipline. We will remind them of the price that must be paid for defying Rome.'

'Are there enough of us?' the militia commander asked. 'Less than three thousand against fifty thousand?'

Valerius hesitated, unsure of his next words. Then

a familiar hard-edged voice from a few short weeks earlier gave him his answer. 'If the militia cannot hold Colonia its people do not deserve to keep it.'

The words were met with a disbelieving silence. He saw the shock on Falco's face and a moment later a roar of fury filled the room. A militia centurion surged towards him and was only held back from physical assault by two of his compatriots. They hated him now. But that was good. If he could only channel that hatred against the Iceni, then, perhaps, they had a chance.

Petronius called for order. They did not like it, but no one wanted a debate. Valerius carried the procurator's authority and to disobey him meant mutiny.

Still some argued against evacuation, those who wanted to stay with their wives and children and defend what was theirs, but they were in a minority. Everyone in the room knew of Celts no longer in Colonia who were now in the north, sharpening their swords. They remembered the humiliations that had been meted out to their neighbours; fear of their return and Valerius's calm authority did the rest. When the issue was settled, he explained how the exodus must be organized, who would lead the convoy, who would command the escort, how much baggage would be allowed. When he had their agreement, Petronius issued his orders and they filed silently out of the room, each man considering how he would tell his wife, how much she would be able to carry and where he would bury what she could not.

As they were leaving, Valerius drew Falco aside. 'You were right,' he apologized. 'We do not have enough men. But that wasn't what they needed to hear.'

Falco studied him, his expression thoughtful. 'I've heard many calls to arms, Valerius, but none quite so direct. Caligula could have learned much from you.'

Valerius smiled. A double-edged compliment, if it was a compliment at all. But he sensed no lasting damage had been done.

'There is one thing you should know, Primus Pilus,' he said formally. 'When we have fought them, and fought them again, when their bodies lie in heaps before our swords, but still they come at us, then I will retire here, to this temple precinct, to make a last stand. The priests will complain that it is sacrilege, but I am a practical man, and I believe I have the support of the gods. We will stock the temple with what supplies and water we can. If you or any of your men are isolated in the fighting make for the temple. You will be among friends. Now, we have much to do.'

What followed was a night of chaos such as the province had never witnessed.

They poured into Colonia in their thousands. Bewildered families torn from the security of their homes, terrified of what might be to come. Rich or poor, they were all the same class now, homeless refugees fleeing before an avenging army which would show them no mercy.

Of course there were not enough carts to take them all. Valerius ordered that those available be used to transport the youngest children, the sick and the old who could hardly put one foot in front of the other. But what mother would willingly be separated from her child? What daughter from her aged father? In the midst of the pandemonium he came across Lunaris attempting to separate two women as they fought, screaming and cursing, for places on the transport for their children. At another time Valerius would have laughed at the look of bewilderment on the legionary's face.

'What am I supposed to do with them?' Lunaris demanded, holding the pair at arm's length as they tore at each other's hair and ripped dresses from breast and shoulder.

'Throw them in the river,' Valerius suggested. He said it loud enough for the combatants to hear the real intent in his voice and the struggling subsided. Lunaris grinned and the two women separated, still spitting at each other, and retreated to opposite ends of the convoy. Valerius helped a blind man, separated from his carer for the first time in ten years, as he wandered along the line, arms outstretched, politely asking if anyone had seen Julia. A little later he witnessed two of Colonia's hard-bitten prostitutes giving up the space they had paid for in gold to a distraught young mother with a squealing baby in her arms and a wide-eyed, snot-nosed infant pulling at the skirts of each leg.

But he couldn't be everywhere. In the first of many accidents, a bewildered five-year-old girl, perched on the rim of an open wagon already doubly over-burdened, tumbled into the path of an iron-shod wheel and shrieked as the bones of her legs were shattered. They did what they could to comfort her but she died within minutes, her eyes still wide with shock.

Three hours after midnight Luca, one of the young legionaries who formed his escort, called Valerius forward to where an angry crowd had gathered by one of the carts.

'What's happening here?' he demanded. The wagon had a raised oilskin canvas secured so the contents were invisible, but the body was settled low over the axles and it was clearly heavily loaded. A bulky woman with her face hidden by a hood sat on the rim, holding the reins.

Luca shrugged at the suspicious faces around him. 'They say something's not right about this cart. They asked the woman to take one of their children, but she won't let them near it. All she does is shake her head. Maybe she's a mute?'

Valerius studied the figure at the reins and noticed that her hands shook as she held the leather straps. Noticed something else, too. By Mars's sacred beard, didn't he have enough to do? He reached out and pulled back the hood to reveal Bassus Atilius, one of Colonia's most successful merchants, fat, unshaven and glaring in a woman's grey dress. Sickened, Valerius took the terrified trader by the neck and threw him on to the ground.

'Kill him.' The shout came from the rear of the crowd.

'Keep them back,' Valerius ordered, untying the straps on the wagon to reveal Bassus's wife huddled among several large boxes. He helped the woman down and picked up one of the boxes and tipped it over the side, where it burst open to reveal dozens of pieces of fine copperware. Other boxes followed, each filled with similar items, including silver plate and ornaments. Bassus grovelled among them as his wife hid her face.

'Please, they are everything I have. I must save them.'

Valerius held up a sack, such as a farmworker might use to carry his midday meal, marvelling at the weight of it. He looked inside to see hundreds of gold *aurei* winking back at him, each coin glowing as if the owner spent long hours polishing them. When he saw the sack, Bassus cried out.

'Kill him,' the voice repeated.

Valerius drew his sword and stared in the direction of the voice. Now Bassus cowered at his feet, pleading for mercy. 'If you want him dead, kill him yourself.'

A growl went up from the crowd, but no man moved.

'At least take his gold.'

'No, we are not thieves. Do you want to sink as low as this man, who would have sacrificed you and your children for a few pots and pans?' He looked out over them, women and boys mostly, but a few older militia men. Not many would meet his eyes. 'His is the greed that is bringing the Iceni to your door. The kind of greed that does not know the meaning of the word enough.' He tossed the gold down at Bassus, where it landed with a hefty clink. The trader grasped the sack to him. 'Luca, find a place in the wagons for the woman, then take this man to the bridge and set him over it. We'll see how many gold pieces it takes to buy Boudicca's mercy.'

For the rest of the night the legionaries were thrown about like dry leaves in an autumn gale, re-assuring, bullying and pleading, sometimes lashing out with fist and boot, until the first purple hint of dawn bruised the ink-black sky above the city and a semblance of order appeared from the mayhem.

Bela, the Thracian cavalry commander, appeared with thirty of his troopers, who lined up on their big horses on each side of the convoy. It would be a frustrating journey for the men, restricted to the speed of the slowest ox cart, but at least, Valerius thought, it would spare their horses for what was to come.

Fighting back exhaustion, he walked along the line of carts, checking everything was in its place and that he'd dealt with all the tiny, niggling, dangerous problems which had arisen through the night. A well-dressed woman he thought might be Petronius's wife glared at him as he passed, as if he was to blame for her plight, but many thanked him, and not just those he would necessarily have expected it from. Others still looked to him for some reassurance. They wanted to know that they would be coming back; that everything would be as it was before. He smiled and nodded, but it was a lie. These women were leaving their lives behind along with their husbands and nothing would ever be the same again. He watched a hundred last goodbyes. Longing kisses and unchecked tears. Heartbreaking pleas to be allowed to stay behind and brave whatever was to come together. A father clutched his newborn babe to his breast until his wife took it from his arms for fear he would hurt it. When the sun came up and he reached the front of the convoy where Bela waited, he knew the cries of the children would stay with him until he died.

The young Thracian stood at his horse's neck, holding his burnished helmet carelessly in one hand, his shale-dark hair ruffled and untidy. Bela had the look of a young Alexander and the confidence to match, but his eyes were solemn and as Valerius approached he sniffed the air. The Roman shot him a questioning look.

'Smoke,' Bela explained. 'But only the smoke of your cooking fires. When they come the smoke will be different because they will burn everything.'

Valerius nodded. 'Your instructions are clear?'

The cavalryman smiled. 'Of course. I deliver my precious cargo and then return, but not before making a personal visit to the procurator.'

'Where you will forcefully express my concerns.'

'Where I will forcefully express your concerns at the risk of my career.'

'And the other messages I ordered to be sent?'

'Janos will carry your personal letter direct to the governor, but it will take some days and I fear he is unlikely to be of help. Petur should reach the camp of the Ninth by tonight if they have not already marched.'

'Let us pray they have. Go, then, and may Mars protect you.'

Bela took his hand and his gaze swept back over the mile-long line of wagons. 'Yesterday we sacrificed a foal to Heros, the chief of our own gods. It was a good sacrifice – but I will accept any help I can get.'

XXXI

Valerius watched the tail of the convoy lumber down the hill towards the gap in the ancient Trinovante walls and the long journey to Londinium. When the road was finally empty he waited for a few moments before turning and walking slowly back through the arch into Colonia.

'Will you inspect my men, tribune?'

Falco stood on the main street outside the goldsmith's shop alongside Corvinus. Normally a hundred people would be in this section even at this hour, buying or selling or just looking. Now it was eerily silent. An empty wicker birdcage rolled back and forth outside one of the other shops and the curtain flapped in an empty doorway.

'It would be my privilege, Primus Pilus.' Valerius

bowed. 'And perhaps you would do me the honour of inspecting mine.'

The militia commander looked pleased at the compliment. Strange that the years seemed to have dropped away from him during the long, punishing night, while the goldsmith's burden appeared to have doubled.

They walked towards the Forum past Lucullus's townhouse and Valerius remembered the day he'd read his father's letter pleading for his return to Rome. A shiver ran through him and he looked up at the sun rising strong and bright over the roof of the great temple. It brought back memories of other suns; fierce Tuscan suns and suns glittering on the azure sea at Neapolis, the sun on his back when he had made love to his first woman and the sun that had highlighted the stark bones on his mother's face a week before she died. There had been so many suns. Would this be his last?

Falco said sadly, 'My slaves buried the *amphorae* with my best wines in a pit outside the east gate. I didn't have the heart to smash them and watch all those years of effort go to waste. A pity you didn't arrive a few days earlier – we could have given them the send-off they deserved.'

'Anything is better than leaving them for the Celts,' Corvinus said bitterly, and Valerius wondered what he'd done with the accumulated treasures and profits of nine years. Buried, most likely, somewhere safe where he could recover them if . . . He realized he'd

338

not seen the goldsmith's wife among the women in the carts. But then there had been so many.

They reached the temple precinct where Lunaris and the soldiers from the Londinium garrison were already working to reinforce the main gateway.

'I want every spare weapon brought here. Spears, swords, bows, even stones, anything that can stop a man.'

'Petronius has the key to the armoury,' Falco pointed out.

Valerius called for his clerk. He scrawled something quickly on a wax tablet and handed it to the wine merchant. 'This is my order to open the armoury and empty it. If he refuses or attempts to delay, break down the doors. Lunaris!' he roared.

The big man laid down the baulk of timber he was carrying towards the gate and jogged across to them. 'Sir,' he acknowledged, his broad face shining with sweat.

'Water?'

Lunaris frowned. 'There's a well in the far corner and a tank in one of the buildings on the north side that's fed by a bucket chain from the river. Only Mithras knows how long we can depend on them.'

'Not for long. Get some men and gather every *amphora* you can find. I need them filled and sealed and then stored inside the temple with a guard over them. Food, too. Have every house searched and what food there is brought here.' He studied the sun again. Its heat was already making the red-tiled roofs of the temple complex shimmer. 'And make sure every man has a full water skin. I don't mind if they die but I don't want them dying of thirst.' He saw Lunaris hesitate. 'What?'

'The temple. We've been having a problem with the priests. They don't want to let us near the place and the Mules are frightened they offend the god. We can't even get into the offices and stores.' He nodded to the buildings of the east range, where two white-robed men stood outside a doorway watching the soldiers suspiciously. Something else he ought to have thought of, Valerius realized. He should have insisted the augurs and their masters were evacuated with the convoy.

'Leave the priests to me,' he said and marched off towards them.

Lunaris grinned. Suddenly he felt a little sorry for the blood-sucking chicken murderers who'd been making his life difficult all morning.

Valerius recognized the younger priest as the augur who had refused payment for telling his future seven months earlier. What was it the man had said? *You have much to gain but more to lose if you continue along the road you have chosen.* Well, he had gained Maeve and then lost her. He had followed his road here, where there was more to lose still. He knew the perils of meddling with the imperial cult. Retribution was more likely to be earthly than divine and the punishments were very specific, very painful and very permanent. But he had a more immediate concern.

He had been ordered to defend Colonia, and defend it he would. Even if it was only this small portion of it. At any cost.

'You are in charge of the temple?' he asked the older of the two, a bulky man with thinning fair hair and frightened eyes that never stayed still.

'Marcus Agrippa,' the priest said, as if his name should be familiar. 'I have responsibility for the Temple of Divine Claudius and I must protest at the high-handed manner in which your soldiers are desecrating this sacred ground. I intend to write to Rome, sir,' he blustered, 'and I will mention your name.'

Valerius smiled coldly and looked around to where Lunaris was now jogging up the temple steps with an *amphora* under each arm. The younger priest recognized the dangerous change in the atmosphere and stepped away from his colleague.

'By order of the governor, this temple and everything and everyone in it are now under military authority.' He had no orders from the governor, but compared with sacrilege it seemed a minor offence. 'I'm sure Divine Claudius as a military man will understand. You are obstructing a vital military operation and under military law may be subject to summary justice. What's inside here?' He pushed between the two men and shook the door, which was solid and obviously locked.

'That is a private area,' the older priest cried. 'There is nothing of military value there.'

341

'Let me be the judge of that.' Valerius put his foot to the wooden panel and the lock snapped, allowing the door to swing open. He looked inside. 'You will take every piece of furniture and every carpet, every statue and every wall hanging and carry them to the temple. Tell the tall soldier there that I want the area between the columns fortified around the area of the *pronaos*.'

'But this is . . .' the priest protested.

Valerius very deliberately slid his sword from its scabbard. The *gladius* came free with an ominous whisper and the edge glinted blue in the morning sunlight. 'Perhaps you did not understand the meaning of summary justice.'

The priest's mouth dropped open and he scuttled through the door, from where there came the satisfying sounds of furniture scraping on the mosaic floor.

'What are you waiting for?' he growled at the young augur.

'I wondered where I could find a sword, sir,' the boy said, nervously eyeing the *gladius*.

Valerius almost laughed, but he knew that would have shamed the lad. Courage could be found in the most unlikely places and he had need of all the courage he could get. He had another warrior. 'Well . . .'

'Fabius, sir,' the boy volunteered.

'Well, Fabius, when you've finished here talk to Lunaris at the temple. Tell him I said to station you in the *pronaos*.'

He walked the seventy paces back to the temple studying his surroundings, seeking out anything that could give the defenders an advantage, or any vulnerable point where the enemy could gain one in their turn. The front wall with the gateway in the centre was the most obvious weakness and therefore the most likely place the Britons would attack. So, when the time came, if he was still alive, that was where he would place his strongest force and he would use that wall to wear them down. He would keep a strong reserve – he shook his head. How could he use a word like strong in a situation like this? As strong as he could afford, then – by the temple steps ready to react if the barbarians broke through anywhere. Yes, he was satisfied he could make them pay dearly for the front wall.

But there were four walls. What about the east, west and north? He considered the east first. Sturdy single-storey offices and storerooms beneath a tiled roof that pitched upwards and ended where it met the wall, which on the sheer outer face was higher by far than the combined height of two men. The north? He realized there was a gap in his knowledge and abruptly changed direction and marched out of the front gate to make a circuit of the outer walls. The inner wall was a continuation of the covered walkway which also included the west side of the precinct but outside, he noted with satisfaction, it backed directly on to the slope which fell away to the flat meadows that edged the river. An enemy without siege equipment would have to be very determined to climb the slope and then take on a surface without the slightest hold for hand or foot. He gazed down towards the meadow, where the thick, sweet grass ended so abruptly against the silver ribbon of the water. That was the key. This was an enemy without climbing ladders and siege towers or the knowledge to manufacture them. An enemy who favoured frontal attack above all else. Yes, it would do. But when he rounded the corner he discovered something that wouldn't do at all. Along the outer west wall an almost continuous line of crude lean-to shacks had been built, which, on closer inspection, were being used to store building materials. Any of them could make a ready platform for an enemy assault.

He stopped at the gate on his way back to the temple, where Gracilis, the Twentieth's hard-case wolf hunter from the Campanian mountains, was supervising the strengthening of the defences.

'Take some men and tear down the huts along the west wall. And while you're at it, clear everything for a javelin throw in front of this gate. I want a killing ground from there to about there.'

Gracilis grinned and saluted. Like all legionaries, the only thing he liked better than fighting and drinking was destroying someone else's property. 'Should we burn them, sir?' he said hopefully.

Valerius shook his head. No point in creating smoke to warn the enemy. 'Just break them up and add them to the barriers.'

A line of legionaries passed water jars into the interior of the temple as Lunaris watched the final pieces of the barricade around the *pronaos* being put into place between the massive pillars. The *pronaos* formed the outer area of the temple and behind it lay the *cella*, the inner sanctum of the cult of Claudius. 'Kind of you to send me the reinforcements,' the big man said. Valerius was puzzled, until Lunaris pointed to where Fabius peered from behind a padded couch propped against one of the columns. Someone had provided him with a helmet several sizes too large and it sat on his head like a cooking pot.

'You may thank me for him later.'

Lunaris looked thoughtful. 'Maybe they won't come.'

Valerius stood back as one of his men carelessly threw a bust of the Emperor Augustus on to the top of the barricade. 'In that case you can join me in the sack when they throw me into the Tiber.' He looked up at the temple above them. 'Do we have any archers?'

'Not among our lot that I know of. A few of the veterans may be hunters and I've seen some of the auxiliary cavalry practising with bows. Why?'

Valerius pointed to the temple roof. 'If we can get a dozen men up there they could cover the whole perimeter. I don't see how the Britons can make a direct assault anywhere but the southern wall, but—'

He was interrupted by a shout from the direction of the gate and turned to see Falco at the head of a line of veteran militia, each with a bundle of *pila* in his arms. The wine merchant's round face glowed pink with indignation.

'Enough to supply an army,' he fumed. 'That damned man. Enough spears for every soldier and this is what's left. Shields and swords too, bright as when they were forged. And for years we have made do with . . .'

'And how is our good *quaestor*?' Valerius asked mildly. 'Will he take his place in the line?'

'Vanished. He hasn't been seen since the meeting. Just as well. If I could lay my hands on him he'd wish he was with the rebels.'

'I doubt we'll miss his presence. Come. We need a stockpile of spears thirty paces behind the south wall, and another by the steps.'

Falco looked at the bustle of preparations going on around him. 'So, you mean to defend the temple. I thought—'

'No, we will fight them first beyond the walls. I am sorry,' Valerius apologized. 'I should have kept you better informed.'

The wine merchant shook his head. 'The last of the militia won't come in from the outlying farms for a few hours yet. Time enough then. We would have heard from the cavalry pickets if there was any immediate threat.'

'We will place any civilians who are willing to fight here, in the temple, with a stiffening of my men. I want only hardened soldiers in our battle line.'

Valerius imagined the terrified merchants, craftsmen and servants facing battle-crazed British champions, the bloody chaos of a splintered shield wall. 'I doubt they'd stand for long and who could blame them. If the Britons do not take fright at the sight of us . . .'

Falco laughed. 'That was a pretty fantasy you spun for the council. I almost believed it myself.'

They walked from the temple precinct back to where the ground fell away towards the river. Below them was the meadow where Valerius had inspected Falco's militia during his first week in Colonia. It seemed a lifetime ago. The river encircled it in a long curve, wide and deep enough thanks to the recent rains to provide an effective barrier against an advancing enemy with a need to move fast.

'I will burn the bridges, all but one.' He pointed to the main crossing that carried the road from Colonia north to Venta. 'That will be our bait. They are fighters, the Britons, but not soldiers. They will be drawn to the bridge because behind the bridge is where we will make our stand and their first instinct will be to annihilate us. Utterly.'

'But what if . . .'

Valerius understood his plan's weakness. 'The cavalry will patrol the near bank to ensure we are informed of any general crossing, but I do not think it will happen. If they want Colonia they must destroy us, Falco. By offering ourselves to Boudicca we can buy enough time for Paulinus to counter-march his legions from Mona. Failing that, the Ninth is only five days away in Lindum; it's possible they are already on their way to join us. If we cannot save Colonia, at least we may be able to win time for Londinium.'

A shout from one of the legionaries working on the temple defences interrupted them. Valerius instinctively turned to the north-east and saw the flare as a beacon blazed at the signal tower on the ridge. He knew the men in the tower would also be straining their eyes to the north and that twenty miles away on the far horizon they could see a tiny echo of the flame they had just lit. It would only be seconds before it was extinguished, he was sure, but it had done its job. He closed his eyes and said a silent prayer for the Tungrian auxiliaries at the station on the Venta road who had stayed at their posts to the end.

They would not be the last.

'She is coming, then,' Falco said solemnly.

'Did you ever doubt it?'

The older man shook his head. 'At least the women and children are safe.'

Bela rode in an hour later slumped over the neck of a blown horse near crippled by the vivid red slash where a sword had sliced its haunches and groaning with the agony of an iron spear point still embedded in his ribs. Two of the Thracians held their commander upright in the saddle long enough for him to make his report to Valerius.

'Cowards. They ambushed us in a wood.' Bela's face shone with sweat and he flinched with the pain of each word. 'They blocked the way with a felled tree and were on both sides of the road. Spears, arrows and slings out of hiding and we had no reply. At first our women stayed among the wagons, but what could they do when one after the other they saw their little ones spitted by arrows or spears? In their terror they sought any way out of the trap. But there was no way. We . . .' His body shuddered at the memory. 'We could hear the screams from among the trees.' He raised his head to look Valerius in the eye. 'They will have spared none.'

Valerius thought of all the escapees he had helped into the wagons less than twelve hours before. The sad, grateful smiles on the faces of mothers torn between the hurt of being separated from their husbands and gratitude that at least their children would be safe. He wondered about the fate of the blind old man and the whores who had given up their places in the cart. Were they picked off one by one by their faceless enemy? Did they rush into the woods to be butchered? It didn't matter. He had failed them all. This was his fault, in his arrogance and his pride. But there were things he needed to know before he could mourn them.

'Bela, who were they and how many were there?' Was it possible Boudicca had already bypassed Colonia and was making for Londinium? The Thracian was on the point of collapse, but this was no time for pity. He had to know. He laid a hand on Bela's shoulder and felt the two men holding him stiffen protectively. 'Tell me,' he demanded.

'A few hundred, no more.' The cavalryman coughed, and a thin line of blood ran from the corner of his lip to his chin. 'Locals, I think, scum taking advantage of the chaos and lured by the prospect of blood and gold.' His head slumped forward and Valerius released him.

In a flat voice the trooper on Bela's left said, 'We charged them six times, and six times they repulsed us. We are all that is left. He would have stayed and died with the rest if we had not carried him away.'

'I know,' Valerius said, patting him gently on the arm. 'Take him to the infirmary and get some rest. Say nothing of this to anyone.'

He sent for Falco, who read the look on his face and turned pale.

'All?' he asked quietly.

Valerius nodded. 'The Thracians did what they could, but there were not enough of them.'

Falco closed his eyes and swayed on his feet and Valerius knew he was thinking of his plump wife, as courageous as any soldier as she sat stiff and erect with their nine-year-old son in the first wagon. But he could not be allowed to think for too long.

'Will your men fight better for knowing or not knowing?'

The wine merchant's eyes snapped open and his nostrils flared. 'You forget yourself, tribune,' he rasped, and Valerius had a glimpse of the old Falco, who had terrorized the Twentieth legion for two decades. 'The Colonia militia will fight and that is all *you* need to know.'

'I need them to fight with fire in their bellies not tears in their eyes.' Valerius kept his voice hard. This man was his friend, but he could not afford to show weakness.

'If I can fight with both, they can fight with both,' Falco said fiercely. 'The answer is that I have served with these men for a lifetime, they are my comrades and they deserve to know. The veterans of the Colonia militia will stand, they will fight and they will die, tribune, and you will go on your knees and seek my forgiveness before the end.' He turned and walked stiffly away, an old man carrying all the burdens of a life on the march on his shoulders in a single moment.

XXXII

Late in the afternoon, Valerius gathered his officers in the long room in the temple's east wing – the one with the painting of Claudius accepting the surrender of Britain. He doubted whether they saw the irony of it. What wouldn't he give now for even one of those four legions displayed there on the wall, their armour and their spear points glinting? With a full legion at his back he would have marched northwards to meet Boudicca and left the rebellion stillborn, her army either shattered or so mauled that she would have no choice but to turn back and regroup. But he didn't have a full legion. He had two thousand of Falco's veterans, the two hundred men he had brought from Londinium and a few hundred of Bela's cavalry.

The young Thracian lay back stiffly on a padded couch recovered from the temple's barricade with his chest heavily bandaged and his eyes fever bright with whatever drug he'd been given to ease the pain. He had insisted on attending the final briefing even though he could barely stand. Falco stood among his cohort commanders with his face set in a mask of grim intent and refused to meet Valerius's eyes. The men surrounding him took their mood from their leader, but there were those who couldn't hide the signs of their grief or their nervousness. He searched for any other suggestion of weakness, but found none. These men still had their pride, even though time had marked them as it had marked the uniforms they wore. He knew some resented his youth, but with Falco's support he had no doubt they would accept his authority. Lunaris leaned against the side wall, his tall frame relaxed and his face expressionless.

'I have had word from our scouts.' Valerius's voice silenced the subdued murmurs. 'If the Britons march hard, their vanguard will be here well before dawn. It is difficult for one man to judge, but the trooper who carried the message believes that Petronius's spy did not exaggerate their strength.' He paused and waited to see if any of them reacted to that terrible truth. There were no doubts now. They would be enormously outnumbered. 'Yet any man who has studied history knows that sheer numbers need not guarantee the outcome of a battle. Alexander had only half as many troops as the Persian Darius when he triumphed at Issus. Caesar himself defeated

Pompey the Great at Pharsalus when he was out-numbered by more than two to one.'

'Not twenty to one, though.'

Valerius was surprised at the intervention from Corvinus, whose support he had assumed. 'No,' he admitted. 'Not twenty to one. But these were soldiers fighting soldiers. We are soldiers fighting barbarian warriors. Does any man here doubt that ten legionaries are worth a hundred of these Britons?'

'No!' At least half of them growled the reply, and Valerius smiled.

'Two to one, then.' To a man, they laughed, even Falco. He allowed them their moment and then continued seriously. 'I do not intend us to fight fifty thousand or even ten thousand. We will burn every bridge but one and the rebels will be drawn to the remaining crossing like wasps to a rotting peach. Only a few thousand will be able to cross at one time and those thousands will die before our swords.' He didn't allow any arrogance to creep into his voice. These men were not fools. 'No, I do not expect to win,' he answered their unspoken question. 'I am no Caesar or Alexander and there are too many of them. Even a veteran's arm must tire. We will bleed, just as they do. That is why I have fortified the temple. At the last we will withdraw here.' And here we will die. They all knew it. No one needed to say it.

'Why not fight from the temple in the first place?' Corvinus demanded, and was rewarded with a rumble of support. 'With close to three thousand men and enough food and water we could hold the grounds for a month.'

Valerius shook his head. 'And watch Boudicca burn your city to the ground around you?'

'She will burn it in any case.'

'Yes, but she won't just leave a few thousand warriors to starve us out and march on Londinium with her army intact. If they are fifty thousand strong now, how many will rally to their cause if they destroy all that is best of Roman Britain? A hundred thousand, perhaps more. Enough even to overwhelm Paulinus and his force. It would be the end of the province. We cannot allow that. By forcing her to do battle we have the opportunity to tear the heart from the rebel army, here at Colonia.'

'Why do we exist if not to fight, Corvinus?' Falco agreed. His voice was tight with emotion. 'Were all those days on the exercise ground just for sweat? No. I have lost everything I loved today and I will not watch idly as the woman responsible marches past to bring the pain I feel to thousands more.'

Valerius knew Falco's was the decisive opinion. Time was running out. There could be no more debate. 'Send engineers to burn the bridges. Prepare your cohorts. We will move into position before dark.' He had deliberated long and hard whether it was better to subject the veterans to a night in the open and the stiffening of ageing limbs, or risk the confusion of deploying in the darkness an hour or two before dawn. 'Bela?' The cavalry commander raised his head with a grimace of pain. 'Pull your horse soldiers back. They can do no more now.'

As the officers filed out he called Lunaris across. 'I want you in the temple and you are promoted to decurion.' The big legionary opened his mouth to protest, but Valerius raised a hand. 'No arguments. I need a man I can trust in command of the place where we will make our stand. We don't know how things will be when we fight our way back here.' He smiled sadly. 'At least with you in command I know I will have somewhere to run.'

As dusk fell, he stood by Colonia's north gate listening to the evening sounds and staring north. It was a blessing to have time to stop and think after a day of constant decision. The night was warm and the air still, and pairs of bats chased unseen insects between the buildings and the trees down by the river. He heard the unmistakable shriek of an owl and felt a sudden deep melancholy. Where was she now? He remembered the sweet scent of her silken hair and the softness of her flesh, the tenderness of lips he had never had the opportunity to kiss often enough, and dark eyes that flashed like wildfire; the wonder of a knowing like no other. She would support the rebellion, he guessed; her father's death had given her enough reason to hate. But would she join it? No. Cearan would keep her safe; honest, dependable Cearan who would now be torn between his duty to his queen and his determination to prevent his people from suffering. How different things would have been if he had taken the throne for himself. With a conscious effort he put the Iceni nobleman from his mind. This was no time to be feeling sympathy for a warrior he might face on the battlefield in a few hours. Had he done enough? That was the question he must ask himself. Was there any detail, however small, he had not considered that might save one legionary's life or cost one of Boudicca's warriors theirs? He felt a twinge of doubt boring into his left temple like a carpenter's drill. Doubts? Of course he had doubts. Even Caesar must have had doubts on the night before a decisive battle, but like Caesar he had to hide his doubts from everyone. He could have withdrawn the veterans back to Londinium with the convoy of women and children and saved thousands of innocent lives. It would have cost him his career and his honour, but that would have been a small price to pay. Was that why he didn't do it, to save his honour? He shook his head. No. Boudicca had to be stopped, or at the very least tested. If he could stop her here, or even make her check for a day, Londinium might be saved, and with it the entire province. He was right to fight here. Right to leave the town and the temple and make her attack him on his own ground and his own terms.

He looked at the sky: the light was dying. *Soon.*

The sound of marching feet on the metalled road behind him echoed from the houses lining the street, iron nails crunching on the compacted surface. He turned to watch them pass. The veterans of Colonia, each one a son of Empire. First Falco, at the head of his command, his sturdy figure hidden beneath a scarlet cloak and his eyes lost in the shadow of his helmet brim. At the last moment the proud head turned and the chin lifted and the old soldier gave Valerius a nod that told him more than any words. He answered the gesture with a salute, his fist clashing against his armour, and he saw Falco smile. Behind their standard-bearers five militia cohorts followed him, parading down the slope with their *pila* on their shoulders and a precision that would have graced an emperor's triumph. Each of them had lost a loved one today and he felt shame that he'd believed they would be diminished by it. Everything about the way they marched could be encapsulated in a single word. Resolve.

Behind the veterans came the bulk of the men he had brought from Londinium, minus the fifty who remained with Lunaris at the temple complex to strengthen the garrison of civilian volunteers. They must be wondering what gods had brought them to this place and this fate when they could still be back in their barracks. And what of himself? Did Neptune laugh when he called up the storm that delayed the ship carrying his replacement? If things had been different he would have been halfway home by now and, Maeve apart, would he have given the island another thought?

He followed in the column's wake as Falco dispersed his men, and then wrapped his cloak around him and lay down among the Londinium vexillation on the damp grass beside Gracilis, who had marched with him all the way from Glevum. There had never been much likelihood he would sleep but his choice of partner guaranteed wakefulness. The Campanian muttered unintelligibly through clenched teeth and from time to time he cried out as if he were already fighting the battle that would come in the morning. Eventually, Valerius could take no more and wandered in the dark down towards the bridge.

The last of Bela's saddle-weary cavalry troops rode across from the north bank as he reached it, guided by the torches of two of Falco's veterans. The unit's commander rode with his head bowed and looked to be almost asleep in his saddle.

'What is the latest news of the rebels?' Valerius reached up and shook the rider's arm, taking in the rank scent of hard-ridden horse. The eyes snapped open and the man stared down at him. He had been one of those who had helped rescue Maeve from Crespo but for a few seconds there was no recognition in his eyes. 'The rebels?' Valerius repeated.

'When we left them they were six miles away, beyond the ridge yonder. I think we were on the army's right flank, but it was impossible to say for certain. They are like a swarm of bees: just when you think you understand their route and their purpose a section will break away for no good reason and march off in a completely different direction. We lost two good men that way, trapped when they got too close.'

'Their numbers?'

The cavalryman shook his head. 'I can give you no numbers. All I can say is they are too many.' Valerius frowned. Insubordination or just plain truth? The horse shook its head, spraying him with sweat, and he caught the bridle to steady it. The troop commander leaned low to retrieve his reins, so there could be no mistaking his whispered words. 'Take your little army away, tribune. If you stand against them they will crush you into the dust and not even notice.'

Valerius looked round to see if anyone else had heard. 'A man could be whipped for saying such things,' he said.

The Thracian smiled wearily. 'A man does not need to fear the whip when he will be dead tomorrow.'

'Will you fight?'

'That is what you Romans pay us for.'

'Then take your troop and spread them out along the bank to the east. Get what rest you can, but I need to know if the enemy plans a crossing elsewhere. Wait until an hour past first light and return here. Bela will have further orders for you.'

The cavalryman held out his hand. 'Matykas, decurion of the first squadron. It was good advice, tribune; at least you're a Roman worth dying beside.'

A few minutes after the Thracians had ridden away Valerius noticed a glow in the sky above the ridge. As he puzzled over it, Falco joined him at the bridge.

'The rebels?' the militia commander asked.

'Perhaps they've camped for the night.'

'A small cooking fire for a large army.'

Valerius grunted noncommittally. He was remembering the two lost Thracian cavalrymen and the tales he had heard of the Wicker Men, the great human-shaped baskets Caesar had written of, into which the Celts threw their sacrifices to be burned alive. He hoped the two troopers were already dead.

They waited, and Valerius knew without looking round that every eye in the meadow by the river was focused on the ridge to the north.

'There,' a voice cried.

The first was to the east, just a dot of flame that, as they watched, flared into something much larger. A moment later it was followed by a second, further west this time, and a third, lower down the slope. Within minutes the dark blanket of the slope was dotted with flames like fireflies on a Neapolitan night.

'They're burning the farms,' Falco said unnecessarily.

Valerius didn't reply, but kept his eye on one particular spark at the top of the slope and to his left, where Lucullus's farm – Maeve's home – was blazing. The fact that it now belonged to Petronius and had been stripped of everything she owned provided only a small consolation.

'Thank you,' Falco said suddenly.

Valerius looked at him in surprise, and shook his head. 'You have nothing to thank me for. If I had done things differently, perhaps . . .' He thought again of the scared faces and the crying children.

'What's done is done,' the militia commander said. 'If they had stayed they would have died in any case. You came to our aid when no one else would help us. Catus Decianus,' he spat, 'set a flame to a tinder-dry thicket and left his people to burn. Paulinus, too. Where is our governor when we need him? Or the Ninth legion, who could have been here now if our warnings had been heeded? They thought we were just panicking old men. But you came, Valerius, and even when you saw your commission was impossible you stayed. We are grateful.

'I have a desertion to report,' he said, before Valerius could reply. 'Corvinus, the armourer.' He shook his head sadly. 'One of our bravest and best. It is hard to believe.'

Valerius remembered the goldsmith's nervous manner earlier in the day. Or was it yesterday? In any case, he couldn't find the anger or the outrage befitting a commander who had been betrayed. How much difference would one man make?

'Can you blame him?'

Falco looked at him seriously. 'We are soldiers, tribune. We fought together in the legions and sweated together in the militia. When the people of Colonia laughed at us as we exercised with our rusty swords we ignored them because it was our duty. We may be old men, but we still believe in duty. And comradeship. And sacrifice. So, yes, I blame

Corvinus, though he is my friend. And, if he is caught, I will nail him to a cross, though he is my friend. If at the end all I can do is die together with these men, I will count it a privilege.'

He turned away, but Valerius called him back and held out his hand. 'I too will count it a privilege.'

As Falco returned to his veterans, Valerius's eyes were drawn back to the hillside where Lucullus's farm still burned, and Boudicca's horde gathered in the darkness.

XXXIII

A dull hint of ochre on the far horizon was the first evidence of the new day, and with it came a subdued murmur that seemed to shiver in the air and which puzzled Valerius until he recalled the words of the Thracian cavalryman on the bridge. Bees, he had said. *They are like a swarm of bees.* And that was it. The sound, which grew in volume with each passing minute, resembled an enormous beehive: unseen but omnipresent, a danger, but not yet dangerous.

Then, beginning in the east, second by second and yard by yard, the darkened slope opposite was illuminated as the sun rose gently from the far end of the valley between Colonia and the ridge. And on the slope they saw their deaths.

Each of them had heard the figure of fifty thousand, but it was just that, a figure. Now they saw the reality and their minds rebelled against the evidence of their eyes. Boudicca's host covered the rise like a vast living blanket of multicoloured plaid, and still they came in their multitudes: tribes and their sub-tribes and their clans, each identified by its brightly coloured banner and led by a chief on horseback or a warlord in one of the small two-wheeled chariots of the Britons. Valerius studied them, attempting to discern some pattern or guiding mind, but he couldn't tell one tribe from another in the shifting throng. The Iceni must be a force among them, with their wronged queen somewhere at the centre of that great mass; the Trinovantes come to regain their homes and their land, and the Catuvellauni to avenge the insults of a decade; men of the Brigantes and the other northern tribes sickened by Cartimandua's betrayal of Caratacus and, inevitably given these numbers, even from Rome's allies, the Atrebates and the Cantiaci, drawn by the scent of blood and loot like carrion birds to a new kill. Through them and around them wove hundreds more chariots carrying the half-naked champions who would take their place at the front of the battle line in the position of greatest danger. Most of the warriors, though, were on foot, trudging through the meadows and the fields with their shields on their shoulders, weary now after their long march from Venta, but still eager. Many would be trained fighters, armed with the best their people could provide, but more would be the farmers, tradesfolk and servants who had picked up anything with an edge or a weight that would kill the hated enemy. All had hungered for seventeen long years for the chance to drive the Romans from their lands; rest could wait. They would be fearful, because there could be no turning back, but that would only make their hate stronger and more dangerous. Among them loped the huge attack dogs trained to tear out an enemy's throat with a single bite. Behind them, each identified by a single column of smoke, lay the way posts of their coming, the villas and farms the veterans and the settlers who followed them had taken years to build, now nothing but smouldering rubble. The militiamen watched with disbelief as a constant dark stream of humanity flowed upriver from the coast, out of the woods and over the ridge to swell the numbers opposite them. This was not an army; it was a nation on the move.

Valerius attempted to study the enemy with a detached soldier's interest, but soon he felt his mind begin to vibrate and his ears fill with a pounding he recognized as the first signs of panic. Despite the coolness of the morning a trickle of sweat ran slickly down his spine. Further along the line he heard a man vomit and another mutter a low prayer to a god who was not listening. Nothing in his imagination had prepared him for this. All his plans and stratagems were shown up for what they were: pointless diversions which would no more harm this enemy than a flea on an elephant's back.

He took a deep breath and scanned the slope again,

but could still find no apparent sign of organization or leadership. The first Britons halted a quarter of a mile north of the river, not through fear but through confusion and suspicion. He knew what they were seeing and he could understand the reaction. They would have expected the veterans to defend the city or to retreat, with their loved ones and their possessions, along the Londinium road. Instead, they were confronted by this tiny force, like a sickly lamb staked out to trap a marauding wolf, and they wondered where the net was.

'Primus Pilus!'

Falco trotted from his position in the centre of the line to where Valerius stood on the left. 'Sir.' He saluted. The militia commander's face was the colour of week-old ash but his eyes held a glint of iron and his features were set and determined.

'March the First cohort forward to within forty paces of the bridge and keep the others in station.'

He had formed his force into three strengthened cohorts of just over six hundred men each. Now those cohorts marched in lines two hundred legionaries wide and three deep, one behind the other, towards the bridge and he strode at their side. The gap between each cohort was ten paces. It was the standard deep defensive formation of the legion, if on a smaller scale. It had advantages and disadvantages, but his choice of battlefield suited it as long as conditions didn't change.

The short advance brought a concerted growl from

the mass across the river, but still there was no general movement.

The bridge was the key. And the river.

The bridge stood less than a spear's throw to his front now with the road from Colonia to Venta curving from the left over the meadow towards it, then continuing across to disappear among the massed ranks on the north bank. It was a sturdy structure, built of oak, seven or eight paces in width and surfaced with thick planking. A wooden rail had been added at waist height on each side to prevent the unwary from falling into the water ten feet below.

He walked forward until he could study the river, keeping a wary eye for any enemy spearmen close enough to do him harm. It wasn't wide – he could toss a stone across it without any great effort – but it was deep and here, and for as far as he could see, the banks were steep and overgrown with trees and thorn bushes, making them an obstacle even if the water itself could be crossed. The line of flotsam told him the spate level of the past two days was falling, but it was still too deep and the current too fast for a fording to be attempted with any likelihood of success. Of course, it could be done, especially to the west where the river narrowed, but it would take time. That was why he had given her the bridge.

'Look!' Falco pointed to the ridge, where a line of chariots flanked by horsemen cut their way diagonally through the crowd. They came at a steady trot, taking no account of those who stood in their way, and gradually word spread of their progress and the cheering began. Fifty thousand voices rose in acclamation. Swords, spears and fists clashed against wooden shields with a crash to rival a thunderstorm, and a hundred of the Britons' animal-headed horns joined the clamour. She was here.

The leading chariot burst clear of the mass of warriors and reined to a halt opposite Valerius, quickly followed by the others. It was too far away to be certain, but the Roman had an impression of hair the colour of burnished copper and a long skirt of azurite blue. She waited, allowing the cheering to build, and, standing in front of the pathetically thin ranks of the leading cohort, Valerius sensed her scrutiny. He remembered the day below Venta's walls and the impression of power she had given. He sensed she was studying him now and for some reason he tensed as if he were trying to stop her from stealing his soul. Minutes passed and the feeling of being dissected from within grew almost unbearable. His legs told him to walk away and he turned, to find Falco at his side.

'I don't think they will want to talk.' The wine merchant was forced to shout to be heard above the noise.

Valerius almost laughed. Before a battle the Celtic champions were always willing to challenge a rival leader, but he agreed it was unlikely to happen today. 'A pity,' he said. 'I could have used the exercise and it would have eaten up a little more time. How are the men?'

'Nervous, but not afraid. They wish it would begin.'

Valerius looked across the river, to where the British leaders were holding some kind of discussion. 'It will be soon enough.'

As he said the words, he saw a spear raised above the lead chariot and a ripple ran through the barbarian ranks like the wind rustling through a field of ripening corn. A moment later the first of the champions appeared, big men in the prime of life, naked to the waist and of proud bearing, with their hair limed and spiked to make them seem taller. They carried long swords or iron-tipped spears and their oval shields were brightly painted with the emblems of their tribes or their clan. They were the elite of their people, bred to war and eager for the fight. For years they had been forced to accept the bitter taste of subjugation and a place at the plough or in the field, but their elders, men who had last fought the Romans on the Tamesa, had kept the old traditions alive. Trained in secret in the lonely places their conquerors never visited, they had honed their skills and worked their muscles. Waiting for the day. Now the day had come.

Valerius and Falco rejoined the militia, the wine merchant taking his place behind the front rank of the lead cohort and Valerius continuing to the rear, from where he would conduct the battle. As he passed through the ranks he had a word of encouragement for every man he knew and many he didn't and they smiled momentarily before their faces resumed the mask of grim concentration that marked a battle-ready legionary.

He remembered the first time he had seen these men, on the day he had inspected them on this very field. He and Lunaris had laughed at their ancient weapons and worn uniforms, their pot bellies and the scrawny arms that looked as if they could barely carry a spear let alone throw it. The faces ran through his mind: old Marcus Saecularis, the sheep farmer, in the centre of the front rank, with the horsehair of his crested helmet announcing his rank to any enemy; Didius, scratching his nose distractedly at the head of his century, who would lend money to any man as long as the rate of return was high enough, but whose last act before donning his armour had been to annul each and every debt; bearded Octavian, named for an emperor, who had stood in the line against Lunaris and his legionaries and had taught them a lesson in humility. And Corvinus, who had never struck him as a coward, but whose position with the fourth century of the Second cohort was left unfilled. Where was he now, when his comrades were about to . . .

'They're coming!'

Strange that the pulsating crash of sword against shield had calmed him to the point where he could watch without emotion the British champions sprint in a great surging crowd towards the bridge. Thousands of them across a front of almost a mile, each racing to be first to reach the Romans on the far side of that narrow barrier. As they advanced and the mass of warriors began to take on individual identity, he felt his heartbeat increase and his breathing deepen.

'Spears,' he roared. Each man had two of the iron-pointed *pila* embedded in the soft grass at his side and a further pair in reserve in the space between the cohorts. Now they chose one and hefted it in their right fists, balancing the weapon for the cast.

The first of the champions were still a hundred paces from the bridge. Good. They would be the fastest, the strongest and the bravest. He saw that many of them had thrown away their shields in their eagerness and their momentum was taking them ahead of their rivals. He counted down in his head. Ten seconds at most until they reached the bridge, then two more heartbeats and . . .

'Ready!'

Bare feet thundering on wooden planking. Two, one. Now!

'Throw!'

Four hundred javelins hissed through the still air for a flight that lasted a split second. The hands that held the spears might be wrinkled and the arms might have lost the awesome power of a quarter of a century before, but they could still throw and at forty paces the target was unmissable. More than two hundred warriors had crowded on to the bridge, eager to be the first to strike a blow against the Romans. Instead, they were the first to die. Heavy spears capable of punching through light armour slammed the champions in the forefront of the attack back against those behind as they took the points in chest, belly or throat. Valerius had known some of the precious weapons would be wasted, but he had to be certain. The entire bridge must be covered in that first cast. Falco had snorted disdainfully and pledged his fortune on it and the wine merchant was as good as his word. Only a handful of the men on the wooden planking survived the rain of spears and most of those were wounded or disabled. The others were pinned by one, two or even three of the weighted *pila*. Already, two hundred bodies writhed and groaned and stained the boards of the narrow bridge with their blood. But behind them came thousands more.

'Ready!' Valerius was well pleased with the result of the first throw. Every warrior now attempting to cross would be impeded by the bodies of the men who had preceded them. He waited until the first of the second surge of warriors stepped on to the dirt of the south bank.

'Throw!'

With each cast another few hundred joined the corpses on the bridge floor until a literal wall of dead and dying obstructed the attack. In their fury, those who came behind frantically bundled the bodies of brothers, friends, comrades and rivals over the barriers and into the river in an attempt to clear a path. They clawed their way forward snarling like attack dogs, only to die in their turn.

'Second cohort, to the front.' In a carefully choreographed movement the cohort behind stepped forward to take the place of those who had exhausted their supply of spears.

'Ready!'

'Throw!'

'Ready!'

'Throw!'

'Third cohort, to the front.'

'Ready!'

'Throw!'

It could not last. He knew it could not last.

Inch by inch, the Britons edged their way across the barrier of their dead. They were the invincibles, but even invincibles would use a shield if it was the only way to survive this slaughter. As the veterans' arms tired, the volleys of spears became more ragged, allowing still more to cross. A dozen turned into a hundred, and a hundred into two. Soon, Valerius knew, unless he stopped them, hundreds would turn into thousands.

'Shields up. Draw your *gladii*. Form line. Forward!'

It took time, too much time. The respite from the spears had given another four or five hundred a chance to cross and still more were crowding behind them, hampered but not halted by the dead and dying.

Now the cohorts deployed in single line, each six hundred strong, and as they marched towards the bridge he saw with relief that they still overlapped the British bridgehead, but only just. Where were Bela's cavalrymen?

He matched step with the outer man of the Second cohort and turned to grin encouragement. It was one of the younger soldiers from the Londinium garrison. He tried to remember his name, but couldn't, only that he should have been back in barracks baking bread for his century. The boy grinned back and in the same instant his right eye exploded like an over-ripe plum and he dropped to the ground as if he were a sack of river sand.

Shit! Valerius looked up to see where the missile had come from, but a howl announced that the Britons who had survived the bridge were halfway across the open ground and about to fall on the front rank of the Roman battle line. So far, the veterans' casualties had been light.

Now there was dying to be done as well as killing.

XXXIV

They died well.

The *gladii* hacked down the first shock of the British attack, and the second, but for every Celt who fell another ten rushed forward to take his place. By now only the mound of corpses and the narrowness of the bridge limited the numbers reaching the near bank. A crack like the sound of a giant axe signalled that the side rails of the structure had given way, throwing dozens to their deaths in the swollen river. Even so, thousands had already crossed and the veterans were only just holding them. Something whirred past Valerius's head, reminding him of the fate of the young legionary. The Britons had no formal units of archers, but many skilled hunters swelled the ranks of that great mass and now they lined the bushes of the far bank, picking their targets with bow or sling. The centurions' steady cry of 'Close the gaps' rang with increasing regularity as the veterans dropped. Three burly Celts pulled Octavian bodily from the Roman formation and hacked him to pieces. Didius took a spear point in the throat and went to his gods without a murmur of complaint. For now, the casualties in the First cohort could be replaced by the men in the second line, but the old soldiers were beginning to tire and the pressure was so great he couldn't gamble on resting a single man. He stepped on a body and looked down to see the baker from Londinium staring up at him with his single eye. It was the first indication that the line was moving back.

Where was Bela?

The sound of a horn gave him his answer and with relief he stepped out of the line and ran back to the higher ground where the cavalry had formed up. Not Bela, but Matykas, the trooper from the bridge who had advised him to take his little army away. The man must have been in the saddle for more than forty-eight hours, and he led only half the horsemen Valerius had expected.

'Your commander?'

The Thracian lifted his head and Valerius saw that only his spirit kept him upright. 'Dead.'

'And the rest?' There must have been a hint of unintended accusation in his words because the man's eyes flared momentarily.

'Dead too. No one ran, tribune. All fell. You put too much faith in the river.'

Valerius fought off a wave of despair. Another mistake. 'How many crossed?' he asked.

Matykas shrugged. It didn't matter now. Nothing mattered. He groaned and straightened. 'Your orders?'

Every Thracian bled from at least one wound. Their spears were splintered or gone and the coats of their worn-out cavalry mounts were flecked with foam. How could he ask any more of these men? 'I need you to take pressure off the flanks.'

The troop commander frowned and looked across the seething horde in front of the bridge as if for a few seconds he'd forgotten the battle existed. Eventually, he nodded and gave the order in his own language.

Valerius saw the reluctance in the men's faces, and the decurion snapped another spate of words. Then he looked down at the Roman. 'I told them that tonight we ride with the stars.'

'I hope it is true.'

The trooper replaced his helmet and tightened the chin strap. 'I hope so too.'

When they were gone, Valerius took a moment to survey the battle from his slightly elevated position. He was by the north gate with the bridge two hundred paces away to his right front. By now it was impossible to count the Britons who had crossed. Several thousand pressed the thinning wall of Falco's legionary veterans and thousands more streamed away to east and west, keener to be among the first to Colonia's spoils than to die on the point of a *gladius*. The Roman line curved like a hunting bow now and was edging inevitably back towards him with its outer wings threatened, three, four, five Celts hammering at each Roman shield. He watched the Thracian cavalry formation split and ride in a wide half-circle that brought the horses of the two depleted squadrons smashing into the British flanks at the same instant. For a moment a flash of bright metal showed as the long cavalry swords smashed down on exposed British skulls, but it couldn't last and the next time he looked they were gone; a hundred lives snuffed out like the flame of an oil lamp.

But those lives had not been wasted. A momentary confusion in the Celtic throng allowed Falco to restore his line and gave Valerius time to run to the militia commander's side.

'We have only one chance,' he shouted to make himself heard above the clash of iron against iron. 'There are too many now. We must form *testudo* and fight our way to the temple.'

Falco turned to him and Valerius saw that though he breathed like an overworked ox his right arm was bloody to the elbow and his eyes shone bright with the elixir of battle that made a man think he was immortal. The lined face was set in a feral snarl and he shrugged off Valerius's hand as if it were a stranger's and turned to go back to the line.

'*Testudo*,' Valerius shouted again. 'We have to form *testudo*.'

For a moment comprehension appeared on the tired features and Falco looked around at the diminishing band of his veterans. Valerius recognized the moment of decision. The little wine merchant sucked in his belly beneath the battered chain mail and came to attention.

'I fear that this is an order I must disobey, tribune,' he said. 'We pensioners have walked as far as we can today. We will stay where we stand and give you as much time as we can buy with our lives. Gather your beardless children and take them where they can do more good.'

'No,' Valerius shouted desperately as his friend turned away.

Falco looked over his shoulder and said very deliberately: 'Get them out, Valerius. Hurry. You only have minutes. I can give you no longer than that.'

He wanted to stay and die with them, but there was still another battle to fight and Lunaris would need his help. 'Londinium vexillation! Form *testudo*, on me.'

The response was automatic and immediate, the shell of the tortoise coming together over and around him. Perhaps a hundred and thirty of them were left, all of them breathing hard and many of them bloodied or limping.

Before he joined the front rank of the formation he took a last look about him. The veterans could barely hold their shields now and any man's sword arm would tire after forty minutes of hard fighting, but

Falco's militia battled on. The Britons had pushed the flanks back until what had been a line was now a small pocket of hacking, grunting, blood-soaked survivors. At the south end of the pocket one opening remained, like the neck of an *amphora*, but rapidly shrinking. Twenty feet away from him, Falco formed a small squad of a dozen wounded and exhausted men in the mouth of the opening. Valerius heard him shout for one final effort, and as he took his place at the front of the *testudo* the old wine merchant caught his eye and with a last salute led his men in a desperate charge that forced the opening back a few precious feet.

'Now,' Valerius yelled. 'North gate at the trot. We stop for nothing.'

As one, a hundred and thirty pairs of legs began pumping with all their remaining strength, and the armoured carapace smashed through the screen of warriors towards Colonia. To be inside the *testudo* after the ceaseless clamour of the battle was to enter a shadow-world where the carnage beyond the shields was of only mild interest to those within. The noise of the fighting and dying was reduced to a muffled roar and the atmosphere was like a crowded sauna shared with wild-eyed, bloodied madmen, stinking of fear and the contents of their fouled underwear, coughing and retching and cursing the gods and themselves. Here, even as your feet tripped over the faces of dead friends, it was possible to believe in a survival that a few minutes before had seemed preposterous.

'Will they get out?'

Valerius looked over his shoulder and saw that the man behind him in the tortoise was Gracilis, the tough Campanian. A sword blow had badly dented his helmet and a ragged wound scored one cheek, probably the edge of a spear that had been aimed at his eyes. It was still bleeding copiously, but Gracilis ignored it.

'No,' he grunted, as something crashed against the outside of his shield. He heard Gracilis whisper what might have been a prayer, but he had no time for prayers. The grass beneath his feet turned to metalled road surface and he made a quick calculation. 'Half left,' he called and the formation altered direction by forty-five degrees. 'Keep your shields up and your legs moving.' Momentum was everything. They were on the shallow slope up through the gate into Colonia. If he was right and the fighting had kept the Britons clear of the gate they should be able to reach the top of the hill, where they'd be only two hundred paces from the temple complex. But every step was agony now. A fire burned in his calves and thighs and his lower back felt as if it were broken. The shield, never light, seemed to have a dozen men sitting on it and he had lost all feeling in his left arm and shoulder. Around him men groaned and cried out as they called on their bodies for an effort that should have been beyond human capability. Flat. He almost shouted out in relief. The road was flat. 'Twenty paces and half left.' His voice was a rasping, wasted thing. 'Not far now, my Mules. Just one last effort.'

He risked a glance between the shields to his front and the horror of what he saw almost stole the last strength from his legs. Hundreds of rebel fighters streamed from the direction of the west gate towards the temple complex. They were trapped. He fought back panic as his mind raced for another way out, but there was none. They couldn't turn back. If they stood and fought they would be annihilated. There was only one answer. It was impossible, but it was try or die.

'They're in front of us, and if they stop us we're dead,' he shouted. 'Step up the pace and slaughter any bastard who gets in the way. Now.'

The Britons on the *decumanus maximus* were not the elite warriors the veterans had faced at the bridge; they were the farmers and wheelwrights, carpenters, potters and smiths who made up the heart of Boudicca's army. Ordinary men, not fighters but willing to fight, and not the shirkers and backstabbers who would come after, when the dying was done. Thousands of them had crossed the river and bypassed the battle in the meadow and now they sought revenge on Colonia for the years of humiliation they had suffered at the hands of the Romans. They destroyed everything that was capable of destruction, regardless of its use or value. In their rage they would batter something innocuous, an old couch or an abandoned bed, as if by destroying the inanimate object they were killing the brain that created it, the hands that made it and the body that had lain upon it. Strangely, although many carried torches and there was a strong acrid smell of smoke in the air, not many of the city's buildings were burning yet. The tiled roofs and lime-plastered walls of the barracks and the houses defied any casual attempt to ignite them. It would take more than a carelessly thrown brand to turn Colonia into an inferno.

But nothing drew them more strongly than the Temple of Claudius, symbol of Roman power and Roman domination, defiler of sacred ground and usurper of true gods, ruiner of kings and destroyer of hopes.

The *testudo* hammered into the rear of the first scattered group and the swords of the front rank hacked down any man who stood before them or simply battered them to the ground where iron-shod sandals smashed into disbelieving, upturned faces. It was called the tortoise but to those watching, astonished, from the doors and windows along the street it appeared more like an armoured galley cutting its way through a human sea, leaving in its wake a flotsam of dead and dying bodies and accompanied by an unearthly clattering, as if a hundred shields were being battered simultaneously against a hundred trees. Closer to the hated temple, the street became more crowded and logic dictated that the sheer mass of British tribesmen must slow the *testudo*, but the power of legs hardened by thousands of miles of marching and driven by an insatiable urge to survive somehow maintained its momentum. Behind his shield in the oven of the interior Valerius felt his mind empty and his exhausted body accept the tempo of the battle line. A screaming, unshaven face appeared and disappeared in a welter of blood. A spear thrust was met by an unbroken wall of shields. A dying man squirming beneath his feet was dispatched with a swift thrust to the throat. The world slowed but his own reactions quickened and it seemed that the gods marched at his side because he was beyond suffering now, in a place where no man could harm him. His body was a weapon of war yet at its centre was only peace. It was the most wonderful feeling in the world and it seemed to last a lifetime, but only moments later a voice he didn't want to hear shouted in his ear.

'Sir, the temple.'

Unwillingly, his mind returned to the real world, the world of pain, and he realized that there was nothing in front of them. To his left, the wonderful, tortured creak of a gate opening sounded like the gift of life. Still in formation with their shields raised, he led the survivors of the battle of the bridge through the walls of the Temple of Claudius.

XXXV

Inside the gate the *testudo* disintegrated into a slumped huddle of exhausted men. Valerius lay back against a wall with his eyes closed. He could hear the shouts of acclaim, but he really didn't care. He was alive. For the moment that was enough.

He removed his helmet and ran his fingers through the damp thickness of his hair, relishing the feel of the cool air on his head and neck. Sweat ran in a stream down his back and his tunic felt as if he'd been swimming in it. Someone thrust a water skin into his hand and he suddenly realized how thirsty he was. When was the last time he'd drunk or eaten? His brain didn't want him to know, but when he placed the skin to his lips the tepid, musty liquid seemed to be instantly absorbed by his brain and the skin was empty before his dust-dry mouth could benefit. He opened one eye. Lunaris stood over him silhouetted by the sun, which was still low and in the east. It didn't seem possible it was less than two hours since dawn.

'Bread?' A hand like an engineer's shovel emerged from the glare to offer a big quadrant of *panis castrensis*, the rough peasant bread of the lower ranks. He took it and bit into it, ignoring the wheat grains, hard as road grit, which threatened to break his teeth.

'More water,' he mumbled, and tossed the skin at the dark mass looming over him.

He knew they were only delaying the inevitable, but all he wanted to do was rest here against this wall with the sun on his face. Let someone else do the leading. Lunaris handed him another skin and he drank eagerly, this time savouring the feel of the water in his mouth and allowing it to run slowly down his throat.

He looked around at the men he'd brought back from the bridge in the *testudo*. Falco had saved them all with his suicidal charge. A fat merchant who could barely fit into his armour had never stopped being a soldier. None of them had. What was it Falco had said – *you will go on your knees and seek my forgiveness before the end* – well, not now and more's the pity. He would have done it gladly just to share one more cup of wine with the old man. He closed his eyes again, and his head was filled with flashes of incidents he barely remembered witnessing. The

Briton with a *gladius* buried in his guts growling like a dog and trying to tear with his teeth at the man who'd stabbed him. The unarmed veteran whose name he'd never know who had thrust himself into a gap in the line and held it with his dying body until he'd been chopped into ruin. Matykas, the Thracian, riding off to die when he could have run, because that's what Rome *paid* him to do. Dead, all dead, yet he lived. Why? His plan had never been to hold the rebels, only to hurt them, yet he felt a terrible sense of failure. And guilt. There was no blame, he understood that. Paulinus and the legate would have applauded his actions. He was a commander who had used the forces at his disposal to do the most possible damage to the enemy. When the time came he had been strong enough to throw them into the abyss. He felt like weeping.

But he had no time for self-pity. 'Are you going to stand there all day or are you going to give me your report?' He used the wall to push himself to his feet. It was an effort. The armour on his back seemed to weigh three times as much as normal and his body felt as if every inch of flesh was bruised.

'Thought you were asleep, sir.' The *duplicarius* grinned, but his relief was clear. He'd had more than enough of the burden of command. 'Three hundred and fifty effectives, if you count civilians, disabled veterans and the ration thieves from the armoury, but not including the women and children in the temple.' That surprised Valerius. He'd thought everyone had gone with the convoy. Another problem he didn't need. Lunaris continued: 'Enough food and water for a week if we go easy. Defences built and manned as ordered, but we're down to the last two hundred javelins.' The statistic made Valerius flinch, though he kept his face immobile. He had seen how effective the spears had been at the bridge. They could be the difference between holding out for hours or days. Lunaris continued. 'I tried to get rid of the chicken murderer who runs the temple, but he didn't want to go. You could have heard him whine in Glevum when the lads started dumping supplies all over his pretty sanctuary and tearing up curtains for bandages. You'd think he'd be grateful we were here to save him from the barbarian hordes, but he as good as accused me of treason. God-botherers are worse than politicians.'

Valerius managed a tired smile. 'You've done well, Lunaris.' He considered the meagre forces at his disposal. In his heart he'd always known it would be like this. He had no choice but to defend what he could and be wary of what he could not. 'We'll put two hundred and fifty men across here in two ranks.' He pointed to an area a dozen paces inside the gate. 'Organize four squads of ten and position them to deal with any breakthroughs. They will be my strategic reserve. I know it's not much, but it will have to do.' He looked over to where the young priest, Fabius, stood uneasily with the other civilians alongside a few resting legionaries, like sheep amongst a pack of wolves. 'The rest we'll leave in the *pronaos* redoubt and when we are finally forced back they will cover us until we can join them in the temple.' He said it matter-of-factly, as if he were discussing the price of grain in the Forum, but the words sent a chill through Lunaris. It did not matter how long the defenders held them, he was saying, or how many they killed; defeat was as inevitable as the next dawn.

Valerius replaced his helmet and the two men walked towards the south wall of the complex and the gate which bisected it. They kept their pace unhurried, aware the eye of every defender was upon them.

Two legionaries were placing the last of the timber baulks to block the arched gateway. The wall on either side of the gate was only shoulder height. Valerius looked beyond it to where the Celts waited in a sullen compact mass, half filling the area of gardens and vegetable plots. There were no taunts or challenges now, only a brooding hate-filled silence that seemed to make the air around him hum with energy. From beyond them came the howls and cries of those looting the city and the thousands more trying to reach the temple through the choked streets.

'When they first appeared we were certain that you had been wiped out,' Lunaris said quietly, and Valerius realized how difficult it must have been for the temple's defenders listening to the sound of battle but able to do nothing. 'There were only a few hundred but they tried to attack the gate and we had to use half of our reserve of spears to see them off. They've been warier since then. Maybe we killed their leader. Now they seem content to wait.'

'They won't attack until Boudicca is here to witness it,' Valerius said with certainty. 'She will not only want to see her revenge, she'll want to feel it and taste it. We still have time.'

Time to wait. And while they waited, the legionaries talking quietly among themselves and dictating last messages to the more literate, Valerius watched Colonia die. It was no haphazard destruction. It was organized, directed and designed to wipe the city from the face of the earth. The rebels had already discovered a stoutly built Roman home was not easy to burn. A torch thrown on to a tiled roof only burned itself out, leaving a blackened scorch mark on the ochre. But they learned quickly. First they cleared the far slopes of the hillside across the river of the tinder-dry, oil-heavy gorse bushes that filled the spaces between the farms and dragged great bundles into the city. While this was done, others were busy on the roofs stripping tiles from the *insulae*, the former barrack blocks, the basilica and the villas in their fine gardens, and baring the pitch-covered wood. Now the torches could do their work, while inside the walls the gorse burned with all the intensity of Greek fire. From within the temple precinct it appeared innocuous at first, just a few tendrils of smoke rising above the roofline. But, in minutes, the tendrils turned into great writhing columns, with the bright red and gold of the fires at their heart reaching high into the sky, speckled with millions of infinitesimal dancing sparklets that lived and died in a second. House by house and street by street the city was consumed by the flames of Boudicca's vengeance. The wrath of Andraste had come to Colonia.

But Valerius knew it would not be enough for her.

She came as the sun reached its peak, carrying a long spear but this time without fanfare because no chariot could make its way along the choked main street, which was one of the few not yet burning. Valerius watched the crowd of warriors part to allow the flame-haired figure to emerge from their midst. For the first time she was close enough for him to study properly. She looked older than he'd imagined, perhaps in her late thirties, and her features were striking rather than beautiful, which he found oddly disappointing: a wide forehead and a nose any Roman would be proud of. A plaid cloak covered her shoulders, held at the breast by a large golden brooch which was outdone by the thick neck-ring of the same metal that graced her throat. But it was her eyes that made her who she was, glittering like translucent emeralds with the raging fires of her desire for vengeance burning in their depths. He remembered his earlier feeling of being stripped bare and experienced it again, her hatred projecting itself to shrivel and unman the defenders. Boudicca stood, stern and erect, surrounded by her advisers and the British nobles who had risked everything to join her. Valerius found himself drawn to one, a warrior with his head swathed in bandages, possibly a survivor of the action at the bridge, supported by a thin man in a grey cloak which shimmered in the sunlight.

He saw the spear rise.

'Make ready,' he shouted, and ran back to the double line of legionaries.

They came in waves twenty deep and if Valerius had more spears they would have died in waves. Instead, only the first two hundred champions were thrown back as they clambered to the top of the wall and the needle points punched through bare flesh, muscle and bone and then flesh once more. But for all the impact the slaughter made on the attackers the legionaries might have been throwing rose petals.

'Forward.' Valerius accepted a shield and placed himself in the centre of the Roman front rank. There would be no directing this battle from behind.

The sweat-stained legionaries marched ten paces in tight ranks behind the protection of their shoulder-high shields, and rammed the iron bosses in the faces of the first men to cross the wall. Valerius felt the impact on his left forearm and punched his *gladius* through a gap at a fleeting seam of bronzed skin. All along the line he could hear the familiar, almost animal grunts as his legionaries forced the short swords into pliant flesh and the shrieks as the points bit home. At first, not enough warriors could breach the precinct to force the defenders back, and the soldiers pinned them against the wall while at the same time ensuring those who attempted to cross behind them had nowhere to land but on top of their fellows. The men on the wall pranced and raged, attempting to find a way to reach the enemy and howling their hate, but their antics exposed them to the few archers Lunaris had managed to place on the temple roof and one after another the well-aimed arrows plucked them from their perches. For the moment, Valerius's legionaries more than held their own, but a hail of spears from beyond the wall landed without distinguishing friend or foe and took their toll on the defenders. A legionary in the second rank screamed and staggered from the line as one of the broad-bladed points pierced him through the thigh. In almost the same instant, the man beside Valerius was blinded by a spear thrust from one of the trapped warriors and reeled back with his hands to his face and blood spurting through his fingers. Valerius found himself facing three of the heavily tattooed rebels.

The first long sword, wielded by a snarling, grey-haired ancient who should have been too old to fight, came at him in a curving arc designed to take his head off at the shoulders. With a desperate parry he managed to block it, forcing the blade upwards and leaving the man's naked belly exposed to a sword point that flickered out of the second Roman line. The Briton went down with a disbelieving howl, just as the second warrior battered Valerius's shield aside with his own. Any blow would have brought the Roman down, but with screaming, sweating bodies crowding on every side his opponent could only make an awkward overhead stroke that gave Valerius the heartbeat he needed to drive the *gladius* under the Briton's chin and into his brain. Still there was no respite. The killing stroke left him open to a howling, red-eyed figure who burst from his left and chopped down two-handed with a massive woodsman's axe. Valerius cursed, knowing he couldn't turn quickly enough. This was where his neighbour, now blinded and coughing his life out among the trampling feet, should have covered him. The axe was angled to strike his left shoulder and he knew his armour would be no protection against such a fearsome weapon. The great blade would cleave collarbone, breast and ribs. He screamed in desperation just as a bulky figure stepped into the gap at his side to lock shields with a crunch and an instant later the blade of the axe appeared through the three layers of seasoned oak of Lunaris's *scutum*. The big man grinned, hauled the shield sharply to one side and stabbed with his short sword. He was rewarded with a groan. Valerius nodded his thanks and returned to the task of staying alive.

The din of the fighting was fit to burst his ears; screams of pain, howls of triumph and the terrible rhythmic grunting, all punctuated by the clang of iron against wood and the spine-tingling *zuuppp* of arrows flying inches overhead. His movements became automatic and it gave his mind the opportunity to rove over the battlefield, some deep-buried sense tasting the scent and sound and feeling the movement of everything around him.

'The right.' He shouted to make himself heard and Lunaris croaked acknowledgement but shrugged as if to say *What do you want me to do about it?* as he fended off a series of blows from the front. 'We have to reinforce the right.'

'You want me to do it myself?' the *duplicarius* asked conversationally.

'What about the reserves?' Valerius ducked as a spear clattered against his helmet and skidded into the rank behind. Every instinct told him that the pressure on the right flank was growing.

'Gracilis is in charge. He knows what to do.'

'I hope . . .'

The howl of triumph from behind could not have come from any Roman throat, and suddenly the right didn't matter at all. Because the Britons had done what they should not have been able to, and climbed the east wall in enough force to attack Valerius's diminishing band of legionaries from the rear.

He glanced over his shoulder and was just in time to see Gracilis's section of reserves smash into a mass of warriors racing from the north-east corner of the complex.

'Back,' he screamed. 'Back to the temple.'

With even three feet of respite he would have

ordered the *testudo*, but there wasn't even an inch; every man was shield to shield and sword to sword with two or even three opponents. The only chance was to stay in formation and retreat one step at a time to the temple steps. The efforts of the archers on the temple roof kept the crisis on the right flank from becoming a rout, but he doubted that Gracilis would hold the attack from the rear for more than a few seconds. When he was overcome, the only Romans outside the temple would be dead men.

Foot by agonizing foot Valerius allowed the line to be pushed back. The pressure on his shield was growing unbearable, the scything blows of the British swords threatening to smash even the *scutum*'s sturdy structure. Beside him, Lunaris snarled and sweated, cursing his inability to fight back.

Every step they retreated allowed more of Boudicca's warriors to pour over the wall. The soldiers of any other army would have broken. But these were Romans. Roman legionaries. They knew how to fight like no other. And they knew how to die.

Only a single, tattered rank remained. Those left behind, the dead and the injured, were trampled under the feet of Celts whose battle frenzy increased with each step closer to the temple that symbolized everything they had grown to hate in the long years since Claudius set foot on their land.

By the time Valerius felt the cool shadow cast by the temple roof less than a hundred men remained, exhausted, each bleeding from multiple cuts, scarce able to hold the heavy shields which were the only things keeping them alive. Then a roar from his left told him the inevitable had happened and Gracilis and his men were gone.

In the same moment, the line broke.

It did not really break; it disintegrated. Where a second before there had been a battered but disciplined defence, now a hundred individual legionaries fought for their very existence, trying desperately to stay alive as they backed up the steps towards the temple that was their only hope. In the maelstrom of flailing sword arms and falling bodies Valerius, shieldless now, battled with the rest. He could still see Lunaris close by, with Paulus, Luca and Messor fighting at his side. The big legionary had lost his helmet and was bleeding from a cut on his scalp, but the discipline of a dozen years of service never left him. He cut and thrust with parade-ground efficiency, never using more energy than was necessary, and killing or wounding with every stroke. The men he faced had long since learned to respect his blade and that respect allowed him to move upwards, one step at a time, towards the temple and sanctuary.

Valerius sliced at a barbarian face and moved towards his friend. Before he had taken a step, a pulse seemed to surge through the group of warriors facing him and from their midst burst the biggest Celt he had ever seen. He was one of their champions, over six feet tall, his body covered in blue tattoos intricately woven into whorls and vague animal shapes, and he was drunk on blood and possessed by the battle rage. Wounds scarred his torso but the urge to kill had overwhelmed his senses and drove him up the steps with his spear held before him in two hands.

Valerius saw him come and his mind automatically worked out how to kill him. The spear outreached the sword by several feet, but he knew if he could get past the point he could pluck the giant warrior's life as easily as plucking a rose. A simple parry to send the spear point past his left shoulder and a back cut to chop the jaw from the snarling face. It was all about speed and timing and he had practised the move a thousand times. But he'd been fighting all this long day and maybe he got careless or maybe he'd used up all his luck. When the moment came, the iron nails of his sandals slipped on the blood-slick marble below his feet and he fell, helpless, on the steps as the tattooed Briton screamed his victory cry and rammed the leaf-shaped blade at his throat.

Paulus saved his life. The *signifer* launched himself across the stairs and diverted the blow with a cut of his *gladius*. Then, standing protectively over Valerius, he screamed insults at the Britons, daring them to try again. With a roar, the big warrior took up his challenge and darted forward, jabbing the long spear at the Roman's eyes. Valerius scrabbled for his sword as a second Briton attacked from the left, forcing Paulus to half turn his shield to fend off the danger. It was only a momentary distraction, but, in battle, moments are the difference between life and death.

The jab to the eyes was a feint and Valerius watched in horror as the spear point dropped and slipped past Paulus's defences before he could parry it. Still his armour might have saved him, but the angle of the attack was such that the iron point found a gap between the plates to take him below the ribs, and the big warrior used his enormous strength to force and twist it deeper as the Roman's eyes bulged and he gave a grunt of shock.

The barbarian loomed over Valerius, so close the tribune could smell the rank sweat of unwashed body. The muscles of the warrior's massive neck bulged and he growled like an animal as he rammed the spear home still further into Paulus's body. Only now did Valerius realize his hand held his sword. With all his strength he stabbed upwards into his enemy's exposed throat until the point jarred against the bone where his spine met his skull. Crimson blood spurted from the gaping wound and vomited in gouts from the open mouth before the Briton finally let go his death grip on the spear.

Paulus was down, but he still lived, whimpering quietly, with that long shaft buried deep in his guts. Valerius staggered to his feet and stood protectively over his dying comrade. But before the Britons could renew their attack, hands pulled him backwards and Lunaris and Messor charged, screaming, down the steps in an attack that made the enemy hesitate. The momentary respite gave another pair of legionaries the chance to pick up their fallen tent-mate and drag him past the statues and the outer columns towards the temple.

They had one chance, but it was fading with every second. Crazed mobs of warriors gathered where Valerius's legionaries had fought to the last, hacking at the things on the ground until they were no longer recognizable as human. A Briton raised a still-twitching heart in triumph, letting it drip blood on to his face before he tore a piece from it with his teeth. Valerius staggered towards the copper-sheathed doors of the temple with the first pursuers close on his heels and then, with a final glance at the noble head of Claudius that was the centrepiece of the entrance, threw himself inside. Lunaris and Messor were the last to escape, backing in side by side and parrying the swords and spears that slashed at them. The work was so close that three barbarians forced their way inside before the men at the doors could bar them shut. The Celts died, screaming, under a dozen swords.

At last they were safe, and trapped, in the Temple of Claudius the God.

XXXVI

Paulus was dying. Agony contorted the *signifer*'s face and his flesh had taken on the waxy, yellow pallor that told only one story. The British spear was still buried deep in his stomach, and Valerius knew any attempt to remove it would only increase his friend's suffering. He knelt at Paulus's side and took his hand. The great strength was fading but he felt a tightening of the legionary's fingers on his and looked down. Paulus's eyes had been screwed tight shut but now he opened them and a tear ran from one corner down his dirt-caked cheek. He tried to say something and Valerius was forced to bend his head to make out the words.

'I'm sorry I let you down.' The voice was only the barest whisper. 'Should . . . should have had the bastard.'

'You didn't let me down. You saved my life. I'm sorry I brought you here. It was a mistake. I've made a lot of mistakes.'

There was no reply and for a moment Valerius thought the *signifer* was gone, but the grip tightened and Paulus cried out, a long drawn-out groan.

When the legionary eventually spoke again the whisper was even weaker and Valerius barely heard the words.

'I cannot,' he said when he realized what he was being asked.

'A soldier's death, sir,' the standard-bearer gasped. 'A good death. We've both seen men die like this. Not . . . for . . . me. Please.'

Valerius hesitated, then bent low and spoke into the young soldier's ear so there was no doubt the words would be understood. 'Wait for me on the other side.' At the same time he placed his sword point below Paulus's chin and thrust. He felt the legionary shudder and perhaps it was his imagination, but there was a moment when he believed he could see the mighty spirit leave the body and fade into the darkness above him.

'For Rome,' he whispered.

He waited crouched over the body as the world threatened to overwhelm him. He had seen too much blood, too much death, and with each friend who passed he felt a weakening of resolve. But he knew he couldn't allow that. He had to defend this temple to the last. Not for Catus Decianus who had sacrificed

Colonia, or the governor who had abandoned the city to its fate. But for Falco and Bela and Paulus who had died to give him the opportunity. Every day he kept Boudicca here was a day's respite for Londinium.

At last, he raised his head and took in his surroundings. This was the place of secrets, the inner sanctum of the cult of Divine Claudius. It was perhaps twenty paces long by fifteen wide, with a floor of tiled marble. It had a single doorway, the one through which they had entered, and no other. An enormous bronze statue of the Emperor in his guise as Jupiter dominated the interior from its position by the far wall, and in niches along the side walls stood other, lesser statues of members of his family.

Lunaris and the exhausted soldiers slumped to the ground close to the entrance, where they knew they would soon be needed. Across the floor and by the walls civilian refugees sprawled or huddled in little family groups, their pale, frightened faces visible in the light of a single spluttering oil lamp. At first the sheer number astonished him. There must be a hundred or more, here either because they had been too late to join the ill-fated refugee convoy or for reasons that became clearer as he began to identify individuals. Petronius, who had refused the militia the arms they needed to defend themselves, wore his sword but had decided his life was too precious to be wasted on the battlefield. He sat with a blank, almost disinterested expression beneath the statue of Claudius among four or five chests that must contain his records, but the true grounds for his defection was undoubtedly the pretty girl, young enough to be his daughter, who nestled protectively in his arms. Numidius, the engineer, had sought sanctuary in the temple he had built and could not abandon, but his scared eyes never left the butchered remains in the doorway and it was clear he was having second thoughts about his decision now. Valerius was pleased to see Fabius, the young augur, had survived, artlessly displaying the sword Lunaris had provided him with, now bloody to the hilt, with an expression of dazed wonder on his face. The sight of Agrippa, the temple keeper, was less welcome. He could already imagine the list of complaints he would have to fend off later. Two of the women appeared to be comparing dresses and a small group of Britons who had worked for the Roman authority sat slightly apart as if they weren't certain whether they were part of this tragedy or not. And others, men who had stayed with their families out of greed or necessity or stupidity. Then his eye fell on Corvinus.

The goldsmith sat with his back against the east wall and his face lost in the shadow, but Valerius saw that he wore his militia uniform beneath his cloak and from his posture his right hand rested on his sword hilt. He had his left arm around his beautiful dark-haired wife who in turn held their week-old son. If Falco had lived he would have killed the former legionary armourer on sight, but Valerius had had more than enough killing for the day. Corvinus was a problem that would have to be dealt with, but he could wait.

'Lunaris, I want an inventory of all food, water and equipment. Numidius!' he called to the engineer, who scuttled to join him with a look somewhere between concern and outright fear. 'You built this place. I need to know everything about it. How solid are the walls?' He stared into the void above. 'The construction of the roof? Is there any way apart from this door that they can get in or we can get out?'

Numidius quickly destroyed any faint hopes of an alternative escape route. 'The walls are constructed of square blocks of stone, fronted with marble. The roof is of wood with marble tiles. I suppose it's possible that with time and the right tools you could break through, but as you see it is thirty feet above you and without ladders and scaffolding is inaccessible,' he said mournfully.

Valerius tried not to show his disappointment. 'Well, if we can't get out at least it means they can't get in.' He sniffed the musty, rank air. 'We need a latrine area, there.' He pointed to the furthest corner. 'If we can't dig a hole, at least we can provide the women with a little privacy. Raise some sort of curtain between the statues.'

Lunaris brought him the list he had asked for, and he studied it carefully. Nothing in the equipment he didn't know about; with enough rope he might have been able to reach the roof, but there was little hope of escaping in full view of fifty thousand Britons and there was no rope in any case. The food Lunaris had stockpiled consisted of basic legionary rations: iron-hard sheets of *buccellatum* biscuit, salt pork, olive oil, *garum* and a few loaves of bread, and was sufficient for just over a week. Water was the problem. Just thirty *amphorae* for a hundred and twenty people, probably four days' supply at most.

Again, he kept his thoughts to himself, but he ordered a guard put on the water.

'What's the point when we're all going to die?' The truculent voice came from a group at the centre of the *cella* floor and Valerius recognized Gallus, a balding young shopkeeper, sitting with the mousy little wife who didn't know about the mistress he kept in one of Lucullus's apartments. 'We might as well eat and drink our fill.'

Valerius put his hand on his sword. 'Any man who attempts to take food or water he's not entitled to will certainly die quickly, but the rest of us still have a chance to live. We have enough water for at least four days if we ration it carefully, and the Ninth legion could be here in two.' The announcement brought a murmur of surprise. 'Boudicca is unlikely to keep her entire force here to deal with less than two hundred people. If we can hold out until then, the Ninth will drive them off. They won't stand against a full legion.' He stared at the man who had spoken, and was rewarded with a grim nod. 'I—'

An enormous crash rattled the massive oak door and echoed around the chamber, followed by a pandemonium of women screaming in terror and men shouting in alarm. Valerius rushed to join his men at the door. The crash was repeated and the bar jumped, but was held in place by the supports.

'Battering ram,' Valerius shouted. 'Put your shoulders to the door.'

The four closest legionaries responded to his cry. Again the crash was repeated, and the men recoiled from the door, holding their upper arms. He called them away, realizing he'd made a mistake. The impact of the ram could shatter bones and he couldn't afford any more casualties.

He found Numidius by his side. 'We have time, I think,' said the older man. 'The doors are six inches of solid oak and the outer surface is sheeted copper. I have had a thought.' The final words were whispered as if the waiting Britons might hear them. Valerius drew him into a corner.

'It was the latrine, you see,' Numidius explained. 'You said we could not dig a hole.'

Valerius stared down at his feet, where the floor was composed of marble tiles each eighteen inches square. 'We can't dig through that,' he pointed out. 'And even if we could you said the foundations of the temple are massive. It would be impossible.'

'Yes.' Numidius frowned. 'The foundations are, but when we built the *cella* we made certain compensations for the British winter.'

'Compensations?'

Numidius nodded, and it was clear he was

embarrassed to talk about his innovation. 'It is not usual, but we incorporated a hypocaust system. It was possible, you see, because the columns carry the weight of the architrave and the pediment directly to the foundations. Peregrinus was most reluctant until he endured his first winter here, but afterwards he was positively enthusiastic.'

Valerius felt his excitement grow. A hypocaust was a system of underfloor flues to carry heat through a building. Depending on the space beneath the marble floor, it could provide a potential escape route. 'So how do we reach this hypocaust?'

'The only way is to remove a tile.'

They bent to study the tile between them. It was mortared solidly into place and when Valerius took his dagger and chipped at the cementing he barely made a mark.

He looked up at Numidius. 'How deep are they?'

'Precisely two inches.'

'And you're sure this will provide an opening?'

The engineer sniffed. 'I built this temple, sir. Trust me to know it. I have carried out what measurements I could.'

The rhythmic boom of the battering ram interrupted the conversation, accompanied by the muted shouts and curses of the men wielding it. Valerius ignored the noise and looked at the tile again. He turned to face the civilians. 'I need volunteers to help loosen this tile. It will take time, but it may give some at least a chance.' It would also keep them occupied and their minds off the fate which awaited them if the chance did not materialize. Four or five of the men stood, and one who claimed to have building experience took charge. Valerius noticed Corvinus didn't move from his position by the wall. Deal with it now, he told himself. No point in delaying.

'Armourer, join me at the door.' Corvinus looked up with raw, ember-strewn eyes. He exchanged a glance with his wife and Valerius detected a nod of approval before he raised himself from the floor. So that was the way of it. Well, it changed nothing.

No privacy existed within the crowded confines of the *cella* but Valerius gave the goldsmith what he could. He took him to one side of the door, away from the soldiers who sat conserving their energy against the west wall. 'You may consider yourself under arrest for desertion and cowardice,' he said. 'When we return within imperial jurisdiction I will see you stand trial for failing your comrades.'

Corvinus flinched as if he'd been struck, but shock was swiftly replaced by a bitter, knowing smile. 'The only thing that will return to imperial jurisdiction is our bones, tribune, if the Iceni leave us even them. Your threats mean nothing to a man who is already dead.' He started to walk away, but Valerius caught him by the arm. Beneath the cloak he felt the goldsmith half draw his sword.

'You would fight me, but not the Britons?' he said, shaking his head in disbelief. 'There is death and there is death with honour, Corvinus. You could have been among the honoured dead by the river, but instead you chose to desert your comrades and friends and hide with the women and children. What will you tell them when you reach the other side? What excuse will you give for abandoning men you fought beside for twenty-five years?'

Corvinus went pale and when he spoke his voice shook. 'Sometimes there are more important things than playing soldiers.' His eyes strayed to his wife, who was watching anxiously with the baby on her shoulder. 'Duty does not always mean duty to the Emperor.'

Valerius brought his face close so Corvinus could feel his contempt. 'Do not talk to me of duty, legionary. I saw an old man walk into a wall of swords in the name of duty. That old man saved my life and the life of every proper soldier in here. Two thousand men – your tent-mates – died in the name of duty while you were counting your gold. Mention the word duty again in my presence and I'll ram that sword down your throat. Now get back among the women where you belong.'

Corvinus turned away with a look of sheer hatred, but Valerius didn't care. Falco had been right. He should have killed him.

Only then did he notice the battering ram had stopped, and that the silence was more ominous than anything that had gone before.

XXXVII

'Fire!'

Lunaris pointed to the narrow gap below the door. Valerius looked down and saw a glowing red line along its length and at the same time the room began to fill with choking black smoke. He knew it was something he should have anticipated when it became clear that no amount of battering would defeat the massive temple door. They would have stripped the copper away along with the mask of Claudius to give the flames a better chance to work on the oak. It didn't matter how thick the wood was. First it would char, then it would glow. Eventually it would burn.

It was only a matter of time.

At the first sign of flames Corvinus's wife let out a terrified scream and clutched her son tighter to her breast. Like a ripple across a pool, the scream spread panic among the other women, turning the inside of the chamber into a smoke-filled Tartarus inhabited by wailing Furies. Valerius shouted for calm, but his voice was lost in the echoing cacophony of sound. Blinded by fear, Gallus rushed from his place on the floor and began beating at the door and scrabbling desperately at the bar, seeking some way out of this hell. Lunaris reacted first. He knew that if Gallus succeeded they were all dead. He stepped up behind the shopkeeper and smashed the pommel of his sword down on the man's skull, dropping him like a stone.

'If anyone else tries to open the door, I'll kill them,' he said, and no one disbelieved him.

Gradually, the screams lost their intensity. Gallus's wife crawled across the floor to her husband and began wailing over him until Numidius and another man dragged his unconscious body back to its position. In the corner, Corvinus whispered urgently to his woman, alternately stroking her hair and his son's head.

Valerius placed the palm of his hand against the inner surface of the door, attempting to gauge the heat. So far, it was only warm, but that would change. From time to time over the next hours he repeated the exercise. Eventually, it became too hot for him to touch and he ordered an *amphora* of precious water poured over the wood and under the gap at the base of the doorway, where it hissed and steamed.

Petronius, ignored by the wall, stirred himself and attempted to reassert his authority by protesting at this misuse of their most valuable resource, but Valerius snapped back at him, all protocol forgotten. 'Don't be a fool. If this door does not hold, do you think any of us will live long enough to die of thirst?'

At intervals, the besiegers tested to see if the flames had weakened the doors sufficiently, for the ram would begin its work again, but, always, they were forced to return to the fire. At first it seemed those trapped must be suffocated by the fumes or driven into the arms of the enemy. Fortunately, the temple roof was so high that the smoke rose to be lost in the gloom above and apart from the initial terror and some mild discomfort it did no lasting harm. But as the hours passed the heat in their crowded tomb became stifling and there was so little air they lay gasping like fish stranded in a dried-up pond, fighting for each breath. Even Valerius slumped exhausted against the wall by the door, his energy close to spent.

It seemed only minutes before a sharp cry woke him from his stupor. His hand immediately went to his sword, but it was Numidius and the engineer's eyes were bright with triumph. 'It's done,' he crowed exultantly. 'The tile is ready to lift.'

Valerius's fatigue vanished and he felt a resurgence of hope. He followed Numidius to where a little group stood around the loosened tile as if they were attending a burial, with the former builder in pride of place. 'We thought we'd leave the last bit to you, your honour.' Thick lines of dust surrounded the marble where it had been chipped away. He could see a distinct gap now, wide enough to take the blade of a knife or a sword. Valerius accepted a dagger from the man who had spoken and knelt, placing the point of the knife deep in the gap and attempting to gain some leverage. When he found it, he placed all his weight on the hilt. The stone rose a hair's breadth . . . and the knife blade snapped at the hilt. A massed groan followed the failed attempt, and Valerius looked up to discover he was now surrounded by twenty or thirty anxious faces. 'Get me two swords,' he said urgently. 'We need stronger blades, one to each side.' This time it was Luca and Messor who did the lifting and the marble tile gradually rose clear, allowing Valerius to push it to one side and reveal the gap below.

The effort was greeted by disbelieving silence.

The opening they had created was eighteen inches square where the tile had fitted, but below it the soot-coated tunnel of the hypocaust flue narrowed by two or three inches. A child might fit into the gap, but no child would ever overcome the terror of slipping into that stygian gloom and where would a child go if it could? Certainly no adult could pass through. Valerius looked down into the darkness and saw a mirror of the despair in his heart.

'I will try.'

He looked up into Messor's youthful, determined features. Was it possible? The young legionary quickly stripped off his uniform to reveal the skinny, iron-muscled physique that had led his comrades to nickname him after the silver fish they caught from the wharfs at Ostia and Neapolis and Paestum. If he could get his shoulders inside the entrance, there was a chance. But Valerius studied the gap again and felt a wave of claustrophobic panic. What if the tunnel narrowed at some point?

He shook his head. 'I can't order you to go, Pipefish.'

Messor steadily returned his gaze. 'I would still like to try, sir,' he repeated, and Valerius wondered at the courage it took to say those words.

Still he hesitated. But if the boy could reach Roman territory . . . 'Very well,' he said.

As Messor crouched over the intimidating black square Valerius passed on the information Numidius had given him. 'You'll eventually reach a small room at the rear of the temple podium where the fire pit is. It is probably two full hours till dark, and if you make it before then you must wait.' Messor nodded in understanding, eyes bright in the boyish face. Valerius handed him a small tight-wrapped bag, the contents of which had been persuaded from one of the trapped Britons. 'Celtic clothing and a dagger. There will be many thousands of the rebels still out there, but in the darkness you should be able to pass among them freely. Pick up a weapon if you can, it will make you less conspicuous, but do not risk discovery. Make for the gate. That is where you will be in most danger, but once you are through it you should head north – not west, north – until you reach the far side of the ridge. Only then can you make for Londinium or Verulamium. The country must be thick with Roman cavalry patrols by now, and with luck you will run into one within a few hours. Tell them they must hurry. Colonia holds, but it cannot hold for much longer.'

He scoured his mind for anything that would help the boy. Messor sat with his legs over the edge of the hole. It seemed impossible that even his slim body could fit into the constricted space below.

'Wait! Lunaris, the olive oil.' The thick, viscous oil would help protect Messor's body from the abrasive sides of the tunnel and perhaps ease his way through the shaft.

The young legionary waited until his comrade had covered every inch of his skin with the liquid, and when he looked up Valerius could see him struggling to conquer his fear. He met the boy's eyes and nodded. 'May Fortuna guide you,' he said. Messor slipped forward into the darkness.

At once it seemed the attempt would be futile, for his shoulders became wedged between the two surfaces. The chamber held its collective breath, but with a wriggle Messor was gone, slipping away like a pale, gleaming eel until finally the soles of his feet disappeared. They waited what seemed an eternity for the inevitable shouts when he became trapped, the screams for help as he fought the implacable force that held him, which would turn to shuddering gasps as his strength ran out. Each of them endured the awful reality of being buried alive in the suffocating darkness below the Temple of Claudius. But the shouts never came, and as the hours passed they allowed themselves to feel something they believed had deserted them for ever. Hope.

Valerius ordered a ration of the precious water distributed before the remaining contents of the *amphora* were poured over the door and the bar, which had turned dark with the intense heat. The state of the doors increasingly worried him. They must be badly weakened by now by the twin onslaught of fire and the relentless hammering from the battering ram. But perhaps Claudius watched over them after all.

Barely had the thought formed in his mind when the priest Agrippa appeared at his side. He had faded markedly in the past two days and in the pale light of the oil lamp his face took on an unearthly opaque quality and his eyes burned fever bright.

'The god came to me in a vision,' he announced in a voice quavering with exaltation. 'He advised me that the time has come to appease him for our presence in his house. Only by making a sacrifice of great value will we be released from our torment and the rebel horde wiped clean from the precinct of this temple.'

'We don't have anything of value,' Valerius pointed out wearily. 'Not unless Corvinus has something hidden under his cloak.' The goldsmith raised his head at the sound of his name and speared a venomous look in the direction of the doorway.

'We have food and water,' the priest insisted, failing to heed the warning in Valerius's voice. 'What could be more valuable in our perilous position?'

Valerius was suddenly death sick of priests and temples and gods. If Agrippa was right it was Rome's gods who had failed to stand before Boudicca and her gods and had allowed them to be trapped in this dreadful place. He had always had at least a little faith in the gods, but now with death six inches away behind that oak door he doubted his faith had been repaid. Perhaps their lives were the price that must be paid for using Claudius to fleece men like Lucullus of their fortunes. He had a sudden thought. 'I won't give up our bread and water for Claudius, because where he is they have all the food they need. But if you insist I will make a sacrifice of something even more valuable.'

Agrippa looked around him at the sparseness of their cramped surroundings. 'I see nothing else of great value,' he said, frowning.

'What could be of greater value to Claudius than you, priest?' Valerius drew his sword slowly from its scabbard, where the polished blade glinted in the glow from the fire, and extended it until the point was an inch from Agrippa's throat. He raised his voice, so everyone in the chamber could hear it. 'I give you a choice. We can sacrifice our food and our water, or we can sacrifice the priest here, who will no doubt go willingly to his god if it will ensure the survival of his fellow men. Food or the priest?'

'Priest,' urged the weary chorus from the floor. Valerius noticed that the loudest call came from young Fabius, the augur.

'Well?'

For a long moment Agrippa stared at the sword as if it were a snake about to strike. 'Perhaps a sacrifice is no longer necessary,' he said in a choked voice and returned to his place on legs that were a little more unsteady than before.

The priest had barely departed when Valerius heard his name called from the far end of the chamber. Petronius. Didn't he have enough to concern him without the *quaestor*'s intervention? 'Keep testing the door,' he ordered the legionary on guard. 'At the first sign of charring, use two *amphorae* to damp it down.'

He made his way through the prone bodies, wondering what Petronius wanted. Their position here posed an inherent difficulty and one he would have expected to raise itself before now. As the senior military officer he commanded the defence of Colonia, and therefore the temple. But Petronius was the senior civil presence, and his position gave him a certain amount of authority, even in this situation. As *quaestor* he would have been entitled to demand control of the food and water supplies. True, he had put up surprisingly little fight when Valerius insisted on using the water to damp the door, but still, this summons – for that was what it was – undoubtedly meant trouble.

Petronius looked more careworn than normal but had made himself as comfortable as possible in his straitened circumstances. While inches separated everyone else in the chamber from his neighbour, the *quaestor* had created a small outpost using the chests containing Colonia's official records which gave him and his companion not only room to move, but the relative luxury of something to sit upon. On closer inspection the girl was even younger than Valerius had imagined, probably somewhere in her mid-teens, with haunting dark eyes and a body on the brink of womanhood. He realized he recognized her. It was the girl from Lucullus's funeral.

The gnawed end of a chicken bone protruded from beneath the hem of Petronius's cloak, a sign not only of a degree of preparation but also that the 'records', or at least some of them, were not all they appeared.

'How may I be of service to you, *quaestor*?' he asked warily.

The answer came as a surprise. 'Come now, my boy, I think we might be a little less formal. I thought you might appreciate somewhere to rest awhile.' Petronius indicated one of the boxes.

Valerius was tempted to turn down the offer, but it seemed genuine enough and it would have been bad manners to refuse. When he'd made himself comfortable he said: 'Now tell me the true reason you wanted me.'

Petronius smiled. 'I underestimated you, Valerius. I believed you were another of those haughty young aristocrats merely using the legion as a stepping stone to greater things.' He raised a hand. 'Do not be insulted; after all, I was one myself. But I saw you and your men fight against impossible odds today and you are a true soldier; a warrior and a leader. It was a remarkable action which cost our rebel queen dear. I doubt she will rest until she burns you out of your lair.'

'The Ninth—'

'That is why I called you,' Petronius interrupted. 'The papers in these chests could be very valuable to her. Intelligence sources and lists of friends of Rome, some of whom are not what the Britons believe. They would be in great danger if the boxes survive and we are taken. Of course, if the Ninth legion is truly coming to our rescue, I need not be concerned.' There was a question in the last statement, but Valerius looked at the girl and hesitated.

'I have no secrets from Mena,' the *quaestor* assured him. 'She is the reason I am here.' He saw Valerius's startled look and gave a tired smile. 'I met her mother four months before I was due to return to Rome following the invasion. She was a Trinovante; Lucullus's sister, in fact. When we found she was with child, I discovered to my surprise that I had a greater duty.'

That word duty again. Valerius found himself torn between admiration and contempt for Petronius. It was difficult to believe that behind the cold and calculating bureaucrat was a lover who had given up his career so that he could be a father to a native girl. Yet this was the same Petronius who had deprived Falco of the arms he so desperately needed.

'Destroy them,' he said quietly. 'Destroy the papers.'

For a moment Petronius's face lost its urbane certainty. 'Your legionary?'

'If he escaped, Messor will ensure the story of Colonia's last stand is known, but beyond that . . . The door may last until morning, or it may not. Even if he reaches the Ninth I doubt they will be able to fight their way to us in time.'

Petronius smiled sadly at his daughter, and reached for her hand. 'Thank you,' he said, but Valerius wasn't sure who the words were intended for. He stood up and walked back to his place beside the door, where the base was now clearly glowing.

'Water,' he ordered, more brusquely than he had intended. His admission to Petronius was the first time he had allowed himself to acknowledge that all hope was gone.

It must have been close to midnight when the fire outside the door was doused. Valerius saw the tense, white faces as everyone in the chamber waited for the first crash of the battering ram and prayed the seasoned oak would hold once more. But the crash didn't come. Instead, a few moments later they heard the sharper rap of a heavy hammer accompanied by a scream that froze the blood of every man, woman and child in the Temple of Claudius. When Valerius put his ear to the door he heard the sound of muffled laughter and a rasping, agonized breathing. The hammer struck again, followed by the scream, and he had to take a step back because he feared the agony of the tortured soul on the other side of the oak would unman him.

Messor. Poor brave Pipefish, who had endured the suffocating hell of the hypocaust only to be taken when he must have been almost clear.

The second scream was replaced by the child-like pleading of a man tested beyond endurance. The pleas drew Valerius back to the door but he could think of no words of solace, nothing that would reach beyond the barrier of pain to the young soldier he had sent to his death. What could he say? That he wished he could take his place? That he wished it was he who prayed for his mother, and to be released from his agony? He leaned his head against the solid comfort of the wood and prayed in his turn for Messor's easy death. When the smoke began billowing into the chamber and the glow beneath the door resumed he knew beyond a doubt that the gods no longer existed, not for him, not for Messor, not for anyone inside this temple to a false god. That was when they realized that the first screams hadn't really been screams at all.

In the hours that followed, the walls of the

chamber seemed to close in and conditions became even more intolerable. The very air, thick with smoke and the stench of roasting flesh, involuntary shit, days-old sweat, and the unique, rancid scent of human fear, grated on the throat as if it were something solid. The latrine area had long since overflowed and those sunk deepest in the lethargy that accompanies lost hope were content to lie in their own waste with their children sobbing beside them. The certainty of death affected people in different ways. Many simply succumbed to despair, but for others, Valerius among them, it had a curiously liberating effect. Ordinary concerns were no longer of consequence. When he thought of Rome and his father and the cousin who would inherit everything that should be his, it was in the abstract, as if he were a third party looking in on all the pointless drama. Even Maeve had faded to a vague, beautiful memory; a kind of comforting presence who would see him safely to the other side.

Petronius had brought writing materials along with his papers and Valerius spent two hours composing a report of Colonia's defence and the courage of the city's militia, of Lunaris's unflinching bravery, Paulus's heroics and Messor's final sacrifice. When he completed the final line, he read it over: *We live on in the hope of rescue and in the knowledge that the Temple of Claudius must be defended to the last breath*. He shook his head. It hardly captured the moment, but by now the words were blurring together and his exhausted mind demanded only rest. He wrapped the scroll tight around his knife, crawled to the hole in the floor and threw it as far into the recesses as possible. When he'd completed the task he puzzled over the rebel attack on the rear of the compound that had broken the defence. It should have been impossible, but plainly was not. He thought he understood how it happened, but not why. But it didn't matter now. Nothing did.

Maeve's face swam into his mind as he slumped into a delirious sleep and he woke trembling, uncertain of the hour or even where he was. Eventually, parched-mouthed and with a pounding head, he roused himself enough to order Lunaris to issue a ration of water, but the legionary shook his head. The last *amphora* was empty.

Thirst affected the old and the young most of all. For hours, Numidius rocked back and forth on his haunches, moaning pathetically, accompanied by a wailing of babes in arms that cut the air like a knife-edge scraped on a brick. Sometime in the night Corvinus's wife capitulated to the cumulative torture of her baby's cries and held him so tight to her breast that the child suffocated. When she discovered the boy was dead she stood in the middle of the room, still holding his lifeless body, and howled like a wolf. Eventually, Corvinus took her gently by the arm and, speaking soothingly to her, ushered her to a dark corner where he cut her throat, then lay down beside the still warm corpses, opened his wrists and slowly bled to death.

Valerius watched the tragic drama unfold and was surprised how little it affected him. Perhaps his mind had been overwhelmed by all that had gone before and all that was undoubtedly to come. Could a man's stock of emotions be used up in the way he had seen a brave man run out of courage? Corvinus might have been his friend; he remembered how proud the armourer had been of the golden boar amulet he had produced for Maeve, and the good grace with which he gave Lunaris his lesson in humility. He had never truly believed the goldsmith was a coward. Corvinus had betrayed the men he had served with for half a lifetime to protect his wife and child. But did that make him a better man or a worse?

'Valerius!' He pushed himself to his feet to answer Lunaris's call. A large area in the centre of the door glowed bright red in the dark and flames had begun eating through the gap between the two oak panels. The bar which had saved them for so long was charred black. One blow from the ram would clearly smash it in two.

'Ready yourselves,' he said solemnly.

Lunaris's eyes shone from his blackened face like twin beacons, red-rimmed and raw from his constant vigil. But Valerius saw something in them – not a message, not a belief. A quality? – he would never have understood if he didn't know it was mirrored in his own. The ability to die without regret: to savour those final moments as a warrior, in the knowledge that you were surrounded by other warriors. He remembered a piece of graffiti he'd once seen on the walls of a gladiator school – *A sword in my hand and a friend by my side* – and for the first time realized its true meaning.

'It could have been different,' he said. 'You could have been a hero on Mona and I could be drinking wine in Rome.'

Lunaris looked into the orange-tainted darkness around him. 'I wouldn't have it any other way.'

Valerius took a deep breath to stifle the thing welling up inside him and nodded to Lunaris to rouse the surviving legionaries. He stripped off his armour and laid it carefully beside his helmet. The others followed suit. No protection on earth would save them now. They would fight to the end, but better a fatal wound and a quick death than being captured by Boudicca's rebels. Messor's screams still rang in their ears and not one among them intended to share his fate. Like them all, Valerius had considered killing himself to ensure it didn't happen. But he was a soldier, and soldiers didn't die like sheep, and now, as he stood among them, he knew he had made the right choice. He lined them up in two ranks and made a play of tugging at sword belts and chiding them for their unwashed uniforms. As he did, he took each of them by the hand and their lean, savage faces grinned back at him, teeth shining in the darkness, and he felt the pride well up inside him.

'It has been an honour to serve with you,' he said.

They cheered him: a hoarse 'hurrah' from throats

cracked with thirst that echoed from the walls of the chamber and startled the civilians lying in their subdued huddles. He felt a boiling surge of emotion and he loved them for it. The anticipation of battle beat like a giant drum on his ears. If a man had to die he could not die in better company. A figure stepped to his side and he turned to find Petronius with a naked sword in his hand, the blade bright with blood.

'I could not let them take her,' he choked, and Valerius nodded.

The door exploded inward in a shower of sparks and flame followed instantly by a howling wave of warriors. Valerius killed the first man with a single thrust but the sword blades and the spear points were too many to resist and they came at him from every angle in a flurry of bright metal. He heard Petronius's death cry at his side as a blade hammered his ribs. Roaring with pain and mad with fear and rage he smashed his sword hilt into a screaming, wild-eyed face. The blow left his right side open and, as he backswung in an attempt to parry a blur of metal that hacked at his eyes, he knew he was an instant too slow. A lightning flash of brilliant colours exploded in his head and he felt himself tumbling into the darkness. Death reached out to him and he welcomed it. The last thing he remembered was a face from his worst nightmares.

XXXVIII

The face that greeted him in Elysium was different. He knew it must be Elysium because it existed in a constant haze where pain was only a distant memory and soft hands soothed his brow and washed his body. Elysium came and went, but the face remained. Just occasionally earthly matters invaded the idyll that was the afterlife, a gnawing sense of responsibility or an unaccountable sadness, but they were small intrusions and always the face would be there to make them go away. Time in Elysium was an irrelevance and the body's needs an illusion. It existed, and Valerius existed within it.

His first indication that Elysium might not be permanent came in a voice from the darkness in a language he knew but didn't understand. And a name that was his own name. The voice was a rumbling, fractured thing and it was accompanied by a sensation alien to the 'happy fields' of the afterlife. Fear. It opened a door through which images marched like the dazzling flashes from the spear points of a distant legion. He saw savage, pitiless faces. A woman crouched and weeping over the body of a dead husband. Swords that rose and fell with merciless precision. And blood. Rivers of blood. Lakes of blood. Blood spattered across a wall, and blood that poured down the steps of a great temple. Screams echoed in his head and though he knew they were his own screams he couldn't stifle them.

'Valerius.' The name again, but this time it was another voice, accompanied by the touch of a gentle hand on his shoulder. He opened his eyes and for the first time the face appeared in sharp focus. Something metallic was put to his mouth and a pleasant liquid ran down his throat. Just before he lost consciousness he remembered her name.

Maeve.

For a time it became difficult to distinguish where dream ended and reality began. Once, he heard a strange whistling sound and woke to find a hooded figure watching over him with a morbid, threatening presence and he knew he must be back in the Otherworld. On another occasion he felt a sharp pain as he fought for his life in a congested chamber, but moments later opened his eyes to find himself staring through a window at familiar stars, in a room that smelled of old smoke and had scorch marks on the limewashed walls.

He knew he was alive the next time he came awake because the stars were in the same place and he could see a tall, slim figure with a mane of dark hair silhouetted against them. 'Maeve?' The name came out as a growl from a week-old puppy.

She didn't move and at first he feared it was another dream, but eventually she turned and moonlight part illuminated her face. She had changed, he saw immediately. His unconscious mind had painted her as she once was, but hunger and grief had melted the flesh from her bones. Now, dark shadows and deep hollows stood out in sharp contrast against the milky paleness of her skin, highlighting each plane and giving her the forbidding, unsmiling appearance of a much older woman. She is still beautiful, he thought, but beautiful in a different way: the way a fine sword can be both beautiful and dangerous.

He lay on a hard wooden bed with a mildewed blanket of rough wool pulled up to his neck and he didn't realize how weak he'd become until he tried to raise himself. His bandaged head throbbed as if it were about to burst open and every limb weighed more than he could lift. She noticed his struggles and quickly crossed the room to pour liquid from an earthenware jug into a cup. But when she raised the cup to his lips he caught the scent of the herb-infused beer Cearan had given him in the wood and he knew instinctively that this was what had kept him asleep.

He turned his head to one side. 'No,' he whispered. 'Tell me.'

A veil fell over her eyes and at first he thought she was going to refuse him, but after a moment's hesitation she began to talk quietly, her eyes fixed on some distant point beyond the window.

She told how Boudicca had ridden south at the head of an army thirty thousand strong, burning and slaughtering anything in her path which was tainted by contact with the despised Romans, and how their ranks had been swelled by warrior bands from the Catuvellauni and Trinovante. 'Each fought to outdo the other in their prowess on the battlefield and in their cruelty, for each felt they had suffered most at the hands of your people,' Maeve explained, as if it somehow excused the excesses: the impalings and the burnings and the rapes.

Of all Roman works, the Temple of Claudius symbolized the shame of occupation and Boudicca had used that symbol to fan the flames of her followers' hatred into an inferno of unthinking and unquestioning rage. 'She ordered them to desecrate the god's image and pull down the temple, stone by stone, and cast it into the river. It is an abomination on this land, she told them, and we will wipe it from memory as we will wipe the Romans from memory.'

When they reached the slope north of Colonia and looked down upon the pathetic force facing them, Boudicca's warriors had laughed at the prospect of meeting the old men of the militia. Others, more experienced in war, counselled caution, but it was the young men who prevailed. So Boudicca had sent them over the bridge to their deaths.

'Three thousand killed and three thousand more with wounds that will keep them from the fight for many weeks,' Maeve lamented. 'They were the mightiest champions of the three tribes and she can ill afford their loss.'

By the time Boudicca reached the temple she expected to see it in flames and the statues toppled. She raged and tore her hair and demanded that it be taken by nightfall and destroyed by dawn. But the Romans in the temple denied her for two more days and, frustrated, she had led her army towards Londinium before she could witness its destruction.

'You know the rest,' Maeve said. 'They spared none.'

He had many questions, but none stayed in his mind long enough to form completely. In the end he realized there was only one thing he truly needed to know.

'Why do I live when everyone else died?'

Maeve gave him a strange, fey look and he became aware of a third presence in the room. A hooded figure rose from the shadows close to the door and limped towards the bed. Valerius recognized it from his dreams and felt a shiver run through him. The hood fell slowly back and he looked into the face of a monster.

Crespo's sword had taken Cearan high on the left side of his forehead, splitting scalp and skull before it cut diagonally across his face. The force of the blow destroyed the left eye socket and turned the eye into a red pulp that was like looking into the mouth of a volcano. Relentlessly, the sword's edge had carved through the bridge of the Iceni's elegant nose, shattering bone and cartilage and leaving a gaping pink-lipped cavity through which his breath whistled noisily. Finally the blade stripped the flesh from his upper right lip and removed three teeth before breaking his lower jaw, which now hung unnaturally low, giving his face a permanent sideways tilt. The result was an abomination of the human visage. When he spoke, it was in the British tongue and only the left side of his mouth moved, so the words emerged as a guttural, unintelligible mumble that still managed to convey the force of his anger. Maeve translated the words for Valerius.

'He has vowed that your language will never cross his lips again and he wishes you to know first that you are his enemy, to the death.' She hesitated as Cearan continued. 'When Boudicca offered you half of her kingdom, you took it all. When she offered you peace, you brought swords. You have killed his wife and his sons, ruined his tribe and defiled its women.'

Valerius attempted to raise himself again, despite the blinding pain it caused, driven by an irrational need to deny it all even though he knew every word was true. Maeve put a hand on his shoulder and forced him gently back.

'His own injuries are of no consequence; it is the

injury to his people which must be avenged. That is why he refused to stay behind when Boudicca took her army to bring down the temple of the false god. He exulted as Colonia burned and in the final attack on the temple his hate and his desire for vengeance drove him even in front of the champions. He recognized you among your soldiers and took his sword to you. When you fell, he thought to kill you, but, at the last, his blade was turned aside by the memory of past friendship and the life he owed you.'

Valerius had a vision of the golden-haired child swept away in the river at Venta. He forced himself to look into Cearan's ravaged face. The single eye burned like a dying ember in a blacksmith's forge and he realized the damage to the Briton went much deeper than the physical disfigurement of his features.

'Still, you might have been cut piece from piece as your comrades were, your limbs hung from the trees like fruit, but Cearan stayed the swords, saying he wanted you for his own pleasure, to destroy you a little at a time in the name of revenge. Two of his men carried you from the temple and then, more secretly, here, to my father's farm.

'Your enemy, the Roman Crespo, is also dead.' Valerius winced as she related the details of Crespo's terrible end. It was difficult to believe any man, however cruel, deserved such a death. Yet, if what she said was true, the centurion's treatment of Boudicca's daughters was as much the cause of the rebellion as druid plotting or Decianus's greed. No amount of pain could make amends for the blood of tens of thousands of innocents.

In the long silence which followed Valerius tried to reconcile the conflicting thoughts and memories and feelings that whirled through his head. Logic said he should hate them both because they had helped destroy everything in which he believed. Instead, all he felt was a melancholy so powerful it threatened to crush him flat. He didn't understand how he could still love Maeve, yet somewhere beyond the pain his feelings for her were as strong as ever. Nothing could change what had happened, but neither could anything wipe away what they had shared. Did she feel it too? If she did she gave no hint. From the first moment he regained consciousness she had never once met his eyes.

'What will happen now?' he asked.

She turned away and he knew she was hiding tears. 'When you are well enough to travel, we will help you return to your people.'

He nodded his thanks.

'But you should know that life comes at a price, Valerius.'

She took his right hand and pulled it towards her as he heard the hiss of Cearan's sword clearing its scabbard. With a thrill of horror he realized the significance of the blazing fire and the stink of boiling pitch.

The sword flashed down and a sting of exquisite agony was the last thing he knew.

XXXIX

When they rode west in the wake of Boudicca's army, Cearan led, on one of his horses, and Valerius and Maeve followed side by side. Valerius was still barely conscious and he only stayed upright in the saddle with her help. They had dressed him in the Celtic fashion and he rode with the hood of his cloak raised to disguise his features. The way took them past the smouldering remains of Colonia, and in a moment of semi-lucidity Valerius saw the city as if through twenty feet of water, shimmering and swaying and never staying still for a moment. The arch of the west gate remained, solid as ever, though the statues which had adorned it lay smashed around its foundations. Beyond, for half a mile, where houses had once stood tall and shopkeepers hawked their wares, nothing remained except a broad field of thick grey ash, interrupted only by the odd charred stump or remains of a wall which had proved too solid even for Boudicca's unbalanced hatred. No living thing moved within the sterile cordon of destruction. No dog, nor cat, nor bird. They had killed them all. Valerius doubted if even the city's rats survived, so total was the destruction.

But the truly remarkable sight lay beyond the swathe of burned ground.

Because the Temple of Claudius still stood.

Fire and smoke had scarred the white walls and the proud, fluted columns. The roof was gone, the thousands of marble tiles torn away and thrown down to shatter on the ground around it. But the *sum* of the most potent symbol of the Roman domination of Britain remained, massive and enduring in the centre of the ruined compound Valerius had been unable to hold. He remembered Numidius's boast that it would stand for a thousand years and wondered if it might, indeed, be true.

'They tried to burn it, but of course stone cannot burn,' Maeve explained. 'Even when they used every ounce of their strength to try to pull it down it defeated them. They smashed everything they could but those tasked with its destruction gave up and left in search of easier employment.'

Valerius veered towards the building, but Maeve took his bridle and pulled him away. 'I do not think you want to see what is inside.' She was right. The memories were too fresh.

But sometimes the gods do not grant wishes, or perhaps they are as cruel and as capricious as their detractors say. When they passed through the gap in the great turf rampart west of the city, Valerius noticed a long avenue stretching into the distance, as if someone had set up a fence on each side of the roadway. Closer, the avenue became an endless row of posts, each topped with a round object.

The crows alerted him to what was to come, thousands of them, wheeling in dark clouds above the road ahead, and then the wind carried the smell to him: the unique, over-sweet scent of rotting flesh. His first thought was that someone had taken a great deal of time and trouble. Each stake stood precisely the same height as its neighbour and each severed head stared directly at the centre of the roadway. The final roll call of the Colonia militia. Some were so mutilated as to be unidentifiable but others he recognized instantly: Falco, Saecularis, Didius and even Corvinus, united once more with his comrades. He searched without success for Lunaris. Farewell, old friend. For Rome. For a mile they rode in silence between the serried ranks of the dead and Valerius felt every blank eye accusing him. Why, of all of them, had he been saved? Swallows swooped between the poles emitting sharp, excited cries, their jaunty flight patterns and scarlet cheeks inappropriately festive as they feasted on the swarms of flies which, in their turn, feasted upon the faces of his friends. Maeve looked to neither right nor left, but he noticed that the colour had drained from her face and a tiny muscle in the corner of her jaw twitched with the effort of keeping her teeth clenched.

Exhaustion or the effects of his wounds played games with his mind. He remembered Cearan taking the rein of his pony and guiding it away from the road and the trees closing in around them, the branches tugging at his cloak like clutching hands. Quiet forest paths echoing with the sound of birdsong. The comforting warmth of Maeve's shoulder leaning against his as she struggled to keep him in the saddle. Two obscenities with vaguely human shapes hanging from the charred doorway of a burned-out Roman farmstead.

They travelled mainly in silence, although Cearan, riding slumped over his horse's neck, whispered incessantly to himself through his destroyed lips, and once he let out a sharp cry that made Maeve rush to his side. By the second morning, Valerius could barely stay in the saddle, but constant draughts of Maeve's elixir somehow gave him the strength to continue. At dusk they halted close to a copse of trees in the lee of a conical hill and, even before she spoke, something in the way Maeve positioned her pony beside Cearan's told Valerius they were abandoning him.

'You must find your own way now,' she said, and although she struggled to keep her voice harsh there was a catch in it that told its own story. A gleam of gold at her throat gave him hope.

'Come with me.' Lack of use made his speech thick

and clumsy and he had to clear his throat and repeat the words before she understood them. 'Come with me and I can save you both.' He wasn't sure whether it was true, but he did not want to live without her.

The dark eyes turned liquid but her determination never wavered. 'You were always a Roman, Valerius, and I was always a Trinovante. For a time we lived a beautiful lie, but no one can live a lie for ever. And now we are enemies.' He shook his head. No, they would never be enemies. 'Have you ridden with your eyes closed?' she cried. 'Things have been done, terrible things that can never be forgiven by you or by me. You want me to come with you, but the only way I will visit Rome will be in chains.'

'You can't win. Boudicca defeated the militia, but it was an expensive victory. Now Paulinus is coming with his legions and when they meet there can only be one victor.'

Cearan's guttural growl interrupted them. Maeve listened and pointed to the hill above them, which was silhouetted against a bright orange glow. Somewhere, another city was burning. 'He says that Londinium is destroyed, and with it Rome's hold over this island. Andraste watches over Boudicca and every day thousands more flock to the wolf banner. Even your legions cannot kill us all.'

Valerius remembered a Silurian hill fort on an autumn afternoon when the relentless legionary swords had harvested one life after another and he wondered if that was true. He made one final attempt. 'I love you,' he said. 'And you returned that love. Tell me it is no longer returned and I will go.'

She closed her eyes and for one moment he believed he had reached the old Maeve. He knew she was thinking about the cave in the woods and the hours they had spent there. But it couldn't last. Her head came up and she turned her pony away. 'Keep north and stay away from the roads.' She threw him the water skin and he caught it with his left hand. 'Use it sparingly. It dulls the pain but take too much and you may not see another dawn.'

He watched her ride off with Cearan. They were almost out of sight when he remembered the question he had wanted to ask.

'You told them about the ladders, didn't you? Without the ladders they would never have taken the temple.'

She turned her head to look back at him but he couldn't see her expression. 'They are my people, Valerius. Whatever I felt for you, they were always my people.' He sighed and all the strength went out of him. She had betrayed him. Yet on this day it seemed a small betrayal among all the others. But she had one more message for him. At the top of the rise she turned in the saddle. 'Avoid Verulamium, Valerius. On your life, avoid Verulamium.'

When he looked up, she was gone.

He rode north in the gathering darkness, allowing the pony to steer its way across pasture and through woodland, instinctively choosing the path of least resistance. The spirits of the night held no fears for him because night was the colour of his soul. Endurance kept him in the saddle, that and occasional pulls at the water skin. While he rode, he dreamed of Maeve; the colour of her hair and the texture and firmness of her skin. In the dream he took her to Rome and she marvelled at the wonders there. But the farther he travelled the hotter the fire in his right arm burned, and the pounding inside his head increased until it became unbearable. He gambled on a longer draught of the liquid, but he must have fallen asleep in the saddle because at one point the pony stopped, snickering gently in alarm. Still with his eyes closed he dug his heels into its flanks, urging it on. It took a few faltering steps, but eventually it would go no further. As the world began to spin and he felt himself roll from the saddle he had the presence of mind to wrap the reins around his left hand.

When he opened his eyes his mind was clear but his body felt as if it had been used for sword practice by a legionary cohort; every muscle ached and his right arm was a savage throbbing trial. Delaying the moment when he must move, he stared up at a sky of perfect eggshell blue through branches thick with leaves that rustled and creaked in the light breeze. Something was missing, though, and he had a stab of panic before he felt the pull of the reins on his left wrist. Surprisingly, his head rested on an object that was soft and pliant that he couldn't remember placing there. A thick scent hung in the air around him but it had become so familiar that his brain took time to react to it.

He rolled over, careful to protect his injured arm, and stared at the thing beside him. A human leg. The body the leg belonged to lay two or three feet away, the flesh white as the marble that clad the Temple of Claudius, except for the obscene red gashes where the limbs and head had been hacked away. Unwillingly, he allowed his eyes to scan the scene around him. His first impression was of a shoal of dead fish on a beach; ivory pale, scattered, random and utterly lifeless. The corpses lay on the grass and among the trees and bushes, some with heads and some without, others with stomachs torn open or genitals removed. Each corpse had been stripped of everything of any value, but what little clothing remained told him they were Roman soldiers, either auxiliaries or legionaries. He struggled to his feet and vomited a thin spew of yellow bile, momentarily overwhelmed by the enormity of what surrounded him. But duty and a soldier's instinct for survival told him he must try to make sense of it.

At first the distribution of the bodies – hundreds, perhaps even thousands of them – confused him. However, as he walked further, he began to discern a pattern. They had been marching south, which made them part of the Ninth, and the lack of a baggage train said they were travelling light and in a hurry. He tried to imagine the order of march: mounted scouts ranging in front, flank guards to the side, legionaries trudging in the van of the column, auxiliaries eating their dust behind, and the cavalry – there must have been cavalry accompanying a force this size – ready to react to any attack. Yet all their precautions had counted for nothing when their commander had brought them through this broad, wooded valley.

He reached a point where the dead appeared more numerous and lay in untidy ranks. Yes. It had begun here: the destruction of a legion. He studied his surroundings carefully before moving warily into the nearby trees. Crushed bushes and dead grass showed where the ambushers had sat, and the many blackened piles of excreta told of a long, patient wait. A large force, and more, if he was correct, on the opposite side of the valley. The attackers had struck here first, along a quarter-mile front, and forced the legion to adopt its favoured defensive line. There would have been no panic. If they had feared the numbers facing them they would have formed a square and fought their way to a more suitable position, but there was no sign they had done so. With their flanks and rear properly protected it should have been a simple matter of shield against shield and *gladius* against sword and spear; a battle the legionaries must win. But somehow a force of similar size had attacked from the rear, making the second line turn and face them. How? Had the cavalry been drawn off by some ruse? Certainly few of them had died here; he had seen, at most, four

dead horses, probably the mounts of the cohort or
auxiliary commanders. And finally, the fatal blow, a
crushing attack on the left flank which had started
a rout. Or not quite a rout. He followed the line of
withdrawal and it was possible to see where small
knots of legionaries had fought to the death to defend
their comrades, but they became fewer and fewer as
they were driven inexorably back. The bodies led him
into an isolated clump of trees with a giant oak at the
centre. The oak formed the bastion for their final
stand. He could see it now, the launch of the last *pila*,
the *signiferi* protecting their unit standards, hacking
and chopping at the multitude surrounding them,
until only one remained, who had fought to his last
breath. He knew all this because, unlike every other
corpse, this small cluster of bodies had been left
untouched; they even retained their armour. One, a
leather-skinned giant still in his wolfskin cloak, lay
a little apart beneath his shield, which showed the
distinctive charging bull of the Ninth on its metal
boss. At first Valerius believed the attackers had been
disturbed before they could desecrate the corpses, but
there was something almost reverential about the
manner in which the last man had been laid out.
The Britons esteemed courage and valour above all
else. Was this their chief or their king's way of
honouring a fellow champion?

He sat by the dead men for a few minutes, attempting to understand the scale of the disaster which had
overtaken them. The whole of the south must have

risen against Rome. An entire legion had been smashed here. Had they died fighting for their eagle? It would account for the ferocity of the defence. But a full legion at the hands of barbarians? It didn't seem possible, yet he had seen the results with his own eyes and he remembered the warriors who had fought their way across the piled bodies to reach the Colonia militia. There could be three or four thousand dead lying in and around the valley. The loss of an eagle would taint every legionary who had ever marched with the Ninth. Worse, the disgrace of a defeat on this scale would be felt in Rome. Paulinus, too, would be touched by it, even if he was a hundred miles away when it happened.

He searched the dead men for personal identification or some weapon to give him at least a chance of fighting back against any wandering band of rebels he encountered, but he found nothing. When he was certain, he swung himself painfully into the saddle and retraced the legion's tracks towards the north.

Where the forces of retribution gathered.

XL

The cavalry patrol found him just as the sun reached its highest point and they would have killed him if he hadn't had the presence of mind to cry out the name of his unit as they approached at the gallop, their long *spatha* swords gleaming and their eyes bright and nervous. The decurion in command circled him warily before, in a thick Germanic accent, ordering him to dismount.

Valerius shook his head wearily. 'I have urgent news for whoever is the senior commander in this area. Take me to see him at once.'

'On whose authority?' the German demanded.

Valerius shook off his cloak and heard the exclamations of dismay at the sight of his wounds. 'I need no authority but my own. I am Tribune Gaius Valerius Verrens, last commander of Colonia, only survivor of the Temple of Claudius, and you will take me or I will go alone. Who commands?'

The cavalryman hesitated. 'Suetonius Paulinus, with the Fourteenth and the Twentieth.'

'Then take me to the governor, but first give me a drink,' Valerius said. 'I have had nothing but some druid's piss since dawn.'

By the time they reached the main column the legions had settled into their marching camp for the night and it took a few minutes before they tracked down Paulinus's pavilion at the heart of the Fourteenth's entrenchments. Valerius noticed a number of men with freshly bandaged wounds. So, they hadn't had it all their own way on Mona; Lunaris had been right about that, at least. The camp of the Twentieth was considerably smaller than that of the Fourteenth, which told him Paulinus had left part of the legion in the west to consolidate whatever gains he'd achieved. Would he have made that decision if he'd been aware of the scale of the rebellion?

The German cavalryman handed him over to a senior tribune on Paulinus's staff, an officer Valerius vaguely recognized. 'Gnaeus Julius Agricola, at your service. The governor wishes to see you immediately, but . . .'

Valerius swayed on his feet and struggled to keep the resentment from his tone. 'I'm sorry, I left my uniform at Colonia along with everything else.'

'No, you mistake me. Please do not apologize,'

Agricola protested. 'It's just that I fear you might fall down and I would be in trouble if I lost you now. The governor has grave need of you.'

The tribune ushered him past the guards to Paulinus, who was staring as if hypnotized at a map of southern Britain pinned to a wooden frame. A second man in a legate's sculpted bronze cuirass stood beside him. Eventually, the governor turned and even through his exhaustion Valerius registered the change in the man. The granite-chip eyes were sunk deep, the heavy brow was furrowed and his skin had taken on a sickly grey pallor emphasized by white stubble that made him look ten years older. Paulinus stared back at him, equally perplexed, his mind clearly attempting to put a name to the unkempt figure in the ragged Celtic clothing and bloody bandages. Valerius could hardly blame him; after all, he would remember a whole young man in the prime of youth, not a haggard spectre with only one hand.

It had been the price of his life.

'You will never bear arms against my people again,' Maeve had said before Cearan raised the sword and removed the right hand with a single clean stroke midway between elbow and wrist. They had used hot pitch to stem the bleeding, but Valerius remembered nothing bar the smell of roasting flesh and the vague knowledge he was no longer whole. During the ride north, the maggots breeding in his mind had been as corrosive as the wounds in his flesh. At first, he wished he'd died along with the rest. What use was a part-man? His soldiering was finished. He could no longer hold a sword or add his weight to a shield wall. Of course, his father would support him, but in his heart he would be little different from the cripples begging hopefully along the Clivus Argentarius. The last stand of the Ninth had rekindled his pride and restored his sanity. The standard-bearers could have run but they had fought, driven by duty and honour and courage, the code they shared with Falco's veterans. If they had suffered death for those values, could he not suffer a life?

Paulinus's reaction surprised him. 'My boy. My poor, dear boy. It is you. I could scarce believe it. You have endured so much. Could any man have sacrificed more for Rome?'

Valerius thought of the six thousand and more who had sacrificed everything for Rome, but the time to remind the governor of that would come later. Paulinus was clearly a man living on the dagger's edge and the slightest push could throw him off balance.

But some things could not be avoided. 'Tribune Gaius Valerius Verrens begs to report the loss of Colonia and the failure of his mission,' he said formally. 'He would commend to you the conduct and leadership of the veteran militia, which was in the highest tradition of Roman arms. They fought to the last man and the last spear, and no blame should attach to them for the city's fall. If blame there is, it is mine.'

'Yet you delayed them for two days, and defended the Temple of Claudius to the end.' The second man combined natural authority with a hangdog expression and he grasped at the positive like a drowning man clutching at the last branch before a waterfall.

'I had the privilege to command the defence,' Valerius admitted. 'No men could have done more.' Memories of Lunaris and Messor flooded back and he staggered slightly as a wave of nausea flooded through him.

'A chair for the tribune, quickly, and water,' Paulinus called to one of his aides. Valerius sat and the governor stared at him intently.

'Cerialis is correct,' he said. The name confirmed Valerius's suspicion and explained the air of defeat which cloaked the other man. Quintus Petilius Cerialis commanded the Ninth legion and was ultimately responsible for the massacre Valerius had stumbled upon. It also answered his question about the eagle. If the Ninth had lost its eagle Cerialis would be dead; Paulinus would have insisted. The governor's voice regained some of its old fire as he continued. 'Since I took Mona we have experienced betrayal, disaster and defeat, thanks to that fool Catus Decianus whose greed and ambition placed this province in deadly peril and sent you, Valerius, into the very gates of Hades. Colonia, at least, was a defeat with honour, as has been confirmed by our spies and the Celts who are already deserting to us.

The praises of its defenders are sung even by the followers of the rebel queen, and the defence of the temple, which they desired most eagerly to overthrow, sung loudest of all. And you, you alone, fought your way clear.' Valerius opened his mouth to deny it but Paulinus raised a hand for silence. 'You are a true Hero of Rome.'

It took time to penetrate, but when it did Valerius felt the room spinning around him. The way Paulinus said the words, with the emphasis on 'Hero', indicated this was more than praise, it was eternal fame. A Hero of Rome would receive the Corona Aurea, the Gold Crown of Valour, from the Emperor's own hands. He would be fêted throughout the Empire, and have access to the centre of power. It was second only to the Corona Graminea, awarded for saving an entire legion . . . and he did not deserve it. He shook his head, but Paulinus was already continuing. 'Now, I must know everything.'

For the next hour Valerius related the story of the veterans' stand against Boudicca's fifty thousand and the final, terrible hours of the Temple of Claudius. Paulinus grunted in approval at the use of the bridge to draw the British champions on to the killing ground and his eyes grew moist when he heard of Messor's courage and sacrifice. But when Valerius tried to describe his own escape he was dismissive. 'I do not need the details. It is enough that you have survived.'

When he reached the ambush of the Ninth, the two

listeners looked away as he related the discovery of the mutilated bodies.

'You were correct,' Cerialis confirmed grimly. 'Four cohorts – two thousand legionaries – and the same number of auxiliaries. Just before we entered the valley, our scouts sighted a sizeable force to the south and I rode to investigate with the cavalry. They struck while we chased shadows. By the time we returned the infantry had been overrun and we were fortunate to escape with our own lives.'

Paulinus looked at him in a certain way and Valerius realized Cerialis still had a reckoning to face, but for the moment the governor needed every man he could get to hold Britain for Rome – and to avenge the thousands of Roman citizens who had already died. Valerius had heard from Agricola how Paulinus had been forced to abandon Londinium to its fate. The governor's features had turned white when Valerius described the horrors he had seen but now the veins in his temples stood out like octopus tentacles and his face glowed red. 'We do not face warriors.' He fought for breath. 'These people are animals and like animals we shall slaughter them. The Ninth and the veterans of Colonia will be avenged. Fifty thousand, you say, and growing every day?' He shook his head and turned to the map, murmuring to himself. 'Too many. I must fight them on ground of my choosing. But where? Where will she turn now that Londinium burns? Where will her thirst for blood take her? East, and back to the flatlands? No, because only victory keeps her army together. West? Possible. If she can bewitch the Silures she will control the gold and Postumus and the Second are already marching from Isca to join us. The south? Easy victories and control of our communications with Rome. Or north?' Valerius felt his stare. 'To destroy us.

'She must fail,' he said. 'An army must eat; she has no supplies and such a swarm cannot live off the land for many weeks. They will be eating their sword belts long before harvest. But it is not enough for her to fail. She must be destroyed, and all who follow her must be destroyed along with her. I swear on the blood of Mithras that I will annihilate her. But where?'

'North.' The word echoed in the silence and Valerius felt the sour taste of betrayal on his tongue. 'She will march north to destroy Verulamium.' Maeve's warning had been intended to save his life; now it would be Boudicca's ruin.

Paulinus disposed his forces as Valerius rose to leave. Verulamium and its people would be sacrificed; he could not reach them in time or fight Boudicca while protecting a column of helpless refugees. In any case, Verulamium, for all its Roman pretensions, was the Catuvellauni capital: let them make terms with their Iceni cousin if they could. He would use his auxiliaries, the light, quick-marching infantry, to lure her on at a pace that would draw the fangs of her warriors. Then he would fight her and beat her, but where?

Agricola intercepted Valerius outside the tent. 'I am to take you to the governor's personal physician. Did he tell you?'

Valerius nodded, aware the tribune referred to the honour he'd been given. 'I mean to refuse it, because I did not win it.'

'It is what I told them you would say, but I fear you have no choice. It is your duty to accept and you do not strike me as a man who would shirk his duty.'

The room seemed to move beneath Valerius's feet and Agricola stepped forward and put out a hand to steady him. 'Come,' he said gently. 'We have delayed long enough.'

'I don't understand. There are a dozen men who deserve the Corona Aurea more, but they are all dead. I lived, but my mission failed and I am no hero.'

'You were brave, you fought and you hurt them?'

Valerius shrugged and Agricola took it as acquiescence.

'Then you are a hero, and my governor needs a hero. Tonight he will draft a report to Rome detailing the happenings of the past month. It will reflect well on no one, it will cost some their positions and it may cost others their lives. You may not have heard, but Postumus, who is camp prefect, refuses to leave Isca with the Second. He fears the Emperor more than he fears Paulinus, but he fears Boudicca more than both. So, defeat and disarray. Paulinus needs a victory, and if he cannot have a victory he will have a glorious defeat. You would not deny the veterans their glory?'

Valerius shook his head. 'They fought like lions and they died like heroes. They deserve to be remembered.'

Agricola took him by the shoulders and stared into his eyes. 'Then make sure they are remembered. Through you.'

By now they were on the threshold of the camp hospital. Valerius paused before walking through the flaps. 'Your logic defeats my argument. Tell the governor I will accept.'

Inside the tent, a small man with sharp features and quick, restless hands rushed up to him like a mother hen. A dark beard and a mottled, balding head made him seem older than he probably was, but the eyes were lively and intelligent. 'Tiberius Calpurnius,' he introduced himself. 'Late of Athens, now of this gods-forsaken mudpatch.'

He immediately began unwinding the bandage which covered the wound above Valerius's right eye, explaining his reasoning as he did so. 'You may feel your arm is more in need of my assistance, young man, but I can assure you it is not. I have seen men who appeared perfectly healthy drop dead at my feet hours after the merest bump with a sword, but a man with a severed arm may last a month without treatment if the blood flow is curtailed and the wound remains uninfected.'

Calpurnius deftly probed the sword cut with his fingers. 'Fortunate indeed. A glancing blow, almost flat. Another inch to the left and you might have lost an eye; a little more of the edge and it would have been the top of your head. Contusions but no sign of fracture, and the wound is healing well, as I would expect in a man of your years. Fainting spells? Blurring of the vision? Yes? To be expected, but if they continue return to me and I will supply you with a draught. Now, the arm.'

Valerius winced as Calpurnius removed the thick cloth bandage to reveal a marbled, purple-yellow stump that reminded him of a piece of rotting meat. Vomit rose in his throat but the physician had anticipated his reaction and placed a bucket at his feet, into which he retched copiously.

Calpurnius whistled soundlessly to himself as he inspected the stump closely from every angle. When he reached out to touch it for the first time Valerius grunted in pain.

'Yes, it would hurt.' The little man gave a tight smile which quickly transformed to puzzlement. 'Again you have been fortunate. I have never seen a battle injury like this. The cut is at the perfect angle, the weapon almost surgically sharp.' Valerius gave a little cry as he probed the blackened, weeping face of the wound. 'A few bone splinters, which I will deal with in a moment. The burned flesh must be removed, or it will mortify, but the unguent, though primitive, has kept infection at bay for the moment.'

He looked directly at Valerius and there was curiosity in his eyes, not quite suspicion, but certainly a question. 'If a saw had been used I would have been quite proud of this myself.'

'As you say, I was fortunate; more so than the man who treated me. He is dead.' The lie came easily; there had been a militia physician but he had been among the first to fall on the field at Colonia.

Calpurnius shrugged. Plainly, the dead held little interest for him. 'A pity. Now, as for treatment. In a moment I will administer a tincture of poppy seed which will render you unconscious and dull the pain. In other circumstances I would suggest that you rest for a few days before surgery, but I sense you are a man of strong heart and healthy lungs and will survive.' He studied the stump again and sucked his teeth. 'I plan to re-amputate two inches above the present level which will allow me to stitch a flap of skin across the wound, thereby protecting it from dirt and disease. It is by far the most effective procedure,' he added, sensing resistance to his suggestion.

'No. I'll keep what I have. Stitch it up, or do what you have to do, but I need to be back on my feet tomorrow.'

'Ha,' Calpurnius grumbled. 'Another young man in a hurry. It will be the death of you, but I will do what I can.' He paused and his face brightened. 'A leather cover, cowhide for thickness and wear. I have the very thing. And then, who knows?'

'Will I be able to carry a shield?'

Calpurnius looked offended. 'One hundred and fifty years ago, Marcus Sergius, grandfather of the odious Catilina, was fitted with an iron hand after his amputation, returned to battle within the week and captured twelve enemy camps. Medicine has progressed considerably since his day. Now, lie here while I prepare the tincture.'

XLI

Valerius rose early on the day of the last battle. Mist disguised the dawn the way a veil hides an ageing woman's fading looks. It came as a pale suggestion of gold lost in a drifting curtain of smoky, ground-locked cloud and with it came Boudicca's host. She had picked up the trail Paulinus had left for her while the ashes of Verulamium and the blackened bones of its inhabitants were still hot. For a week, the auxiliaries had led them on, first north, then west; day after day of forced marches and occasional, tantalizing glimpses of the enemy, the red cloaks and polished armour always on the next hill or beyond the next river. They were like wolves now, the Britons, with the Roman scent as thick in their nostrils as the taint of blood from a mortally injured deer as it stumbles towards its final refuge. Thirty days of constant movement, fighting and killing had worn them thin, but the hunger still remained, and with it the hatred. The wrath of Andraste and Boudicca's need for revenge never diminished. She had spilled enough blood to fill a lake and sent enough souls to the gods to satisfy even their legendary appetite, but still it wasn't sufficient. Only by smashing the legions and killing the man who led them would she and her people find peace.

As the ghosts of trees appeared a few hundred paces to his left Valerius knew it would be soon. The rebel camp fires had been visible on the horizon when Paulinus's legions bedded down in their positions for the night. They would have been on the move for more than an hour now, ready for another day chasing shadows. But the shadows were no longer going to run.

From the murk, the familiar, inhuman sound – the buzz of a million bees – filled the air, then the weak sun staggered above the eastern horizon and the mist shredded and burned away. The buzz faded to a confused, unnerving silence, and from his position at the governor's side Valerius looked out over countless thousands stretching into the distance in a sinuous black column of humanity. Paulinus had spent days manoeuvring towards this position so that Boudicca would be drawn behind him, funnelling her army into the killing ground. The five thousand men of the Fourteenth legion formed a triple defensive line across the narrow valley at the head of a long, gentle slope. Five cohorts of the Twentieth who accompanied Paulinus anchored his flanks against the valley walls. Among them, he set up his 'shield-splitters', the ballistas which could fire heavy metal-tipped arrows a quarter of a mile. Beyond them, the cavalry ranged to discourage attempts to bypass or attack the vulnerable flanks. Behind the legions, the auxiliaries waited in reserve, ready to exploit any success or to die in their turn. For there would be no retreat.

'This is my weakness and my strength,' Paulinus had explained as he laid out his battle plan. 'We will have only one opportunity to destroy her. Even if we win a great victory but leave her army intact, we will be so mauled as not to be able to fight for another thirty days, while she would scarce need to draw breath. Our end would be long and slow, but inevitable. We must fight her to a standstill, draw every warrior on to our javelins and our swords, kill and keep killing until no man stands. The position I have chosen means that my soldiers must fight or die, but her confidence and the vast host she leads ensures that Boudicca will never turn back.'

Agricola broke the silence that followed. 'But if we hold them and she does decide to withdraw . . . ?'

'Then we all die.'

It took the rebel queen time to bring her forces to battle. Valerius could make no estimate of their numbers, but his eyes told him the army had swelled enormously since he had first seen it on the slope above Colonia, perhaps even doubled in size.

Covering an area a thousand paces wide and three times as deep, they seemed as many as the birds in the air or the fish in the sea. The silence had vanished now, replaced by a muted roaring akin to standing too close to an enormous waterfall; a relentless, surging rise and fall that seemed to shake the very air.

His lack of emotion surprised him. He sat on his horse, with the reins still unfamiliar in the grip of his left hand, and watched Boudicca's forces deploy with the dispassionate detachment of a spectator at a cockfight who had already gambled his last *sestertius*. Fear had no hold on him because a man could only die once and he had died at Colonia. But how could a soldier fight without passion? Maeve had robbed him of his hand; had she also deprived him of his soul?

He drove her from his head and studied the scene again. A visible thickening was apparent in the numbers at the base of the slope as more and more warriors joined the throng edging its way towards the Roman line a mile distant. A few chariots forced their way to the front and he recognized the glitter from the torcs and arm-rings of the rebel chieftains, but of Boudicca herself there was still no sign. Beyond the mass of fighters he noted the dust cloud as the rebel baggage train and camp followers caught up with the main force, deploying to the left and right for a better view of the battlefield, determined to witness the destruction of the red scourge that had blighted their lives for almost two decades.

Maeve was out there somewhere, he was certain of it. Cearan had been determined to rejoin his queen and where he went she would follow, in the knowledge that only she stood between his sanity and the total disintegration of that shattered mind. He closed his eyes, attempting to visualize her among the great swathe of humanity. When he opened them another glint of gold from the van of the rebel army stirred a memory. *If you didn't love me why do you still wear the boar pendant I gave you?*

By now it was mid-morning and Paulinus watched in silence as the rebel forces filled the slope in front of him, his shoulders hunched forward, eyes glowering from below the gold-embossed brim of his helmet. He had made his decisions and given his orders. He had no thought of failure because failure was death. The massive head came up as a new figure entered the stage.

Boudicca.

Her fiery mane flowed behind her in the breeze and she stood tall and proud in her chariot as she emerged from the chanting sea of warriors and spun to a halt on the green sward twenty paces ahead of her army. She had her back to the Roman line and Valerius could feel the dismissive contempt in her gesture. As he watched a brown blur flew from beneath her feet and scampered across the field to his right. At first he was puzzled, but then he remembered one of Boudicca's emblems was the hare. The omen must be positive because an enormous, snarling roar greeted

466

her that sent a shiver through every Roman. At the same time, hundreds of banners, proud symbols of the combined might of the tribes of southern Britain, were raised in acclamation.

He heard her voice for the first time, deep and almost manly, and caught snatches of speech carried on the wind but could make nothing of the words. Paulinus must have heard it too, but if he did the governor dismissed it. 'Come,' he ordered, and Valerius and Agricola joined him as he rode along the front of his legionaries, who stood silent and motionless.

'You fought well on Mona, my Mules, but I have brought you here for a little more javelin practice.' The words carried along the line and Valerius could see men grinning at the unlikely familiarity. 'Those who stand before you have murdered, tortured and raped Roman citizens, men, women and children; innocents whose only crime was to attempt to bring civilization to this land. They butchered and mutilated your comrades of the Ninth, and the brave veterans of Colonia who fell defending the Temple of Divine Claudius.' He paused and the silence was filled by a growl, like an enormous dog gathering itself for the attack. 'We offered them our friendship, our trust and our aid, and they took all with smiles of thanks, but when we turned our backs they reached for the knife and the sword and the spear, as is their way. They believe you are already defeated.'

'No!' The massed roar carried across the valley and echoed from the banks.

'They are the true face of barbarism. They are your enemy. They show no mercy and they deserve no mercy. Give them none. For Rome!'

'For Rome!' The words erupted from ten thousand throats and Valerius felt the ice in his belly melt and the first stirrings of life return to his heart.

'For Rome,' he whispered.

An enormous clamour of horns signalled the enemy advance and the Roman ranks opened to allow Paulinus and his aides through to relative safety. From behind the rear cohorts of the Fourteenth Valerius watched as the Britons surged up the slope towards the waiting legionaries. The slope was long and it took time for the first warriors to reach the small stakes the centurions had placed forty paces ahead of the line, the optimum killing range of the *pilum*. Within that narrow corridor no legionary would miss his target. As the Britons charged, the ballistas tore gaping holes in the front ranks, the big arrows gutting two or three men at a time before they spent their power. Four cohorts made up the first of the Roman lines, including the elite, reinforced First; more than two thousand men. They had time only for a single cast before the howling mass of Britons fell upon them, but that single cast scythed down the vanguard of the attack as if it were made of summer grass and not flesh, blood and bone. Yet Boudicca had an endless, willing supply of fighting men, and those men, it seemed, had an unlimited supply of courage. Only the wealthy were equipped with shield and sword; most fought with spears. When one fell, he was replaced in an instant, and when he fell in his turn, two or three more fought to take his place. Celtic iron and Roman shields met with a clash like the combined fury of the gods, and Celtic iron still outnumbered Roman by ten to one. But once more Valerius witnessed the way the very numerical superiority of the attackers played against them when they met men determined to stand their ground behind the shoulder-high shields. Those in the van-guard of the assault were forced directly on to the Roman line by the weight and numbers of those behind. How can a man fight when he barely has room to breathe? The legionaries grunted and snarled insults as the long swords and wide-bladed spears sought them out, and the Britons grunted and snarled back as they heaved and battered at the impenetrable wall in front of them. But it was the Britons who were dying. Between each pair of shields a *gladius* punched with the speed of a striking cobra and every blow took its toll with murderous precision. From behind the front line, the cohorts of the second and third lines hurled volley after volley of javelins into the packed ranks in front of the shields. In the first fifteen minutes of the attack Valerius estimated that Boudicca lost five thousand dead and injured. The wounded pleaded, squirmed and wriggled amidst their own gore beneath the feet of the uninjured, only to be trampled and suffocated. Centurions ranged behind the Roman front line shouting themselves hoarse and ordering replacements for men badly wounded or too exhausted to raise their shields. One by one, these fell back to ease parched throats and grab a crust of bread before they were kicked and bullied back into the killing machine. The rotation kept the shield line from cracking and the little swords jabbed out relentlessly, killing or maiming with every thrust. As long as their supply held out the nearly three thousand men of the six supporting cohorts kept up the rain of spears, the heavy lead-weighted missiles plunging down on the mass of flesh below.

By noon, the British casualties were already enormous, but Paulinus's battle line had weathered every crisis. An hour later, Valerius sensed a weakening of the British resolve. It was nothing tangible; the pressure on the front rank was as relentless as ever. But hour after hour of pushing at the backs of their comrades to no apparent purpose had doused the fire in the hearts of those in the centre and rear. Paulinus noticed it too, and his head came up like a deerhound hitting the scent. He looked out over the battlefield and saw his enemy at a standstill, the rearward ranks lethargic and neutralized. This was the moment, he realized, when the battle was his to win or lose. If he didn't act, the certainty was that he would eventually be defeated. His men could wield a sword and bear a shield for only so long. A legionary's strength was finite like that of all men. The alternative was a gamble, but a gamble he must take.

'Sound "Form wedge",' he ordered. The cornicen at his shoulder put his horn to his lips, and the distinctive call rang out along the line.

With swift, orchestrated movements the centuries of the first two lines transformed into the devastating arrowhead attack formations and launched themselves into the face of the Celtic attack. The wedges carved great swathes through the rebel ranks, and behind them came the Roman reserves still in their disciplined lines, their shields beating down any who escaped between the arrowheads.

'Send in the cavalry,' Paulinus ordered, and the auxiliary horsemen smashed into the British flanks, adding to the carnage.

Valerius held his breath. Now was the time for Boudicca to withdraw her forces and save what she could. Only twenty thousand or so had been involved in the actual combat; the rest were spectators. If she retired, Paulinus would have to fight her again tomorrow, and the day after that. But it was not within her power to do so. The thousands of booty-laden ox carts and chariots of the rebel baggage train acted like a dam against which the Romans forced back the great seething pool of Boudicca's followers. If one man fell, ten fell with him and all were crushed beneath the feet of their comrades as they milled and wheeled, looking for somewhere to run or someone to fight. Paulinus turned his horse away.

'Spare none,' he said.

* * *

Boudicca watched the Roman wedges smash into her stunned forces, the shock waves of their coming fracturing resolve even in the rear where she stood by her chariot with Banna and Rosmerta, helpless to alter the course of a battle she had wanted to fight on another day in another place. In that moment, she recognized her defeat. Andraste had deserted her.

She turned to the two girls and they were surprised to see her eyes damp with tears; it was the first time she had wept since the Romans came to Venta. Neither of them had shared her frightening hunger for vengeance, but they had never left her side. Now they prepared to share her fate.

She reached for the vial which hung at her throat below the golden torc. It was blue and made of fine Roman glass, but she found no irony in that. The contents were a poison of her own manufacture, tested on Roman prisoners who were among the fortunate few to meet a quick and painless end. She found her hand shaking as she raised it to Banna's mouth, but the blond-haired girl raised her own hand to steady her mother's before swallowing deeply from the container. Rosmerta swiftly followed suit, her face a mask of determination belied by the frank terror in her eyes. Boudicca's heart swelled to bursting. How she loved them.

Gwlym looked on emotionless, untroubled by sorrow or pity or fear. Like him, they were all tools of the gods. Victory or defeat had never been of consequence. What mattered was that Boudicca's name and deeds would live through the ages. Before she consumed the last of the poison Boudicca called him to her. 'When it is done, take us to a place they will never find us. Bury us deep. If I cannot defeat the Romans in life, I will defeat them in death.' She put the vial to her lips and drank, then raised her hands to touch each of her daughters on the cheek for the last time. 'Farewell,' she said. 'We will meet again in the Otherworld. Life will be better there.'

The sun dipped low towards the western horizon as Valerius allowed his horse to pick its way warily through the dead. He didn't know how many there were, only that a man could walk from the top to the bottom of the slope and from east to west across the valley without ever placing his foot upon the earth.

He rode like a blind man, the memory of a single face anchoring him to reality. His senses had long since been overwhelmed by the sights and sounds and smells of butchery on a scale beyond the imagining of any who had not witnessed it. A spectral miasma hung over the battlefield, like a low, thin fog, and he imagined he could taste death on his tongue and feel it clogging his lungs.

The slaughter had continued all through that long, hot afternoon and Paulinus's thirst for revenge had proved as unquenchable as that of Boudicca. When his officers reported that their men could no longer go on killing because they lacked the strength to wield their swords, he had replied: 'Let them use their daggers.' And when the last Celtic warrior bled out his life beside his comrades and the exhausted legionaries lay down thankfully to rest among their victims, he had stormed from his tent and pointed to the thousands of women and children cowering where they had been rounded up by the cavalry. Soon the screaming began again.

Valerius realized the futility of his quest when he reached the thousands of abandoned carts and carriages, their contents strewn about them in a frenzy of looting by the auxiliary cavalry. But something, stronger even than the knowledge that his own sanity depended on the outcome, kept him in the saddle.

It was near dark when he recognized the long chestnut hair fluttering like a fallen banner below the overturned ox cart. In the distance, he imagined he could hear the cry of a hunting owl.

Glossary of Roman military terms

Ala – A cavalry wing normally composed of 500 auxiliary horsemen, but occasionally 1,000 strong.

Auxiliary – Non-citizen soldiers recruited from the provinces as light infantry or for specialist tasks, e.g. cavalry, slingers, archers.

Ballistas – Artillery for throwing large arrows and other heavy missiles of varying size and type.

Century – A unit of the legion, numbering eighty men.

Cohort – A tactical unit of the legion, normally containing six centuries (480 men), apart from the elite First cohort, which had five double-strength centuries (800 men).

Decurion – A junior officer in a century, or a troop commander in a cavalry unit.

Denarius – A silver coin.

Duplicarius – Literally 'double-pay man'. A senior legionary with a trade or an NCO.

Gladius – A deadly short sword carried by legionaries.

Governor – A citizen of senatorial rank given charge of a province. Would normally have a military background.

Legate – The general in charge of a legion.

Legion – A unit of approximately 5,000 men, all of whom would be Roman citizens.

Mithras – God of an Eastern religion popular among Roman soldiers.

Prefect – An auxiliary cavalry commander.

Pilum – A heavy javelin used to demolish enemy attack.

Primus Pilus – 'First File'. The senior centurion of a legion.

Principia – A legionary headquarters building.

Procurator – A civilian administrator subordinate to a governor.

Quaestor – A civilian administrator in charge of finance.

Scutum – A legionary's rectangular oak or birch shield.

Sestertius – A Roman coin worth a quarter of a *denarius*.

Signifer – A legionary standard-bearer, most senior of which is the *aquilifer* who carries the eagle.

Spatha – A long cavalry sword.

Testudo – Literally 'tortoise', a unit of soldiers with shields interlocked for protection.

Tribune – One of six senior officers acting as aides to a legate. Often, but not always, on short commissions of six months upwards.

Acknowledgements

Thanks once again to my editor, Simon Thorogood, and the team at Transworld and to Stan, my agent at Jenny Brown. I'm indebted to Philip Crummy's brilliant work, *City of Victory: Story of Colchester – Britain's First Roman Town*, for providing me with the foundations of Colonia.

Claudius

Douglas Jackson

'What stands out are Jackson's superb battle scenes . . . I was gripped from start to finish'
BEN KANE, AUTHOR OF *THE FORGOTTEN LEGION*

ROME 43AD. Emperor Claudius has unleashed his legions against the rebellious island of Britannia.

In Southern England, Caratacus, war chief of the Britons, watches from a hilltop as the scarlet cloaks of the Roman legions spread across his land like blood. He must unite the tribes for a desperate last stand.

Among the legions marches Rufus, keeper of the Emperor's elephant. Claudius has a special role for him, and his elephant, in the coming war.

Claudius is a masterful retelling of one of the greatest stories from Roman history, the conquest of Britain. It is an epic story of ambition, courage, conspiracy, battle and bloodshed.

'Rightly hailed as one of the best historical novelists writing today'
DAILY EXPRESS

9780552162494